By:

Nathan Roten

Edited by: Jordan Roten & John Hudspith

Cover Design by: Damon Za

Interior Layout by: 12stone Press

ISBN: 0-9906378-4-0
ISBN-13: 978-0-9906378-4-4

Find out more at:

www.AegisSeries.com

Keep in touch with Nathan at:

www.NathanRoten.com

DEDICATION

To my dad, Jack Roten. Thank you for being a loving father, a dedicated husband and an incredible, godly role model. You will always be my hero.

You are sorely missed and deeply loved.

FREE DOWNLOAD

RECOLLECTION
THE AEGIS CHARACTER STORY
OF GRAHAM DAWSON

WITNESS THE NIGHTMARE
THAT STARTED IT ALL

YOUR FREE GIFT IS WAITING

Recollection is available as a free download exclusively to newsletter subscribers.

Join Graham as a young boy as he experiences his first encounter with the power he has yet to discover and the nightmare that started it all.

Sign up for the author's New Releases mailing list and get an exclusive free copy of RECOLLECTION: the first book in the AEGIS character story saga!

Consider character stories as the extra seasoning packets for the main novels that enhance their flavor. Each is a stand-alone story that reinforce the main storyline and gives you unique insights into the event that made them who they are.

To get your copy, simply click here to get started:
NathanRoten.com/free

Cast Of Characters
From Catalyst Grove

Graham Dawson- Fifteen-year-old orphan from Greenwood Orphanage who once struggled to keep a mysterious power hidden, has now been shown to have a remarkable and unique power called *The Aegis.*

Damien Ortega- Eccentric best friend to Graham and Aquatic- one who has the power to summon and command water.

Kel Stewart- A strong-willed orphan from a different Orphanage- Oak Ridge, because of a tragic car accident. Kel discovered she has the gifting of a Pusher, the ability to push energy into solid surfaces.

Ailey Bennett- The youngest of the group of children that has been through Catalyst Grove, and basically a sister to Kel. Shy and caring, Ailey's gifting is a Bridge, which can connect other people's giftings together through physical touch.

Alex- Leader of the Aegis Group, respected builder of the town of Portfield, and pending adoptive father to the four orphan teenagers.

Cavaness Foster- A mostly callous and abrupt man who has a reputation in the town for having special powers. Cavaness holds command under Alex as a highly-developed Pusher.

Chase Campbell- A sarcastic twenty-one-year-old who has taken Graham under his wing. Chase was also a former resident of Greenwood and the one to extend the invitation to the others to be a part of Aegis, persuading them by revealing his power as a Surge; one who can move and think at incredibly high speeds.

Brian Murphy- An equally as sarcastic member of Aegis and Former, a gifting that allows him to form objects out of energy and use them in various ways.

Eric Branson- Formal military Green Beret. Eric has the power of a Spark, one who can create and use electricity for his own purposes.

Olivia Winstone- Strict Matron of the Greenwood Orphanage, who pushes the children to be better in all aspects of life.

Silas Serene- Villain in opposition to Aegis, under the

direction of a mysterious master. His power is unknown. After the explosion in the cavern, Silas was left crippled but managed to provide the location of the other Aegis training facilities to his master.

Silas' Master- Unknown name or power, but is alluded to be the immortal, younger brother in the story of _The Unseen War_.

PUSHER

A Pusher can fire energy into solid surfaces and then have that same energy deflect at any angle. The general application of this gifting is used with the earth. The subject will propel an energy shot into the ground, calculate the desired depth and angle of trajectory, and then allow the energy to deflect, causing the earth and rock to explode upwards. More advanced methods can use solid surfaces such as metal to either propel the material surfaces themselves or allow the energy blast to deflect outwards to areas that would not be possible from a standard, direct blast.

BRIDGE

The Bridge gifting is generally developed in the introverted personality, whereas the subject prefers to work in the background, not wanting to be the main focus of attention. Fueled by the desire to empower others, the Bridge can make a connection between one or more people, acting as a conduit. This allows each person's gifting to flow to anyone in physical contact with the Bridge. These powers can be used individually or in combination with all participating members. Many Aegis members label the Bridge as the 'Wild Card' due to the exponential combinations of attacks possible.

AQUATIC

The Aquatic is a very rare gifting that allows the subject to manipulate the element of Dihydrogen Oxide: H20, and can absorb oxygen from the water to remain submerged for prolonged periods. Due to the properties of electrolysis, an Aquatic can use the power provided by the catalysts to control the physical state of water, causing it to move wherever they desire.

SURGE

The Surge gifting is rapid movement. The modern English dictionary defines a *surge* as a sudden and powerful movement. The subject possessing a Surge gifting can move at supernatural speeds in both mind and body, as well as attack at higher rates of speed than any other gifting.

FORMER

The Former gifting allows the subject to form objects out of the raw power provided by the catalyst. The possibilities of types of formed objects are near limitless, only restrained by the creativity and imagination of the person. The former can create offensive and defensive attacks in various forms and connect their vision to whatever they create, making them most useful as scouts and spies.

SPARK

The gifting of the Spark gives the subject full ability and control over electricity, both in its manipulation and creation. The electric charge may be created from the catalyst band or controlled by an outside source.

THE AEGIS

The gifting of the full power of the Aegis is a prophesied power that will alter the balance of power between the two immortal brothers.

CONTENTS

1

THE FALL OF RAVEN

Screams cut through the black smoke and raging flames.

"Get the children out!" screamed a male voice. "Jael, did you hear me? Jael. . . Jael!"

The man tucked his head in the breast of his coat, which reeked of smoke and sweat. He coughed and gagged as he shouldered into the haze. A wave of purple energy shot past his leg. He strafed and ducked around the corner. He climbed over heaps of rubble and fallen wood beams. The smog thinned enough for him to see the distant walls crumble under flashes of purple and yellow blasts.

He pulled his head from his jacket like a turtle from its shell, mortified at the destruction before him. Footsteps pattered close behind. He instinctively pivoted, ready to attack. The catalyst bands radiated underneath his skin as yellow energy pulsed in his palms, ready to fire. He struggled to see through the smoke-filled tears stinging his eyes.

"Director Blair, thank The Ancient," said the young woman, clearly panicked. She doubled over, panting and struggling to breathe. She coughed while wiping away a clot of grit and ash from her cheek. "Sir, the Grove has been destroyed. There are no survivors, not even the recruits. What do we do? Raven is being overrun."

"How many Victus have you seen?" said Blair.

"Too many to tell and way too few of us." Tears streaked the remaining ash. "How? How did they find us?"

"They found Alex's Grove in the States. When they found that, they also detected the energy signatures. Corbin sent out a message, but it was too late."

As Director Blair spoke, a shadow approached behind a broken stone wall. He stepped forward, pushed the woman out of the way, took a fighting stance, and fired a steady flow of energy at the assailant, who crashed into and broke the remainder of the wall. Blair reached down, retrieved his teammate, and led her into another room.

"We don't have much time. Use the secondary corridors and gather who you can. We can't fight scattered. Go!"

The woman nodded and ran toward the arched doorway, but before she could round the corner, two purple darts cut through her chest and sank into the stone wall behind her.

"No!" screamed Blair.

The lights hanging from the ceiling surged as the bulbs blew out. The light rose from the filaments at Blair's command, surrounded the intruder, and blinded him. While the man shielded his eyes, Blair sprinted to him, landed a swift punch to the gut, and flipped him over his shoulder. The man tried to see who hit him, but Blair fired a burst of energy, which flung him backward, knocking him unconscious.

He quickly surveyed the room for other intruders and

returned to his friend. A trail of crimson on the wall marked her descent to the ground. He tried to wake her, but she did not move. He felt her neck for a pulse, but there was none. He gritted his teeth so hard he thought they would break. He steadied his breathing, choked back tears, and rested his forehead on hers.

He stood to his feet and turned in time to catch a blast of energy to his chest. He staggered back a few steps until he regained his balance. He prepared to retaliate, but seeing that his assailant held another Aegis member captive, he refrained.

Blair held his hands up in surrender. "Enough. Just tell me what you want, and I'll cooperate."

"What do I want?" asked the woman in gray camouflage. Her green eyes squinted as she smiled. "I want this place to burn."

"Mission accomplished. Anything else?" Blair said flatly.

"Come now, where are your manners? You should always begin with some pleasantries when a guest enters your home. I don't even know your name. Mine is Kyla."

Her hostage fought her grasp, and she pulled him sharply back to her.

"Hello, Kyla. What brings you to my doorstep?"

"Again, with the rudeness. How can we have a conversation when I can't even address you by your name?"

"You couldn't care less about my name. I assume all you want to know is if I'm in charge of this facility. . . and I am."

"Well, don't sugar-coat it," said Kyla, still holding the young man in a painful pose. "Strong and blunt. A man of my dreams."

"I'll be the man of your nightmares if you harm one hair on his head."

"Cooperate, and he will go free."

"Then get on with it. You still haven't told me what you want."

"Where is the boy?"

"You're going to have to be a bit more specific."

Kyla punched the hostage in the ribs. His knees buckled, but she pulled him back up to his feet. Director Blair saw a familiar figure run through the smoke behind Kyla as he stood. His heart fluttered. *Jael!* She was running toward the central command room where Transit Mirrors were mounted.

"Hey! Over here!" yelled Kyla. "You know who I'm talking about. Where is he?"

"He certainly isn't here. I'm unsure where you're getting your intelligence from, but you missed the mark."

Kyla groaned in anger and flung dozens of small purple orbs in the air above Blair.

"I never miss my mark. The boy. . . where is he?"

Blair watched Jael pass the entryway to central command toward another hallway where five or six infiltrators approached.

"I do not recall him ever visiting Europe, come to think of it. You don't look European, either. How far have you traveled to come and tear my house down?"

"I don't have time for your stalling tactics. Tell me now, or I'll take you down and move on to your friends for intel."

Blair looked up at the orbs and then beyond Kyla, stealing another glance at Jael. She was still going down the wrong corridor. If she made it much further, she would be ambushed. He had to help her.

"You seem more like a combatant than an executioner. Why don't we make this a little more interesting?"

Blair balled his fists, and the catalyst bands under his skin illuminated. With a grunt, he threw both hands to the side, releasing powerful bursts. The wall to his left exploded. The blast to the right hurled past Jael and brought down the first section of the corridor in a rain of stone and dust. Jael fell backward and scooted away from the crumbling hallway.

Kyla positioned her orbs closer around Blair. She started looking in Jael's direction, but he wouldn't let her.

"That was just a warm-up. If you want to know where he is, you'll most assuredly have to fight for such a precious bit of knowledge."

Kyla pulled her attention back to Blair. "You know, I actually believe you. . . the part about the fight, anyway. But I know when a man has set his resolve." She glanced down at her hostage. "Guess I'll just have to find someone else to help me."

Kyla grinned and looked into Blair's eyes. The orbs surrounding him brightened like purple fire. Blair watched Jael backpedal to the correct entryway that would ensure her escape. Just as Jael turned to look his way, Blair noticed Kyla was picking up on his genuine concern. He quickly directed his attention to the young man Kyla held captive.

"Don't worry. Follow your instincts and remember our cause. Always remember why and for whom we fight."

Jael turned to see the orbs poised around Director Blair. Her eyes widened in terror. Kyla turned to see Jael standing in the stone doorway.

"Duck!" yelled Blair.

The young man fell to his knees as Blair fired a burst of energy into Kyla's stomach. The impact made her stumble backward, but she quickly planted her foot to stop her momentum. Teeth bared, she threw her arm forward, commanding all her orbs to crash down on Blair.

"Leon!" Jael screamed as she watched Blair disappear behind a purple inferno.

Kyla shot another glance at Jael, who stood frozen in terror. Kyla grinned as she picked the young Aegis member back off the floor to pursue Jael. Before she could take two steps, the young man threw a pulse of energy into the ground with one hand and fired a blast with the other.

The ground rippled as the energy tunneled forward. The blast connected with and tore apart the stone wall of the entryway Jael stood in. A small piece of rock ricocheted and struck Jael in the cheekbone. She stumbled back, cradling her head in her hands. The Pusher energy then unearthed and brought the entire entryway down. The young man smiled as he saw Jael escape behind the cascade.

Kyla grabbed him by the shoulder and spun him around.

"Congratulations. You saved one person. Too bad you won't live to enjoy the accomplishment unless you give me what I want."

She grabbed him by the throat and lifted him on his toes. Her emerald eyes bore a hole in his heart.

"Tell me where they are keeping Graham Dawson."

2

Alex's Search

Alex stood alone and motionless, lost in thought. He cast aside a padded chair to get a closer look at the six large mirrors hanging above the elaborately carved wooden desk. Two of the six had fractures in the glass, stretching like spider legs. Alex stared intently through the shards at his reflection, noting the pain in his eyes.

He sighed and turned around. He crossed his arms and leaned against the desk to view the transit mirrors that adorned nearly every square inch of the remaining three walls. Light poured in from the only set of windows housed on the opposite wall from the desk. They were wide and squatty but still allowed light to bounce from the mirror's shiny surfaces, giving the room a unique and ambient glow.

After a moment, Alex walked to the center of the room,

passing each column of mirrors and glancing at each of the hundreds of mirrors adorning the vaulted wall space. Row upon row, he squinted, searching and shifting from one to the next with waning patience. His jaw tightened as he moved from mirror to mirror.

Solemn and resolute, he extended his hand, forming an apple-sized, translucent orb in his palm. He tossed it in the air, allowing it to hover and pause in front of each high-hung mirror. Though no catalyst band gleamed from underneath his skin, his eyes had turned to amber as his vision connected to the orb above.

Time faded, and his frustration intensified as he searched every mirror in his possession. After peering into every possible portal, he enabled the orb to dissolve. With a great weight on him, Alex returned to the desk, seeing multiple versions of himself reflected in the fragments of fractured glass. He glanced one final time around the room, then whispered into the silence as if his question would carry through the portals.

"Where are you?"

3

Power Up

"Fire!"

Graham pulled his hand back, his catalyst band radiant. He kept his eyes on the glowing target, tracking its velocity. A small ball of light formed in his hand. He threw it forward, releasing a blast of energy ahead of it, calculating its speed so that they would make contact at the right time. Chase called it 'leading the target.' The target erupted in a flash of light, and the blast absorbed into the back wall.

Again and again, Graham would fire in rhythm, hitting the small orbs tossed into the air to the beat of the music blaring over the loudspeakers. This time, it was *Eye of the Tiger*.

"Okay, let it rest during the chorus," said Chase. "This time, I want you to turn your back to me. Let your mind clear, and just before the beats of the bridge hit, I want you to spin around and react. I will have all the targets suspended. Your job is to observe their placement and hit as many as you can." Chase rubbed the palms of his hands together in preparation. "Once the beats finish and he says *'eye of the tiger'* again, I want you to try to surge."

Graham massaged his dominant wrist. They had been at it for hours. His hand was starting to go numb from the repetition. He wanted to take a break, but he knew that wasn't an option. Not now. Not when so much needed to be done in such a short amount of time. He turned around, closed his eyes, shook the fatigue from his hands, and flexed the numbness from his fingers.

The song continued to play. Graham focused on the words.

"Surge. . . really?"

"Yes, really. Anyone can fire small bursts, but it takes real skill to keep the energy flow going. You've got this."

Graham shrugged. "Okay. Just tell me when."

He then turned his back, shaking his limbs like a boxer walking toward the ring, anticipating the pending fight. Chase watched, half focused on the timing of the music and half on Graham's mental routine. He chuckled, cracking a grin.

"Amazing. What a kid."

The music played until the iconic beats returned. Graham balled his hands into fists as small shafts of light stretched out from between his fingers.

"Fire!"

Graham jumped and twisted around, spotting three targets before his feet hit the ground. The beats of the song resounded through the large room. With each one, Graham fired several attacks, hitting each orb.

Chase cupped his hands together and propelled a larger target above his head.

Graham widened his feet into a horse stance, with one

foot set back for stability. He put the heels of his hands together, holding his fingers outstretched and parallel to the ground so that his hands looked like a small set of wings. In a single motion, he pulled his hands into his chest and then flung them forward with a grunt.

This time, instead of a singular blast leaping from his palms, a constant and steady stream of energy rushed out. His back arched under the intensity. He tried to hold it steady, but the raw power was overwhelming. The surge connected with the wall a few feet below the basketball-sized target Chase had made. As Graham tried to control its direction, the surge carved a deep fissure up the wall.

Graham quickly lost control. The power snaked all over the room, leaving a broad, scorched trail along the wall and ceiling. Chase ducked just in time to avoid being hit by the rogue energy. Graham clenched his shoulders tight to tame the attack, but to no avail. He twisted his body abnormally until he fell backward, disconnecting his hands to catch his fall. When he did, the attack pulsed and vanished.

The line Graham carved into the wall gradually faded as if an invisible eraser restored the room to its original state. Chase stood up straight again while the charred line above his head absorbed into the wall.

Graham's cheeks grew hot with embarrassment. In just a few strides, Chase was beside him with an encouraging pat on the shoulder.

"Don't let that one get under your skin. You did better than I did the first time I tried that move."

"I highly doubt that," said Graham.

"It's true. Sure, I had to duck to keep from being decapitated, but at least it was just me. I was the first Surge discovered in this region. As I trained, we had ten visiting staff from the other regional headquarters. Everyone wanted to watch me go supersonic."

"What happened?"

"Let's just say that the wall is not the only object I

damaged that day. Sometimes, when people get caught off guard by the surge, they can lose all sense of composure, especially if they're not used to being in combat. I'm sure they didn't expect the show to be interactive."

Chase grabbed a bottle of water and a towel from the nearby table and threw them to Graham.

"We'll stop here today, and I can pick out a few more songs for tomorrow. You did great with the normal blasts, and your aim was dead on. Next time you try the surge, squeeze your chest and lats as tight as possible like you're trying to compact yourself into a tight ball. It will help stabilize you."

Graham nodded as he took a swig of water. He loved how Chase made training fun, choosing songs and making him hit targets to the rhythm. He could spend a whole day in training sometimes, and it would only feel like minutes had passed. Cavaness, on the other hand, was all business and no play, or rest for that matter. He would bark commands, and Graham would follow them. One hour felt like a year when Cavaness was training.

"How are the nightmares? Had any in a while?" asked Chase.

Graham leaned his head back and swallowed the last of the water.

"I haven't had one for a while, until last week. Now new pieces are showing up."

"Oh, yeah? What new pieces?"

"After the blast of light, I see someone come and pick me up. He's talking to someone, but the voices are muffled. The sun is behind him, so I can't see his face."

Chase did not act surprised.

"Makes sense. You had to get from the woods to the orphanage somehow. Did you get the feeling this person was helping?"

"I don't know. I think so. He was gentle."

"Well, if I were you, I wouldn't give it a lot of thought.

Your mind will continue to push things to the surface as it sees fit. Just let it happen. Speaking of the orphanage, how far along are you with the adoption process? Are you getting close to being here full-time?"

Graham wiped his forehead with the towel.

"I don't know exactly, but Alex said our final house visit will be sometime this week. Once they assess and approve, we can leave Greenwood for good. I've hated going back and forth these past, what. . . four months now? I can't wait until I have one home."

Chase draped an arm around Graham's shoulder as they left the training room. "I know it's a pain to go back and forth, especially since Ms. Winstone insists you keep up your class and coursework while you visit here. It's a lot to juggle. I'm surprised you have the energy to handle it all. It will be a distant memory soon, though. It sounds like you'll be here carving channels into the walls night and day before too long."

"Shut up, or I'll carve a channel through your face."

"Oh, you'll try, but you'll fail," said Chase, grabbing Graham in a headlock and twisting his knuckles through his hair.

Graham wiggled free, pushing Chase away with a laugh. They continued down a long corridor until they reached the vast, vaulted living room of Falcon.

"Anyway, it's Mr. Kobble that's keeping the standards high. I haven't seen Ms. Winstone for weeks. I heard she had to take a leave of absence. Someone said it was family trouble," said Graham.

"It's hard to believe that Ms. Winstone would be able to spend any amount of time away from Greenwood. Whatever the emergency is, I'm sure it's pretty serious to keep her away for that long," Chase replied.

They strolled beyond the front foyer just in time to greet Branson, who was walking through the front door.

"Hey, Eric," said Graham.

"Hey, big guy. How did training go today?"

"Mostly well. The surge move threw me on my butt."

Branson shot a look at Chase.

"You made Graham try a surge? What are you smoking, Chase? That's at least a level-ten technique. You know that."

"Graham blew out the cavern ceiling from Catalyst Grove like dust on an old shelf. I wanted to gauge where he was, and I was right to do so. He held it for over five seconds."

Branson's scowl of disapproval quickly changed to surprise. "Really? That long, huh? Well, I stand corrected. I'm impressed."

"Thank you," said Chase.

"I wasn't talking to you. I was talking to Graham, and you're still crazy for doing it. You're just lucky you had good results. Otherwise, Cavaness would have been all over you," said Branson, setting his black duffle bag beside a small end table. "Anyway, I'm not here to chat. I need to take Graham over to the house in Millstone. Alex has just been notified that the final visitation will happen in an hour, and he wants all the kids there with him."

"Really? Kel and Ailey will be there? I haven't seen them but once or twice since the Grove. I'll go get changed real fast."

Graham flew upstairs to change out of his sweaty clothes. Branson continued talking as he knelt to sift through the contents of his bag.

"The Council will meet in a few days. There will be people missing, of course, but everyone still available will be there. Alex will be making the announcement. Let's pray the council will accept it."

"The reality is right there in front of us all. How could they not?" replied Chase.

"Denial is a powerful illusion. The council will want to save face and protect their pride at all costs."

"It's hard to believe we all have the same origin. How can we all start in the same place with the same purpose and let it turn into this?"

"Give mankind time and power," Branson said gravely, "and anything can happen."

4

A Farewell To Oak Ridge

"This may be our last day here," said Kel, turning to Ailey as she hung up the phone. "Alex just called and told us to pack up. We're going to the house in Millstone for the final visitation review with the adoption agency. If they give their approval, then we can stay!"

Ailey, who had been lounging on her bed, sat up quickly and became a flurry of motion. She ran over to the entrance of their bedroom, where Mr. Pitman had provided two large suitcases. She grabbed a case and threw it onto her bed before whirling around and whipping clothing out of her top drawer. Laughing at the younger girl's enthusiasm, Kel retrieved her suitcase as well. The girls rummaged through their drawers, pulling out all their belongings and packing them away.

"How have your training sessions been going? I find it a little odd that they only take us in there one at a time."

Ailey gave a thumbs-up. She signed the name for Branson and Murphy, pointed to her chest, then pointed to the underside of her wrist where the symbol for her gifting resided.

"You've been working with Branson and Murphy, huh? What cool party tricks have you learned now?"

Ailey signed her words to Kel proudly.

"You can't be serious. Branson formed an electric dove and set a table on fire?"

Ailey nodded, and then her fingers were in motion again.

"You're so lucky," Kel sighed as Ailey finished. "I wish I could work with someone other than Cavaness sometimes. He's a good teacher, but he pushes so hard. It's like he thinks we will fight in the apocalypse tomorrow. He won't let up for anything."

Kel grabbed the final handful of her clothing and folded everything carefully. She paused before reaching for the single trinket on the top of her dresser. She half smiled as she held up the small metal figure of a dolphin jumping from a wave. Ailey noticed the figurine and put her arms around Kel's waist.

Kel returned the hug and placed the dolphin on top of her clothes. "It's funny how time marches on so quickly. I catch myself wondering what she would be like now – how she would look and act, or what her laugh would sound like." Kel glanced down at the small girl with arms still wrapped around her and smiled. "I imagine she would be a lot like you."

Ailey shrugged, blushing.

"But I do have you." Kel took Ailey's hand and squeezed in excited anticipation. "And hopefully, today, we can officially call ourselves sisters!"

As they finished packing up the few belongings they had, there was a light knock on the door.

"May I come in?" asked the voice on the other side.

"Yes, sir, Mr. Pitman."

A short, balding man wearing a three-piece suit stepped inside. He was neither fat nor skinny; in fact, there was very little that helped him stand out in a crowd. He held his arms out as he continued through the door.

"My dears. I will surely miss you. I already do." He gave them each a warm hug and kissed them on the top of their heads. "A Mr. Brian Murphy is waiting for you downstairs. He tells me your final visitation is today." His voice quivered slightly as he spoke. He cleared his throat before he continued. "You must forgive me. I'm afraid I'm a bowl of mixed emotions today. It's always a blessing to see good children sent to good homes, but it's equally difficult to let them go."

After the girls zipped their luggage closed, Mr. Pitman took the two suitcases in his hands and followed the girls downstairs.

"You are two of the good ones. I wish you well, with every good fortune. Heaven knows you deserve all the happiness in the world, especially after your close call at Portfield Manor."

Mr. Pitman gave a final, fatherly hug to the girls and then picked up their bags to take them to the car. Kel and Ailey made their way to a few other rooms to say their goodbyes and best wishes but practically flew down the stairs as soon as they had finished, hoping to get back to Falcon as quickly as possible.

"I can't wait to see the boys," Kel panted as they ran side by side. "I really miss them. It's been months. I wonder if they've been practicing as hard as we have."

Ailey didn't slow her pace. Her focus was solely fixed on making it to the car first.

Murphy had parked beside the prominent water feature outside of the orphanage. From a distance, it looked like he was admiring the four stone oak trees, which stood on top of a small arch resembling a hill or mountaintop. Once the girls got closer, though, it was apparent to Kel that his attention was on something much higher than the fountain. His head was cocked skyward, with his irises glowing amber. He didn't even glance at the girls, seemingly oblivious to everything around him.

Ailey reached him first and slammed her hand against the front fender of the car, then held her hands up high in victory. Kel followed closely behind, but her foot slipped in the gravel and she stumbled forward, nearly crashing into Murphy's leg. Catching her fall at the last second, he scooped her up with one arm and set her back into a proper standing position, all while still looking overhead. Once she stabilized, his eyes returned to brown as he looked at her and smiled.

"Easy there, ladies. Alex would prefer you not to be all scratched and bleeding for the visitation. You do still want the adoption to go through, right?"

"Of course we want it to go through! We've been dreaming of this day for months now." Kel glanced at Murphy curiously. "What were you looking at anyway? I thought we were supposed to be selective about when we use our powers in public."

"Just checking in. . . and don't worry. You may not have thought I wasn't paying attention as you came barging toward me, but I was well aware." He smiled as both girls' cheeks colored. "Besides, to anyone else, I was just looking up at the clouds. Much more subtle than firing an invisible blast of energy."

"I suppose. Are we headed straight to the house? Will Graham and Damien be there?"

Murphy looked down at his watch.

"Damien is there now, and Graham should be on his way. If all goes well, we should have a big celebration tonight but don't forget that the Council is meeting soon. We can't lose sight of the bigger picture."

Murphy opened the car door and let the girls climb into the back seat. As she turned toward the front, Kel realized they were not alone in the car. Ailey noticed the youthful woman in the passenger seat as well. The woman's long brown ponytail swung around as she turned her head to look at the girls.

"Hello," said Kel awkwardly. "We weren't expecting anyone else to be here. Are you a friend of Murphy's?"

"Friend and ally," said Murphy, sinking into his seat.

The stranger held her arm up and pulled back her sleeve, revealing her illuminated wrist.

"Hi. My name is Jael," she said warmly with a European accent. "Brian and I are friends, but, like you, we are also teammates."

Ailey sat transfixed.

"I didn't know there was another woman in our core group," Kel replied.

"There are plenty of women in Aegis. You'll see many now that you will see the broader network. I am from Brussels. Not born and raised, mind you, but that is where I have lived for most of my adult life."

"You're from Europe? I have *always* wanted to go to Paris," said Kel. "Do you have any family there?"

"Some extended family in the Netherlands, yes, though they are not activated," replied Jael.

"Is that where you are originally from?"

"Yes, from Rotterdam. It is a beautiful little port city. You should visit after you see Paris."

"I would love it. What about you, Brian? I don't think you've ever told us where you are from."

Brian gazed into the rearview mirror.

"Tiffin, Ohio. Just one state over. I grew up on Lake Erie every summer and attended Cleveland Browns games in the fall. It's no Paris, but it's a nice, quaint town. My parents are dead now, but I still have a cousin there. We used to be pretty close, but we had a falling out years ago. Now, she only calls when she needs my help. Of course, now I'm at Falcon year round, so it's hard to keep a relationship going with anyone outside those walls."

"Well, you never know. Maybe you two can patch things up. You have to hold onto the family you have." Kel turned back to Jael. "So, was there an Aegis headquarters in Brussels?"

"Yes, I was stationed at one called Raven. That is, I was before Victus overtook it."

Jael timidly cleared her throat, and the mood instantly dimmed. Now that she was facing the girls, the remnants of heavy bruising on the right side of her face were evident, like a faint paint spill on the underside of her skin.

"I'm sorry to hear that. I'm glad you are okay." Kel squirmed a bit as the mood dampened. She bit her lip momentarily, searching for what to say next until she remembered the unknown word Jael had just mentioned.

"Who is Victus?"

Putting the car in reverse, Murphy draped his arm around the headrest of his seat to back out of the driveway. "Victus is why Alex recruited you. That is who we fight against."

The car whipped around the entryway to Oak Ridge. Murphy flung the gearshift into first gear as if throwing someone to the ground.

"Do you mean Silas – they have a name? Why weren't we told this?" Kel asked.

"It didn't matter until now. You know the meat and potatoes of the story. You know why the Council is meeting later this week. I guess we have just been so focused on getting you all developed that we forgot to mention names."

"Names and people change, but the cause will remain the same. That much I'm sure you are well aware of," said Jael quietly. "I was one of the lucky ones. I happened to retreat into a room with a trans in it. By that time, most of my friends were already dead. I wanted to go back, but in my desperation, I had taken the mirror with me, so I couldn't. I didn't even know where I was for a time, but eventually, I made it here."

Ailey signed a question to Kel. "Ailey wants to know what a trans is."

"It is short for Transit Mirrors. We acronym everything. It's a habit we all got into back at Raven."

"I've been telling Jael about you guys, bragging about how you knocked two of us unconscious during the catalyst stage. She's very excited to see what you all can do," said Murphy.

"Yes, I have heard a lot about your development, though I would love to hear it from your perspective. Grove stories are always so fascinating. There are never any two alike."

"Um, sure, I guess. Back in late summer, Chase came to our orphanage and eluded to things – things which I could do but am not supposed to be able to do – and told us that we weren't the only ones." Kel paused, cutting her eyes to Ailey. "When I say we, I mean Ailey and I. We met with Chase a few more times before he offered us an invitation to come and meet others who were like us. He also showed us his superspeed ability to convince us he was for real. I was pretty reluctant, but Ailey was almost frantic to go, so we did.

"I thought we would only meet people who could already do impossible things, but shortly after we arrived, Graham and Damien came through the door, and they seemed even more clueless than we were about what was going on. We met them at Portfield Manor, where we were given the catalyst bands. The rest, I'm sure you know."

"No, please. I love details," replied Jael.

"Well, I don't know how it's done in Brussels, but we were blindfolded with a hood and taken to a big warehouse. We were tied to chairs and left to figure everything out on our own. We eventually escaped that room because I accidentally blew Graham's chair into pieces with the Pusher power I still didn't know I had. We worked our way down to the entrance, where Ailey accidentally used her Bridge power to help us escape the building. We ran into the woods and were then funneled to a large ravine, which led to an underground cavern, where Damien figured out he was an Aquatic. At that point, we all had shown evidence of our power, except for Graham, which made him even more determined to take the lead, I think."

Kel gave a soft smile when she mentioned Graham's name.

"Since we couldn't find a way out, we decided to take a stand against the others in a large open space in the woods. It was pretty gut-wrenching. They did a good job of making everything seem real, especially the pain from the energy shots. We all wondered why Cavaness had zeroed in on Graham. I think I passed out from pain somewhere around that point. I remember seeing Graham almost break through the barrier and reveal his power, but then, he stopped short. The real horror began when Silas took everyone by surprise with his group. Vickus?"

"Victus, yes," corrected Jael.

"Victus." Kel shuddered and then continued. "They took us back through a transit mirror to the cavern we had been in previously. He tied up Damien with those awful, smoky chains and tossed him into the water. That's when Graham lost it. He freaked out and almost imploded the entire cavern. By then, I was out again, and when I woke up, we were at the Falcon headquarters. Everyone ended up being okay, and Alex confirmed that Graham was the one everyone had been looking for. . . the one who would unsettle the balance of power."

"Remarkable," said Jael. "A Pusher, Bridge, Aquatic, and Graham. Just the thought! It's hard to believe the person with the full power of the Aegis is finally here. You know, we were close once before. There was one guy who was so strong that we thought he was the one. Of course, time eventually revealed that was not the case." Jael looked down in remorse. "Poor soul."

"What about you? What can you do?" asked Kel.

"I am what people call a Lumos. I can manipulate physical light and take energy from other people and absorb it into my body. But more than that, I can also retain their memories and knowledge."

Murphy slammed on the breaks. He had almost missed a stop sign.

"Come on, trim the hedge, will ya? I can barely see that thing. You know, I never have liked the Millstone district. Ever since the factories shut down, the place has fallen into shambles. Honestly, I have no idea why Alex keeps a place here."

He steered the car past the intersection and through the small, ruddy town. Jael told the girls a story about how she learned five different languages in three days. Kel was intrigued but found it hard to focus while being tossed around by all of the potholes in the road.

"There it is. Just up that hill. Not bad for a humble little town, huh, Jael?" Murphy wove the car through another series of potholes to a considerable estate at the crest of the hill, overlooking the north side of town. It was a large brick home with beaming white columns gracing the length of the front side. It was not nearly as big as Portfield Manor, but it was still remarkable.

"Here we go – with fifteen minutes to spare. Why don't you two go in and get settled? I'll take Jael back to Falcon, where we will eagerly await the good news."

The girls stepped out of the car and walked toward their temporary home.

"It was great to meet you both. See you back at Falcon. Good luck in there! I'm sure it will go well."

Both girls waved, and Ailey signed thank you to Jael as they walked up to the front door.

Murphy turned the car around and drove toward Portfield.

"How's the leg?" he asked once they were back on the main street.

"It still aches, but I can walk without a limp now. Alex has been good at helping the healing process along. Speaking of. . . do you think he can get me back there? I have to know if there were any other survivors." Jael tucked a lock of hair behind her ear and shrank back into her seat. "I can't believe I just left like that. How selfish and stupid. I didn't even try to find out who was leading the attack."

"Your survival instinct kicked in, and you followed it. There's no shame in that," replied Murphy. "I'm sure we can get close. We'll have to wait until after the Council meeting to act, but I'm sure we can do something."

They both sat in contemplative silence until they reached Falcon.

5

An Official Welcome

Three figures were huddled side by side in the big kitchen. The white granite countertops looked like clouds resting on top of the dark mahogany cabinets. The kitchen looked like an unused showroom with every tool and appliance in its place.

Damien stood at the kitchen sink, holding his hands to each side of the running water pouring from the faucet.

"Good. Now, try moving the water back and forth very gently. I want you to focus on the amount of force you apply."

Alex stood beside him, determined not to miss an opportunity to train. Damien focused on the water, carefully swaying his hands. At first, only his hands were moving, but after a few seconds, the water began to bend and sway with the motion of his hands. Damien smiled.

Graham knew that most of Damien's training had been like this. They had started him off with the strongest attacks he could generate. The next day, they wanted him to simply create light ripples in a pool of water so that he could embrace the concept of finesse and controlled force.

He was beginning to swirl the stream in a circular motion when a loud voice jolted him.

"Careful with that!" screamed a female voice.

Damien jerked, and the stream of water bent upwards and sprayed him in the face. He quickly deactivated his power, allowing the water to return to its natural flow.

"What the heck, man! Why did you–"

"Aren't you happy to see us?" asked Kel.

Both boys stared at each other in surprise momentarily and then rushed to hug them. Graham swept Kel up in a bear hug, almost knocking Damien over, who had done the same with Ailey. Alex leaned against the doorjamb, crossing his arms and smiling at the reunion.

Ailey signed, asking how they were doing. Kel opened her mouth to translate, but Damien answered.

"I'm great, Ailey. Especially now that you two are here!" He smiled at Kel. "I've missed you both so much! How have you been?"

Ailey gave a thumbs-up.

"How did you know what she said?" asked Kel.

"I've been doing a little studyin' up on sign language. I figured since my new sister speaks another language, I should try to learn it."

"I'm impressed." Kel's eyebrows arched. "Why are you wet?"

"That would be your fault," Damien said, bumping her shoulder.

Kel grinned. "How about you, Graham? Have they been working you as hard as they have us? I swear, I'm so exhausted when I get back to Oak Ridge that I can barely make it to my room before I pass out."

"That's pretty much how it's been for us, too. Chase and the others don't seem to want to waste a single moment," Graham replied. "I think the destruction of Catalyst Grove got them pretty determined."

"Indeed it did," interrupted Alex. "We can't use you in the fight until you have reached a certain level of capability. It would be neglectful to do otherwise. Since you must return to your respective orphanages regularly, we've had to be very intentional, targeted, and focused during your training time. It will only become more intense, I'm afraid."

Alex started to say more but was interrupted by a knock on the door.

"I will explain more tonight."

He walked past them to the door. Kel and Ailey turned to each other and began conversing in sign language. Damien turned to see what was on the T.V. but quickly became disinterested.

"Every time I come over here, Alex has the news on. How do people watch that? Honestly, it's just one horror story after another."

"Good afternoon, Mrs. Quell. Please, do come in," said Alex.

A very wide lady stepped through the doorway with white pointed glasses and a clipboard.

"Hello, children," said Mrs. Quell, holding her arms open.

"Hi, Mrs. Quell," said Kel as Ailey waved. "Good to see you again."

"You as well, my dears."

"May I get you some tea?"

"Tea would be wonderful. Thank you, Alex. How are the other children getting along? Well, I guess they are not children anymore, are they?"

"No, ma'am. They all grow up so fast. Jessica has recently moved to the Midwest, but Chase is still here, and they are both doing just fine. Had he known you would be the one to come for the final assessment, I'm sure he would have wanted to be here. He grew quite fond of you during the visitations. You do have a way with them."

"Thank you, Alex. That's very kind, though it's not hard to get a child's approval when you have candy in your pockets," she said, giving the kids a conspiratorial wink.

Alex moved into the kitchen and resurfaced with a cup and saucer. A small tag dangled beside the handle, twisting from its string. Two cubes of sugar rested beneath the paper tag.

"Two lumps, correct?"

"Oh, sweet boy. You remembered how I like my tea!"

Alex handed the cup to Mrs. Quell, and they continued to catch up as they walked throughout the house. Room by room, she scribbled on her notepad and checked off boxes on her form.

"How does he do that?" asked Graham, lowering his voice.

"Do what?" replied Kel.

"He doesn't know a stranger. He could talk to the wall over there."

"Who knows?" Damien shrugged. "Some people are just good at talking, I guess."

The morning went by quickly. The four children swapped training stories as Mrs. Quell surveyed the house until Alex finally led her back to the living room.

"Shipshape, as usual. These are fine conditions, Alex. I just need to speak with each child, and then I can give you my final answer."

"Please take your time. I have set up a few chairs in the corner there," said Alex, leading them to a set of blue wingback chairs. "I will be here if you need anything."

"Thank you very much. Ailey, sweetheart. Why don't you come over first?"

Kel walked Ailey over to Mrs. Quell and offered to help interpret.

"How are we doing? Do you think we will pass?" asked Graham.

Alex did not respond, being too distracted by the report that had just come on the television. Graham tapped him on the arm.

"Hmm?" Alex began to turn his head toward Graham, but he kept his eyes on the screen as long as he could. "I'm sorry, Graham. What did you ask?"

"How are we doing?"

"Oh, just fine. Mrs. Quell and I go way back. She was the one to assess this same house when Chase was adopted. She's quite familiar with my home and my dedication to children. As soon as she interviews you all, I expect good news."

Before Graham could respond, Alex turned his attention back to the newscast and an update given by a member of the United Nations.

> Today, I bring news of a growing global threat. This threat is not a political entity, nor is it contained in physical borders. We do not yet have a name for this force, but we have credible intel that suggests this movement is on the rise and is now gathering momentum on an international scale.
>
> Rest assured that we at the U.N. are monitoring the situation and are tracking all possible terrorist ties. It is our goal to be transparent to the global community. We will provide another official report once we have more detailed information, but for now, we simply want you to be aware and alert. Keep a watchful eye out for suspicious activity in your community. We are asking you, the general populace, to take arms. Not with guns and weapons but with a watchful eye and decisive action to report suspicious activity. We must be unified and determined to terminate this mounting threat before it can grow legs. If you have anything to report, please call the number at the

> bottom of your screen. We have staff available
> around the clock to take your call. Thank you for
> your time and attention."

Graham suddenly understood what Alex was listening to and stared intently at the television screen.

"Wow, are they talking about Silas?" he asked.

"I'm not sure, but I have my doubts," replied Alex. "The general public is unaware of our fight."

Alex's tone seemed grim, especially on a day when everyone was in good spirits at the expectation of a finalized adoption.

"Well, if it's him, then I hope they send him to the chair unless he can absorb electricity. Then they can hang him."

"That is a hefty sentence for anyone, even someone like Silas," replied Alex.

"He would've killed us all if he had the chance. I don't see why he should be around to hurt others if we can help it. Isn't that why we're training? To take out guys like that?"

"Graham, dear. Would you come on over," asked Mrs. Quell. "You're the last one, sweetheart."

Graham was so captivated by the report and Alex's reaction that he had lost track of time. The other three were already back on a couch, picking up where they had left off in their training stories. Alex gestured toward her, and Graham conceded.

Mrs. Quell only had a few questions for Graham. There had been multiple visits during which she had gathered most of the information she needed. After a few minutes, Mrs. Quell put the cap back on her pen and flipped the pages back into place in her notebook.

"Well, I think we're all done here. Thank you, children, for taking the time to speak with me. I know you'll be very happy here."

"So you approve?" asked Damien, not masking his excitement.

Mrs. Quell took a final sip of her tea.

"Yes, Damien. You have a wonderful home here, and with Alex, I know you will be well taken care of."

Alex thanked Mrs. Quell for her time and walked her to the door. The girls hugged each other, squealed a bit, and did an odd sort of jumping dance. Damien and Graham mockingly did the same until Kel punched Graham on the arm.

"So this is it, then? We're official?" asked Graham.

"*Pienso, hermano.*" Damien leaped over the back of the couch and rested his hands behind his head as if lying in a hammock. "Ahh. . . home, fake home."

"I know. It's a shame we won't stay here much. It's pretty nice," said Graham.

"Yes, but I still like Falcon better," Kel interjected.

"Sure, it's nice, but there's not much to do here other than relax," said Damien. "Falcon has the training rooms."

While Damien and Kel continued talking, Graham let himself relax. The last few months had been a whirlwind of activity, and he needed a breath of relief. Every now and then, he could still feel twinges of pain in random parts of his body, which he assumed was from the explosion of energy at the Grove. He had Silas to thank for that, which made his blood boil. He couldn't shake off the hate he felt for the man. His anger continued to rise until he caught a glimpse of Kel and Ailey celebrating. Then, he realized he had a reason to celebrate and focus on something unrelated to this war or his abilities, which put his heart at rest. As he signed in delight, he felt an armrest across his shoulders.

"Welcome home, officially," said Alex.

"Thanks, Ale– I mean, Dad? What exactly do we call you now?"

"You can call me whatever you like. If you are used to Alex, then you are free to keep calling me that. We will be around other members of Aegis often, so 'daddy' may prove to be a bit uncomfortable for all involved."

"Yeah, you are probably right," Graham grinned sheepishly.

Alex smiled and patted his shoulder before moving to the others and doing the same. Then, he motioned to the door.

"Let's not keep everyone in suspense longer than we need to."

Alex held the door open to let them pass. "Tonight, we celebrate. Tomorrow, we must prepare for the fight ahead."

6

The Flow of Power

Silas leaned on his cane as he spoke, careful not to let the tip slip on the slick marble surface.

"My lord, the plans are coming together, just as you said they would. The intel from Kyla suggests we move forward with the siege."

The man in the darkness paced back and forth. His long, black coat dusted the floor as he walked.

"Good. And you are certain she is trustworthy?"

"I have no reason to doubt it, my lord."

"Very well. We will move forward and proceed with the plant as planned. Everyone will move into position as we discussed, but to ultimately succeed, we need more people. How many of Alex's people were captured from the training groves?"

"Hundreds, my lord," said Silas, shifting his cane from one hand to another.

"More bands will need to be created for them. It makes no difference to me who will be used for their creation. You may choose."

Silas stared at the floor momentarily, nodded, and walked out the door. Moments later, he re-emerged with one of his subordinates, who appeared quite timid.

"My lord, I present to you, Walker Ashman. He was the man who fired the pulse that destroyed Alex's Manor in Pennsylvania."

Silas turned to Walker. "You may address him as Kaiser, your Emperor."

"Walker Ashman. Not many are given permission to be in my presence, as I am sure you are aware."

"Y. . . yes, sir. I am deeply honored, my lor– Kaiser."

"Come with me," he said, placing a hand on Walker's shoulder, ushering the tense man to a narrow channel carved into the marble floor. It looked like it had once served as a water feature but was currently dry. The channel was a few inches deep and nearly twelve feet long. At the end of the trough was a small, square platform.

"Kneel here," said the Kaiser, pointing at the platform.

"For your actions at the enemy's training facility, you will be given the honor of enabling hundreds of men and women to fight for Victus."

"Thank you, my lord. Victus is the way of the future, and I, along with my family, am honored to fight for its cause."

"Only a select few are given the honor of equipping more brothers and sisters to become one of us. Close your eyes now and embrace your destiny."

Walker breathed deeply and closed his eyes. Silas stood back from the ceremony, cleared his throat, and looked at his wristwatch.

As Walker knelt on the cold slab, the Kaiser touched his shoulder. His hand radiated with a purple hue while intense waves of energy pulsated into Walker's shoulder, filling his body with pure, raw power. Walker sighed with satisfaction as the power flowed through his veins. He smiled in pleasure as every cell in his body awakened with the infusion of energy.

"Embrace the power and let it fill every part of you."

"Yes." He sounded elated. "Yes, I can feel the power flowing in my veins, into my very being. Thank you. Thank you, my lo–"

As Walker confirmed the infusion of power, a jagged silver dagger plunged into his chest. The five-inch blade buried to the hilt. A crimson circle expanded around the handle, soaking his white undershirt with blood.

Walker's eyes bulged as he grunted and stuttered in shock.

Kaiser pulled the dagger out of Walker's heart and kicked him forward over the trough, where he fell like a toppled inkwell, his blood spilling underneath him and pouring out toward the opposite end of the stone gap. Though the blood was a rich crimson, it radiated with a purple shimmer from the fusion of the Kaiser's power. He then took a white rag and wiped the blood from the silver dagger.

"Your sacrifice will enable more to fight in our army, just as I have said."

Walker's arms and legs were sprawled out, bridging the gap of the trough in the marble floor. Blood seeped from the corner of his mouth and his face grew pale as the remainder of his life force drained from his body.

"M. . . my family," he managed before his words became incoherent gurgles.

". . .will be well aware of your fate," said the Kaiser.

Kaiser bent down within inches of the dying man and whispered into his ear.

"When you are given the order to time a blast correctly, I expect you to follow through. You failed. The men of Aegis survived, and now you have paid the price."

Silas kept his gaze on his watch, seemingly irritated at the length of time it was taking Walker to die.

The Kaiser straightened up, keeping his back to Silas.

"Assemble the prisoners and have them prepared for the catalysts."

"Yes, my lord. I will have them ready in a few hours."

"Silas."

"Yes, your lordship?"

"As we prepare for the plant, I am charging you to ensure our cover is secure. We must confirm who is on our side and who is not."

Silas bowed slightly, as far as his injury would allow.

"It will happen just as you have said."

7

A Ceremony of Culture

"Welcome Home!"

Streamers hung from every corner of Falcon's living room. The dining table was covered in food, making Thanksgiving supper look like a midnight snack. Branson, Murphy, Chase, Jael, and Cavaness were all there, applauding them through the door. What a wonderful and slightly odd scene. Only odd because Cavaness was obviously forced into the cheer; not at all looking natural.

"Go on, then. Be sure to get more than one plateful. You will need the extra energy for tomorrow," said Alex.

The kids quickly mingled in and started eating.

Jael watched Ailey as she scarfed down her first plate of food and prepared to get a second.

"Hey, Ailey. Do you have a moment?"

Ailey nodded, wiping crumbs from the corner of her mouth.

"I would like to do something, but I want to ask for your permission first. Would you mind if I learned sign language? I have not had the opportunity or need for it yet."

Ailey smiled at Jael's offer and desire to connect. She pointed to herself and made a fist with her thumb to the side, which is the sign for the letter 'A.' She then swooped in the air in the shape of a smile.

Kel happened to glance over at them. "That's the sign for her name. She's saying her name is Ailey."

Jael chuckled. "Thank you, Kel, but I don't need to learn like that. That would take far too long." Jael looked back to Ailey. "Do you mind if I put my hands on your head? I promise to only look at the language skills."

Ailey thought for a moment. Kel watched Jael, very interested to see what would happen next. Ailey looked unsure of what may happen, but her curiosity conquered her concern for the unknown.

"Atta girl. Now, you will feel a tingle, but it won't hurt. I promise."

Jael leaned in, placed her hands on Ailey's head, and closed her eyes. Her wrists began to glow, as did most of Ailey's scalp. Ailey shuddered as if a cold chill had run down her spine. After about five seconds, Jael removed her hands and sat upright.

"How fascinating!" Jael both said and signed together. She then ceased to talk and used only her new signing skills.

"That's incredible. What did you say this power was again?" asked Kel.

"Lumos. I like to think of this gifting as a two-sided coin. Illumination has two different realities. There is physical light, which I can manipulate, but there is also the illumination of the mind. We can acquire knowledge, memories, and life skills at the more advanced levels through touch.

Jael pointed to the ceiling, where a massive chandelier hung, comprised of at least fifty individual lights shaped like flickering candles.

"As for physical lights. . . I think I'll just show you."

Jael held a hand up toward the chandelier. Her pupils changed to amber, and her wrists radiated like burning coals. Simultaneously, the light emanating from the filament in each candle's lightbulb rose out of the glass and remained suspended a few inches above. Jael moved her fingers like she was playing a piano. As she did, the tiny balls of light began to jump over one another in a brilliant display, dancing like fireflies around the light fixture. Everyone in the room stopped what they were doing and stood mesmerized by the light show.

"What in the world is that?" asked Graham. His sense of wonder magnified as the glow of the dancing lights mirrored in his eyes.

Cavaness pointed to Jael. "That's her. It's pretty spectacular, isn't it? I think this gives her more joy than anyone else." Graham looked over, and it seemed true. The joy radiating from Jael's eyes was almost as dazzling as the lights above. "She's had it rough. She came from our European section called Raven, which Victus overtook shortly after the destruction of the Groves. As far as we know, she was the sole survivor."

"That's terrible. How did she find you if she was in Europe?"

"She had a mirror that transported her into the region. You remember the training. Once she put out the vibe, we found her."

"She's lucky we did instead of the others."

"That was a risk she was willing to take. I think it worked out for her," said Cavaness, watching Jael enjoy the moment.

Jael noticed that everyone was watching, so as a grand finale, she commanded the lights to fly around the room, weaving in between each person. The balls of light zoomed around and then suddenly froze in mid-air. Everyone tried to take hold of the lights, grasping and waving their hands through them. She let them play for a few moments, then directed the lights to slowly rise into the air and return to their glass encasements.

"Magnificent. Truly magnificent," said Alex. "I think this is a perfect way to begin the ceremony."

Damien leaned in close to Kel. "Uh-oh. I hope they won't put hoods over our heads again."

Kel elbowed Damien in the side. "Shhh."

"We intended to do this once you had first accepted the adoption papers, but unfortunately, we had been interrupted. Once you were recovered from the cavern, we all decided it would be more meaningful to proceed tonight."

Chase and Branson walked around to stand with the kids.

"Serving is a privilege. Though most of the human race is unaware of our activity, we want to take a few moments to celebrate the revealing of your gifting, alongside your official adoption."

Chase placed a hand on Graham's shoulder and squeezed.

"As in any large community, there are naturally sub-cultures within it. Take America for example. From a very young age, you've learned to hold a strong sense of national pride by pledging allegiance to the flag of this great country. But, within this country, we naturally group ourselves into smaller cultures such as state affiliation, religion, ethnicity, or career. We all take great pleasure in being associated with the place where we grew up, the cultural heritages, and the talents we grow into."

Alex pointed to seven metallic symbols on the wall behind him.

"Our specific giftings have generated communities within Aegis, each having their own subculture, or tribe if you will. Tonight, you will not only be officially recognized under the flag of Aegis but also by your respective tribe. As we move beyond these walls to meet others like us, you will have the opportunity to meet others like you. Aquatics who can control water, Bridges who love to serve strategically by combining giftings, and Pushers who calculate their quakes. As time passes, you will be welcomed into your own community of like-gifted men and women."

Alex paused to let the kids look at the symbols.

"Of course, there are a plethora of giftings. . . many more than seven. I chose these seven specifically because these are the gifts on which each of our seven regional headquarters – our seven outposts – were founded. They were and are the seven pillars on which our society was built."

Some of the symbols were already familiar to Graham, but he did not recognize a few. Ailey stood on her tiptoes and peered at the icons. The light from the chandelier above reflected streaks of gold across their glossy surfaces.

"These symbols are an outward sign of the pride of a community I hope you will grow to love. Once the Council has had its say, we will begin reaching out to the other Aegis communities. With any measure of luck, you will meet up with others like you very soon."

Alex walked over, took his drinking glass in his hand, and held it high.

"Now, when you have eaten your fill, I have something else I want to show you."

8

Full Impact

Graham had never seen the third floor of Falcon before. There were only two rooms there. Alex had led them past the first door to where the second was already ajar. He took the handle and opened the door, revealing a bizarre and spectacular sight. It was dizzying to see all the reflecting light. As Graham walked into the room, he was overwhelmed by the sheer number of mirrors mounted on the walls, floor to ceiling, covering nearly every square inch of wall space.

"Are these all transit mirrors?" asked Jael in apparent amazement.

"Yes, they are indeed," replied Alex.

"It must have taken an eternity to create these. How in the world is this even possible?"

"Every wall is built stone by stone. This is no different. It's just a very old wall," Alex said.

Damien, Kel, and Ailey spread out to take it all in. The room was a marvel. They did not know what went into or how long it took to create a trans, but decades of effort were represented here even if it took only a week for each one. Kel stood directly in front of a mirror and noticed her reflection was not staring back. She shuffled over to the next one, which had the same result.

"What?"

Kel heard Damien's clunky footsteps as he shuffled from side to side. He had realized the oddity as well.

"Why is there no reflection?" asked Kel.

"Most mirrors like these hang on public display, so the Weaver who made them will usually keep the reflective properties in place. For these, it was not necessary. Knowing the nature of this room, I am certain that the Weaver simply wanted to salvage as much time as possible. The light can reflect off the surface, but that is all. The purpose of these mirrors is not to look at yourself but to the needs of others. This is why I have brought you here."

On the adjacent wall from the door was an ornate wooden desk. It was the only piece of furniture in the giant room, which made it appear much smaller than it really was. Alex led them to it, pointing to the mirrors hanging over the top. Though almost every trans differed in small ways, the ones that hung over the desk differed drastically in style and size. They were much larger and oval, with a type of wooden crown stretching across the top of each one. Within the ornate crown was a bird, and the emblem of a gifting was held in each of their beaks. As he continued to observe, he quickly noted that these had a reflection and that two of the mirrors were cracked, as if someone had slammed a fist in the middle of them.

"What happened to these?" asked Graham, pointing to the broken mirrors.

"That is why we are here. It's also why we pushed you to your limits in training," replied Alex. "These six mirrors represent our entire network. They connect to each of the regional headquarters. There are six others worldwide, and we are standing in the seventh."

Alex took a step back and gestured for Murphy to continue. Cavaness remained still, planted like a tree with his arms crossed, waiting to hear Murphy's explanation of the events.

"Okay, where do I start? I don't think you have heard the whole story." Murphy looked over to Alex. "Do you want them to hear it all?"

Alex nodded.

"Right. I'm sure you haven't forgotten what Silas did the night you were activated. It would've been bad enough if stealing you was all he had done, but the damage was much more widespread. When Silas found Catalyst Grove, he could detect its energy signature."

As Murphy spoke about the destruction, Alex and Cavaness watched Murphy and Branson's reactions.

"It is kinda hard to explain, but in a nutshell, the power that protects the new members as they navigate the Grove is the same for all training facilities. Unless you are really good at masking your energy signature, others like us can track it. We don't know for sure, but based on my knowledge as a Former, I'm guessing that once Silas detected the unique signature, he could send that information to every Former under his command. They could blanket the sky with their scouts, which are the tracking balls I used to find you in the forest. It probably didn't take long based on their number of Formers."

Cavaness glanced at Alex and shrugged with a look of uncertainty. He cleared his throat.

"Branson, why don't you take over? Your military mind will be able to explain the next part."

Murphy stepped back and let Branson pass, who stood

before the others, his hands clasped behind his back.

"Once they knew the locations, I'm sure it only took a few hours to form their frontline attack. You begin with what you know the most about. The training facilities were the first to go. Their positions were compromised, and we could do little to protect them. We were able to send news to a few of our teams, but in our estimations, over seventy percent were destroyed by Victus."

"Who is Victus? No one has mentioned that name to me," blurted Damien.

"Remember the Unseen War? We are Aegis, formed under the direction of the Elder immortal. Victus is the group formed under the Younger. It's the organization for which Silas fights. I don't know if you remember what he said the night he took you, but it's because of those two words that Alex has called the Council together."

"I don't think I heard what he said."

Branson seemed to continue with caution.

"Vae Victus."

"What?"

"I'll let Alex explain that one. Now, as I said, seventy percent of the Groves were laid to waste. We were able to evacuate the other thirty percent. Once they were clear, we destroyed them."

Branson paused to let that fact sink in. Cavaness watched intently.

"You, along with the other recruits who were being developed that night are the final inductees. We couldn't risk any more of our outposts being discovered. Any other form of power that linked one place to another would have been detected. Our ability to recruit is no longer an option. It pains me to say this, but you are the last."

Graham was sure that he did not fully understand the impact of what Branson was saying, but his stomach still felt as though it were going to drop through his feet. He couldn't wrap his mind around that amount of destruction. Things were a lot more serious than he had ever thought.

Jael tried to suppress her emotion, but hard sobs pounded their way out of her body.

"Sorry… I'm sorry."

Her whimpers echoed through the room as she dashed out the door. Branson bowed his head in respectful remorse as she glided past him. Murphy also stood still, his gaze fixed to the floor. Cavaness and Alex took note. Once she had left the room, Branson cleared his throat and continued.

"Her Outpost was hit hard, as you may already know." Branson pointed to one of the two broken Trans. "There must have been something in their training facility that linked to Raven. It was overtaken."

Jael's cries could still be heard faintly. Branson pointed to the other broken mirrors.

"Albatross was also destroyed before we could make contact."

Branson, even as a trained soldier, could not help but pause to control his emotions.

"Victus hit, and they hit hard. We allowed ourselves to believe that we couldn't be discovered. We became prideful, and many have paid for that arrogance with their lives."

Branson paused again. Murphy's gaze remained fixed, and the muscles in his jaw tightened as he gritted his teeth. The joy of the party from downstairs fell flat under the despair of their current circumstances. Gloom permeated the room as a moment of silence fell over them. As Alex walked over to address everyone, Jael slipped back through the door. Ailey signed to her. Jael forced a smile through her sorrow and signed back.

"We have pushed you beyond any reasonable limit for your age. I know you have questioned why you could not train together as a team. This is why. Over the past months, each of your mentors has used these mirrors to go on scouting missions to find the best points of attack to regain control of our fallen outposts. They have each gone in shifts, leaving only one behind to continue your training. We need you and your gifts, but I will not send you unprepared to the heat of battle. I have pushed these men just as hard as they have pushed you. Tomorrow, the Council will meet. If I am to convince them of just how powerful and dangerous Victus has become and the destruction they have created, we must also provide our plans for a counterattack."

Alex walked over and removed a broken Trans from the wall.

"I have created replacements. Before we can go on the defensive against Victus, we must go on the offensive and re-establish connections with all seven outposts. If we can make contact with the regional directors, they can, in turn, gather their forces within their region. We cannot fight as scattered sheep. Our number one priority must be to gather together and fight as one. To protect our weakened network, we must successfully reset the mirrors. Once each mirror is set in each outpost, they will connect and activate uniquely."

Alex placed the mirror on the desk and put his hands in his pockets.

"The Council will not see it this way," said Cavaness to the kids. "They will want to use reason and negotiate with Victus. You know nothing of our culture or way of life. Not yet, anyway. I wish you could've seen it even ten years ago. It would've been a much better picture than what you are about to see. You will hear all sorts of nonsense in that meeting tomorrow, so I don't want you to be caught off guard by their naivety."

Cavaness could see the confusion in their eyes and the struggle to comprehend everything being said, so he chose his next words carefully.

"Understand this. You cannot reason with evil. It's a force that refuses to bow to logic. Evil has one purpose, and one purpose only. . . to destroy and conquer."

9

New Memories Reveal

Pillars of black mist twisted through the trees, causing the branches and leaves to bend and twist. The wind began to howl, and the sound of cracking limbs caused Graham's father to turn around and take a hard stance in front of his family.

Graham's nightmares had been fewer since coming to Aegis, but every so often, they would return. He didn't always see the morphing of the black mist, but this time, he stood opposite a pair of black panthers. They sprinted out of the forest and grew larger and taller. Their fangs and gleaming purple eyes towered upward, twisting in a circular motion and morphing into the pillars of black mist he was now seeing through his two-year-old eyes.

He could hear himself cry in fear. He looked down to see

his little hands balled into fists and shaking. *Was this real?* Graham could feel the wind in his hair and the terror in every heartbeat. It was as if he were reliving the moment in his two-year-old body. He had always felt a certain degree of his parents' fear, but never had he felt the raw emotions of both their fear and power before.

Graham cried out again as he heard his father scream at the fog, warning it to stay back. Then, something happened that he had never seen before. His dad pulled back his hands and fired a massive wave of energy at the smoke. Graham watched as his father's wrists beamed with a brilliant yellow shimmer. He turned around to see his mother lying on her side. Her arm was bent underneath her head, her body limp and motionless. Wisps of black fog curled around her and darted toward his dad. Seeing this, Graham lost control and screamed at the top of his lungs.

The ending was always the same, but he did get a glimpse of his body before blacking out. His shirt whipped and twisted as if the wind was emanating from himself. He watched as the light grew more intense, starting from his chest and radiating outward. He had always guessed the light's source, but now he could know for sure. It was coming from him. There was no doubt now that he was the reason for being an orphan.

Graham fell to the side, facing his mother, who was still unconscious. His vision became blurry, his head swimming. The world went dark, as it always had, and Graham fully expected to wake up in a cold sweat. He thought it funny how he could be semi-coherent during a dream like this, consciously waiting for reality to return. Still, the nightmare had become so ingrained in him that it eventually became natural. As he pondered this odd ability, he noticed he was still dreaming. The scene was black, but it wasn't because he was now awake.

It felt like he was in a room with terrible lighting. Like seeing people through a thick fog, he could make out hazy shapes. Opening his two-year-old eyes, he noticed his mother was no longer lying on the ground. He could see a vacant space and what he guessed to be a cluster of trees nearby. He felt two hands slide under his armpits. Someone was picking him up. He looked and saw a shadowy figure holding him at eye level, but could not make out who he was, or even if it was a he.

"Hey there, Graham-cracker. Wake up, little buddy. Come on, be strong," said the stranger.

The voice was indeed male, but he snapped out of the dream before Graham could get any more information. He sat straight up in bed. Nothing was hovering. Ever since the application of the catalysts, the supernatural effects of these nightmares had stopped.

He could only focus on the new part of the dream. *Who picked me up? Was that my dad? Are they still alive?* His heart raced at the thought, and he could vaguely remember being called Graham-cracker, though he couldn't recall who gave him the name. He was sure his mom was not on the ground, right? He tried to remember again, but he could not summon the scene. *She could have been carried away, but what if she was okay? What if she walked away? What did this mean?* Graham rubbed his eyes with his palms and tried to take it in.

He had to know more. He woke up with such a rush of adrenaline that he knew he would never go back to sleep, but he wanted to try. Maybe his dream would pick back where he had left off, and he could know for certain that his parents were still alive. He looked over at the nightstand beside his bed. 2:35 glared back at him in red numbers. He wanted so badly to rush to Alex and tell him what he had just seen. He knew he couldn't, though. Not at this time of night. Graham grunted in disappointment and reluctantly slipped back under the covers. He grabbed his rubber ball, his one treasured possession, which he'd had for as long as he could remember, and tossed it in the air.

Having his own room was still odd. He enjoyed the solitude, but after a lifetime of sharing a room with a cluster of noisy sleepers, he still struggled to adjust to the silence. Graham slowly let go of consciousness as his eyes grew heavier with each toss. Only one question lingered in his mind as he drifted into sleep.

Were they still alive?

10

THE COUNCIL MEETING

The following day came much too quickly. Graham woke up groggy, fumbling around his room until he could put on clothes and brush his teeth. He wanted to find Alex and tell him about his dream, but as he entered the dining room, he noticed that everyone was still eating in silence. For a celebration, last night did not end well. The sad atmosphere had dispersed throughout the mansion, lingering throughout the morning. Graham was glad to see that at least Jael seemed to be in better spirits. She hummed a tune as she continued preparing for the meeting. He sat down to a plate of scrambled eggs and bacon, still steaming and smelling like heaven. He devoured the plate in three bites, wiped his mouth, and followed everyone else upstairs to the room of mirrors. Alex reached up and pointed to a mirror at head level.

"This is the one. This trans will take us to a small bakery about a mile from Council Hall. Pair up and remember to take a deep breath right before you enter." Graham was sure Alex was speaking to him more than anyone. "It makes the nausea a little less intense. Once we are there, you will need to mask. Remember your training and focus on suppressing your catalyst energy. Victus has never been spotted in the area, but we must be cautious."

Graham stared at the mirror as Alex spoke. There was not much to distinguish this mirror from the rest. They were all slightly different, but unlike the outpost trans, the rest had no markings to set them apart. It was as if Alex had memorized every destination, which wouldn't surprise Graham. It seemed like anything was possible where Alex was concerned.

As in Portfield, each adult paired with one of the kids. They took a deep breath as the adult in each pair put their hand to the center of the mirror. Their bands illuminated, and they vanished.

It had been a month since he had gone through a trans, and the breathing technique was worthless. Graham emerged with every muscle in his body tensed, as did the others. All he wanted to do was vomit. Graham slowly unclenched his fists and pried open his eyes to see a storage room with shelves holding bags of flour on each side. He looked to his left, and to his relief, Damien and the others were in no better shape.

"We need to come out in stages and mingle among the customers so it's not obvious that we have emerged from the storage closet," said Alex.

"But first, it's time to mask," said Cavaness. "Just like we taught you."

Graham put one hand over the other. His top hand remained facing downward, his lower hand twisted palm side up. He then clasped both wrists and closed his eyes in deep concentration. The bands illuminated for a second, letting the light spill between his fingers, then slowly faded as if they were on a dimmer switch. He slowly exhaled and looked down. The bands were still visible, but just barely. The dim light pulsated for a few more seconds and then faded away.

The others had done the same. Once finished, Cavaness held out a hand and swept it through the air, stopping briefly in front of each person. "Good. I can tell you have been practicing. I can't detect any energy."

Two by two, they walked through the back door into the bakery's lobby. After a few minutes passed, the next two emerged. Everyone must have been on a break from work. It was mid-morning, and the place could hardly fit another body. Murmured conversations filled the room. Order bells rang while the man behind the desk yelled, "Order up!" followed by a person's name. As Alex passed the front counter, one of the workers turned his back to the crowd and pulled his fist to his chest.

"Best of luck today, Alex. The council may be hard-headed, but plenty of us are on your side."

"Thank you, Landon. That means a lot. Do you have someone on standby to run this place?"

"Yes, sir. Everything is in order. Just give me your word, and I'll be there."

"Good man. I should think you will be called upon very soon."

"I am at your command."

Landon gave another salute and turned back to the next customer in line, whose fingers were dancing across her cell phone, utterly oblivious to anything happening around her. Weaving through the masses, the Aegis team gathered outside, pouring out onto the city sidewalk.

"Where are we?" asked Kel.

"Do you not recognize Time Square?" replied Alex, pointing to the iconic buildings and screens.

"You mean where they always do the New Year's Eve party on TV?"

"Yes, it sure is. I was coming here the night you became one of us."

Graham was stunned. He had no idea what Kel and Alex were talking about. He never bothered to watch the ball drop on TV. All the other kids at Greenwood took any chance they could to watch TV. The living room was always so crowded then. He had always taken that as his chance to seclude himself and get a little peace and quiet. Now, he wished he had. He had never seen such tall buildings in all his life. They dwarfed even the three old buildings in Wellington. There were people, cars, food, and flashing lights everywhere he looked. His nostrils filled with a bizarre mixture of car exhaust and hot dogs. It was magnificent.

Alex smiled, enjoying the wonder in Graham's eyes. Even Jael was a bit enthralled. He allowed them to take it all in for a moment before continuing.

"We need to split up. I doubt we will be able to navigate this crowd in one pack. Let's pair up again and stay about ten paces apart, staggered throughout the masses."

They stayed to the right of the center row of buildings and then took a series of turns through the city blocks. It took a while to walk a mile on a crowded New York morning, but eventually, they arrived at a towering skyscraper. The exterior was made entirely of glass. They entered and glided through the main lobby to a hallway which led to a cluster of elevators. Fortunately, no one else wanted to get into the elevator with them, as ten bodies were already enough to fill the small space. Alex reached towards the columns of buttons and pressed number thirty-three.

The elevator ascended quickly and stopped with the chime of a bell and an electronic female voice confirming that they had reached the thirty-third floor. After taking a right out of the elevator and a few left turns, they arrived in a short hallway that dead-ended into an exterior glass wall. There was one door on the left wall and no doors on the right.

"Here we are. Once we enter, I want you to make your way to the visitor's section and find a seat together," said Alex to the kids.

Graham turned toward the door but quickly noticed that everyone else was facing the opposite direction. He turned around just in time to see Alex's hand against the wall with a glowing doorway appearing beside it.

"Quickly now, we do not want any unexpected visitors."

They shuffled through the secret doorway in the solid wall. As Alex passed through, the door vanished. They now stood in an unfinished section of the building. This room was comprised of bare metal studs, some random sheets of hanging plastic, and bundles of wire, as though the construction workers had abandoned it.

What an odd place for such an important meeting. Graham was underwhelmed.

"Do you see the visitor's section?" asked Graham.

"I don't see any kind of section," replied Damien. "I think we went through the wrong portal."

"We are exactly where we need to be," snapped Cavaness. "This is not a time for joking."

Alex stood with his hands in his pockets, gazing out over the city skyline and the people on the sidewalk below. Jael stood beside him.

"We take a lot for granted, don't we?"

Jael nodded. "Yes, we certainly do. I still find it hard to believe they are all unaware of what is happening. Can they not feel it? Do they not sense the evil that is growing all around them?"

"You have been so accustomed to our world that you forget what it was like before you came. You know and can sense it because you have seen it first-hand." Alex pointed to her wrist. "That has allowed you to see it. On the other hand, they have chosen to keep busy with their day-to-day lives, unaware or ignoring the subtle calling signs on this side of the veil. It's not all their fault, though. The veil is thick, and you must remember that long ago, they wanted it this way."

Jael shook her head in disbelief.

"That's why we do what we do, Jael. Day in and day out, we train, develop, and fight against Victus so that, in the end, they will know the truth."

Alex glanced behind him to Graham. "That time may be much sooner than we all realize."

Cavaness led the others over to the window where Alex stood.

"The meeting is about to begin. I think it's time we go in."

Alex placed his hand on the large glass window. As he did, an invisible wave of energy rippled across the surface, causing the window to turn off its transparency. In place of the view of the city below, it displayed an open foyer filled with busy people.

Graham looked to each side, plainly seeing the city through the panes of glass to either side. Like Falcon, this place was cloaked and hidden from the outside world.

Branson herded the kids through the passage into a large room like the lobby downstairs. There were windows all around which mimicked the windows of the building they had just come from. Kel and Ailey looked beyond the city, squinting and holding their hands out to block the sun.

Graham marveled at the sight. The Council Hall stretched out between two buildings like a catwalk. They were literally hovering over the city street. He watched as a pair of birds lazily glided toward him. They darted back and forth around each other in what Graham thought might be some form of tag. Graham was so entertained with their playfulness that he did not realize how close they were to him. They were so close, in fact, that he was scared they would hit the cloaked building. He reached out as if to warn them of the invisible threat. He held his breath as they were about to slam into the undetectable window, but instead of hitting the glass, they simply vanished. Graham looked around, hoping to see the birds flying inside the foyer, but couldn't find them.

"Hey Graham, come take a look at these two birds. They are dogfighting like those two planes from the movie we saw last summer," said Damien.

Graham sprinted to the other side of the room, and just as Damien had described, he could see the tail end of the two birds fluttering about without a care or concern.

"They just flew right through us! I watched them on the other side of the room, and they disappeared through the window."

"Crazy, man," said Damien.

"Crazy? It's unbelievable! How's that even possible?" Graham replied.

"Yes, ma'am. That is correct. Yes, four. Okay, thank you very much. Good day." Alex finished his conversation with the receptionist. He gave four green badges to the kids, a crimson-red badge to Chase, and a dark gold badge to the others.

"What are these?" asked Graham.

"These are your security badges, color-coded by tenure. Green for newcomers, yellow for beginner levels, red for intermediates, and gold for veterans. The council wants to understand who you are at a glance." Alex opened the door beyond the reception desk. "You need to sit together by color. Greens are to the far left as you go inside."

Alex looked at the clock on the wall and smiled as he ushered them inside.

11

A CALL TO REASON

Alex had broken off from the group to prepare for his speech. Graham grew nervous looking around the great hall. The ceiling was towering. The roof's framework sloped to the four corners of the massive room, held up by four massive pillars, which were hewn into giant human statues, each in a different pose.

The first was of a robed man with one hand over his heart and the other outstretched, clasping a flaming torch. The torch's flames whipped and curled around the beam that held the ceiling. The man's gaze was fixed toward the sky. Bold letters at its base spelled the word **TRUTH**.

The second statue was of a warrior on the defensive, fighting off an attack. His lower half was facing toward the center of the room, but his upper half was twisted around with a shield stretched upward, holding the roof structure. His offensive hand had curled fingers, poised for attack. A catalyst band was carved into his wrist, and the underside of his shield held the Aegis Sun. The inscription at its base was **VALOR**.

The third statue appeared to be a lady reaching down to pull another person out of a trap or pit. She held a glowing sun in one hand and had a firm grip on the other person's wrist with the other. Graham thought the orb-like sun in her hand must again be the Aegis symbol. The person in distress was disturbing. Her body was only visible from the waist up, giving the appearance that she was trapped inside the floor. There was a look of terror in her eyes, and tentacles had wrapped themselves around her torso, creeping up around her shoulders. It would have been a bleak picture had the misery not been balanced out by the care coming from the other woman. **COMPASSION** was the word carved into the base of this pillar.

The fourth and final pillar was a woman holding a swaddled newborn baby. She was the only statue who did not have a hand upward, holding the roof system. Instead, she focused solely on her child, holding it in a loving embrace. They looked inseparable. Graham followed the trail of her robe down the length of her arm, where he noticed that her sleeves were pulled back, revealing her catalysts. He was quite impressed with the woodworker's ability to carve the bands in such a way as to show they were glowing. They looked as if the wood itself had a glow of ember underneath the surface. It was a beautiful depiction of love and protection. A large rectangle stood out from her robes, and on it was the word **LOVE**.

Looking above her head, Graham noticed the Sun again, stretched out over the mother. The bottom flare was sweeping the crest of her head while the other curled up the roof beam. All four beams arched upward until they met in the middle. There was also something hanging from the center where they joined. Graham shifted so that he could get a better view. It appeared to be a sword or dagger.

"It's quite a sight, isn't it," said Chase. "Kinda makes you feel like an ant. I still can't figure out how they built this place without anyone knowing,"

"What are the statues for?" asked Graham.

"They represent the universal virtues on which Aegis was built. If I know Alex, I am sure he will reiterate their significance to the council. I don't think they even pay attention to them anymore." Chase looked saddened as he spoke. The last few weeks seemed to have matured him. Where Chase would usually try to inject a heavy dose of sarcasm, he now spoke with a more serious tone. "Attributes like virtue seem to be a cozy, happy thought rather than a firm reality these days. I hope you can cut through all the bull you are about to hear." Chase pointed to the statue of the armored soldier. "The council doesn't see things in those terms anymore. They've let a twisted sense of diplomacy warp their view of reality. They act as though they can solve the world's problems over a cup of coffee. Remember what Cavaness said."

In the center of the meeting hall stood six people, one of whom was Alex. The podiums were placed in a circle so no one had a place of prominence over the rest, like a modern-day version of King Arthur's table. The conversation had already begun. Stadium seating for all the members stretched across every wall, allowing everyone a good view. Graham, Kel, Ailey, and Damien sat in the middle of the group of newcomers. The others had mingled in their respective crowds, listening to the ongoing conversation below.

"We are comprised of civilized nations now. Surely you see that," said a thin, aged man.

"That depends on your definition of civilized," replied Alex.

"You must look at the achievements of the past sixty

years. Victus has been nearly silent. Don't you think they understand that we must coexist?" asked a tall, middle-aged woman at the podium facing Alex.

"Have you ever stood in the eye of a hurricane, Ms. Mills?" asked Alex.

"No, I cannot say that I have."

"It's eerily silent. As soon as a section of the storm passes, it appears to be perfectly normal again. It is a deceptive force. The opposite becomes reality as soon as you think the worst is behind you. Ladies and Gentlemen of the council, I stand among you today to tell you that Victus is rising. Time is their chessboard, and they make calculated moves. In chess, there are periods of positioning your pieces before you strike. I assure you, this is no different."

"That may have been true in the past, but things change, Alex," said the plump, balding man to his right. "We have successfully negotiated with members of Victus to stop their vile antics and listen to reason. Weapons of war change over time. Our ancestors fought with rocks. They gradually advanced to bronze and steel. Horseback riders developed into chariots. Swords and bows were upgraded to guns and tanks. Now, we have intellect, reason, and logic."

"Mr. Lee, can you not see that they are using these very tools against you? Their so-called 'negotiations' are a Trojan horse. Evil does not sit at a table and negotiate. It schemes. It devises plans. It deceives. Evil does many things, but compromise is not one of them."

Alex addressed the other members of the council with an impressive combination of calmness and authority. With every question and point of view described, Alex stood his ground on his view of reality.

Graham looked over to a dark, muscular man on the front row of the veteran section. His arms were crossed, and he shook his head in obvious frustration. It was difficult to tell who he was upset with, Alex or the council.

The balding man spoke up once again. "One immortal

being cannot possibly conquer another immortal being. Don't you see? The only way forward is a shared existence. There is absolutely no point in two immovable forces fighting against one another. Surely you, of all people, can see the logic in that."

Alex paused. The room fell silent and felt torn in two with tension.

"There is a popular fable about a scorpion and a frog. Have you heard it? As the story goes, a scorpion wanted to cross a river to continue his journey, but, of course, scorpions do not swim. As he stood at the water's edge, a frog hopped by. The scorpion asked the frog why he was hopping away so fast, and the frog told him that a hungry snake was hunting him. The scorpion told the frog that if he allowed him to cross the river on his back, he would stand guard against the snake should he try to follow. The frog was worried because he knew scorpions sting and kill their prey. 'How do I know you will not sting me?' asked the frog. The scorpion assured him that he would not sting him because if he did, then they would both drown. The frog looked into the distance and saw the bending of the tall grass and knew that the snake was closing in, so he made his agreement with the scorpion. He hopped in the water, allowing the scorpion to crawl onto his back. The frog waded into the middle of the river, feeling very relieved and grateful that the scorpion had kept his word until he felt a sharp pain in his lower back. 'What have you done?' the frog gasped in panic. The scorpion's poison was paralyzing his muscles, and they began to sink below the water's surface. 'You have killed us both!' The scorpion remained calm as they both sank into the depths. 'Sorry, old boy. I cannot help it. I'm compelled to sting you because that is my nature.' Within moments, they had both drowned."

Alex made eye contact with each council member before continuing.

"It doesn't matter what makes sense. Evil will always

strive to destroy and conquer because that is its nature. You cannot change that nature any more than you can persuade a flower to eat bees or a lion to stop killing and eat grass."

The council members looked at one another, perplexed. Cavaness and the others were murmuring under their breath, silently pleading for them to listen to Alex. Graham was doing the same. How could they not agree with Alex after that? He knew he was biased after being taken by Silas and nearly killed by him. He understood the flicker of madness behind the sophisticated exterior. He could hear his calm voice as he threw Damien into the water to die.

"Alex, we are beyond parables," said a black female council member. "They are beginning to negotiate. We have seen the fruit of our efforts. Wouldn't you rather see them come to the light that Aegis stands for? That is an attainable and noble goal."

"Surely you don't mean that!" exclaimed the swarthy man on the front row of the veteran section. "You *cannot* be serious."

"I would remind you, Mr. Corbin, that this meeting is a discussion between council members only. I would advise you to hold your tongue," said the thin man.

Alex looked over to Corbin, and with a smile, he gestured for Corbin to sit back down. He turned his focus back to the council.

"On a case-by-case basis, Madam Reynolds, I would agree, however, speaking for Victus as a whole. . . I wonder what your sister would have said."

Madam Reynolds gasped as shock spread across her face. "How incredibly inappropriate to bring that up, especially here. You have no right to–"

"Madam Reynolds, I don't mean to offend, but I think you have forgotten what they are capable of. I only wish to remind you of what the leopard's spots look like."

"And I will thank you for leaving my deceased family out of the discussion. That was over two decades ago, and we have made substantial progress since then. Alicia would be proud of our achievements." Madam Reynolds paused to compose herself. "Every organization has its fanatics. That does not mean that they are all that way. We can convince the majority to see the truth."

"Forgive me, Madam Reynolds, but you are wrong on this. Victus has existed for thousands of years. You speak of manmade organizations, and your logic applies only there, but when the leader at the helm is one of those fanatics, you have an entire enterprise that operates under that influence. Water pours from the top of the waterfall, drenching every rock underneath. This is the case for Victus, and the one pouring the water is infinite."

"And if we light the fire from the bottom, it will consume to the top. We will begin with the foot soldiers, and the influence will carry up to the Kaiser himself," said Ms. Mills, stepping in to allow Madam Reynolds to regain her composure.

"Be careful, then, that you are not consumed by the fire you create." Alex took a breath and cleared his throat. "And let's move beyond that name, shall we? Kaiser is just his title and a false one, I might add."

The balding man cut in. "And it is a name that need not be repeated in this great hall."

Alex shook his head in disappointment. He took a sip of water from the glass on his podium before continuing. "The majority of the vote of this council will stand, but I stand as a witness to your decision. Looking over the past few thousand years, what do you see as the fruit of their labors? Do you see reason? Do you see the slightest bend towards change? Just because we live in a modern society doesn't mean their passion and motivation will match the age. Since the enlightenment, each generation has claimed to be the modern, sophisticated society that will overcome bias and usher in an era of peace, yet evil remains all the same."

Alex looked back to Graham. He signaled for him to step

forward. Graham looked around hesitantly, but after seeing Alex motion again to come, he sheepishly stood up and went to Alex, who bent down and whispered in his ear.

"Go stand in the middle. I will tell you what to do in a moment."

Graham obeyed, and though his legs did not want to carry him forward, he swallowed the lump in his throat and forced them to obey. He stood in the council circle with his hands halfway in his pockets, awaiting further instruction.

"Ladies and Gentlemen of the council, I present to you Graham Dawson. He and three others here today were among the final wave of recruits. Silas himself destroyed our training facility and took these children captive. Children. Just before vanishing through a transit mirror, he made a declaration. He left four of our men to die in a crumbling building, and as he departed, he left them with the words, 'Vae Victus.'"

The council members looked to one another and began to murmur.

"I need not remind you what that means, as I am sure you are already very well aware, so I ask you, Mr. Lee. . . show me their reason in destroying our training facilities, murdering thousands, and declaring war? Can you negotiate with that?"

Mr. Lee remained silent.

Alex continued. "If you want to understand their reasons, let me show you their true motivation. Graham, please pull up your sleeves so everyone can see your wrists."

Graham did as Alex asked and made eye contact, asking with his eyes if he should do what he thought Alex was asking of him. Alex nodded in confirmation. Graham gritted his teeth and balled his fists, holding his wrists upward so the council members could see the emblem in his glowing catalyst bands. As the light grew brighter, the Aegis sun and the dagger-like shape that held the symbol were visible.

The entire meeting hall erupted with chatter. The council

members looked at Graham in utter disbelief. While Madam Reynolds whispered to the man beside her, Corbin stood up and cupped his hands around his mouth.

"What more proof do ya need? Ya really think dey'll listen to reason knowing we have *him* on our side?"

"Silas experienced first-hand what Graham is capable of," said Alex. "When kidnapped and taken hostage underground, Graham attacked. His power took over fifty feet of dirt and rock and flung it into the air like a handful of sand."

Alex turned to Kel, Damien, and Ailey and motioned for them to stand, along with the others from Falcon.

"This boy and his friends nearly died that night, and so did their mentors. Thousands of others in Groves around the globe perished that night, both experienced Aegis members and recruits alike, because Victus knew we had found Graham. Do you honestly believe they will now sit at a table with you and negotiate a peace agreement?"

Alex immediately retrieved Graham from the circle and walked him back to the green section, allowing his question to linger. He bent down to whisper. "Thank you, Graham. I know that was uncomfortable." Alex ushered him to his seat and returned to his position.

"As is our policy, we will meet twice more to discuss all of the evidence and viewpoints before coming to a vote. Unless you have anything further, I move to adjourn," said Mr. Lee.

Ms. Mills raised a hand and seconded Alex's motion to dismiss.

12

CORBIN'S RECRUITMENT

As the Council members stepped away from their podiums and left the room, Corbin jogged to Alex as the others from Falcon gathered around. They huddled in the back corner of the hall in front of the Valor statue.

"How can dey argue against that. . . and *you*, of all people," he said in a thick Cajun accent.

"They are blinded by their motives, Corbin. When seeds like that are planted and take root in the heart, it is nearly impossible to weed them out. If we are not careful as we attempt to remove them, the entire heart will be uprooted."

"Yeah, well, sounds like a few of dem could use a new heart anyway. Maybe the old one needs rippin' out. I can't believe dey think Victus will shake hands and be buddies. So what now?"

"Now, we act. We can't wait for the next two sessions to take place. We must assemble teams and reconnect the fallen headquarters. We need a complete force, and right now, we're scattered." Alex put a hand on Corbin's shoulder. "Thank you for your support. It was a bit out of place, but it was appreciated nonetheless. We need men and women with your zeal to continue our fight."

"Thanks, Alex. I appreciate that," said Corbin in his relaxed, suave tone.

"How many do you have left from your team?" said Alex.

"Ever since we got word from you that night about the Groves, we've been spread pretty thin trying to make contact within our region. I only left a handful with me at EagleEye, keep'n five or six others. Three are veterans, but the others aren't above level eight."

"Can you trust one of the three veterans to remain in charge?"

"Yeah, I think ol' Bru Bennett can remain over the HQ. . . why?"

"Come, we need to speak where there are fewer ears."

Alex took them through a side door to a smaller conference room where the council members met privately. Alex took a seat at the head of the table. Corbin sat beside him and Cavaness to the other side. Chase and Branson also sat, along with Graham and the other kids. Murphy leaned against a large window.

Alex finished his train of thought once everyone was seated. "Corbin, I need you to assemble the other two veterans and help us regain the other outposts. We don't have many leaders left."

"Sure, Alex, whatever you need."

"What giftings make up your team?"

"Well, let's see. If Bru remains at the HQ, that leaves a Snype and a Scorcher, and of course me as a Former."

"Not a bad combination. Your team is best suited to go to Europe and recover Raven. Gather your team and supplies and meet me in the bakery tomorrow at midday."

"Sure thing. I've been waitin' to release a little frustration anyway. Might as well do it on some Vics."

Alex ignored the comment. "I will provide the details tomorrow, though, from Branson's reports, the building is almost visible again since no one is left to replenish the power source for the veil that conceals it. Since the trans has been destroyed, the closest drop-off point is approximately ten miles away on the outskirts of the city. You will need to assess the damage, make contact with the local team, and replenish the power source. If the general populace begins to see the building, we will have city-wide panic to deal with."

"Understood. I'll gather the team and supplies. We'll find them, Alex. Rest assured. If anyone's left, we'll bring 'em back."

Cavaness leaned forward to join the conversation.

"In the meantime, we will assemble and send two teams and make contact with the Director of the other fallen outpost."

"My gosh, how many are destroyed? I thought we got the word out in time," said Corbin.

"Two for now," said Cavaness in his usual deep, gravelly voice. "Albatross and Raven have gone dark. Since the mirrors were destroyed, we have been assessing their closest drop-off locations, conditions, and security status."

"Man, we are worse off than I thought. You really think we can reconnect the network?"

"We must do all we can," said Alex. "Victus has made their move, so we must make ours."

13

RALLY CRY

A legion of men and women stood in a round cobblestone courtyard, looking up at the man standing on the balcony, leaning on his cane. Questions of why they were gathered floated through the crowd as they waited for Silas to speak. The sky overhead was overcast and dark, nearly the color of the stone floor beneath their feet.

"A few short months ago, we discovered that our very way of life was threatened. All over the world, the Aegis group had been secretly recruiting and training their army to eradicate our way of life."

Silas analyzed the crowd for reactions and for fighters.

"We are the way, the cure, and the future of this disheveled planet. Within Victus is peace, security, and the ability to build a better world. Aegis, on the other hand, stands in stark contrast. They defend the current system, the status quo, and see no issue in living in the shadows of the normal realm. The veil that divides our world from the rest of humanity will not remain forever, and when it's gone, the masses will see the world in its true form. Make no mistake. . . even now, the one who will tip the balance has been found by Alexander and the Aegis group. With this young boy, they have been given their marching orders to take us out permanently."

Shouts of anger and resentment came from the crowd below. Silas allowed them to quibble as he leaned on his cane. Once satisfied with the crowd's discontent, he held a hand in the air, commanding silence.

"We must assemble and retaliate quickly. Aegis is already on the move, and we are now like a boxer on his back foot, having to fight from the defensive. Today, we will choose many of you to fight. What happens in the coming days will go down in history as the day Victus took a stand and gained the advantage over the enemy. We are living in a time foretold thousands of years ago, and you are chosen by fate to be a part of its fulfillment. You can be the one who tips the balance of power in our favor. We will advance on several regional Aegis outposts to confront them directly. Kill who you can. Intimidate and strike fear in the hearts of the rest, but remember, the ultimate goal is to capture the boy named Graham Dawson. He is the boy who holds the ancient powers, the same as your Kaiser. The same as Alexander. Find him and capture him *alive*."

Many in the crowd erupted in cheers and shouts while others stayed where they were, talking amongst themselves, questioning what was said. As excited fighters stepped forward eagerly, a small cart was wheeled in behind the crowd, draped with a black cloth that swayed as it moved over the uneven cobblestones. When the cart had reached the center of the courtyard, the wheelers stopped and stood as guards on each side.

"I see many of you are still undecided. Whatever your reason for hesitation or lack of evidence, let me clarify my next and final point. Sometime yesterday, an agent of Aegis infiltrated our camp and murdered one of our own."

The two men took hold of the black fabric and pulled it from the metal frame to reveal the body of Walker Ashman. His arms and legs remained sprawled out in the same position as when he was left to die on the marble slab. His eyes were still open, strained in terror. Sharp cries of shock came from many in the crowd.

"Look upon our fallen brother and ask yourself how safe you feel. Walker was one of our fighters, yet he did not die on the battlefield. No, he was killed on our very grounds, in his home, where he was supposed to be safe. He had a wife and two children. He was a father and husband, simply fulfilling his duty to our community, martyred because he stood in the way of their mission to destroy us. For those unconvinced, let this fallen hero be the heartbeat of our battle cry against Aegis."

With Silas' final remark came waves of rallying cries. Not a single person stood idle. There was a rush toward the doors underneath the balcony.

Silas shifted his fedora and turned to walk back through the open doors to recruit from his pool of qualified fighters.

"Let the games begin."

A smaller crowd now stood before Silas in a great hall adjourned with framed paintings and an exceedingly wide mirror, each waiting patiently for instruction.

"Today, we will advance our plan to claim victory over Aegis. You have been selected because of your talent, dedication, and vigor. Take a good look at one another. You are now brothers and sisters in arms. Those of you who have little experience will be led by others who are veterans. Advance and conquer. Through this battle, we will finish what we started with the Aegis training facilities. *Vae Victus* - our declaration of war - has been proclaimed, and you are the agents of which this declaration will manifest."

"Vae Victus!" each said with a raised fist and beaming purple bands.

"Go now and prepare for victory."

The crowd mingled and began exiting the back of the room—determination filled every footstep.

"You two, stay here," Silas said.

A woman with shoulder-length, jet-black hair and emerald-green eyes stepped forward. Her hair blended with the black and gray digital camouflage, enhanced with interceptor body armor plating. The man beside her also stepped forward. His clothing nearly matched hers, yet his camo appeared to be used in arid terrain, as well as his sandy blond hair. The name E. Hopkins was stitched on a small, rectangular piece of fabric on his chest. A third man lingered at the outskirts of the room, listening.

"Kyla, Ethan, you will lead your teams into the heart of two Aegis outposts. Kyla, you will hold the South American outpost we have already overtaken. Ethan, we have intel on a new outpost in Eastern Australia. You will lead this siege, and do not bother being discrete. There are many moving parts to our plan, each action building upon the other to achieve a larger purpose."

"Yes, sir. . . and I respectfully prefer Hopkins, sir. Ethan is a family name I'd rather not use."

"As you wish, Hopkins," replied Silas.

"Sir, if I may." A man in the back of the room stepped forward.

Silas squinted to see who was talking.

"Show yourself," Silas commanded.

A thin man walked into the light. He was solemn, and his eyes were puffy and bloodshot, yet his presence carried an air of power and resolve. His teeth bared like an angry dog as he spoke.

"Sir, send me. On my honor, I will not fail."

"You have already been selected. Your superiors will give you your assignments," Silas dismissively replied.

"Forgive me, sir, but you do not understand. You just put my slain brother on display, and I will do whatever it takes to avenge his murder. Send me, and I will annihilate any Aegis in my path."

Silas peaked an eyebrow.

"What is your name, son?"

"Seth. Seth Ashman."

Silas looked him over. "Yes, of course, you favor him quite well—same hairline, eyes, and cheeks. Alright, Seth, you have my attention. Go with Hopkins to Australia and be under his command. How much field experience have you had?"

"Roughly sixty hours logged in battle, sir."

Silas turned to address Ethan.

"Use Seth as you see fit, but use his ambition strategically."

"Yes, sir."

"Seth, go now and ready yourself," said Silas.

"Yes, sir."

Kyla and Ethan remained with Silas as he explained the bigger picture and their roles in it. As he finished his summary, he concluded with a reminder.

"Remember, Alexander is completely unaware of his own man's involvement, as are the rest of his team. When you fight the mole, he will make it seem real, but rest assured that he is working to advance our cause. Retaliate, but in the end, go with his lead. He is but one cog in our great machine."

"Understood, sir," said Kyla.

"Yes, sir," replied Ethan.

"And remember," said Silas, "the ultimate goal is to get

Graham Dawson. We can destroy every facility Aegis has, but as long as that boy is with Alexander, they will have the upper hand. Kill who you want, destroy what you can, but when the dust settles, you are to have Graham Dawson captured and delivered to the Kaiser."

$$14$$

PREPARATIONS

"You heard a lot of chatter yesterday that I'm sure you did not fully understand," said Alex, addressing the kids.

Branson sent a surge into the training room's wall, where it scorched across the wall in a sizzling black trail. The wall gradually absorbed it, regaining its normal complexion.

"You know that this room absorbs our blasts. You have seen that for months now," said Branson. "What you may not know is what Falcon does with that energy. Yesterday, Alex told Corbin that the HQ in Europe was close to becoming visible. Can you guess why that may be?"

"He said there was nobody there to feed it energy," said Kel.

"That's right. There is a veil over each regional office, just like what we have here over Falcon. It allows us to remain hidden and undetected. The Weaver who created the veil designed it to connect to certain rooms, enabling it to be powered. As powerful as any Weaver may be, such a massive cloak can't be sustained purely by the power he injects into it. We must feed it to remain hidden, demanding we continue our training and development. To protect this outpost, we must advance."

"So, how long does it take to wear off?" asked Damien.

"It depends on how strong it was before it stopped receiving energy, but at least for Raven, the veil is beginning to thin out after three months. We can start to see through it, but the general public can't. Not yet, anyway. But they will soon."

"Thank you, Branson," said Alex, moving to the middle of the room. "We will have a training session together later this morning as a team, and then we must begin securing the outposts. Graham, I want you and your team to stay here for the next hour and train together."

"My *team*?"

"Yes, your team. One of the extra benefits of sending people through Catalyst Grove in groups is that a leader always emerges. For this group, that is you. You need to lead them in how to work as a team to overcome any obstacle or opposition. After an hour, you will have a short break, and the others will join you."

"Um, okay, I will. Thank you," Graham stammered.

He was grateful, but how could he possibly teach his friends how to do something he didn't know himself? He had never led anything or anyone. He was never even the captain of the kickball team back at the orphanage. He wouldn't back down, though. If Alex chose him, there must be a reason, even if Graham could not see it yet. He hoped so, anyway. He started brainstorming how their powers could combine. *A Pusher and an Aquatic could create quite a tsunami. . . but when would they use that? No, that would be too much damage. What about using Ailey and pushing water through the ground? Yeah, that would be pretty cool, but what about me? What can I bring to the table? I can enhance the strength of whatever they're doing, but that's about it. Hmmm, I wonder–*

Chase caught Graham off guard during his daydream. He looked up and saw that the others had already left the room, except for Chase.

"What were you thinking about, little bro?"

Graham loved it when Chase called him that.

"I was just thinking about how we could use our powers together. We only have two main powers. Ailey is a Bridge, so she can only assist, and all I can do is bring a little more power to the punch."

"I think you'll discover much more than that as you go along. It has always helped me to think reactionary. In any given situation, what would be the first response from each person? Figure that out, and then think about how to combine those instincts to work together. If I know you like I think I do, you'll do just fine."

"Thanks, Chase. I hope you're right."

"I'm always right."

"Yeah, except for when you're wrong."

"I wouldn't know what that's like."

Graham chuckled. "You're crazy. So, when do you head off?"

"We'll leave after lunch. I'm excited to go but a little bummed that I won't get to continue training you."

"Oh, I haven't even thought about that. Who's going to take over?"

"Alex will stay behind and train you all. He believes he can prepare you for a mission before too long."

"Well, it won't be the same without you. I wish you could stay and let Alex go."

Chase ruffled Graham's hair, causing it to stick out at odd angles.

"Me too, buddy. Me, too. I'll let you get to it. Don't forget what I said, and good luck."

"Thanks."

"You'll do great," said Chase as he exited the room.

Branson stood in the supply closet, rifling through the supplies for the mission ahead. He took a throat mike, an earwig, and a walkie-talkie from the box and put them on. He twisted the black knob on the top of the radio between his fingers and heard it crackle to life in the earpiece, tuning it to a specific channel, and then did the same with two other radios. "Testing– One, two. Testing– One. Two. Three."

Cavaness was walking past and heard Branson's voice on the other side of the door, so he leaned in to listen. He could hear Branson giving test commands and the resulting granular voice from the other sets. Once the testing quieted, he could hear Branson turn off the other units and speak again. Cavaness kept a stone face and leaned in closer. He tried to make out words, but all he could hear was mumbling. He gave Branson a few moments, then flung open the door.

"Everything in order?" he barked.

Branson calmly removed the walkie-talkie from his lips and looked at Cavaness.

"Yes, sir, I believe it is. COMs are all working."

Cavaness studied his reaction. "And who were you giving instructions to?"

"Sir?"

"It sounded as though you were speaking with someone else."

"No, sir. Just repeating a few lines an old war-time buddy of mine used to say. It's a little ritual I do before each mission to clear my head and focus on the task at hand."

Cavaness stood silent for a moment. He walked over to

Branson and glanced down at the unit, taking note of the channel it was on.

"Finish up and come into the dining room. Alex will be back soon from his meeting with Corbin. He wants everyone gathered together when he returns."

"Yes, sir."

Cavaness walked into the dining room, where he noticed Murphy outside, leaning against the balcony rail. He opened the sliding glass door and stood beside Murphy. There was a moment's pause before Murphy turned around, but Cavaness could see his eyes returning to their natural color.

"Hey, boss. What's up?" said Murphy.

"You okay, Murphy? You've seemed distant these last few weeks."

"Yes, sir, I'm doing just fine. I just thought I'd keep an eye in the sky occasionally to keep watch. . . you know, after what happened."

"And, what do you see?"

"Nothing to report. All is clear as far as I can tell."

"And what about your counter-measures?"

"Counter-measures? What do you mean?"

"Didn't you say during your last level evaluation that tracking scouts could be compromised?"

Murphy thought for a moment.

"No, I haven't. . . I mean, I haven't seen the need, being that we are veiled. Even if another Former latched on to my scout orb with one of their own, they still couldn't see what I see. They would only be able to let their scout travel with mine, and I always let them dissipate in the distance. I never bring them back to me."

"Regardless, you still need a Plan B, and though I appreciate the initiative, never do something like this without telling Alex or myself. Understood?"

"Yes, s–"

Cavaness cut him off, barking at Murphy like a drill sergeant. "Now, what happens when they latch on?"

Murphy stammered a bit to answer, obviously not used to this sort of treatment.

"If I'm advanced, say level twenty or so, then I can latch a scout to another scout. It is hard to do, and few are capable, as far as I know. You have to be even more advanced to have it attach without detection. It would be like me trying to slide a coat over your arms and shoulders without you knowing it. It's insanely difficult, and as I said, even if I could latch on to another orb, all I'd be able to see is what the orb sees and ride it to whatever destination it is traveling to. Any trained Former with half a brain knows to dissolve their scout in the field. To bring one back home would mean ushering your enemy to your doorstep." Murphy met Cavaness' stern gaze. "Why are you grilling me?"

"Because I don't like things happening in secret, even if they're well intended."

"Understood. Now that you know, am I good to keep watching and protecting our outpost?" said Murphy in apparent frustration.

"You may carry on after you tell me your defensive measure."

"Alright. You'll have my report before you leave."

15

FULLY RESTORED

"How are we coming along, Silas?" asked the Kaiser.

"Kyla's connection with him is still proving useful, and I do not think any of the Aegis team is aware of its existence, my lord."

Silas limped across the herringbone marble floor. He looked in much less pain since the explosion that caused his handicap, but it was evident there was still residual pain.

"Kyla's test runs have proven to be above and beyond all we thought possible. The blood connection has given us everything. It has put the training facilities under our boot, and now it will lead us straight to Alexander himself."

The Kaiser closed his eyes and lifted his head as if catching a pleasant scent.

"It's wonderful to know Alexander is being betrayed by

one of his own. The irony is simply delicious. We can never trust those closest to us. In the end, not even blood ties are stronger than greed and power lust. Ensure she continues with great caution. Alexander is no fool. His subordinate cannot be caught during a transmission."

"Understood, my lord. I will reiterate."

"Good. And what have we gotten so far? What are Alexander's plans?"

"He means to regroup by contacting and recapturing the fallen regional outposts. We can't know how many he has in all, but we have found and destroyed two of them near their closest training ground. We have a third in sight now and are about to strike."

"When?"

"Tonight, your lordship."

Kaiser paused. He clasped his hands behind his back and peered at the floor in contemplation.

"No. Have your men hold off until we hear back from Kyla. Have her give the signal and see if we can discover their timetable. We have an opportunity before us, Silas—a vital and rare chance. I will make the preparations, but you must follow my instructions to the letter. Do you understand?"

"Yes, your grace."

His eyes peered through the darkness at Silas. "Come to me."

"My lord?" Silas asked.

"For this to succeed, I need my army at full capacity, so come here and receive strength."

Silas limped and stood still with a tight grip on his cane.

Kaiser bent down and vigorously rubbed his hands together. A purple mist rose from the friction like smoke above a fire before his hands erupted into flames of pure energy. He firmly grasped Silas' leg. Silas clenched his eyes and gritted his teeth. He braced himself to endure the coming pain, but in a breath of relief, he quickly relaxed with the soothing heat.

The Kaiser's energy engulfed Silas's leg in a purple haze, and in a flash, the power plunged into his flesh, radiating from within. Silas's eyes were still closed but no longer clenched, and a sinister smile spread across his face.

The Kaiser straightened up and made eye contact.

"You have been given this gift for my service, to deliver Alexander and Graham to me. Do not disappoint me again."

Silas sighed in relief, regaining his new sense of confidence.

"For your gift, I will not fail you." Silas bowed his head and departed.

16

It Begins

"Alright, fearless leader. What are we going to break today?" asked Damien.

"When Chase and I started, we always warmed up by firing a few bursts. That is what he calls the normal blasts. Why don't we start there?" said Graham.

Each of the four took a step back into a fighting stance, ready to fire rounds into the back wall of the training room.

"One. Two. Three!"

Yellow balls of energy burst from their hands, hurling through the air like giant fireflies. Once they hit their target, they left behind black scorched rings on the back wall of the training room. After about thirty seconds, Graham yelled for them to stop.

"Good. Let's rest for another forty-five seconds and do it

again. Did any of you do this with your mentor?"

Ailey nodded. Kel and Damien both said no.

"We always began with concentrated shots into the ground. We didn't focus much on this type of attack," Kel said between heavy breaths.

"Most of my training consisted of different stages with water, usually in tubs and containers," said Damien.

"Well, then, I guess we have a lot to learn from each other." Graham looked at the clock on the wall. "Okay, in one. Two. Three!"

More bursts filled the room. Black marks peppered the wall, each fading into the invisible veil. They fired as many bursts as they could in their thirty-second timeframe.

"Time!" yelled Graham, panting.

"Holy cow, this is rough," said Damien, struggling to catch his breath just as much as Graham.

"Come on, soccer star, where's your endurance?" asked Graham.

"Man, this is a totally different type of endurance."

Ailey hunched over with her hands on her knees. Tiny beads of sweat glistened on her forehead. She mopped her brow with her sleeve and rubbed the small scar on her neck. Kel took notice and walked over.

"You okay?"

Ailey signed a few sentences.

"Really? Have you asked Alex about it? Maybe he can help."

Ailey signed again.

"If it happens when you're training, it sounds like more than just the scarred tissue."

"What's going on?" asked Graham.

"The scar on Ailey's neck has been aching every time she trains in here," said Kel.

"Maybe her body is just not used to the extra stress. I've heard that some people who break bones in their feet can tell when bad weather is coming. It could be that her scar is trying to figure out how to handle the changes."

"I don't know. I would feel better if someone had a look."

Graham watched as Ailey continued to massage the odd feeling from her neck.

"Okay, I'll bring it up with Alex after everyone has left for the pillars, outposts, regional offices, or whatever we're supposed to call them."

"Thank you. That would be a relief."

"Sure. No problem."

"So, what's next?" asked Damien.

Graham thought. "Well, after a warm-up, we usually worked on precision. Lately, Chase would throw targets in the air. He would make me turn my back to him, and when he gave the signal, I would turn around and hit as many targets as possible. Do you want to try that?"

Before anyone could answer, Cavaness poked his head through the door.

"Alex is back. Why don't you grab a bite to eat and meet us in the dining room? It is almost time to set off."

"Yes, sir."

"Good man."

Cavaness slipped back out and closed the door.

"I guess a warm-up is all we get to do right now. Let's go see what Alex wants."

Graham and his team entered the dining room to greet Alex, who had brought Corbin and two others back with him. The man to Corbin's left could have been his twin brother, though his frame was taller and leaner, and he had a head full of thin braided micro dreads. He had the same dark tone to his skin as Corbin and wore a black jacket. Corbin looked like he might be in his mid-forties, whereas this man seemed ten years younger.

"Hello, sir. It's a pleasure to see you again," the man said to Alex as he bowed his head slightly and put his fist to his chest. "I'm Lucas from EagleEye."

"Welcome to Falcon, Lucas," said Alex.

The woman to Corbin's right introduced herself next. She was fairly young, perhaps in her late twenties. She was of average size and build. Her black hair came a little past her ears, fanning outward at the bottom. She wore brown cargo pants, a mustard-yellow long-sleeve shirt, and a military-style, sleeveless red vest with pockets across the front. Her blue eyes were like gleaming sapphires.

"Hey, everyone. My name is Sonia. I look forward to serving with you."

"Thank you for answering the call, Sonia," said Alex.

Alex then went around the room and introduced the rest of the team. They all picked at the food on the table, telling stories about the hecticness of the past month and how they were affected. Corbin was happy to report that no one at their regional catalyst grove had been killed. There were a few minor injuries, and two recruits nearly drowned, but they had escaped the worst of it. Jael spoke of Raven and how opposite her news was. She told the story with impressive control. Once everyone had their fill, Alex led them to the third floor and into the room of mirrors.

"Wow. Pretty impressive, Alex," said Sonia.

"Alex, you never told me you had a gateway into the entire world," said Corbin in amazement.

"This is not something I'm keen on publicizing. I wanted you all to see this as a sign of hope. I know our current situation looks grim and dark, but let this room be a ray of light that cuts through that gloom. We can reconnect our network and fight Victus in full force."

"Just tell us what to do," said Corbin.

Alex led them over to the wooden desk. He pointed out the shattered mirrors and the need to reconnect.

"For a body to function and thrive, it must have a good

circulatory system. Blood goes into the heart and pumps through vessels to the rest of the body. Right now, parts of our network are cut off, and we need to restore our circulatory system."

Alex pointed to seven new sets of mirrors on the desk, one stack for each outpost.

"I have made these with a few enhancements. They each have the usual divots to the right of the glass, but these also have one singular divot to the left. Secure the facility and mount the mirror. Once set, you must place your thumb in this special indention. It will remain pending, awaiting activation of the rest of the mirrors."

Alex took hold of a mirror and held it up for all to see.

"All seven are interconnected and have the same enhanced properties infused into them. Upon activating the seventh and final trans, the specially crafted power infused into the mirrors will become active, providing the security and protection needed for each region."

Alex put down the trans and removed a lighter from his pocket. He turned the small wheel with his thumb. Sparks flew from the flint, and a tiny flame appeared.

"Do you see this flame? Though small and delicate, no matter how hard the darkness tries to overcome it, it cannot. The light of the flame will always overpower the darkness. Similarly, the success of this mission will cast a ray of light to dispel the current darkness hanging over our broken network. We must succeed. It is of the utmost importance to regain the captured outposts and reconnect them, or else we will miss our only opportunity to bring all parts of the body together and regain the upper hand."

"We won't let you down," said Chase. "We'll fight until the last breath if that's what it takes."

Cavaness glanced at Chase and clasped his shoulder. "We are ready, Alex."

"We second that," said Corbin. The rest of his team nodded in agreement.

Branson reached under the desk and slid out a large cardboard box. He opened the top and removed COM units for each person. He pointed to the walkie-talkie set and pointed to the controls.

"These are what you would expect. Keep the microphones tight around your throat. The vibration of your voice will activate the unit, allowing us all to hear what you are saying, even in a low whisper. Keep it on the correct channel for your team. Press this red button, and the indicator light will confirm you are broadcasting to all channels, so we will all hear your chatter. This way, you can keep the earpiece in at all times and only hear what you need to hear. Got it?"

"That sounds great, but surely these things can't reach around the world," said Jael.

Chase stepped up to answer. "They can through these," he said, pointing to the mirrors. "We may be on opposite sides of the world, but since these create an instant link with one another, we will always be within range, just as long as you keep them within five miles of yourselves."

"Very cool, my man," said Corbin.

Graham watched everyone take the COMs and set them in place. He longed to go with them, wishing to be helpful. Graham wanted so badly to hit Silas with a surge. He watched Chase as he stuffed the earwig in. He was such a natural leader. Graham was so thankful that he had someone to model himself after. He wanted to be able to take command like that one day.

"Alex, when do we go?" Graham was so focused on being in the fight that his thoughts escaped his mouth before his brain could stop them. He felt slightly embarrassed at the blunt inquiry but held a good poker face.

"Soon enough, Graham. I appreciate your eagerness, but you must realize the severity of these missions. You were fortunate in the cavern, but you must be prepared and controlled when you face your enemy this time."

Chase shot Graham a smirk and a wink.

"I have a feeling that once you go out into the field, you may wish you were back in the training room." Alex turned his attention back to the group. "To make communications easier, each team will have a simple codename. Corbin, your team will be EagleOne. You will take your team and go to Raven."

Chase snickered and pointed at Murphy, who, in turn, mouthed a silent *shut up*.

"Cavaness, your team will be FalconOne. You will take Chase and Jael and set off for Albatross."

"Yes, sir," said Cavaness.

"Murphy, you and Branson will remain here and assist in developing Graham and his team."

"Understood," said Murphy and Branson together.

"Graham, will you hand out the bags?" asked Alex, pointing to the COMs box.

Graham nodded and retrieved backpacks from the box, handing them to each team.

"Thank you. As I said, you must mount a set of mirrors in each outpost. Take these packs and designate one among you to carry it. They look heavy, but I assure you, they will not be much of a burden."

Alex was right. Lucas picked one up and tossed it in the air like a beanbag. It couldn't have weighed more than a few pounds, which was quite impressive for a pack of mirrors of that size.

Once everyone had their supplies together, Alex stood before them and pulled his fist to his chest. Everyone followed suit. The clap of the salutes filled the room. It was a solemn moment. Everyone held their posture, taking in the seriousness of the mission ahead. Without a word, Alex lowered his hand and turned to the mirrors, removing all six from the wall to replace them with the new trans.

He reached for the HawksNest trans, which is the outpost of the Spark based in Eastern Australia. His hand was inches away when the mirror began to vibrate. It rattled against the wall and nearly fell from its hook, then shattered and vomited tiny glass shards. Alex had to cover his face to keep from being pelted.

Sonia and Jael gasped. The sudden break took everyone aback.

"What just happened?" asked Kel, her voice as nervous as her expression.

Alex stared at the broken mirror. "HawksNest has just been taken."

"What? It can't be. I was just there a few weeks ago, visitin' with the Director. Dey seemed so prepared," said Corbin. "Sir, that area is still fresh in my mind. I believe Lucas, Sonia, and I can take it back. Send us there first before it takes more damage."

Alex kept his attention on the shattered trans.

"Corbin, how familiar? There will likely be a large number of Victus there. We may need to consider sending two teams in," said Cavaness.

"You just leave it to us, Cavaness. We've got two long-range and one close-combat here. We're ready to go into the heat of it. Just show us the drop-off point, and we *will* rescue HawksNest."

Alex turned and looked deep into Corbin's eyes, then at the other two team members.

"Alright, but remember, they'll have enough numbers to capture a fully staffed outpost. The risk of casualty is quite high. Understand what you are about to get yourself and your team into. Be sure of the course you're about to take."

Corbin nodded. "I'm ready and willing, and so is my team."

"I know you are, but are you willing to take full responsibility for the outcome of your decision. . . for leading your team into such conditions?"

"Absolutely," Corbin said, not fully understanding the question.

Alex then returned the gesture, accepting Corbin's

response. "Then Raven must wait. HawksNest is the new priority. Chase can show you the closest point of entry," said Alex.

Chase took Corbin to a trans near the back wall, mounted just above their heads.

"This will take you about an hour, by foot, outside the city. Be sure to conceal before you step outside and keep tabs on anyone who may be following you. Good luck."

Corbin gathered his team around him. "Don' worry. We'll get it up and runnin'."

"Go and remain on guard," said Alex.

Corbin stood in front of the trans, with Sonia and Lucas placing a hand on each of his shoulders. He reached up and rested his hand on the center of the glass, and they vanished.

Cavaness and Chase lined up in front of the trans that would take them close to Albatross. Chase glanced over his shoulder to Graham and his team. "You guys better keep at it while we're gone. I expect to see a few level-ups when we get back. Take care of yourselves." Chase winked at Graham.

Ailey started to tear up. Graham could tell that she did not like everyone leaving simultaneously. He didn't like it either. Usually, he would have welcomed the silence of an empty house, but that had changed while he was here. He had grown accustomed to being around the others so much that he no longer felt the need for seclusion. Oddly enough, he did not know if he could get used to the silence.

Cavaness walked over and kissed Ailey on the forehead. "Don't worry. We will be back before you know it. Keep at your training. We need you to be strong. Can you do that?"

Ailey nodded with a quivering lip.

"How long do you think it will take to re-establish the outposts?" asked Kel.

"It's hard to tell until we get there. The scouting missions showed Albatross heavily guarded by Victus. It will take some time to break through."

"Please, be careful."

"We're prepared, Kel. Don't waste your energy on worry. Use it to get stronger in training."

"Yes, sir."

Kel wrapped an arm around Ailey and watched Cavaness, Jael, and Chase disappear.

Alex walked over to the kids and smiled warmly.

"Are you all okay?"

"Sort of. It's just odd to think that we'll be the only ones here for a while," said Graham.

"Yes, it'll be different here. It's funny the things we take for granted, isn't it?"

"Yes, sir, it is."

Watching the others leave sparked a memory from the council meeting. It was a term that was never fully explained. Graham concentrated, trying to remember what the words were.

"Alex, at the council meeting, you mentioned Silas saying Vae Victus as he destroyed Portfield Manor. I remember him saying that to Cavaness. What does that mean?"

"That's a good question but not a simple answer. You see, the name Victus has a dual meaning, which is why I'm sure it was chosen. Its most basic meaning is *life*, specifically a *way of living*. They claim that true life and meaning lie in their power and culture. They call themselves *The Way*. They deceive people with the illusion that their victory is the world's only possible way forward, and to go against them is to deny the purpose of the evolution of life itself. Victus has a special power that the rest of humanity does not. That, they claim, makes them superior in every way. In contrast, because we see our power as a responsibility to care for and protect the unactivated, we are seen as standing in the way of progress. As time moved humanity forward, the term also took on a negative meaning, separating people into two groups: the conquerors and the conquered."

Alex took a broken mirror in his hand, tying his words to

the recent damage.

"Vae Victus was first used over two thousand years ago. It worked so well as a psychological taunt that they still use it today, though what began as a taunt eventually became a declaration. Its secondary meaning translates into *woe unto the conquered* and is only used now when they declare war. They hope to mentally defeat us with these words before the punch is thrown on the battlefield."

Graham swallowed hard. A darkness fell over him at the thought of those chilling words. They didn't seem so bad until Alex explained them. Graham knew there was a fight ahead, but the word *war* seemed to sit much heavier on his mind.

"You will remember, from the story of The Unseen War, that the two immortals were eventually pitted against one another. They are known now as the Patriarchs. We were named Aegis, after the original bands, which means protection. On the other hand, the younger immortal decided to take on the inverse, which is to conquer." Alex spoke clearly and concisely, as if from memory. "That is what we are fighting against, and that is the sort of evil we must get the council to recognize."

"Where are the brothe–" Graham was in mid-sentence, but Alex gracefully cut him off.

"Our teams have gone out on their missions, and we must begin ours. Come, it's time to train."

17

FALCON

Murphy and Branson stood to either side of Alex in the training room. All three wore similar, cream-colored, and loose-fitting clothing, like martial arts clothing, but in a more structured fashion. The pants were simply pants with wide legs to allow for free and easy movement. The top was a little more elaborate, with military-style shoulder straps and a Celtic-type trim to the collar and cuffs. The front fastened at an angle from the left shoulder down toward the center. Over the left chest was a small sun emblem, with a much larger one printed on the back.

Alex remained in his usual suit pants and matching vest.

"Since this is the first time you have been in the training room together, I thought it best to review the basics before we get into the thick of your training. As you've already noticed, Murphy and Branson are wearing unique clothing. These are our sparring uniforms. I have infused the material with the same type of power that covers Falcon. These uniforms will connect to the power of your bands and provide some extra protection while you train."

Alex gestured Murphy and Branson into the middle of the training room, facing one another. Once in place, Alex continued.

"First, let's start with the primary attacks. You have concentrated on a single attack up until now—the *Burst*. We all share four different types, regardless of our individual giftings, though we only use three under most circumstances.

As Alex paused, Murphy and Branson each fired a single blast at one another. Each ball of energy slammed into the other's chest, yet their sparring clothes seemed to either absorb the attack or disperse it, leaving them unharmed.

"The burst is the easiest and most natural attack, not unlike a quick jab in boxing. I'm sure you remember it well from your time at Catalyst Grove. It is used in close combat and distance fighting, primarily for stunning or distracting your opponent. That said, it can also do extensive damage at higher levels."

Graham watched and listened intently. He did not want to miss a single word, but as Murphy and Branson each provided visual examples, he inadvertently rubbed his chest as his mind flashed back to Silas and how different those bursts felt compared to Cavaness's or Chase's from the Grove. He could almost feel the pain surge through his body again.

"The second is called a *Charge*. The charge is quite like it sounds, holding a burst attack for a time before releasing it, increasing its strength. The charge is most helpful in creating entryways through solid walls, distractions, and intimidation. While it could be a forceful attack on your opponent, most do not use it in combat because it takes time to build your energy and would give them time to counterattack."

Murphy remained still this time while Branson took a fighter's stance. A growing yellow ball of light expanded in his palms until it grew to the size of a watermelon. He then released it with a grunt. The charge slammed into the wall, spraying like an exploding firework.

"The third is called a *Surge*. While it is named the same as the Surge gifting, it's not exclusive to them. A surge is an ongoing energy attack that looks like a long, fiery tube of light. It's far more powerful than a burst and is quite taxing."

Alex paused again to allow for a demonstration.

Branson and Murphy nodded and turned toward the opposite side of the room, away from the others. They both planted a foot firmly behind them, then cupped the heels of their hands together, arms extended. With a grunt, they both unleashed a wave of energy from their hands. The attack collided with the far wall in a flash of light, leaving a sizzling trail of black as the surges arched across the wall. They allowed the attack to last roughly five seconds before stopping.

The two men lowered their hands and turned back to the others while the black streaks from the energy slowly disappeared into the wall.

"How much does it drain you when you do it?" asked Damien.

"Depends on how long you allow the flow to continue," said Branson. "You're a runner, right? Think about running on the soccer field. Bursts are like a light jog half the length of the field. Surges are like an all-out sprint for laps."

"How do you hold it in place?" asked Graham,

remembering how hard it was for him. He was a little jealous of how easy they made it look.

"It's like bear-hugging a fighting tiger," said Murphy, half joking, half serious. "The nature of that attack is to spread out, so it takes a lot of focus to keep it tight in a single stream. You have to use every muscle in your body: your core, thighs, triceps. . . everything to keep it concentrated. That's one reason why it takes so much out of you. Releasing a surge for ten seconds would be roughly the equivalent of running full speed for approximately one mile."

"How's that even possible? I can't run half a mile, much less sprint for a full one," said Kel.

"Conditioning your body is simply a matter of focus and time," said Alex. "You possess an exponential amount of the former but a small amount of the latter, which is why we are pushing you so hard."

Kel nodded.

"The fourth and final attack is called a *Detonare*. It is used only in dire circumstances, as it expends nearly all your energy at once when performing an attack, much like a bomb explosion. Everything in the vicinity is destroyed and will, without doubt, kill anyone in the blast radius: all but the one performing it. I hesitate to mention it as you will likely never use it. However, I want you to be aware."

The seriousness of the attack turned Graham's attention to Chase and the outposts. "Wouldn't it be better if we were out there with them?" said Graham, almost cutting Alex off. "Couldn't we advance quicker if we were in the field?"

Branson crossed his arms and stared at Graham. Murphy grinned, waiting for Alex's response.

"I admire your courage and dedication, Graham, but sending you all out as you are now would be irresponsible at best and a death sentence at worst. I am not willing to send undeveloped fighters to the battlefield. That's a Victus tactic. Their strategic advantage is to overwhelm us by the size of their forces. We overcome them by forming close-knit teams of high-level fighters. For example, ten novice levels would not match a single veteran skilled to level twenty."

Alex walked to a locker near the entrance and removed a long parchment rolled up like a scroll. He unfastened a small ribbon and unrolled it, showing everyone what it contained.

"I assume you have heard about power levels. It's not a rigid structure and will be subjective based on your advancement in the basic offensive and defensive maneuvers you just learned and your progression in your specific giftings. That said, we have compiled fundamental milestones based on the statistics over the years of what is recognizable as an advancement in ability. You can think of these as grade levels in school, outlining levels one through ten. Level ten will be your first major breakthrough."

Graham remembered his conversation with Chase at the Manor and got very excited at the number ten. *Didn't Chase say something amazing was supposed to happen at ten?* Before he could ask the question, though, Alex continued.

"There are no badges, certificates, or awards for level advancements. They are simply our judgment in rank based on your training. Our standard is that no one is deployed into the field to combat Victus unless they have reached level ten. Reaching level ten is your primary objective."

Branson stepped up beside Alex, arms still crossed, gesturing with one hand as he spoke.

"Beyond the levels, you will also need to learn tactical maneuvers. You have already established teamwork. We saw this at the Grove. It's a great first step, but you'll also need to learn how to fight as a single unit and anticipate one another's moves before they happen. You must learn each other's strengths and weaknesses along with your own. In any given situation, we will teach you to discern when you should attack or let another team member attack based on the immediate threat."

While Branson was talking, Murphy had joined him and Alex at the front of the room.

"I'll balance out Branson's tactics with lessons on adapting to your environment, using your surroundings to your advantage. Adaptation is the creative side to combat. . . to improvise and overcome."

"And I will work with you to develop your specific gifting," said Alex. "Three teachers for three different skill sets. We will work in rounds throughout the day. When you look at it, it's amazing how often good things come in threes."

Alex took the parchment and laid it in front of Graham. "I'll give you a few minutes to review and familiarize yourself with the levels before we begin training. When you're finished, I'll post it on the wall for inspiration when you are tired to endure and continue advancing."

Graham held the top and bottom of the scroll with his hands to prevent it from rolling back into a tube. The paper itself was old and stained with age. It appeared to be much older than he was, even older than Cavaness. The golden sun crested the top in gold foil. There was a brief introduction below, followed by a simple list with a large number stamped in the same golden foil as the sun. Words in an old English font explained what each number represented:

1. A successful completion of the training grounds will render the emblem of the subject's gifting in the vacant circle of the catalyst bands.

2. With concentration, command the catalyst band to appear at will.

3. Track and hit three fast-flying targets with bursts.

4. Fully suppress the catalyst energy, leaving no trace of Dynamis Energy.

5. Hold a charge for ten seconds before releasing it into the target circle.

6. A protective shield can be formed and maintained from the Catalyst band.

7. The laying on of hands to another's catalysts results in a healing transfer of Dynamis Energy.

8. A Charge can be produced and executed in tandem with Bursts.

9. A Burst can be absorbed by the Catalyst Band and reused.

10. A Surge can be successfully held on target for ten seconds.

Graham did his best to internalize the list before handing it to Ailey, who was already peeking over his shoulder to view it. He smiled and passed it to her. Ailey's eyes lit up as the light reflected off the golden numbers. Her lips mouthed the words as she read.

Alex gave time for the list to pass to Damien and Kel. Once Kel finished, she returned it to Alex, who then rolled it back up.

"Now then. To advance, you will need to know where you stand currently. As you have seen, the first levels are easily obtained. We have analyzed your rank as you have trained over the past months. You're all unique in that you were captured by Silas just after obtaining level-one status. While this was a horrible experience and could have killed you, that dark cloud in your past was not without a silver lining. As scary as it was, that event acted as an accelerant to your training. Graham, because of the extreme nature of how you obtained your gifting, you are currently at level six."

"Wow, nice amigo!" blurted Damien.

Ailey wore an excited grin.

"That's great, Graham," whispered Kel. "Way to go!"

"Damien, you, too, were pushed beyond normal limits due to your submersion. You are currently a level five. Kel, you and Ailey both are level fours."

Ailey took Kel by the hand, fingers laced and squeezed with delight. Kel squeezed back.

"It's all too easy to have an unhealthy focus on your rank, so try not to get too caught up in the numbers. Most importantly, do not let the advancement of others create envy, but rather let it be an opportunity to encourage one another. If you are on a higher plain, let it be leverage to pull others up with you, not look down on them in superiority."

Alex took a few pins from the locker and mounted the list onto the wall.

"Now that you know where you stand and the expectations placed on you, it's time to begin. You will train ten hours daily, alternating sessions with us throughout the day to squeeze the most out of every hour. From this moment on, you will need to eat, sleep, and breathe this training, and when you reach exhaustion, remember Chase, Cavaness, and Jael, who are on the front lines. Murphy, you're up first."

With a nod, Branson and Murphy guided Damien, Ailey, and Kel to the center of the room.

"Graham, you will join them in a moment, but right now, I need you to come with me."

18

ALBATROSS

ALBATROSS OUTPOST
Pueblo del Sol - Argentina
4:00 pm local time

"Rats," said Chase.

"No, these are capybaras, I think. These are much bigger than rats," said Jael. "One of the less pleasant things about stealthily traveling through a trans is sneaking up on whatever is on the other side."

Large rodents the size of adolescent pigs scurried about the damp, dark room lit by slivers of light peering through the wooden slats that made up the exterior wall.

There were a lot of Spanish speakers mingling outside of the hut. Cavaness signaled for Jael to join his eavesdropping.

"I think it's just locals. Jael?"

"Yes, they're chatting about local politics. We are fine."

Chase looked around the dingy room for anything useful, but all he could see was a wooden table made of branches and a small, overturned chair.

"It's not exactly the Hilton, is it?" said Chase.

Jael snickered, which made Chase grin. Cavaness ignored the remark completely.

"Follow me and keep together, but in loose formation. Keep staggered and alert."

Both nodded.

Cavaness cracked open the door and let the afternoon light pour into the small hut. He shielded his eyes from the sun as they entered what looked like a marketplace. There were rows of wooden huts configured in horseshoe patterns with bright clothing, blankets, trinkets, and sculptures.

Many of the locals flocked to Cavaness to sell him their inventory. As they crowded around him, Chase and Jael mingled in with the crowd, headed south.

It was easy for Cavaness to keep track of them, being shoulder-high above everyone around him. Satisfied with their position, Cavaness waved his hand dismissively at the sellers.

"No gracias. Perdón."

The commotion faded to silence under his words. He started heading south, and the locals quickly made a gap to avoid being trampled by the giant man.

The rural village was seated on the outskirts of the forest, so they quickly disappeared into the woods.

The locals turned back to their shops, all except for one man. He, too, was a local who looked like the others, except for the small earpiece concealed behind his left ear. He noted where the Aegis members entered the forest and spoke into the hidden microphone using his broken English.

"Just like you say. They in Pueblo del Sol, going southeast.

You got a big man who is leader. He with a young boy, early twenties, and a woman in her late twenties. Three in all."

He listened for a moment and then replied. "Yes, sir. I will follow. They should make it to you by nightfall."

The three tromped through the forest for hours, watching for any sign of Victus.

"Do either of you need a break?" asked Cavaness.

"Maybe in a bit, but I'm good for now," said Chase.

"I'm fine," said Jael, taking a swig of water from a plastic container. "But I would like you to fill me in on some details. I never ventured outside my region, so where are we going, exactly?"

"Albatross is the name of the Aquatic Outpost. A waterfall empties into a river that supplies water to most of the surrounding villages. It's a long way from the village we emerged from but not too far from others. The distance is a precaution," said Cavaness.

"Okay, makes sense. And who are we contacting?"

"The two director's names are Adrian Garcia and Marcio Torres. We don't know if they were present when Albatross was attacked. That's what we need to find out."

"And the outpost itself?"

"We must reclaim it, but finding the directors is our top priority. Retaking and re-establishing Albatross comes afterward."

"If Adrian and Marcio are captured, then they're likely being tortured for information. Victus doesn't care about an outpost. They care about what it represents. . . a regional rolodex," said Chase.

Jael stopped suddenly, grabbed her head as if dizzy, and braced against a tree. Her feet crossed as she staggered to the side.

Chase took her arm. "Jael? You okay? Wait, that was a dumb question. Of course you aren't. What's wrong?"

Jael's head twitched, her eyes snapped shut, and her jaw clenched.

"I'm. . . I'm alright. I just. . . sometimes, I have these intense flashbacks. I think it is because you were talking about Victus trying to get to all of the regional personnel. I can't get them out of my head. . . the attackers, that is. I can never see their expressions in detail, but I can see the wicked smiles."

Chase held her steady until she signaled that she could continue under her own strength.

"You can't remember who any of the Vics were?"

"No, I wish I could. There were too many of them, and it was all so sudden. I couldn't concentrate on anything but survival. I just remember the death of a friend and the woman that killed him. It's her twisted grin that I see when I close my eyes, that and the shadows of the people I left behind."

The local Vic moved through the forest with the stealth and skill of the animals that inhabited the jungle. Staying far enough behind to remain unnoticed, he went in blurred movements from trunk to trunk and trunk to limb, far above the forest floor. Finding the perfect vantage point was always easy for a Surge.

Underneath the collar of his brown linen shirt was a black stripe with two small microphones cradling his Adam's apple, pressing them closer into his throat.

"At this pace, they only a few hours out. They moving up the valley at marker thirteen."

"Roger that," replied a female voice through the man's earpiece. "We're on approach. T-minus twenty-five minutes from your current location."

"Copy that."

"Check back in if they change course."

"Sí, señora."

Jael's cheeks were getting flushed. She bit her lower lip for control, which was her habit, her telltale sign of the pounding emotional storm within. "So, how far off are we from the waterfall? I assume that's where the actual outpost is."

"A few more hours at the pace we have been going," said Cavaness in an uncommonly patient tone. "We must be cautious from now on. Albatross was one of the first to fall. We must assume that they have been building defenses ever since."

Cavaness waved Chase forward to lead the small group.

"Give us an assessment. We'll stop every thirty minutes and do the same as we approach."

Chase jogged to a thick stump and jumped to its center, staring into the distance. His eyes darted back and forth rapidly as if they were pulling data from every nook and cranny of the jungle. After assessing everything around them, he hopped from the stump and rejoined the others.

"No traps set as far as I can see, but we do have a tail forty yards behind us. I have a feeling he's been with us since we left the village. Want me to take care of him?"

"No, leave him be unless he knows you saw him," replied Cavaness.

"No, I don't think he's aware."

"Good. We'll use him when the time is right."

"How are you so sure there is nothing around us?" asked Jael. "Surely your eyesight isn't that good. This place is all trees, leaves, and blooms."

Chase smirked and scratched his tricep, which was his telltale sign of shyness.

"It's not what I can see, necessarily. It's what I analyze. Nothing in the surrounding terrain would lend itself to being a trap— no unnatural bend to branches, no odd pattern to the vines, and no abnormalities in the trees to be used as a snare. Plus, we are too far out yet. I doubt they would bother constructing anything here. The perimeter would be too wide. That is why our friend is following us."

"Wow, impressive, Chase. I didn't know you were a strategist," said Jael playfully.

"Being a Surge comes with many advantages. I get the speed of body as well as the speed of thought."

"Lucky for us."

"You may want to hold that thought until my assessment proves right."

Chase and Jael exchanged smiles.

Cavaness rolled his eyes and walked between the two of them, waving them on as he passed. "Let's keep moving. I'm sure our friend back there is feeding our location to his team."

19

HAWKSNEST

HAWKSNEST OUTPOST
Newcastle, Australia
6:00 am local time

Corbin hit the ground running. He briefly checked each room as he ran, ensuring the building was empty. His team glided across the floor on his six. They flew past a few small common areas, beyond a vacant side room, to a larger foyer. Corbin flung the front door open and down the porch steps without hesitation. To his surprise, it was pretty mild outside. The house was a small shop in a string of similar buildings in a small Australian suburban community. Corbin pulled a GPS unit from his pocket and searched for the coordinates provided by Branson.

"We've got a bit of a hike ahead of us. Sonia, I want you ta keep us on track, but we need ta stick to side roads. I doubt they'd have time to send scouts out yet, but I don't wanna take no chances."

Corbin tossed the GPS unit to Sonia.

"Whatever you say, sir."

"Lucas, you stay close by, but try ta stick to high ground where you can. I'll track in the sky, but you'll need ta be in position to react. Looks like we gotta travel about three or four miles."

"Yes, sir."

"Alright now, let's go rescue the Aussies."

Corbin flung five or six orbs into the sky. He placed his hand on Sonia's shoulder to guide him as his eyes changed color, his vision now focused through the scout orbs. Sonia led them south, down the hill toward the central part of town. They sprinted down the road and behind the next row of shops, navigating through a few minor intersections and down a stretch of back alleyways.

"Where are we anyway?" asked Lucas.

"We're on the outskirts of Newcastle, Australia. Don't ask me why dey would put an outpost way out here, 'cause I don't understand it myself," replied Corbin, who was already beginning to sweat through his shirt. "We're headed to Nobby's Headland- dat cylindrical mount of earth on the long stretch of beach."

The trio continued sprinting through Newcastle's back alleys. Corbin kept his gaze in the sky as he looked at the town below for a few more moments until his eyes returned to their natural brown.

"It's too dang populated. I wouldn't be able to find 'em unless dey was holdin' a Victus sign." As he spoke, he grabbed Sonia's wrist to view the GPS unit and looked at the coordinates.

The town was large but quaint. The smell of the salty sea permeated everything. Many of the larger buildings were brick, and because it was a port city, most of the decor was naval- anchors, seagulls, fish, and thick white rope. Periodically, they could hear the dinging of bells and the bellow of barges off in the distance. Now tucked in a back alley, they huddled together and planned their next move.

"Try getting on dat rooftop der and tell me what ya see." Corbin pointed south. "We're headed that way."

"Will do, sir," said Lucas. He scurried up the side of the building, headed toward the southern stretch of road ahead. Once there, white noise crackled through the earwig.

"Sir, the main road curves around the contour of a beach. The only thing due south is a long stretch of sand leading to a small island-type peninsula. Is that the Headland? I see a cylindrical mountain with a cluster of white buildings at the peak. From this view, it does kinda look like a nest."

"Is der any cover between here and der?" asked Corbin.

"Not really, no. Once we're past the next few buildings, we'll be exposed. It's just a stretch of beach until we reach the outpost. There's no way to remain hidden."

"Good thing we have you then, isn't it," said Sonia.

"Let's go out in the open first. Maybe we can flush a few out for ya. You stay there and pick 'em off," said Corbin.

"Copy that," replied Lucas.

Corbin and Sonia sprinted toward the beach. They must have looked very out of place. Everyone around them was dressed in swimwear, yet they were decked out in full military garb. They got a few odd looks as they ran past. As their feet hit the sand, they slowed their pace to mingle as best they could.

"Zoom in on rooftops and the skyline above. I'm not completely sure how dis place is set up, so we have to be ready for anything," said Corbin.

"Checking now," said Lucas. He put one foot on the small knee-high wall in front of him and rested an elbow on his knee. He leaned slightly forward to get a better view. As he did, his eyes turned amber, and his pupils contracted like a camera lens.

"I've got a lot of people, but nothing suspicious. There are no hidden positions behind the veil that I can see. At least no one posted up top. There's a small structure at the base-ocean-side. You can find a way up from there. Keep to the right and–"

A glare caused Lucas to flinch. He blinked a few times and then tried to look again, only to feel a sharp pain in his collarbone. The shot threw him backward. Corbin and the others heard the grunt through the earpiece and turned around.

"Lucas! What happened?"

There was radio silence.

"Lucas, report!" yelled Corbin as best he could without attracting the crowd's attention.

"Uh. . . run. . . another Snype is. . . ahhhh. . . on the main rooftop." Lucas writhed in pain, holding his injured shoulder and struggling to get his words out.

"Move!"

20

FALCON

Graham followed Alex down a maze of hallways until they reached an office, which seemed almost as grand as the commons area of Greenwood. Thick timbers looked as though they were holding the room in place. An extensive wooden desk sat at the opposite end of the entrance, but instead of sitting at his desk chair, Alex took a seat in a leather chair and asked Graham to take a seat in its twin, just across from him.

Alex sat on the edge of the cushion with one hand balled up in the other, rubbing his thumb along the soft space between the other thumb and index finger. This made

Graham a bit nervous. He had never seen this room before, and though Alex always had a calm and peaceful demeanor, the seriousness of the moment was evident. He started having flashbacks of being in Ms. Winstone's office.

Alex stared at the floor for a moment, deep in thought, eyes unfocused.

"How are your nightmares, Graham?"

This question caught him off guard. He was expecting a speech, a scolding for wanting to jump into battle hastily, or maybe an update on the teams. He certainly did not expect a heart-to-heart conversation.

"Um, okay, I guess. I still have them, but the hovering objects have stopped. I guess these bands have given my power an outlet."

"I'm glad to hear that, but what about the nightmare itself? Are you still seeing the same fragments repeatedly, or are you getting more pieces to the puzzle?"

"It's mostly the same things, although there's a little more to it before I wake up. I'm at the same picnic with my parents, and the swirling walls of smoke attack us as usual. My dad defends us, everyone screams, and the light flashes. That's when I always wake up, but now, as the light fades, I see a shadow of a person walking toward me. At first, I thought maybe it was my dad or mom, but I don't think so. If it were, I wouldn't be an orphan."

Graham's voice was somber, and his eyes fell to the floor. He often thought about his parents, wondering how different life would be if they were still around. He wanted to believe they were still alive, but he wouldn't let himself be fully open to that. Not even with the new pieces to his dreams.

Alex nodded, acknowledging all that Graham was saying.

"It's as I suspected. Even though you know what the blinding light is from your dreams, your unconscious mind will not stop searching the archives of your fractured memories until it uncovers what happened to your parents."

Graham finally broke his gaze from the floor and met Alex's eyes.

"Graham, I told you months ago that I would help you figure this out, and I want to reassure you that I've been actively fulfilling my promise to you. While I don't have any new information from my sources right now, what you have just explained to me allows for one confirmation."

A streak of excitement shot through Graham's chest. He gripped the arms of his chair in anticipation.

"Years ago, we received a report of a young child who had performed an extraordinary display of the dynamis power we possess. This story was the first spark of hope, the first sign that the person who would be the bearer of the Aegis power was now among us. I wasn't given the details of where you were found, and because we knew Victus would come searching, we had to act fast. I gave orders for you to be taken to a facility where you were to be protected, but I also commanded that your location be a secret. I tell you this because while I didn't know the exact location where you lost your parents, I do know the person who shows up at the end, and he assured your parents you would be safe before they went into hiding."

Graham stared at Alex, trying to understand what he was saying. His hands went numb. His heart fluttered, and his breathing became heavy.

"My parents are alive?" His voice held a mixture of relief, pain, and confusion. "But, the screams. . . the light? If they didn't die that day, then why did they leave? Why did they go away?"

Graham didn't notice, but with every breath, his anger grew. His fingers gripped the chair's arms so tight they looked as though they would pierce the leather. Without thinking, he got to his feet, and as he did, the chair floated from the floor. Heat rose in Graham's cheeks as hot tears pooled.

"And why didn't you say anything? If you knew the story when I told you my nightmare, why didn't you say anything then?"

Alex remained seated, unaffected by Graham's change in mood and the supernatural side effects.

"Take a breath, Graham. One deep breath."

Graham obeyed, and the chair fell with a heavy thud.

"I had to let your mind discover this veiled figure on its own and give you the space to understand who this person was, or more importantly, who it was not. Had I told you beforehand, your mind would not have been working with its own memories, and thus you would have been in a constant state of doubt, which is far worse than a period of uncertainty."

Graham didn't want to believe that. He would much rather be angry at Alex, his parents. . . at the world. Some part of him, deep down, knew that what Alex was saying made sense, but he would not accept it. All he could do was shake his head, let some tears loose, and fix the chair back in its original position.

"Leave it. I will fix it." Alex stood and set Graham's chair upright. Graham fell into it as though he'd been pushed.

"There's a voice inside of you that is trying to say that your parents have done a terrible thing in leaving you, so listen to my voice instead. To sacrifice a lifetime spent with your child to save his life is among the greatest acts of love I have ever witnessed. This is the truth about your parents."

Graham was annoyed that he could not keep his lower lip from quivering. He held his breath and strained to stop his tears, but they would not obey. He couldn't tell if they were a result of the pain of rejection he felt from being abandoned or the relief that washed over him knowing that he hadn't killed them.

"So where are they now? Where did they go?" asked Graham as he wiped a tear with his sleeve.

"They went dark. No one has heard from them since that

day. I think they understood what you were and chose to separate themselves from you so that Victus could not use them to find you."

Graham's heart felt like it had been stabbed, and the thought of his parents going into hiding because of him only twisted the invisible knife further in. He had not killed them, but instead, he had sentenced them to a lifetime of exile. He wasn't sure which was worse.

"We have to find them, Alex. I owe them that. What about this veiled person from my dreams? Where is he? Maybe my parents told him something."

"That is the first thing I thought of, but we have not had contact with him for some time. He has a complicated history, but I am using other assets to find your parents."

By this time, Graham was pacing in front of the chairs. He did not know what to think or say next, so he let his legs pace and his mind race.

"I told you this because you deserve to know, Graham, but it's not the main reason I brought you here."

Graham stopped pacing, but it was evident that his mind was still on the hamster wheel.

"I need your full attention, Graham."

Graham cleared his throat and suppressed more tears. He turned toward Alex and apologized.

"No apology is needed, but thank you. The main reason I wanted to speak with you has to do with your team. You are the leader of three other people who now look to you for guidance and support. Your physical training will take up much of the daytime hours, but where they stop, you must continue. I want you to meet with me every night to learn the foundations of our way of life: our ideals, our constitutions, and our organizational structure."

While Graham appreciated the extra investment, his heart grew even heavier at the thought of the additional effort required of him.

"You must go the extra mile for your team and lead from

the front, and to do this, you will need just as much knowledge as experience. This is the heavy mantel of servant leadership."

Graham's mind went to his friends, wondering what they were doing downstairs. He flashed back to when Damien had almost drowned, and the sight of Kel and Ailey's limp forms over Cavaness' shoulders as they retreated from the cavern. The memory sparked his protective nature and took momentary precedence over the feelings of his parents' sacrifice.

Alex looked at Graham as if he could see into his thoughts and feel his emotions. He sat with elbows on his knees and smiled.

"You have their soft nature. I can see it in your eyes."

Graham snapped out of his flashback, unsure how to respond.

"Focus on the here and now. It's a lot to ask, given what I have just presented you with, but I need. . . we all need you to focus on getting stronger. I'm sure the mystery of your parents' whereabouts will unravel in time. For now, I'm asking you to leave this in my hands. Can you do that?"

"I will try."

"Good man. As I have more information, I promise to inform you. For now, it's time to learn and train."

21

HAWKSNEST

HAWKSNEST OUTPOST
Nobbys Headland: Newcastle, Australia

Corbin and Sonia sprinted in a sporadic pattern, so the Vics could not easily anticipate their movement. There were not many people in the stretch of sand between the town and the hill, but the vacationers who were looked at Corbin and Sonia as if they were mad. The land was flat and bare, with nothing to shield them from attack. Little purple darts flew around them as they sprinted. Their only hope was to make it to the base of the large hill so the Snype would no longer have a line of sight.

"Lucas, talk ta me, my man," said Corbin, panting.

"I. . . I got hit in the shoulder, but I'll live."

Lucas shuffled over to another wall, resting his back against it. He held his shoulder and winced in pain as he removed a small mirror from his pocket. He held it up, searching for the other Snype, and rotated it until he could make out a small figure. He craned his head up just above the wall. A streak of purple shot past his face, leaving a burn mark across his cheekbone. The purple dart pelted the stone wall behind him and broke off a small cluster of rocks. Lucas melted back behind the wall.

"Are you serious! You gonna play like that, huh?" Lucas whispered to himself. His eye twitched as the welt below reddened. He patted his cheek to check for blood. The sight of the wet, red line across his hand only fueled his retaliation. "Let's just see how quickly you dodge a tower."

Lucas stood up and twisted around toward the hill in one swift motion. He flung his hand forward, firing six small, yellow darts from his hand, and sat back down behind the wall as quickly as he had stood up. He listened as the darts made contact with the metal radio tower mounted on the building, just behind the tiny sniper perch. He heard the creak and moan of the metal as the tower's base twisted and snapped. The structure leaned forward and toppled over. He waited for the sounds of the tower crashing into the roof. That was his signal.

Lucas bolted up again and zoomed his vision in on the rooftop. He could see a cloud of dust and mangled metal. A shadow darted through the dust. He calculated the man's speed. He held an inverted hand under his chin, just in front of his throat. Streaks of yellow energy flowed from his fingertips down into the palm of his hand and formed a small, yellow dart. Lucas followed the target and fired three consecutive darts, which soared through the air and connected center mass in the man's chest. The shadow stumbled backward and disappeared into the rubble.

As Corbin and Sonia sprinted closer to the base of the hill, they could hear Lucas over the radio.

"The Snype is down, but not for long. As strong as his darts were, I'd say he's a veteran. This wouldn't have been his first time being hit."

"Roger that. We're movin' as fast as we can. Good work. Glad you're alright," said Sonia.

"You're not out of the woods yet. Four bogies are coming toward you, sea-side. Most tourists have cleared out from the beach and are fleeing from the crash up top. You don't have time to worry about concealment. Get to the base of the outpost ASAP."

"You don't have to tell me twice," said Sonia.

"I see 'em. They're too spread out, Lucas. Try to herd 'em closer together for us," said Corbin.

"Copy that."

Lucas peered at the coming threat. A handful of Vics tried to spread out and surround Corbin and Sonia. He fired a burst, causing sand and dirt to cover the woman on the right side of the pack. She shrugged and held her hand up to block the sandy splatter. Without realizing it, she instinctively started moving closer to the others and away from the explosion. Darts and small, forceful blasts peppered the shore on either side of the approaching enemy, causing them to squeeze together.

"Is that tight enough?" asked Lucas.

"Thanks, we'll take it from here," said Corbin.

Sonia was quicker and more athletic than Corbin, so she was already ahead of him. She fired a few blasts to keep the approaching threat in tight formation. A few purple blasts hit the sand at her feet, causing her to lunge sideways, tumble into a roll, and land on one knee and outstretched leg. A fiery orb formed in her cupped hands. With a heavy grunt, she hurled it toward them. The blast was a mix of pulsing energy and orange flame. The fiery attack streaked across the ground, laying down a black line of scorched earth. The four Vics on approach back-pedaled to a halt just before reaching the small fire wall.

"Guys, you've got more of them setting up on the rooftops. I'll do my best to cover you, but you had better get to the base of that hill fast," said Lucas.

"This is gettin' real old, real fast," huffed Corbin. "Sonia, give us some cover after Lucas distracts our friends up top. I'll take care of des clowns."

From behind the flames, the others fired bursts. Corbin stretched out a long wall of energy, bowing outward. The wall deflected the purple blasts back toward their makers, who dove in all directions to avoid their own attacks. Corbin's formed wall continued forward, but the bottom started rolling up like a retracting theater screen until it looked like a long rod. Before the others could react, the rod hurled through the air and slammed into their chests, knocking them over like bowling pins.

In the meantime, Lucas was on the rooftop, firing Snype darts at the opposing rooftop. One would duck while the other would form a small shield from their wrist to deflect the shots.

While they were distracted, Sonia created more handfuls of fire and flung them toward the rooftop. They sailed through the air like comets, each ball descending with a long fire tail trailing behind it. Her shots licked the entire rim of the circular hill on which the buildings above rested. A fire wall crackled upwards, creating a temporary barrier between them and their attackers.

"Get down here, Lucas. We're gonna need you inside," said Corbin, approaching the four Vics who were still trying to recover from the hit. He formed a large ring above them like a giant halo and commanded it to descend, trapping them in the middle as it constricted. He gave a nod to Sonia, who fired a ball of fire into the rim, causing it to erupt into flames.

The others huddled with their backs to one another, trying to escape the heat of the blazing ring.

"Oh baby, just like Johnny Cash," mocked Corbin. "You

just stay steady now. Don't do anything daft and make me constrict it more. Ya with me?" He motioned for them to start walking toward the hill. "Move it. If we are not inside in the next sixty seconds, you'll get way more than an Australian sun tan. Oh, and tell your boys up top to stand down."

One of the men spoke a few commands into the mike on his wrist.

"Much obliged. Now go."

Corbin searched for an entrance as they approached the base of the hill. The stone pattern was nearly identical everywhere, except in one spot, where the stone was stacked in a crude and jagged arch.

"You got forces on the other side of dat door?" Corbin asked the man who had spoken in his COM unit.

The man remained silent. Corbin looked at the name patch on the man's jacket.

"Hopkins, my man. I asked you a question. Now, don't make me get mean."

The blazing circle constricted a few inches, and Sonia caused the flame to intensify. The four Vics flinched, trying to escape the heat, sweating from the intensity. Hopkins shook his head.

"No. All teams are positioned outside."

Sonia allowed the fire to dissipate a little, giving them a bit of relief.

"See, that wasn't so bad, was it? Things always go better when you play nice. Now, if you're lying, dis ain't gonna end well for you. Sonia, give us a little cover, will ya?"

Sonia nodded and waited for Lucas to meet them before laying out a curtain of fire behind them. Corbin held a hand up to the rock, and the crude arch started to glow. The stones beneath the arch faded away, revealing the once-hidden entrance to HawksNest.

"Go," barked Corbin.

In seconds, they were in, and the archway stones

reappeared back in place, sealing them inside.

22

ALBATROSS

ALBATROSS OUTPOST
Remote Jungle- Argentina

Chase, Cavaness, and Jael continued deep into the jungle, surrounded by lush foliage with leaves wider than cars. The trees towered into the sky with thick vines twisting their way up the trunks. Each person would alternate leading the pack, holding up leaves and branches for the others to pass under. The forest felt alive with the rustling of plants, the swaying of trees in the heavy breeze, and the sounds of various birds and wildlife calling out to one another in their native tongue.

As Jael ducked under the outstretched arms of a colorful, exotic plant, she came nose to nose with a toucan. She smiled at the bird, seemingly impressed with its acceptance of her presence. She giggled a bit to herself and began talking to the bird and waiting for a reply. Her focus was so honed in on the splendor of their surroundings and the life contained within them that she did not see the looming threat hidden in the distance.

Cavaness took the lead, passing Jael. Chase followed closely behind, his eyes in constant motion, analyzing the path ahead. Cavaness suddenly stopped and threw his hand out, signaling the others to remain still. Chase shot him a curious look, but Cavaness simply put his finger to his lips and pointed straight ahead. He snapped his fingers to get Jael's attention. She turned around to see Cavaness point two fingers to his eyes, then to the top of a tree, towering in the distance. He then pointed up into the sky and back down at the tree.

Jael strained to see out into the distance but finally found what Cavaness saw. She nodded and stared directly at the sun.

Chase also got a lock on the man far up in the trees. He then calmly walked behind a large fern. The others followed.

Cavaness leaned toward the others and whispered, "He's not alone. He could be a Former, but I would guess he's a Snype. We need cover. Jael, I need you on that. I'll distract him while Chase goes in for the hit."

"Understood," they said in unison.

"Be prepared. The rest of the body will retaliate when we take down the eyes."

"How many do you think?" asked Jael.

"It's impossible to tell in this place, but I've seen movement in at least five other areas," replied Cavaness.

"Only six Vics? I'm insulted," said Chase.

"These won't be amateurs. If they're guarding, then they are Vets. Don't underestimate them," barked Cavaness.

Chase lost some sarcasm and readjusted as if he had

practiced this before. "Yes, sir. Understood."

"Good. Jael, go."

Jael immediately gazed into the sky once more. She lifted her hand up, her band blazing and her eyes changing to amber. She curled her fingers as if she were cupping the sun in the hollow of her hand, then rotated them. The sunbeams that penetrated the lush greenery began to shift and focus on the tree which held the Vic. The beams focused in like a spotlight, causing such a glare that even she had difficulty looking at it.

Cavaness stepped back with one foot and pushed a wave of energy into the ground. The tremor rippled through the ground and up the trunk of the towering tree. It began to bend and sway under the invisible force, and a person's lower half became visible behind the leafy cover.

"Got 'em. Cavaness, a little boost? Give me ten yards," said Chase.

Cavaness nodded. "Go."

Chase sprinted forward while Cavaness fired another wave into the ground. As Chase approached the ten-yard mark, he kept his stride but bent his knees in anticipation of the lift. Right on cue, the blast erupted from the ground underneath his feet, but instead of hurting Chase, it propelled him skyward toward the tree. Chase squinted as he tried to see beyond the light, shading his eyes with his hand.

Just as predicted, blasts began to fill the forest. There were at least three Vics in front of them and another two flanking each side. They had walked right into a trap.

Purple and yellow attacks filled the air. Cavaness fired bursts with one hand while pushing energy into the ground with the other. His gifting was suited for fighting in buildings with adjoining, solid surfaces. A dense jungle, however, with limited visibility and no connected surfaces to push energy into, was far more challenging to work with. He looked to his right to see how Jael was faring, but she was gone.

Chase soared through the air and connected with the man perched in the tree. He had come at him with outstretched arms, firing blasts into the Vic's chest as he descended on him. The Vic fell backward into the trunk, his head slamming hard into the rough bark. Chase's momentum carried him to a neighboring branch. He jumped to it, took hold of a thinner branch above, and swung completely around. Swiftly, he jumped right back to the attacker and landed a punch square to his jaw.

The Vic's head snapped back with the blow and hit the trunk again. His knees buckled, and he slumped down, unconscious.

Cavaness continued firing blindly through the overgrowth in the general direction of the purple blasts. He strafed to his left as a purple ball flew over his shoulder.

"Jael!" yelled Cavaness.

A glint of light caught his eye. She had sent a small beacon in the sky in reply. At least one other Vic saw it because a few attacks began to fly in her direction. Cavaness ducked behind a fallen tree for cover to formulate another plan. He shifted upward to look around, then sprang to his feet and fired a surge into the ground. It surfaced fifteen yards to his left underneath a tall, thin tree. Earth and roots erupted into the sky behind the tree, causing it to snap at its base and topple.

Cavaness jumped out from behind his cover and sprinted toward where the tree would fall.

"Jael, duck!" Cavaness reared his glowing hands back, throwing his entire body into it with a heavy grunt. There was a massive flash of light, and the tree hurled through the air at the attackers.

"Watch out!" came a cry in the distance.

The leaves and ferns bent and swayed as the Vics scrambled to retreat from the path of the spiraling tree. Fleeing just in time, one man turned around and formed a purple wall of energy to shield his team. The tree crashed into it with such force that he fell backward, hitting his head on a rocky outcrop. The tree slammed to the ground, rolling a full rotation before coming to a halt. The Former remained motionless.

The second distraction provided enough time for Jael to come into contact with another attacker. This time, it was another woman, a little smaller than Jael, with black hair and balled fists. She immediately swung at Jael, who ducked under the punch and landed one of her own to the woman's oblique. She grunted and flung an elbow that connected Jael's temple.

Jael let the hit carry her around full circle, twisting her body so that she was facing the other woman. She held her hands parallel to the ground and threw a surge at the Vic. The black-haired woman saw the attack in time and fell to her side, firing a burst at Jael's feet.

Jael lifted her foot to evade the attack and twisted around again, now standing perpendicular to her attacker. The two went back and forth, trading blows and blasts, each equally matched in their defensive maneuvers. Attack after attack, the two ended up six or seven feet apart, both breathing heavily. They studied each other, trying to find a way past their defenses.

The black-haired woman pointed a finger and, through labored breathing, said, "Wait a minute. I know you. Yeah, you're the one who turned tail and ran away at that other outpost. What was it. . . Raven? You fight pretty well for a coward."

Blood rushed through Jael's face. "You? You helped destroy Raven?" Her lips pulled back, baring her teeth.

She could see that she had hit a soft spot. "That putrid junk hole? I did you a favor by knocking that place down. Oh, I'm Kyla, by the way. I would have introduced myself before, but I was too distracted to offer pleasantries." Kyla cracked a malicious smirk.

Jael's jaw dropped at the grin. The evil grin that she had seen before. Her eyes widened. "You!"

Kyla's eyes darted from Jael to the space behind her as she spoke.

Jael took a deep breath. Though a radiant amber, her eyes could not hide the strained blood vessels. "People died. My people. good people."

"Only the strong survive. Evidently, your friends were just not that strong."

Kyla's eyes darted again, now seeing her Victus comrade sneaking up behind Jael.

"We don't say Vae Victus for fun. Those who join us live and *thrive*. The others perish. Do the math. You seem pretty skilled, even though you're a coward. No one's perfect, I suppose. I might even consider letting you come with us."

"What, join you? You murdered everyone I care about!"

Kyla dove to the side while Jael was mid-sentence. The man behind her wielded a jagged branch above his head, ready to strike. In an adrenaline rush, the man yelled and reared back even further, but a giant blur knocked him violently to the side before he could swing it. Two men rolled over, one unconscious on top of the other. As they came to a halt, Jael looked to see where the second man had come from. She saw Chase landing on the ground, his shoulder still slumped forward from having just thrown the Vic.

Meanwhile, Cavaness was surrounded. The Vics had positioned themselves on all sides and marched closer together, pinning Cavaness in the middle. However, the convergence did not cause much concern. He stared at them as if welcoming their approach and calmly waited until the Vics were nearly shoulder-to-shoulder with one another.

Cavaness made eye contact with those before him, then peered over his shoulder to those behind him.

"The way I see it, you have two options right now, and only one works out with you still standing. You've been brainwashed into believing that you are the way. . . the new generation of righteous humanity." He paused for a moment, keeping his stance firmly planted. "You're wrong."

"You're outmatched, old man," mocked a stout man to his left. "Look around you. You're outnumbered ten to one."

Cavaness stood in silent reflection, taking his time to reply.

"You aren't listening. You think you are superior to those who are unactivated, but I think you can feel the darkness of those bands eating away at you." Cavaness held his hand up. His catalysts were still gleaming, but the scars over them were still visible. "Trust me. I know what I'm talking about. Submit now, and we will help you. You think your power is your own and makes you valuable, but ultimately, you are all disposable pawns."

"You are not gonna talk your way out of this, gramps. Now, shut up, or I will shut you up myself."

Cavaness took one final look at his attackers. The man talking was a veteran, but many others were young and inexperienced. They couldn't have been more than level sevens at best. He looked sternly into their eyes. Many shifted nervously and broke eye contact. He lowered his head, huffed in disappointment, and balled his fists.

"Alright, fine. We'll do it the hard way."

23

FALCON

Alex walked by the training room and peered inside to see Murphy teaching the kids how to use the burst attacks. He watched through the door window momentarily, satisfied with the progress. He then held a hand out and released seven plum-sized orbs toward the ceiling, where they hovered like Christmas lights. While they remained suspended, Alex waved his other hand, causing the glowing orbs to fade from bright yellow to translucent and become completely transparent.

He flicked his wrist, dispersed the invisible tracking balls wherever his mind commanded, and headed upstairs to his office.

He sank into his desk chair and pulled a walkie-talkie handset from the top drawer. He turned the dial at the top to channel six.

"Agent Red, this is Falcon. What is your current status?"

A few seconds went by before a reply came through.

"This is Agent Red," said a woman's voice through the static. "I'm still tracking down a hot lead, but no sign of him yet, I'm afraid. Check back in twenty-four hours, and I should have more. Over."

"Very well, and thank you. Falcon out."

Alex sat the unit down on the desk and stared at it briefly before turning on three monitors, which crackled to life in color and sound, giving him feeds from three different news stations. Each station reported the ongoing coverage of the developing terrorist group announced by Ambassador Klein of the U.N.

Alex muted two of the three screens, focusing on the middle one with KBN News. As before, anchor Lauren Flowers was reporting on the recent updates given by the U.N.

> Today, Ambassador Klein reported new intel concerning the global terrorist group, which has yet to brand itself with any label. They are believed to have advanced technology, which gives them the capability of mass destruction. Though their true identity and motivation are still unknown, we have just obtained footage of a recent attack near Nobbys Headland in Newcastle, Australia. As you can see on the screen to my left, this is live footage from an anonymous source taken from a cell phone. While the footage is shaky, it captures a glimpse of their advanced weaponry.
>
> Focus on the woman to the right of the screen. Watch as she extends her hand upwards to the hill above as it erupts into flames, nearly incinerating the

innocent men and women above. Also, notice the man to the left. He also seems to be controlling a group huddled together in terror. We believe these unknown attackers are among the top leadership of the terrorist organization, and every possible resource is being utilized to identify and track them down.

We ask those in Newcastle to remain in their homes until the suspects are captured. The U.N. is asking that the worldwide community be on watch and to report any similar instances. The number to call is at the bottom of your screen. That's all for tonight's broadcast. Join us tomorrow evening for more breaking news and live coverage of the annual Macy's Flower Show in New York. For KBN News, this is Lauren Flowers.

Alex remained silent, leaning back in his chair with his arms crossed. He processed the footage for a few minutes and then closed his eyes.

In his mind, he could see the feeds coming from the orbs he released downstairs. They had dispersed throughout Falcon in search of Branson and focused on Murphy. While the scout orbs Murphy had formed could only produce infrared-like images, Alex could produce orbs with the same clarity as his own eyes.

He watched Branson sit at a table with COM gear scattered over its surface. He was scribbling notes in a journal.

Alex moved the orb so that he could peer over Branson's shoulder to read, which turned out to be tactical notes he had prepared for his next session with Graham and the others. He then focused on the contents of the journal. The handwriting was hurried and messy, which was far different from the precision handwriting in the tactical notes. He was writing as fast as his hand could go as if his thoughts would forever escape him if not corralled on paper. His hand had a slight tremble as he wrote.

Alex could see that he was writing about a war. Branson was detailing an account of his platoon in Iraq, having been separated from his team after a mortar had gone off in their compound. He wrote of the fear and hysteria the enemy caused in the small village and the result of the attack. He scribbled in a frenzy his entire experience and something about a small child. Looking at Branson's face, Alex could see his eyes were puffy and red. He rubbed his trembling hand down his cheek and frustratedly pushed the journal aside.

Branson twisted his neck side to side and took a deep breath. He mumbled a few words under his breath, cleared his throat, then took all the COM gear and checked the batteries in all the handsets. Branson then turned to each channel, requesting a check-in status from each team. He continued flipping through, stopping on channel twelve. Branson held the walkie in his hand for the longest moment, staring at the number 12. His knuckles turned white as he gripped the unit so tight that Alex thought he might crush it.

Soon, his watch beeped, snapping him out of the moment. He turned his wrist over to see the time. Five minutes to three o'clock. It was time for his training lesson. He gathered all the COM gear into a satchel, wiped the dampness from under his eyes, and continued toward the training wing.

After the shift change, Alex followed Murphy through Falcon. He had gone through what seemed like a routine of unwinding, snacking, and retiring to his room for rest. Murphy removed his shoes, removed the contents of his pockets, and set them on top of his dresser. He then walked over to an armchair in the corner and plopped down, resting his head against the padded back. He closed his eyes, locked his fingers across his belly, and rested his elbows on the chair's arms.

He appeared unusually exhausted. Alex tried to get a feel

for his mood, but he could only detect his fatigue. Just as his body began to relax, the flip-style phone on his dresser buzzed with an incoming text message. Murphy sighed, pushed out of the chair to his feet, and walked over to the dresser. Alex focused on the small digital display.

Is it safe to talk?

Murphy danced his thumbs over the buttons.

Yes, I'm alone, but make it quick.

Moments later, his phone vibrated with an incoming call. He shifted the phone to one hand and hit a button.

"Are you safe?"

Alex could not hear the conversation on the other side of the line, so he had to focus solely on what Murphy was saying, trying to process the intent of the conversation as Murphy paused to listen to the caller.

"No, I can check, but it can't be right now."

Murphy paused to listen.

"Don't worry about me. I can handle myself. I just want you to be safe, away from danger."

Another pause.

"No, I will remain concealed to avoid suspicion. You know it has to be that way. Now, tell me what happened to you. I need details, or I can't help."

Murphy leaned on his dresser as he listened to the caller for a longer duration.

"Okay, I'll send a scout out later. For now, I want you to remain where you are and stay calm. I have a shift change and will be unavailable until about seven o'clock. Once I'm done, I'll check on things, okay?"

Murphy snapped the phone shut and tossed it on the bed. He walked over to a pair of French doors leading to a small balcony outside his room. He crossed his arms and stood transfixed on something beyond the building. The vitality in his eyes continued to drain as he looked out through the trees toward Wellington.

Alex opened his eyes and sat back up straight in his chair. He stared idly at his desk, shaking his head in disappointment.

"Oh, Brian. What have you done?"

Kyla slid her phone back into a duffle bag just past the small transit mirror she had used to retreat to Albatross. She walked back into the corner of the cave, where streams of water poured from the ceiling. The reception hall of Albatross was carved into the rock tucked behind a large waterfall. Kyla stared at the sheet of water on the far side of the hewn hall. The roar of the water was so loud that she had a hard time reporting to Silas.

"So, I assume he agreed once again?"

"Without question," replied Kyla. "He's sending another scout this evening. We should be finished up here in plenty of time to make it over there."

"Splendid," said Silas in his usual phlegmatic voice.

Silas walked over to address two men bound in black, vaporous chains in the far corner of the room. He leaned over the first man, his hands clasped behind his back and his cane tucked under his arm.

"You see, Adrian? We have many ways to obtain information. If you don't want to talk, then you are only bringing more unnecessary pain on yourself. We'll just get your friend and compatriot, Brian Murphy, to lead us to Alexander and Graham. Besides, I rather enjoy watching you writhe in pain. Watching you virtuously endure it brings me joy as if there were some ultimate meaning to your persecution."

Silas stood and retrieved his cane, shoving the tip into Adrian's ribs. A pulse of energy shot down the length of the shaft, making Adrian grunt in pain.

"Although you may want to give some thought to whom you are protecting. Not everyone in Aegis is on your side, you know. Speaking of which, your allies are coming and will be here shortly. Do you think they will rescue you, or will you be an acceptable casualty to regain Albatross?"

Silas turned to address Kyla.

"ETA?"

"I'd say about another hour and a half."

"Well, I suppose we should get Adrian topside to greet our guests."

Kyla nodded. "And what of our Aussie friends? Have we made progress there as well?"

"Yes, much better than we had hoped. We are getting good coverage on the outside, and the pieces are in place on the inside. Everything is coming together, just as planned."

24

ALBATROSS

A brave young Vic lunged at Cavaness, who was still focused on the group's leader. Not bothering to look his way, Cavaness held a hand out and pushed a wave of energy toward the kid, causing him to backflip before slamming into the ground. With the first attack out of the way, the entire group converged.

Chase ran over to the two men to see if they were still

conscious. The woman who was attacking Jael had disappeared into the foliage. After assessing the condition of the two men, Chase got to his feet and gazed off into the distance.

Jael stood beside him, putting a hand on his shoulder. "Thanks. That could have been a lot worse."

Chase did not reply. She looked up to see his eyes darting rapidly from side to side.

"Chase?"

A few moments passed until he refocused, noticing Jael's concerned stare.

"Oh, hey. No problem. Glad to help. That branch would have left a mark."

"Where were you? It was like you were in a trance."

"I'll explain later. For now, we need to find your new friend and fast. She's a Vet, probably the leader of this crew, and we need her to talk."

"What about Cavaness? He's surrounded."

"Cavaness can take care of himself. We need to go now. Don't worry, we won't be far."

Chase took Jael by the hand and started west through the path of broken underbrush. They had just passed a cluster of abnormally huge red-petaled plants when Chase fell to the ground with a heavy grunt. A small breeze blew in front of Jael, and she was knocked down, too. A blur circled them until a man came to a halt. Their friend from the village had come to play.

Chase looked up to see the middle-aged man wagging his finger back and forth like a teacher scolding a student.

"Ah, ah, ah. Where do you think you're going?"

"Nowhere in particular, just–" As he was talking, Chase moved at full speed around the man and landed a punch in the small of his back.

The Latino man whirled around and fired at Chase, who did not attempt to run but instead allowed a thick shield to form from his wristband and deflect the shot. The shield was rectangular-ish with jagged points at the top and bottom as if three lightning bolts were tied together. As quickly as it had formed to protect Chase, it had vanished once it had served its purpose.

Chase returned the sentiment, nearly hitting the man square in the chest, but he sidestepped the shot. Pound for pound, Chase and the Latino man went at it in streaks of yellow and purple. Each took turns attacking and counter-attacking, never being able to hit the other.

"Don't leave, Jael!" Chase said from the cloud of hazy motion. "They're trying to split us up. Go and distract some people for Cavaness while I deal with this guy!"

Jael hesitated. Revenge flickered in her eyes and tensed her jaw. She balled her fists and moved toward the path where Kyla had fled, but something stopped her. Her focus frustratingly shifted to where Cavaness was fighting. Grunting, she turned from Kyla's escape route and ran toward Cavaness.

Cavaness fired multiple pulses into the ground, separating his adversaries to prevent them from pairing up for an attack. Mounds of dirt and foliage burst from the ground between them. The leader of the small pack ordered the others to move in while he let loose a vine-like string of electricity from his outstretched hand.

Cavaness dug his heels into the ground and crossed his arms in front of his face. A circular shield formed from his catalysts with the small V-shaped Pusher symbol at its center. The shield appeared just in time to block the blueish-purple tendrils of electricity. The shield remained formed as long as the bolts continued to pour out.

"Now, you fools!" screamed the leader.

Two boys charged Cavaness on each side and grabbed

him by the crook of the arms while trying to summon chains to bind him with. Another stared into the sky like Jael but could not produce a result from his strained efforts. The final boy hung from Cavaness's forearm, trying to uncross his arms. The initial convergence of the four youths had made Cavaness sway slightly, though he hardly budged.

Jael rushed to the scene in time to notice one of the boys trying to use the sun's rays to blind Cavaness, so she, too, gazed into the sky to command the light and thwart his efforts.

As the boy took hold of Cavaness' wrist, he understood what the boy was. He was trying to siphon away the energy and get inside his mind. He was another Lumos. Cavaness wore a disgruntled look, quickly growing tired of the whole charade.

The boy who had been knocked down was back in the fight, joining the other two behind Cavaness.

"Enough!" Cavaness barked.

He made his shield to dissipate, allowing the electricity to hit him in the chest. He gritted his teeth, grunted with the shock, and quickly flexed his arms to pin the Vic's hands between his forearms and biceps. The electricity from the Spark flowed from Cavaness into all who had a grip on him. Each of the boys went rigid and convulsed. While still in his defensive stance, Cavaness reared back and snapped his arms forward, flinging all four boys toward their leader. When they collided, they scattered like bowling pins in an electrified cluster of arms and legs.

The three others behind Cavaness looked nervously at each other. Slowly, Cavaness peered over his shoulder at them with fire in his amber-shaded eyes. They gasped and immediately fled in different directions through the forest.

Chase and the other Surge continued to go at each other at unimaginable speeds. They moved about the forest in faded streaks of light. At first, they fought linearly but quickly reverted to using the terrain to throw the other off. Chase streaked up a tree trunk in a streak of yellow to gain even more velocity and descended toward the Vic, firing bursts on the way down.

The blasts peppered the forest floor, but none reached the intended target. All sorts of glowing streaks of light filled the jungle as they continued their battle.

Chase finally caught a break. As he leaped from tree to tree, he snapped off a small branch, then ran around the base of a cluster of trees, trying his best to run in a predictable, figure-eight pattern. Once Chase had made his fourth lap, he came to a dead stop. Turning around, he pulled the branch back like a baseball bat and swung for the fences.

Just as he had hoped, the man was close behind. Noticing Chase had stopped, he lunged forward to tackle him. As Chase swung, the branch hit him in the upper thighs, sending him into a mid-air somersault and crashing to the ground. The man tried to yell, grabbing his legs, but there was no air to produce sound. The fall had knocked the breath out of him. He could only mouth a silent scream.

Panting, Chase threw the branch to the ground and walked over to him. He knelt with one knee on the ground and the other on the man's chest. He waited for the man to catch his breath and swung his fist in a blur of yellow. Lights out.

Jael watched as a few young Vics scattered into the forest and could not contain her amusement. Meanwhile, Cavaness had already reached the convulsing mound of men. The leader of the group, regaining consciousness, tried to push the two kids off of him, but they were so out of it that he was fighting off dead weight. He almost had one ready to roll off the side when he saw Cavaness' head block the sun.

Cavaness knelt and pushed down on the heap, pinning the man beneath his own subordinates. The kids writhed and grunted under the added pressure. The man tried to wiggle free, but his arms were pinned.

Cavaness put more pressure on him as he spoke. "You think you have the advantage because you took our training facilities? You think you can beat us by capturing our outposts? Think again. The power you think is yours can be taken away, and so can these infantile, diapered rookies you call an army. These boys have no idea what they signed up for, and I am taking them from you so they can see the truth."

The man stared back with a twisted expression. "You're wrong. We are The way. . . the future. You are the conquered. Go ahead and take them. For every person you remove, ten more will take their place. You can't win against our numbers. Despite your well-laid plans, Kaiser will have his rule."

As the man focused on Cavaness, he failed to see Jael approach from behind. She also knelt, cupping his head in her hands. Translucent, purple vapor stretched from his temples to her palms. He was caught off guard enough for Jael to begin the extraction process before he could put up a defense.

"Never you mind about our plans. Let's see what yours are," said Jael.

The man's eyes rolled back into his head, eyelids fluttering as Jael closed her eyes in concentration, absorbing the vapor of memories as they flowed into her hands.

The man's tense muscles relaxed as she continued to extract his knowledge. His head fell to the side as he slipped into a deep sleep.

Jael continued to take knowledge and energy away until she was satisfied. The vapor stopped falling from his temples as she cut the connection.

"Not good," Jael said.

"What? What are they planning?" asked Cavaness.

"I don't think he has the whole plan. I got the impression that they keep the information compartmentalized, but from what he told me, they plan to execute Adrian and Marcio on our arrival. They're bait to lure us in with. Beyond that, I am not sure."

"Here, maybe this guy has more to share," said Chase, pulling the unconscious Latino by the collar.

He dragged the man between Cavaness and Jael and then sat down with a thud.

"You okay?" asked Jael.

Chase was still breathing heavily. "He's heavier than he looks."

Jael grinned and shuffled over. "Alright, let's see what you have to tell us."

Just like before, Jael closed her eyes, held her hands to the man's temples, and extracted whatever she could find in his mind. After a few minutes, she clenched her fingers again and sighed.

"Sorry, I think this guy is just a foot soldier. His mission was to be our tail and inform the group. There is nothing more beyond that, although, to your advantage, you really put a holy fear in him. I don't think he has ever met another Surge before. He's frightened of you."

"At least something came of all that," replied Chase. "I'd bet money Kyla is the other one with intel, but we will never beat her back to Albatross. We've got to come up with a plan."

Kyla's name set Jael's teeth on edge. Cavaness took notice.

"What?" asked Cavaness.

"That woman, Kyla. . . she was at Raven." Her eyes teared

up at the mention of her former home, but she swallowed the emotion. "She led the attack that killed my people, my. . ." Jael cleared her throat. "She deserves to be in the ground, same as them."

Cavaness put a light hand gently on the back of her neck.

"A time for vengeance will come, but until then, the way to defeat her is to thwart her current mission."

Jael closed her eyes, taking deep breaths. Cavaness' words did not seem to bring much comfort.

Meanwhile, Chase knelt and unzipped the backpack that Jael had laid at her side, searching for something specific.

"Okay." Jael had regained her composure. "Let's frustrate her plans. How do we go about it?"

"We are the closest to Alex, even more so than Adrian or Marcio. They want us alive to find Alex, but the endgame is Graham," said Chase.

"Is he really that powerful?" asked Jael.

"He reached power levels near thirty during the catalyst stage."

Jael's eyes widened. "How's that even possible?"

"It's possible because we live in the time foretold in the Unseen War. There's no mistaking that Graham is the one prophecied about," said Cavaness.

"He shouldn't be alive after that much power ran through him as a rookie. It nearly killed him. He was unresponsive for three days. If he can reach level thirty on day one, just think of what he can do once he's trained," said Chase.

"As much as you hate Kyla right now, remember that she's still a pawn," said Cavaness. "The balance of power lies with Alex because Graham is the one who is tipping the scales. And as important as Kyla thinks she is, she's a disposable resource, just a single arrow in a very large quiver. You must always consider the bigger picture and act on that perspective."

As Jael wrestled with that idea, Chase continued to rummage through the pack until his hand found a notebook-sized mirror.

"There. Got it." Chase tilted the small mirror so he could see the front. "Time to send these guys to The Wasteland."

"Well, good riddance," spat Jael. "I'll search these other two guys before you send them off."

Jael walked to the man who had nearly bashed her with a tree branch, making no effort to avoid kicking him as she stepped over.

Chase watched her bend down beside the big man. He fumbled the mirror around in his hands, keeping his eyes on Jael in the distance.

"What are the odds that Adrian and Marcio are still alive?" asked Chase.

Cavaness stood with his eyes focused on Albatross.

"Hard to tell. It depends on who's leading this group. For our sake, I hope they are. They're good men. Strong men. They have built a huge network of people here, and we need to keep it connected."

"And if they are still alive, what's the plan to keep them that way?"

"I don't know, but we've got plenty of time on our way for you to figure something out, as long as you can focus on the mission instead of her."

Chase immediately blushed. "Hey, I just–"

"You like her."

"Well, yes, but. . ."

"But nothing. That's the way it is. Accept it and move on, but don't let it distract you from the mission. The stakes are too high."

"You know, I really hate your perception sometimes."

"Somehow, I think you'll get over it."

"I'll keep focused as long as you keep this to yourself."

Cavaness nodded with a hint of satisfaction.

Chase took a knee beside the other Surge. He grabbed the man by the wrist and allowed a ripple of energy to flow into him, causing his purplish black band to appear. His eyes fluttered lazily, mumbling incoherently.

Chase held the small mirror to his palm.

"Wake up, dude. It's time to go on a little trip."

25

FALCON

FALCON HQ
Portfield, Pennsylvania

"To be effective, you must learn the ins and outs of each other's capabilities," said Alex. "Up until now, you have not had the chance because you have trained individually. Now, we'll work on training together as a team."

Alex led Kel to the back wall and asked the other three to stand about ten feet away.

"First, remember that everyone has three most commonly used offensive attacks. The most basic is the *Burst*. The second is the *Charge*, and the third and most difficult is the *Surge*. You can attack with these and use them as a counter-attack. Now, I want you to understand what a gifting-specific attack is like. Kel, I want you to push a pulse into the wall, bend it, and try to hit one of the others. Be sure that it's not too strong."

Kel analyzed the distance and trajectory between her position and the position of the others. She cracked her knuckles, held her hands together close to her chest, and then fired a pulse into the wall. It absorbed into the wall and quickly propelled back toward Damien, who was already poised to react. Damien let loose a burst just in time to connect to the invisible force approaching him. His counter-attack made contact, but it was so close that it knocked him onto his back when the two forces collided.

"Great shot, Kel. That was near-perfect precision. Damien, what did you notice?" asked Alex.

"It was hard to judge because I couldn't see it, but I could sense it coming."

"I couldn't have said it better, myself. A Pusher's pulse is invisible to the naked eye, but the catalysts' power has given you all a sixth sense in detecting other power sources. The true name of this power is best described in Greek and is called *Dynamis*. Our culture has a lot of terminology, so I will do my best to give it to you in small amounts. When you hear the word dynamis, think about a stick of dynamite and the power contained within it. The English word dynamite came from this term and is the power originally used by The Ancient to create all we see. Whenever we speak of the gifting or powers we use, whether visible blasts of light or invisible pulses, we speak of dynamis. Does everyone understand?"

Everyone nodded.

"Good. Kel, please continue, but this time, don't stop. I want you to keep pulsing until I give a signal."

"Okay, I'll try," Kel replied.

She reared back again and fired pulses into the wall. Graham and Ailey successfully countered with small attacks. Damien also fired a blast without being knocked down. With each successful hit, Kel pushed stronger pulses into the wall. Graham kept his hands cupped together and tried to match his attack to the same intensity of Kel's pulse. He fired so quickly that he retaliated too hard on the last shot, sending the pulse violently back into the wall. Seconds later, the pulse propelled back out at its original angle and flew just beyond Kel, nicking her arm and spinning her around onto her side.

Graham cringed. "Kel, are you okay?" he asked in a slight panic.

"Oww. . . yeah, I'm fine. I didn't expect it to come back at me."

Graham jogged over and helped Kel to her feet, glad to have a chance to hold her hand again.

"You'll find many nuances to your giftings as you advance. Don't take anything for granted, and try to anticipate what could be possible," said Alex. "This is a perfect example. A pulse is like a pinball. You must take care, not only in your calculations but also in your timing. As you just experienced, your target can also use it against you if they know it's coming."

"Yes, sir. I'll keep that in mind," said Kel.

"Damien, why don't you come up next."

Damien switched places with Kel beside Alex, who led them over to the other side of the room. Several circular tubs filled with water sat near the wall.

"Until now, we have been working on the offensive attacks so you could develop as quickly as possible. Now, I want to show you some basic defensive maneuvers. People with giftings like Damien, Branson, and Casey Hagan can manipulate and command elements in the physical world, such as water, fire, and electricity. These are much harder to defend against with a burst or a surge. Putting a barrier between you and the natural force is a better tactic in these instances.

"If you remember, when you were in the clearing at the

Grove, Brian Murphy had formed a wall to block the wave of water that Damien had thrown at him. You can perform a similar feat. You cannot form large walls like Brian, but you can create momentary barriers, like a shield, that will protect you. The key is timing. It will only last a few seconds until you are quite advanced."

Alex led Damien in between two of the tubs. He spaced out the others so that there were eight or nine feet between them.

"Damien, I want you to focus on volume. Start with approximately one gallon and launch the water toward Graham. As you continue, increase the volume a bit each time. Graham, as odd as it sounds, I want you to clear your mind and allow the catalysts to work with your defensive instincts. Your natural reactions are almost always the correct ones. You will need to ball your fists, but let instinct do the rest, and don't worry about perfection the first time. The worst that can happen here is that you get a bath."

Graham stood between Kel and Ailey, so he felt on center stage, making it all the more awkward. *Just react? This was going to be a disaster- A wet, embarrassing disaster.*

Damien was surprisingly serious, looking highly focused on the task. He held both hands to his right side at waist level. His bands activated as a small stream of water funneled upwards out of the tub. Damien must have been practicing hard over the last month. The water had not only formed into a near-perfect orb but appeared to be churning like boiling water, which Graham thought was a taunt. *He's peacocking.* Damien looked from the water to Graham and grinned. *Oh no.*

"Bottoms up, amigo!"

Damien flung his hands forward, and the water followed. Graham braced for the attack and crossed his arms at the wrists, shielding himself. As his arms crossed, his bands overlapped, and as the light intensified, a force emerged from them. It was mostly circular, about the size of a hubcap, but morphed into all sorts of odd shapes, much like the substance in a lava lamp. The water splashed against the newly formed barrier and rained to the ground. Because of the shifting shape, a little water splashed on Graham's shoulder, but for the most part, he was dry.

"Nice going, Graham!" said Kel while Ailey clapped.

"That was pretty sweet, dude. Even I will admit that," said Damien.

"Indeed it was," said Alex, "Most people can only form a shield about the size of a teacup saucer the first time. Well done, Graham. I hope you all took notice. Since this was Graham's first time, its shape morphed, but the more you practice, the more stable the barrier will become. As you get better, it will retain its natural, intended shape. As you just witnessed, the barrier remains connected to your catalysts. Unless you are a Former, it will remain this way. Ailey, why don't you try it next."

Ailey nodded and tilted her head side to side, cracking her neck to loosen up. She then interlaced her fingers and pushed her palms out, cracking her knuckles.

"*Listo, amiga?*"

Ailey nodded again.

"Alright, then."

Damien used the water to his left this time. He flicked his wrists, causing a stream of water to funnel upwards to twice Damien's height. He caught it on its descent as if tossing a baseball and propelled it forward. Instead of taking the hit full-on, Ailey shifted so that her right side faced Damien, making her a thin target. She held her arm up so that it was perpendicular to the floor. Her wrist gleamed, and a tall, skinny oval appeared from her catalyst band. It lasted only moments. She clenched her eyes shut and tensed as the shield deflected the water. As the water splashed to the ground and the barrier dissolved, she opened one eye slightly to see the result. She surveyed her clothes and looked up at Alex with a beaming smile.

"Ailey! You did it! There's not a drop on you," said Kel. *"Buen trabajo, chica!"*

"Wonderful job, Ailey. I could not have asked for a better example," said Alex. "Not only did you completely block the water, but your instinct told you to turn to the side, making you a difficult target to hit."

Alex paused so everyone could congratulate Ailey.

"Okay, Kel. Let's see what you can do."

Without hesitation, Damien held his hands out to each side. Small tendrils of liquid sprang from the tubs and circulated his hands. Kel took a breath just as Damien threw the water toward her. She turned to the side, remembering what Alex had said about being a smaller target. Mimicking Ailey, she stretched out her arms while a thin semi-circle formed and flickered on and off like a fluorescent light. The shield protected only about half of her body when the water connected. A small wave curled against the barrier, but a sizable stream slammed into her side, soaking the back of her body. The light immediately vanished, leaving Kel dry on one side and dripping wet on the other.

Damien held back his laughter as best he could, which was not much. Kel looked at her drenched arm and flung it down, splattering the floor with water, then shot Damien an irksome glance.

"I believe you tried to think through it too much," said Alex. "That usually happens when we train like this, so try not to be discouraged. You were taking mental notes while Graham and Ailey took their turn. It's only natural to mimic other people's success. Next time, try to make it your own."

Damien could not help himself. As his muffled chuckling expanded to all-out laughter, he was too preoccupied to notice what Alex was doing next to him.

Alex swiped a flat hand through the air like a knife, as if he were hollowing out the inside of a large bowl, moving gracefully like an artist's brush on a canvas. As he finished his movement, a sliver of water was severed from the top of the tub and rose into the air. With a few flicks of his wrist, the levitating water somersaulted in mid-air and rushed toward Damien, who was just now noticing it from the corner of his eye. He shifted sideways in shock. Alex gently pushed his palm forward, and the water flung forward faster, like an arrow from a hunter's bow.

Damien panicked and took a firm stance similar to Graham's, fully facing Alex. He crossed his arms in front of his body and formed a barrier in an oddly shaped triangle, trying to fold his body behind it. To his disappointment, the barrier had only covered his face and shoulders. The rest of the water slammed into his stomach, saturating him from the chest down. As the glowing shield dissipated, Damien remained as still as a statue, wide-eyed and stone-faced, trying to process what had happened.

"You're an Aquatic?" asked Graham, much louder than he expected.

Alex turned to Graham, stuffing both hands in his pockets. "You could say that, though I am not limited to it."

Graham thought for a moment.

"Whoa. What else can you do?" asked Kel.

"To be perfectly honest, everything." Alex again held his hands out, palms up. He held eye contact with Kel as one hand erupted into flames while the other electrified with small bolts darting from his forearm to his fingertips. He smiled as they all watched in amazement. Alex then clapped his hands together. The sparks and flames melded together and whipped around his hands like a small twister as the elements morphed into a yellow mist and flung the strange fog into the air, forming the seven outpost symbols above their heads.

The formed mist remained suspended so they could take a good look. Once Alex felt they had time to take it all in, he turned his palms downward, commanding the yellow mist to settle at their feet like morning dew on a grassy field. As the fog covered the ground, it also stuck to Kel's body,

Graham's shoulder, and most of Damien's body.

Alex made circular motions with his hands, and the mist began to churn. The mist absorbed all the moisture on the floor and the kids, forming sacks of yellow clouds around them, which then floated back toward the black tubs and dissolved, causing the water to rain back into them.

The room was electrified with wonder. Graham could not understand how Alex could produce and masterfully command the elements. He had seen others from the team do spectacular things, but this was simply majestic.

"Now then, that should be enough for today," said Alex, as if he had just done something completely ordinary. "I want you to feel free to come here any time, day or night. It is always open for you to train. Beginning in the morning, we'll look at your giftings as a group and discover how you can work together as a team."

Graham fumbled over his own words. "How can you do everything? Don't we all have one specific power?"

Alex smiled and walked back over to Graham. "For you four, yes, but for me. . . well, there's a reason why I am the leader of Aegis."

"Because you are the immovable force the Council was talking about," Graham said.

"Does that come as a shock to you?"

Graham swallowed hard with the confirmation of exactly who he was talking to. Damien and Kel looked at them inquisitively.

"No, not a shock. I just don't know how to address someone who has lived for thousands of years."

Damien and Kel's look of curiosity morphed into shock.

"Well, that's quite easy. Just continue as you have been."

"So, back at Portfield Manor, when you said you were of the line of Alexanders, you were really saying that you *are* the line of Alexanders. Each generation was just another version of yourself?"

"That's quite keen, Graham. Yes, each picture, like the one

in Greenwood, is indeed me."

Graham wanted to stay in his lane, but the question posed in the Council meeting had been eating away at him.

"If you don't mind me asking. How does the conflict end between the unstoppable force and the immovable object?"

Alex smiled. "That is the age-old question now, isn't it? But we can talk about this later. Right now, you all need to rest. I want you all to meet after dinner to discuss how to use your giftings as a team and come to the training tomorrow prepared to enact your plan. Cavaness, Chase, and others depend on you to develop quickly, and we mustn't disappoint them."

26

HAWKSNEST

HAWKSNEST OUTPOST
Nobbys Headland: Newcastle, Australia

"No!" Lucas gasped as they entered the main hall of the HawksNest outpost. "What have you done?"

The once-majestic interior of HawksNest was now nothing more than heaps of rubble and ruin. The entire diameter of the hill was one large room, four levels high, with circular doorways spaced every so often around the perimeter. What once had been elaborate carvings in the structure's walls and pillars were now scorched and cracked with chunks of rock broken out from the blasts that had torn the great hall apart.

Corbin seethed. "Tell them to get in here now!"

Hopkins obeyed and called his team into the great hall. "It won't matter now. You can kill us, but it won't save this place or your other outposts."

He held a steady, sinister gaze. "Look around you. This place is destroyed along with the people stationed here. Do you think salvaging it will make a difference? No, I think deep down, you know that's pointless. You have already been defeated."

Though it must have been excruciatingly hot, the man leaned close to the flame to pronounce their victory.

"Vae Victus."

Corbin remained still with his arms crossed. "Are you done? Man, you guys are longwinded. What I wouldn't give for one time, just one time, where you guys didn't go into a self-righteous monologue."

As the other Victus members entered, they looked surprised to see their teammates entrapped by a suspended, flaming ring. Sonia twisted her torso, flinging the backpack off her shoulder and onto the ground in front of her. She sifted through the contents until she found what she was looking for. She pulled out a small mirror, but it was not one that Alex provided. She set it on top of a heap of rocks.

"Tell them to go through," said Corbin.

"Where are you sending them?" asked Hopkins.

"Oh, it's not just them. It's all of you. And don't worry about *where*. You wanted us scattered, so I'm simply doing the same. You better believe I'm not hauling your ugly mug around this joint."

No one moved but waited to see if the others would obey.

"Hey, man! What did I say about playing nice? Tell them to go through, or I will knock them all out cold and throw them through."

"No," Hopkins said calmly.

"So that's how it's gonna be?" said Corbin.

"That's how it's *gonn-a* be," he replied, mimicking Corbin's slang. "What's the sacrifice of a few pawns?"

"You can't be serious," said Lucas, getting ready for a fight.

"Oh, I am serious. Dead serious. No retreat, no mercy. The sacrifice of a few will save the whole. Go ahead, make us martyrs. In doing that, we will–"

"Oh, shut up." Corbin signaled to Sonia, who extinguished the fire in the ring with a snap.

Corbin immediately constricted the ring. Hopkins was able to duck in time, but the ring caught the other three around the crown of their heads, causing their heads to slam together with enough force to knock them out.

The group of Vics stationed on the hilltop burst through the doorways of the third level of the outpost.

While Corbin focused on Hopkins, Sonia and Lucas focused on the others, who had now scattered like rats throughout the outpost. Yellow and purple blasts filled the room, creating dust clouds and infusing the great hall with an ominous haze.

"Look around you!" yelled Hopkins. "This place is already a tomb. Soon, it will be yours as well."

27

FALCON

Graham sat in a side room with his newly declared team. The room itself was an offshoot from the main living room, constructed to facilitate casual conversation, being tucked in a nest of windows and oversized chairs with a side table in between them. In the middle sat a round table with seven wingback chairs. The four of them sat at the table, munching on some fruit and bagels, trying to get their energy levels up before their next session.

"It's still hard to believe we're here for good, isn't it?" asked Graham to no one in particular.

"I honestly haven't had time to process much after the

workouts," replied Kel. "But yes, after being surrounded by forty or fifty other kids, it is hard to get used to only a handful of people."

Ailey nodded slightly as she satisfied her ravenous appetite with fistfuls of fruit. Graham couldn't help but enjoy watching her attack her plate with as much intensity as her workouts.

"I know it's only been a few months since we got here, but it already feels odd with Chase and Cavaness gone. I hope they're doing okay."

"How's it working with Chase?" asked Kel. "You two seem to connect pretty easily."

"It's great. I feel like we're the same person sometimes, and he really knows how to get me excited about the training. I wish he were here now."

"He'll be back before you know it," said Damien. "In the meantime, you'll just have to settle for us."

"By the time we're done training, you may feel like you have had to settle for me," replied Graham.

"Please, there is no settling here. I love our team more than anything," said Kel.

"Heck yeah. We even took out our teachers as a team and didn't even have any training," replied Damien.

"That's true if you can count beating someone who was only giving twenty percent in the first place," said Graham. "Listen, I know we don't have a lot of time until our next session, so I wanted to get rid of the elephant in the room."

"What are you talking about?" said Kel.

"Well, you heard Alex. He has made me the team leader, even though I don't really feel like one. I'm sure it's only because I'm *the one*, but I want you to know I didn't ask for this."

Kel reached over and squeezed his hand. Graham blushed but kept his hand steady.

"I'm sure that's part of the reason," she said, "but I don't think that's all there is to it. I, for one, am happy about the decision. And somehow, I think you were given that responsibility precisely because you don't think you deserve it."

"You're strong, dude, even if you are still learning to control it. You've got no issues with me," said Damien.

"Yeah, but even while we were growing up, you always stayed one step ahead. You were the one who didn't mind confronting people," replied Graham.

"And when Silas had us, you were willing to trade your life for ours. That's all I need to know," said Damien.

"So, you guys truly aren't put off that Alex set me as the leader?"

"No, we're relieved. Honest," said Kel.

Ailey wiped her hands with a napkin and signed something to Kel, looking slightly awkward as she spoke with her sticky hands.

"And Ailey is happy about it, too. She says you are like the older brother you always read about. You know, the one who protects you," said Kel.

Graham blushed just as much in reaction to Ailey's response as he did to Kel's touch.

"Wow, I don't know what to say. Thanks, guys. That takes a lot off my mind. Alex has encouraged me to be completely open and honest with you. He said that's the best defense against any divisions that could occur with our team, so I want you to feel free to be open with me about anything, even if you think it will hurt my feelings."

Everyone at the table agreed.

"In that respect, I want you to know that Alex has asked that I do extra training and study with him after we finish as a group. He said I'm supposed to learn about the ideals and constitutions of how Aegis has been established. I'm not sure what this will accomplish, but I wanted you to know about it. I don't want any more elephants."

"Sounds as exciting as munching on a handful of dry saltine crackers," Damien said with a shrug. "Better you than me, amigo."

"You're probably right about that, but whatever it is, he wants me to understand something."

As Graham finished his words, he failed to see Murphy walk up behind him.

"Understand what?"

"Oh, hey Brian. I don't know, really. Just something Alex told me. Is it time for the next round already?"

"In fifteen. I just wanted to give you a heads-up. Anything I can help with?"

"Um, no, not really. It's just something that will take some time to figure out. We'll get ready."

Murphy kept a controlled tone, yet his facial expressions didn't quite match his voice.

"Well, if you're sure."

Graham and the others stood up, pushed their chairs under the table, and walked toward the kitchen. Murphy remained where he was, watching Graham as he put his plate in the trash and disappeared down the hallway. Murphy took his phone out of his pocket and flipped it open to look at the time. He anxiously fumbled it in his hand, then thrust it back into his pocket. Branson emerged from the COM room as he walked down the hall.

"You're up in ten,"

"Yes, I know," snapped Murphy, not breaking stride.

Branson shot a curious stare at the back of Murphy's head. He opened his mouth to speak, but Murphy had already passed from sight around the corner.

28

ALBATROSS

ALBATROSS OUTPOSTRemote Jungle- Argentina

After hours of trekking through the forest had passed, they finally reached the outskirts of the Albatross facility. The entire exterior was a towering waterfall whose roar could be heard far off. Chase bolted down from a tall tree and back to the group.

"They've got Adrian on the lip of the waterfall and four others scattered along the riverbank," said Chase. "And he's bound with Former chains, so he can't command the water."

"So, they plan to cast him down to the crags. If the rocks don't kill him, then he'll drown," said Cavaness. "Is the man behind him the Former?"

"No, I don't think so. He's holding his hand like a Snype.

And he's poised to fire a shot at the base of Adrian's skull. I guess they don't want to leave his death up to the rocks."

"We've got to get Adrian's abilities back. We need to take out the Former first," said Cavaness.

"So, how do we flush him out?" asked Jael.

"We won't have to. Adrian will strike when he has the opportunity. We just need to create that opportunity," said Cavaness. "If it were me, I would make it as hard to get to me as possible, especially knowing the enemy was on approach. Those chains are the only reason they're not all dead, and if they are strong enough to restrain Adrian, then we are dealing with a very powerful Former. I'd be the Former is the one furthest from him."

"So, we have a Snype and a Former to take out first, then who knows what after that," said Chase, rolling his eyes. "I thought this was going to be hard."

Cavaness ignored Chase's sarcasm. "Is there anything else you could pull from that guy's head?"

"No," replied Jael. "Just the standing order is to kill the directors upon our arrival."

Chase defaulted to Cavaness, letting him make the next judgment call. Cavaness looked into the sky and then over to the treetops leading to the outpost.

"We've only got about thirty more minutes of sunlight before the sun sets behind the tree line. I'll warn Adrian. Chase, you're on the Snype. Jael will take care of our cover."

"How will you warn him without Victus knowing?" asked Jael.

"It's an old code, but it should work. Your COMs working?"

"Yes," replied both.

"Good. Just get into position and wait for my signal to move in."

Adrian stood tall and confident despite the current circumstances. His long white hair fluttered as the breeze licked across his weathered face.

"In my fifty-two years on this earth, I have never seen such a bold-faced attack," said Adrian in his thick Spanish accent. He tilted his head to better address the man behind him. "You really believe you will take control, don't you?"

"The only thing I know is what I'll do next if you don't shut your mouth and turn back around," said the Snype.

Adrian conceded and turned around but continued talking.

"You're young. You realize you are playing an important role in starting World War Three, right? I advise you to be absolutely sure of the side you fight for."

The young man slapped a hand on Adrian's shoulder with a flicker of rage dancing in his eyes.

"One more word, old man, and I won't wait for your friends to get here."

Adrian nodded and fixed his sight on the crashing water below, and then something new caught his attention. He looked into the distance to a pool of water with small ripples emanating from the center as if someone was strumming a guitar string underground. The pattern was most irregular. He searched the sky to find the source of the disturbance but could not find what was causing it.

Cavaness hid in the thick overgrowth, nearly fifty feet from the waterfall's base. Careful to use the correct level of intensity, he continued to push small pulses of energy into the ground toward the pool. Three short pulses, three larger, then three smaller ones once more, followed by a twenty-second pause. Once the surface had settled, he repeated the same thing. Three small, three large, and three small again. He continued this pattern, watching for any sign of acceptance from above.

"I understand!" said Adrian, almost yelling.

The Snype was not happy with the random declaration from his hostage. He kicked the backs of Adrian's legs, making him fall forward to his knees. He grabbed Adrian's neck and squeezed tight, causing his bands to appear. The streaks of light pulsing from his fingertips into his palms reflected on the skin of Adrian's neck.

"I warned you!" yelled the Snype.

"I understand your position," said Adrian loudly, tense with the man's firm grip. "You were promised a place of prominence, no? Perhaps a seat at your master's table? It would be a tempting proposition for anyone. I'd be willing to bet your lady friend on the hill who constructed my bonds received a similar offer. How many seats do you think there are at his right hand? I'd wager you'll have to fight for it in the end. Are you prepared to kill her for a position? Is that what you want?"

"That's it! You just spoke your final words!"

The light on his palm grew more intense in preparation for severing Adrian's spinal cord. Still, the brightness was no comparison to the radiant light beaming off the water's surface, as if someone had increased the voltage of the sun. Its rays bent at unnatural angles into the eyes of every Victus member. They held their hands to the sky to block the glare, but the rays would move around their fingers.

The Snype, confused by the spectacle, let his attack fade and shoved Adrian forward over the cliff instead. His moment's hesitation, however, gave just enough time for Chase to rush in. He stormed to the edge of the water, leaping across protruding rocks. He wrapped one arm around the Vic, slamming the side of his head into the man's eye socket while simultaneously grabbing Adrian by the back of his shirt. Chase used his falling enemy as a counterbalance to help pull Adrian backward, away from the cliff's edge. The intense pulse Cavaness fired coursed up the waterfall, assisting Chase's efforts.

Chase pinned the man down, holding his arms to the ground by the wrists. The Snype's fingers curled, and small light flashes streaked from his fingertips into his palms. With a quick burst, he fired tiny darts, which whizzed past Chase's head like bullets. One shot nicked his left temple, painting a red stripe through his hairline.

Chase struggled to keep the man's shots from penetrating his skull. Any closer than that last hit, and he was a dead man. The underbrush to the side of the falls danced and swayed as Cavaness sprinted to the crest of the waterfall. Chase smirked but quickly lost his temperament after hearing Jael's struggle upstream. The veins in Chase's forearms bulged as he strained to keep the constant flow of darts away from his head, but as the veins grew more pronounced, so did the ones in the Snype's biceps as he hurled darts as fast as he could produce them.

Both men grunted, two opposite forces matching the other's fervor in a display of endurance and will. Any movement on Chase's part would result in a lost focus on the Snype's wrists. Unfortunately, his speed was not an ally. All he could do was resist and hope to outlast his opponent. That hope, however, began to fade as he felt the man's wrist turn ever so slightly in his grip. The Snype grinned through bared teeth.

"Goodbye," he seethed.

Streaks of light bolted down his fingers for the attack. Chase saw the tip of the dart form in the man's palm. Just as he released his shot, a thick, tubular wave slammed into his head. The Snype instantly lost focus, flinging limbs and gurgling as he fought the water that had overtaken him. His dart loosed and sprang toward Chase, who strafed, but not enough to avoid getting struck. The dart carved another gash in his temple before flying past and carving a rut in the muddy bank.

Chase touched the blood running down his cheek as he watched the perplexed Snype fight against the pounding water. Looking over his shoulder, he saw Adrian crouched on one knee, balanced with one hand on the ground and the other outstretched, commanding the water. The river flowed to either side of him, but he was on dry land, cradled by a waist-high wall of water all around him. One stream of water reached out to the Snype like a liquid tentacle, the light blue water contrasting the deep amber of Adrian's eyes, glowing like iron rods in a fire.

Jael had the higher ground when she made her move, about the same time Chase had gone for the Snype. She leaped from a mound of dirt, catching the other woman completely off guard. In the descent, Jael hooked an arm with hers, sinking her elbow into the base of the woman's neck, then twisted her body and flung the dazed woman into the river. She then jumped onto her body, leaping from her like a frog to cross safely to the other side. Only half conscious, the woman twisted around toward Jael and tried to form some purplish object in her hand. Without looking, Jael fired a burst, hitting the woman in the head. The force of the blast threw her legs in the air and sent her spiraling toward the edge of the falls. Jael encountered two other Victus men, poised to strike as she landed on the other side.

The ground shook. A ripple from underneath the ground quaked beyond Jael and surfaced in front of the two Vics. Rock and earth erupted, spraying them with organic shrapnel. Jael graciously nodded to Cavaness on the hill and sprinted toward the men. Though he was cradling his head in his hand, one of the attackers had enough awareness to see Jael coming. He flung a hand forward. Flames flared, reaching out toward Jael in an infernal embrace.

She felt the heat before she saw the flames, leaping into a side roll to avoid the inferno. As she deflected, the other man threw bolts of electricity at her. The majority of the attack scathed the ground next to her, but one streak connected with her thigh. Jael shrieked as the shock rippled through her leg and up into her abdomen. Her leg stiffened, and her stomach painfully contracted. The man's hand sparked as he hurled another cluster of bolts toward Jael.

Adrian was finally free to command the water and missed no opportunity to use it fully. With his sole focus given to capturing the Snype, he was unaware of the arrival of the unconscious woman lapping against his cradle of water like a piece of driftwood. He quickly stood and flipped his wrist. The water obeyed and sent a wave toward the shore, depositing her on the bank when he heard a shriek in the distance. He turned to Chase. "Go, help your friend," he said. "I will handle this one."

Chase caught a glance of Jael just before a bolt of electricity knocked her down, nodded at Adrian, and left him alone with the Snype entrapped in a liquid cocoon. Adrian swept his hand through the air, commanding the water surrounding the man's head to peel away, though the rest of him was still encapsulated in water.

The Vic coughed and gagged, taking deep breaths.

"Where is Marcio being held?" Adrian waited patiently for the man's response once he regained his senses.

"Somewhere where they will have plenty of time to see

you coming." The man tried to laugh, but only raspy coughs followed. "He'll be dead before you can see the whites of his eyes."

Adrian detected a faint glow in the water around the Vic's hands, so he caused the water to pour back over the man's head. The Vic let loose his darts wherever his hands happened to flail.

"That was a mistake," Adrian said calmly to the attack.

The man groped for a way out of his watery bonds, but no matter how hard he tried, he could not escape the liquid imprisonment.

"No matter. You have told me all I need to know. I have no further need of you."

Adrian again allowed the water to fall away from the Vic's head. Another thick tentacle of water reached out and grabbed him. It pulled him back into the riverbed and stood him upright, where he bobbed like a buoy at sea.

"I do hope you will take my advice from earlier. It's never too late to step on the right side of the proverbial line in the sand."

The Snype bared his teeth and started to respond, but instead, a wall of water pushed him over the edge of the falls. His liquid capsule protected him from the fall, carrying him safely to the base of the rapids and whisking him far away downstream.

 Chase convulsed on the ground. He had made it just in time to take the hit for Jael. He had wanted to block it with his shield but could not produce it in time. The Scorcher raised his hands to strike when a ripple of energy flowed up the tree beside him. A branch snapped from the trunk and cartwheeled through the air, nearly wrapping around his mid-section. The force broke the branch in half. Small fireballs burped from his hands as he crashed to the ground in pain.

Cavaness was close to the riverbank now. He caused the entire riverbed to quake. The Scorcher could hardly get up under normal circumstances, but the quaking made it next to impossible to stand. He remained as a lump, unable to do much more than moan. The Spark raised both hands to electrocute Chase again, but the earth's rumble impaired his ability to aim. He let loose two bolts from his hands. One bolt flew aimlessly into the air, but the other found its target. Chase raised his arm and produced a glowing, jagged shield from his wrist just in time to absorb the shock.

The brilliance of the bolts grew as the Spark continued his attack. Chase leaned into them, grunting and taking strides toward his attacker, step by step. It was apparent that the electricity was affecting Chase. With each step, his eyes strained, and his muscles contracted in irregular and uncontrolled patterns, but it did not stop him. Despite the constant flow of electricity, he remained on course, determined to take out the target.

Jael cringed at the light display, hiding her eyes under her hand to see, but too much was happening. She tried bending the light of the voltage, but her gifting would not work on electricity emanating from a Spark.

As Chase got within arm's length, the quaking stopped, which allowed the Spark to throw perfectly aimed bolts at Chase with both hands. Chase winced and fell to one knee. The shock was almost unbearable. His back arched as every muscle contracted and spasmed until, all at once, it stopped. Chase peered beyond his energy shield in time to see the force of Cavaness's punch lift the man off his feet and into a backward somersault. Cavaness stomped the ground, opening up a long crack in the riverbank. The Spark quickly fell into the newly formed fissure, lying in what looked like an organic coffin. With another, less forceful stomp, the ground around the fracture shifted and closed in like an accordion, pinning him in.

"You okay, kid?" asked Cavaness.

Still on one knee, Chase held a trembling hand up, asking for some time to recuperate. He took a few deep breaths, steadied his heart rate, and closed his eyes in concentration. After a few moments, his hand was able to hold still.

"I'll live. Gi. . .g. . . give me another minute or two." Chase closed his mouth and breathed through his nose. His eyes flicked beneath his eyelids.

"Is he going to be alright?" asked Jael.

"He will be," replied Cavaness.

"What's happening? I mean, what's he doing right now?"

"He's purging the shock. Normally, it would take hours for something like that to wear off, but since he's a Surge, he can do it in minutes."

"Cavaness, she's gone," Adrian cut into the conversation.

"Who's gone?"

"The one I laid up on the bank. The one who created my bonds. She's gone, likely on her way to warn the others."

Cavaness looked at Jael and pointed to the two men on the ground. She acknowledged and walked over to them.

"How could she even get under the falls?"

"She's a Former. She would have no trouble using her gifting to open the falls like a curtain. If Marcio is to live through this, we must go now."

"Give Chase a few minutes, then we'll go in after Marcio. Do you know where he's being held?"

"I wasn't told directly, but I have an educated guess."

"How educated? Enough to bet Marcio's life on it? You know better than I that one wrong move in there, and he'll be executed."

"No one is more aware than I, Cavaness. If I were in their shoes, it is where I would go."

"Of course you are. I mean no disrespect. I just need to be sure that you're sure."

"I'm as confident in his location as I was in your SOS

signal, Cavaness. Come to think of it; I remember coming up with that emergency signal with your grandfather back when the Pushers were regular visitors here. He came up with the idea, as a matter of fact, and quite by accident. The best inventions seem to happen that way, don't they?"

"I only remember stories. I wasn't even sure I was giving you the right letters."

"It was enough for me to know you were out there, and that's what matters. Thank you, by the way, for what you and your team did just now. It seems it has placed me in your debt."

"I remember doing some damage here in my youth. Let's consider ourselves even."

"Very well. I accept."

"You accept what?" asked Chase, rubbing his hand across the back of his neck.

"Your heroics, young man, toward myself and that young lady over there." Adrian pointed to Jael, who had just finished reading the memories of the Victus soldiers.

"Nothing you wouldn't do for me, I'm sure."

"Indeed. I would like to think so."

Jael joined the group. "Marcio is being held–"

"In the Honor Hall," Adrian finished.

"Yes, the Honor Hall. How did you know that?"

"Because it's a wonderfully strategic place to hold captives and to escape when necessary. It's quite open, with second-story balconies around the perimeter and multiple exit points. Keeping Marcio in the center of the room would ensure they have eyes on all means of egress and with time to react."

"So, we go in through the front door, guns blazing, and hope for the best?" asked Chase.

"Be serious," snapped Cavaness. "We'll have to move in with stealth and precision. They're expecting us, so we'll have to get creative."

"We will not go in through the front," said Adrian. "I agree with a stealthy entry. However, we can do so from over there." He pointed to a big cluster of rocks clumped together amidst a group of berry bushes.

"We're going to tunnel underground?" asked Jael.

"The tunnel is already there. It's a springhead, and its streams are exposed within the outpost. We can go through the underground water system and take them from behind."

"And we just hold our breath as we wade against the current?" asked Chase.

"Let me handle the water. I'm fairly good with it."

29

HAWKSNEST

HAWKSNEST OUTPOST
  Nobbys Headland: Newcastle, Australia

"I've got Hopkins!" yelled Corbin. "Get them to stop stirring up all this junk!"

Hopkins had already escaped through the cloud of dust provided by his subordinates. Corbin released three scouts into the air to triangulate everyone's location. They scattered about the vaulted room like marbles in a miner's pan.

"You got my location?" yelled Corbin, crouching behind a big chunk of stone blown from a nearby column.

"Yes!" replied Lucas and Sonia.

"Second level, three o'clock!"

Lucas fired darts with both hands aimlessly into the thick

wall of soot and dirt. Sonia loosed bursts in the same direction. The plethora of attacks in the room echoed through the outpost, and the yelp and the thud of the man on the second floor confirmed at least one successful hit.

Corbin's searched the room with his scouts. His irises changed to amber, and his pupils dilated. Through the orbs, he could see dark yellow shadows dart back and forth among the different levels of the outpost. Corbin could see himself crouched behind the boulder, but he still could not get a fix on Hopkins. A glowing shadow positioned itself on the third level behind him. He saw the hand invert and tuck underneath the person's chin.

"You sneaky. . ."

Corbin commanded a scout to kamikaze into the Vic. She cried out as her head snapped back. The two other scouts whirled behind her and propelled into her shoulder blades, throwing her over the railing. In a split second, she had landed on top of another Vic on the ground level.

"Mmmhmm, that's right."

Corbin crouch-walked to where she had landed and hit them with a few bursts to ensure they were out for the rest of the fight.

Sonia emitted random balls of fire amongst the three levels to help them see through the haze, but nothing they connected with was flammable, so the light did not last. She tried a few more times but reverted to the standard burst attacks after seeing the paltry results.

Lucas had already ascended to the second level. His Snype nature would not let him stay on the ground floor like a fish in a barrel. He ran around the balcony until he reached the next staircase.

"Come on, Corbin. Give me something," said Lucas.

"Working on it, baby, but they're good at hidin'."

Lucas stood tall behind a stone column on the third floor. He peeked his head around the side, his micro dreads flicking the air beside him. He pulled his hand up beneath his chin but stopped mid-way. The shot to his shoulder threw him sideways. He pulled his hand up to attack, but his shoulder wouldn't let him, so he let his arm down and shifted to the other side of the pillar to use his off-hand. His vision zoomed in, searching for Hopkins or his subordinates.

"I still can't see much. Sonia, cover yourself as much as possible, but light this place up," said Lucas.

"Are you kidding me?" said Sonia in mid-attack. "I'm not going to be your bait."

"We've got your back. Trust me."

"Honey, you've been with us for six months. You're not skilled enough for me to trust you."

"Just do it," said Corbin. "Give the kid a chance."

Sonia hesitated, shaking her head in disbelief. "Fine, but I'm toasting you both if I get shot." She positioned herself in the middle of a pile of rubble and raised her hands. Flames erupted and mushroomed into the air, lighting up the room.

Lucas and Corbin searched the balconies but could not get a location on anyone.

"Keep it comin'," cracked Corbin's voice over the COM.

Sonia gritted her teeth and intensified the fire.

Corbin spotted a hand reach out from behind a doorway on the second level, poised for an attack.

"Behind you!" yelled Lucas. "Corbin, duck!"

Corbin rolled to the side as electrified hands grasped the air where Corbin's head was. In mid-roll, Corbin barked the location of the other man.

"Second floor, your ten!"

Lucas leaned further out and spotted the hands in the doorway, ready to launch his attack at Sonia. Lucas fired a dart that pelted the rounded doorjamb just in front of the attacker. Though he did not hit his mark, the distraction was enough to throw off the Vic's aim. The electric bolts whizzed past Sonia's shoulder, then pelted the rubble behind her. She strafed to the right, rolled over her shoulder, and ran for cover under the cantilevered balcony floor.

Corbin approached and landed a heavy punch on Hopkins, throwing him forward, but Hopkins was able to regain his balance. He turned to face Corbin, throwing bolts as he twisted. Corbin deflected the attack with a glowing, circular shield. Electricity danced over its surface.

Lucas cursed his poor aim under his breath. He closed his eyes, cracked his neck, and refocused. After a calming sigh, he repositioned his hand and focused on the wall, calculating where the Vic was standing. Streaks of energy pulsed from his fingertips into the palm of his hand. The pooled energy grew wider until it was three times the size of a standard Snype dart. His hand shook under the surge of power as the intensity of the dart charged like a battery.

The Vic was setting up for another attack. Lucas could see the purple glow emanating from behind the stone. He grit and bared his teeth, brilliantly white against his exceptionally swarthy skin. The intensity of the building energy made his hand tremble, but he steadied it the best he could, locked onto this target, and loosed the dart.

With the power of a cannonball, Lucas's attack burrowed clean through the stone, leaving a golfball-sized tunnel through it. The Vic yelped just before being hurled into the adjacent wall. The thud of his body was nearly as loud as his shriek.

Corbin threw a wide burst under his shield at Hopkins' feet, who jumped, but not quickly enough. One foot cleared the attack, but the attack hit his other ankle, causing him to stumble forward. The electric bursts stopped as he fell onto Corbin's shield.

Corbin braced and absorbed Hopkins' weight, then fired a wide ray of energy like a solar flare from the shield, sending Hopkins flailing through the air to a nearby rock pile. He painfully rolled to the side, clutching his ribcage, scurried to his feet, and ducked behind the remains of a tall column.

Corbin's scouts had remained suspended around the

outpost. He unclenched his fist, causing the shield to disappear, and clapped his hands together. The two remaining scouts dove and circled the column to either side. One hit Hopkins in the temple, while the other hit him mid-thigh on the opposite side, throwing him sideways to the floor.

Sonia ran toward Hopkins with glowing hands, ready to end this fight. Hopkins, half-conscious, saw Sonia and clapped the floor. Electric bolts crawled along the stone toward Sonia like an army of spider legs. Just as the bolts reached for her boot, Sonia leaped to a nearby boulder.

A small dart pelted the stone floor just beyond Hopkins' outstretched hand. The bolts from his hand dissipated. While Lucas distracted him, Corbin clamped his hands over Hopkins' wrists and formed oval shackles, covering his hands up to his elbows.

"There. Keep your sparks to yourself," said Corbin.

Electricity danced inside the glowing, yellow bonds but could not escape them.

"Now, about that martyr thing," said Corbin as he punched Hopkin's jaw. "You ready to make good on that one?"

Sonia crossed her arms, enjoying the spectacle.

Hopkins spat blood and smiled. "You don't have it in you."

Corbin reared back for another punch, but Lucas gently held back Corbin's arm.

"Don't let him antagonize you. He knows he's beaten. It isn't worth it."

Corbin held his fist in the air just a bit longer for good effect and then put it down.

"Get him out of my sight."

Sonia pulled the small trans from her pack. Corbin pulled Hopkins by the collar onto his knees. Sonia held the small mirror so Hopkin's hand was inches from the glass. His band activated with a dull, purple glow.

"Don't worry, your buddies will be right behind ya," said Corbin.

"Wait, where are you–"

In an oily mist, Hopkins traveled through the transit mirror before he could finish.

"What a judgmental prick," said Corbin. "Hope we don't have to deal with dat fool again. Why don't you two clean up the remaining Vics and send 'em to the Wastelands while I look around."

Lucas and Sonia ran to collect the others.

"You're lucky, you know that?" said Sonia.

"What?"

"I almost got fried. I don't know what made you miss that guy, but that was way too close. So much for trusting you to have my back."

"Hey, I did have your back, and you look in pretty good shape to me, " Lucas replied, clearly taken aback.

"You never miss."

"Yeah, well, I've been shot twice now, so I was using my opposite hand. All things considered, I think I covered you pretty effectively."

Sonia glanced at Lucas' arm, which was slightly curled and held close to his chest. She could tell he was in pain.

"Shooting southpaw, huh? Alright, I'll give it to you. Not bad for your weak hand, though you still could have told me that to begin with."

"Alright, sure. Next time, I'll ask the Vics to hit pause while I bring you up to speed. And what was that about me being the new guy? You know I'm the best shot around, right?"

"It's a little different when you are the bait. No offense. I'm used to sending in others as bait."

The two continued their quibble as one held the trans, and the other pressed the unconscious person's hand to the glass, sending them through to the other side.

Meanwhile, Corbin combed the lower levels for survivors.

Many had evacuated, or at least he thought so, due to the lack of help or body count. He continued down the hall until he heard murmuring in the next room. Corbin formed a scout in his hand, connected his vision to it, and threw it down the hall. It rolled along the floor like a radiant marble, passing under the doorway at the end of the hall. As it passed under, it diverted to the right, hugging the baseboard.

Six or seven men and women huddled together in the center of the room, looking terrified. Though smeared with soot and grime, most appeared to have survived without harm. A few had small blood trails coming from various nicks and scratches. The man who seemed to be wounded the worst also appeared to be the calmest and most emotionally stable. Corbin focused in. He did not look like a villain, but he was oddly quiet. Once he felt safe proceeding, Corbin dissolved his scout and knocked on the door. Muffled gasps escaped in reaction.

"Hey, it's okay. This is Corbin. Alex has sent me to get ya'll out of here. I'm gonna open the door, so please do not attack. I'm Aegis, okay?"

Corbin turned the knob and slowly let the door creak open, poking his arm through the crack. The crowd huddled in fear and disbelief.

"It's okay, it's okay. I'm one of you, see? Look at my band."

Corbin clenched his fists and caused his bands to show, proving his allegiance.

"See there?" he said, pointing to the sun emblem. "My team has fought off Victus. We're here to take you to safety."

In unison, the group relaxed.

"Corbin, as in Corbin Blanche, from EagleEye?" asked the man in the group's center in a thick Australian accent.

"One and the same, my man. And you are?"

"I'm Braxton Kim, one of the two directors of HawksNest. I believe you met with the other director a few weeks ago." Braxton was unaware of the blood caked in his blond hair or the gashes on his arms, or he did not care. The two men shook hands. "Thank you for what you have done here. We had assumed the worst."

"Don't mention it. It was a pleasure taking out those knuckleheads, especially their lead man. How many of you were here when you got hit?"

"Fortunately, we were only at half-staff when we got blindsided. Some made it out through transit mirrors, but we still miss a few staff."

"Where's the most fortified area here for 'dem to run to?"

Braxton thought momentarily while the people around them began to disperse from the room, asking one another if it was truly over.

"Likely to either the training arena, The leadership commons, or the upper level for escape."

"And where are those first two areas?"

"Training is base level. Return to the main hall, take the third doorway on the right, and follow it all the way down. The leadership commons is opposite the doorway to the training arena. If we split up, we can find them faster."

"Sorry, baby, no can do. Our orders are to return you and any survivors to Alex *pronto*."

"Corbin, I cannot leave my people behind. Surely you understand."

"Don't worry. You aren't leaving anyone behind. That's what my team is here for. If there are any survivors here, we'll find 'em. You, on the other hand, are needed back at Falcon HQ. Orders are from the top, my man."

Braxton clasped Corbin's arm. "Give me your word that you will not leave here until you have searched every last room and moved every boulder to find my people."

"You have my word."

Braxton appeared to relax with Corbin's promise, perhaps for the first time since HawksNest was attacked. He turned to the rest of the group.

"Attention, please."

Everyone fell silent and faced him.

"Corbin and his team have successfully eliminated the threat. We have all been asked to retreat immediately to Falcon. As many of you know, we are still missing personnel. While we have direct orders, myself included, to meet up with Alex and his people there, Corbin and his team have vowed to stay here as long as it takes to find them. I ask that you honor Alex's request and follow Corbin to Falcon, trusting that the others will soon follow."

Braxton pounded his chest, saluting Corbin for his service. Corbin did the same and led the pack of Aegis members to Sonia and Lucas, who had already sent the remaining Vics through the trans and had prepared the trans leading to Falcon.

They traveled through the mirror one by one, saluting Corbin's team before vanishing in a thin mist. Braxton was the last to step through.

"Where was the old trans before it was destroyed?" asked Corbin.

"Two rooms before you get to the leadership commons on the left."

"Good. Alex will brief you. Once we finish here, this will be the new way to Falcon. Alex has crafted new mirrors."

"Very good. Godspeed on finding the last of our people."

Corbin nodded and ushered Braxton through. With everyone gone, the outpost had fallen eerily silent.

Corbin took one final assessment of the damage around the main hall. "Man, they hit hard and fast, huh? Alright, we need to look for more survivors. Braxton thinks there are still a few left. Spread out, and let's take it one level at a time. Sonia, you go that way," said Corbin, pointing toward the training arena. "Lucas, you search over there, and I'll go over 'der. Radio in if you find anyone, warm or cold."

They all scattered, searching in their designated section. Lucas held his throbbing arm close to his chest while weaving around piles of rubble to get to his section of the outpost. He passed a mound of what looked like chunks of gravel with large timbers cast over the top like scattered toothpicks. He rounded the corner and saw gray fabric protruding from the pile. He would not have thought much about it except that it moved.

Lucas diverted to investigate. The rubble shifted more, and as it did, a finger unearthed, followed by another. Smothered grunts came from within as the person, half buried, struggled to get free. Lucas could see the upper portion of the man's head wedged under one of the broken timbers.

Lucas' eyes widened. His jog turned into an all-out sprint.

"Hang on, I'm coming!" he said. "Corbin, Sonia! Get over here and help me dig. We have a live one!"

FALCON

FALCON HQ
Portfield, Pennsylvania

Once again, Graham sat by the fire in Alex's office. Alex pulled a watch from his vest pocket and pushed the small pin at the top, flipping open the front cover. He glanced at the time, gently placed it back in his pocket, then walked over to his desk and retrieved a leather-bound book. It was larger than most normal books, and the binding was tattered and worn. The cover's perimeter had a thick rectangular border, and a three-dimensional, equilateral triangle was stamped in the middle. Contained within the border lines were symbols. As Alex gave him the book, Graham immediately recognized a few. The Pusher and Aquatic crests were the easiest to spot, though they were among many others he did not recognize.

"What's this?" asked Graham as he cracked open the book.

"This is the bedrock of who we are. Like any secure building begins with a firm foundation, a successful organization stands on a mission statement. This book contains the written constitutions for each outpost we fight to reconnect, detailing their virtues, convictions, and resolutions."

Graham flipped through the pages, taking note of their age. Each page contained an elegant layout of handwritten paragraphs, each beginning with the crest of each outpost.

"This is where you need to begin. I want you to spend a few hours tonight poring over these pages while putting yourself in the authors' shoes. These men and women penned their outpost's moral fabric, and these pages are the physical representations of their deepest beliefs. While we fight behind the scenes of humanity's perceived world, I want you to grasp the virtues and convictions we defend. When you are finished, you should have a good understanding of what happened at the council meeting. I must step out for a moment, but please settle in and absorb as much as you can."

Reading was never Graham's passion, but if it meant that much to Alex, he knew he had to try.

"Okay. I will read through it. I promise."

"Thank you, Graham. I have made some tea if you would like some while you read. I'll be back soon to discuss."

Alex patted Graham on the shoulder, then left the office, leaving Graham to his reading.

Graham reached for the silver platter with an elegant, intricately crafted tea set. The teapot had elaborate designs hammered into every side, even in its claw feet. There were two small cups, a bowl for sugar lumps, and a cream server. Graham had never had hot tea before, so he was still determining what to do next. He poured some steaming tea into a cup, took a sip, and immediately winced at the bitter taste. He grabbed the small silver tongs, dropped a few sugar lumps, and tried again. Much better.

Alex entered the mirror room and sat at the desk with the newly fashioned mirrors hanging over the top. As before, he leaned back and closed his eyes to focus on the scout orbs he had created earlier that day. He had the remarkable ability to keep them in place and active while being focused on other activities, which was not the case for others gifted with the Former powers.

Alex had caused all the orbs to disappear except for two, which remained in Murphy's room. He leaned back in his chair with his feet crossed and fingers laced together, resting on his lap, watching and listening as if he were physically in the room with Murphy.

Murphy punched in a text message, telling the person on the other end that he was sending his scout now. Once he finished, he laid the phone underneath his training clothes so his power wouldn't short-circuit the electronics.

Murphy then walked to the French doors, opened them slightly, held up his hand as his eyes changed color, and fired an orb into the sky. The frigid February wind formed goosebumps along his forearm.

Murphy's scout ascended into the sky. As he pulled his arm in to close the doors, Alex sent one of his scouts into the night sky to follow. As both orbs flew westward, Alex's orb closed in. Foot by foot, then inch by inch, the orb moved in and gently attached itself to Murphy's. Using his other orb, Alex monitored Murphy's expressions, who seemed unaware of the connection that just took place.

With the orbs connected, Alex now only had to sit back and spectate. He noted where Murphy was navigating and watched as the town of Portfield shrank into the distance like a falling rock disappearing into an abyss. The scout flew with impressive speed, but not so fast that Alex could not track where they were. So far as he could tell, they were well over the border of Ohio. The orb began to slow its pace and descend. Alex spotted Lake Erie in the distance and used that as a reference point while he continued to deduce and understand where Murphy was going.

The orb settled into a rural suburb outside of a small city. Using the interstate street signs for names, Alex now understood them to be just south of Bellevue. As the orb descended further, Alex caught a glimpse of a brief flash of light and the slightest bump to Murphy's orb. A third orb had joined. The faint disruption did not seem to alarm Murphy, but it was evident to Alex, who simply allowed the situation to unfold.

Murphy had navigated to an average middle-class home in a small suburban community. The house was nothing out of the ordinary. It was a typical ranch-style home that looked like it had been built in the seventies. The siding was a generic white vinyl, and the roof sagged in random places. The house sat on about half an acre of land, of which Murphy had begun circling the perimeter. The scout weaved in and out of trees, through patches of shrubbery and hedges, and then back around to the front yard. He then searched the neighboring homes, swept the streets, and settled back at the white house. He followed basic pre-meeting recon procedures to ensure no one was spying on the conversation.

Once Murphy was satisfied with the sweep, he passed by the living and dining room picture windows. A woman with black hair and a slender physique sat in a bathrobe at the dining room table, with a cell phone placed just above a book she was reading. Alex tried to get an ID on her, but her elbow was planted on the table with her cheek cupped in her hand, which caused her thick, black hair to dangle like a curtain over her face. Occasionally, she would shift in her chair and take a sip from her coffee mug, but she would not look up.

For twenty minutes, Murphy continued to execute the recon procedures, then returned to the window to check on the woman until he was satisfied that everything was calm and safe. In a burst of light, the scout dissolved into the evening sky. While the scout orb dematerialized, Alex caught a glimpse of what he had suspected and one thing that he did not. With Murphy's scout gone, his orb was beside the other scout orb. They could likely detect Alex's presence if this Former were a seasoned veteran.

Alex turned his orb to look inside. Instead of being seated at the table, the woman was now standing directly in front of the window with her hands pressed against the glass and her amber-colored eyes staring into the sky where the orbs were. She had thrown the robe to the ground and wore a combat uniform underneath. Jael's handiwork stretched across the tail end of her left eye, and heavy bruising covered the upper half of her cheek.

"Kyla," Alex said under his breath, though he did not seem surprised.

With a gentle flick of her fingers, she commanded her scout to fling forward, connecting it with Alex's orb.

Graham flipped through the stiff pages. The decades of use gave the book a unique musty smell, which Graham strangely enjoyed. The handwriting was written in cursive, so it was hard for him to read at first because he was used to modern print.

He wanted to begin with something familiar, so instead of starting on page one with a crest he did not recognize, he flipped a few pages to find the constitution of the Aquatics.

He was impressed at the level of artistic detail that went into both the crest and the border of the page. Every detail was designed to emulate the flow of water. As he read, even the flow of the text read like a flowing current.

> *We exist for the flourishing of the human race, in the honorable pursuit to attribute honor to the collective name of Aegis and to the Ancient who has given us all we see and enjoy. Through the institutions of passion and courage, we will seek to serve humanity, working to enlighten and protect them from a very real and present danger.*
>
> *Our battle is not against flesh and blood but against the powers of darkness. In every encounter, we strive to illuminate the hearts and minds of all mankind, even our enemies, for they, too, can be persuaded should they see and understand the truth. In every circumstance, and with the full power of our giftings, we will strive to bring this light to every living soul.*
>
> *Water flows in creeks and rivers in nature, bringing vital nourishment for grass to grow, trees to bloom, and flowers to blossom. Water is also the element of life, providing a flood of daily nourishment to the physical body. In like manner, it is the initiative of the Aquatics to infuse our members with passion and courage, which is the spiritual element of life.*
>
> *Moreover, water holds the balance of life and death in its fluid hand, giving full measure to both. In small doses, it brings restoration to a parched mouth, yet in its full force, it can desolate entire cities.*
>
> *Opening the eyes of the unactivated to these truths and this purpose is our responsibility to bear and the scales we seek to balance.*

Graham reached over to take another sip of sugar water mixed with a bit of tea. He had to remember that five lumps of sugar in one cup of tea was the perfect combination.

So far as he could gather, the Aquatics concentrated on

infusing passion and courage into everything and being obsessed over every aspect of water. He could definitely see the passion aspect in Damien. He had always thought his Latino blood gave him his unique vitality, but maybe it was also because of this.

Graham thought about all the times Damien had his back in the orphanage, how he had almost had the term 'loser' penned in permanent marker across his forehead, and how Damien had pretended to be friends with the bully to be there at just the right time to save him from that embarrassment. There were multiple times on the playing fields at Greenwood when Damien would stand up for kids who were mocked for their lack of athleticism. He had no issues getting in a bully's face and putting them in their place. And how could he forget the times he stood up for Graham in Ms. Winstone's office? Yes, passion and courage fit Damien perfectly.

He did not expect to begin thinking of his friends as he read through the constitutions of the ancient outposts, but he was really enjoying this. What other insights could he gain about the others? Who should he analyze next? Graham thought for a moment, then eagerly flipped a few pages until he rested on the page of the Pusher.

Alright, Kel, let's see what you're made of.

"Hello, Kyla," said Alex calmly.

Alex could shield the vision of anyone who tried to see through his scout. Kyla could only peer into a black void, and the anger showed on her beet-red face.

"Who are you?" she barked. "And how on earth are you talking to me?"

"I think the more pressing question is what you are doing, Kyla?" replied Alex.

"So, you know who I am?"

"More than you realize."

"Then tell me how you are communicating with me, or I will order our people to inflict even more damage on your precious outposts and the people we've captured."

"There's no need for threats, Ms. Reeves. I see no reason to conceal my identity from you."

Kyla looked as though she was taken off guard at the mention of her last name.

"You must rank pretty high to know my full name. So, let's have it."

"I'm not near the top, Kyla. I am the top. You are speaking with Alexander."

Kyla's complexion drained of color, and she quickly tried to dissolve her scout, but it would not succumb to her command. Alex removed the darkness from his orb just enough for Kyla to see his face and nothing more.

A faint shriek escaped her mouth as she devoted all her energy to destroying her scout. The small ball of light danced up and down in the night sky, then began to twist and twirl at high speeds. If the unactivated neighbors could see the energy zipping outside, they would have witnessed a magnificent light show.

The scouts streaked through the air at the front of the house, leaving trails of light wherever they went like a comet bouncing off invisible barriers, but no matter how hard she tried, she could not detach or dissolve her scout. Whatever Alex wanted to say, he had her full attention whether she liked it or not.

The motion slowed down, and the orbs came to a standstill near where they had first connected. Alex cleared his throat and continued where he left off, unaffected by the frenzy that had just occurred.

"Now that I have your full and undivided attention, I want to send a message to your boss."

Murphy paced in front of the balcony door for another few minutes until whatever thought process was running through his mind had finished. Then, he walked to his dresser and retrieved his cell phone from under his training clothes. He dialed the number and waited for Kyla to pick up, but no one answered. He ended the call and punched in the number again. After a moment's pause, he ended the call again and threw the phone on the bed in frustration, pacing the length of the room.

Something was wrong, and the concern was written all over his face. Kyla always answered the phone.

Murphy retrieved the phone from his bed and tried several times with the same result. This time, he decided to leave a voice message.

"Kyla, you need to pick up. I sent a scout and found nothing, but we need to talk things through. If there's a plan to attack you, I'll stop it, but I need you to answer the phone. Call me back when you get this."

Graham consumed the Pusher constitution. He wanted to know what made Kel tick, how to read and understand her better. He couldn't stop grinning as he read the opening paragraphs.

> *We exist for the benefit of the human race in the honorable pursuit to attribute honor to the collective name of Aegis and to the Ancient who has given us all we see and enjoy. Through the institutions of discipline and integrity, we will seek to serve humanity with a steadfast hand.*
>
> *The pulse of a constant struggle between good and evil runs throughout human history. The changing dynamics*

of this war will always require consistent discipline, focus on the main objective, and fidelity toward the cause. Through the constant pursuit of improvement and refinement of heart, we conquer the enemy and protect our fellow man.

Knowledge crafts the sword, and wisdom guides its strokes.

Wow, I can see Kel and Cavaness in this, thought Graham. Kel's determination to follow the rules, sense of self-worth, and loyalty were evident.

Over the next hour, Graham dug into the meat of every constitution, trying to understand the essential virtue on which each outpost was built. It also gave him the added benefit of knowing what motivated his teammates.

After the final page, he started to close the book when he noticed the back of the final page also had writing on it, but it was different from the rest. Graham tipped the book so the last clump of pages flopped on his thumb, leaving the final page standing up like a wild hair. The writing was different from the others. It was handwritten as if it was someone's last-minute annotation. He looked at the bottom of the page and, in a sophisticated signature, read:

On these statutes, we will overcome the darkness to fulfill the purposes for which we were created.

–Alexander.

31

HAWKSNEST

HAWKSNEST OUTPOST
  Nobbys Headland: Newcastle, Australia

"Hang on. We got ya," said Corbin.

Dozens of small orbs positioned under the heavy timber. Once Corbin was satisfied with their placement, he took a step back.

"Alright, you two get ready to blast that thing once it's airborne, got it?"

Sonia and Lucas nodded their agreement and took a fighter's stance.

"On three. One. Two. Three!"

Corbin caused all his orbs to explode simultaneously, throwing the timber upwards. Sonia and Lucas fired blasts in sync, propelling it backward and away from the victim beneath the rubble. With room to move now, the man braced his hands and pushed himself free from the rock and grit. Lucas ran to him and helped him to his feet.

The man appeared bewildered and dazed. Lucas helped him down from the rubble and sat him on a nearby section of a broken column.

"Hey, you okay?" asked Lucas.

The man lifted his head and looked at Lucas with a blank stare. Corbin studied the man, then looked to Lucas, gauging his reaction.

"Hey, tell me your name. Do you know your name? You still with us?"

The man brushed the dust from his hair and then rubbed his eyes. His face was long and thin with high cheekbones, though it was hard to see any facial features through the soot smeared on his skin.

"I. . . uhh. My name is Ka. . . No. Bale." His eyes shifted around the room. "My name is Bale. Where am I?"

"So, you don't remember where you are?"

The man put his forehead in his hands. "It's all a thick fog," he said with a little more strength. "I remember a lot of screaming and explosions. People running around frantically. . . with accents. British, I think, or maybe Australian. There was a woman hurt on the floor over there." He pointed to where he'd been trapped.

"I pushed her out of the way when I saw the beam fall. Purple flame was consuming it, but it wasn't on fire."

Bale's eyes widened, and he stood up at the mention of the energy attack.

"Vics! Victus hit us. We had no idea. . ."

Sonia gently touched Bale's shoulder and persuaded him back to his seat. "Easy. Just take it easy." She then gestured to Lucas to continue questioning.

"Did they say anything, make an announcement, or give any proclamations?"

"Yes, the first man in screamed something like Hay Victus or something similar. It all happened so fast."

"Vae Victus?" asked Corbin.

Bale looked to Corbin inquisitively. "Yes, Vae Victus. That sounds like it."

"What is that?" asked Lucas.

"It is their way of announcing pending destruction and victory over their enemy," said Sonia.

"And it looks like they made good on it," said Bale.

"Not entirely. We still took them out in the end," said Lucas. "They're gone now, so you can relax."

"I don' mean to be crass in a time like dis, but we need to be sure you ain't fooling around, my man," said Corbin.

"How do you mean?" asked Bale.

"I mean, we gotta be sure you are one of us."

Corbin scrunched his sleeve up around his elbow. He made a fist and forced his catalyst band to appear. He rotated his wrist so Bale could see both emblems: the sun on the top and the Former on the underside.

"Your turn."

"You can just force it to show?" asked Bale.

"Yes, you sure can, and it is fairly basic. How long have you been activated?"

"About a year and a half. I went through the training facility in the summertime, so I guess it's nearly two."

"Two years in, and you can't reveal? Sorry, baby, that don' seem right," said Corbin, bracing himself. Lucas looked at Corbin, taking note of his hesitation, then took a similar stance.

"Whoa, hold on," said Bale, throwing his hands in the air. "We're all on the same side here. I've been trained and equipped and sent on multiple missions. Just because my superior failed to show me something so trivial doesn't mean I'm a Vic. Just tell me how it's done, and I'll show you."

Sonia stepped closer and bore her arm.

"You charge up for a burst, but instead of releasing the energy, you let the band absorb it."

As she spoke, she illustrated by doing it. Her band lit up, showing the Aegis Sun on one side and an emblem of flame on the opposite side.

"Alright, sounds easy enough."

Bale unbuttoned his cuff and rolled up his sleeve. He focused intently on his arm, balling his fingers into a fist. A shimmer of light flashed around his wrist like a glowing rubber band, and then the light slowly ran down his forearm, revealing a golden catalyst band. His brow furrowed as he continued to focus on producing his proof.

Corbin took Bale's hand and rotated it to see the emblem of his gifting. A small circle in the center connected with lines to many other circles around the perimeter.

"I guess we have more in common than I originally thought. Another Former is always good to have around."

Bale lowered his hand and rolled his sleeve back down.

"So, we are good then?" asked Bale.

"Good enough to help us in what we gotta do next," replied Corbin.

"You still must be vetted with our leadership," said Lucas.

"I'll handle da vetting with Alex," said Corbin. "Can you walk?"

"Yes, I'll be fine. I just need some water."

Sonia reached into her satchel and tossed a plastic bottle to Bale. Bale popped open the top and gulped half of it in seconds.

"You know this place? Were you stationed here full-time?" asked Corbin.

"Yes, I moved here about eight months ago," replied Bale, coughing intermittently.

"Good, den you can help us search for survivors. We need to groom this place and get back to headquarters ASAP."

"Great. I'll be happy to help search. How many have you found already?"

"There was a group that had taken shelter down there," said Corbin, pointing. "We were on our way to search the rest of the outpost when we found you. We're splitting up. Sonia is headed there, Lucas over there, and I'm taking this room. Why don' you start with the door next to mine? We'll go up a level once we're finished down here."

"Alright," said Bale, taking a drink of water.

He chugged so quickly that a trickle of water fell on his lap. He scooted his hand across his mouth to catch the rest. Bale ran over to where he was assigned, tripping over scattered rock as he approached the door. He stopped and cradled his head in his hands until he regained his balance.

"Bale, back here in twenty!" yelled Corbin, unable to keep a straight face.

"Keep an eye on this one, Lucas," said Corbin. "He don' look too skilled."

"Give him the benefit of the doubt, Corbin. The man was basically pinned under a tree," said Lucas.

"Got it," said Bale, his voice trailing down the hall.

"Yeah, I guess you're right," replied Corbin.

"I'll help him along," replied Lucas, getting to his feet.

"Meet back here in twenty," said Corbin.

Each dispersed to their designation section of the outpost to look for survivors. Once the allotted time had passed, they met in the central hall and spread to the second and third levels.

Bale was the first to return. A few minutes later, Sonia returned with two women, a teenage girl and a young boy. Lucas had not found anyone else but had a few things tucked under his arm. Corbin had one unconscious man draped over his shoulder. Bale walked behind Sonia and Corbin to Lucas.

"I thought you were supposed to get survivors, not some books, to occupy your time," said Bale.

"I happened upon the library while I was searching. I'm taking these back, per Alex's request."

Bale reached for the books, looking at the spines. Lucas pulled back.

"I don't know what these are about, but I got the impression that it was a sensitive request."

Bale pulled his hands back. "Alright. I didn't mean to pry. I'm a reader and spent a lot of my spare time in there is all."

"We need to get these people out of here and back to EagleEye," said Corbin.

"Why not Falcon?" asked Lucas.

"Alex will have his hands full if Cavaness' team and we send him all the wounded. When I found this fella, I contacted Alex and told him I would take whoever we found back to our place."

"Then what?" asked Sonia.

"Den, we wait for Alex's next objective," replied Corbin.

Sonia nodded. "Alright, let's get you downstairs to a safe place," she said to the women. She walked a few steps and looked back to see the three still huddled together, with the boy between the two women looking terrified. His face was black with ash except for the streaks of tears on his cheeks.

"Come on. You can trust me. We'll take you to a place where this won't happen again."

The boy tried to walk, but the women held him back with protective hands.

"May I?" asked Bale, stepping around toward the survivors.

He reached out toward their heads. They timidly pulled back away from Bale, but he moved in fast and cradled their heads in his radiant hands, which were glowing like street lamps against a midnight sky. Their eyes softened as their eyes glazed over. Sonia and Lucas watched with intrigue.

"Shhhh. Listen to my voice and be at ease. There is no threat now. Relax and clear your head of any memory of what happened here."

To their surprise, what Bale was doing was working. Both women looked like they had just woken from a whole night's rest. Lucas stared at Bale.

"I had medical training before I entered all this, focusing on neurological science," said Bale. "When I was activated, I figured out a way to access and push energy into the various areas of the brain, influencing memory and emotion."

"You're full of surprises," said Lucas.

Bale did not reply. He had already focused back on the women to inspect his work.

"We need to go now. Follow us."

Without hesitation, they followed. The boy looked intrigued at the change in his caretakers but seemed content enough seeing their peaceful demeanor.

"Alright Sonia, take us to where we are going," said Bale.

Sonia corralled the others and walked toward the stairs, with Lucas bringing up the rear with the teenage boy. Bale stood where he was, satisfied with the effect of his treatment. He sighed in relief and looked around at what remained of HawksNest, which wasn't much. As the others neared the staircase to the lower levels, Bale caught movement out of the corner of his eye. Two men in black were hiding among the remaining timbers holding up the outpost's roof structure. They shuffled to position themselves over Sonia and the others with fiery bands blazing. They leaped from the beams to pounce on their prey in perfect sync.

Bale turned and yelled.

"Sonia, Lucas, look out!"

32

FALCON HQ
Portfield, Pennsylvania

"The Council may buy into his lies, but I do not. Eventually, they will see it," said Alex.

"What makes you think I even have an audience with the Kaiser?" replied Kyla.

"Call it intuition," said Alex confidently. "I assume he alerted you to the Former's blood connection. Tell me, how long have you been using it to get Brian to discuss our plans? I must say, this is a disappointment."

"Well, Brian was always a fool."

"Oh, Kyla. You misunderstand. I'm not talking about Brian. I'm talking about you. I sense such a misplaced hatred in you."

Kyla appeared vexed by the sudden focus on herself.

"We all have our reasons for doing what we do."

"I want you to hear this from my mouth. Before this is all over, you will see your master for what he really is and your so-called position for what he really has planned for you. You are at the wrong end of the spear, my dear, and I would hate to see you run through."

Kyla remained stubbornly silent.

Alex's orb began to illuminate as bright as the midday sun. It was so intense that Kyla had to turn her back completely.

"You see, if your Kaiser were in my shoes right now, he would use the connection with the scout orbs to infuse energy directly into your brain, causing excruciating pain, which he could make last for however long he wished before he allowed the temperature in your skull to rise high enough to melt your brain. He would not hesitate to sacrifice you if it meant advancing his plan."

Though the light was intense, Kyla was not in pain. Her hands cupped over her eyes, but the light had also penetrated her mind. Closing her eyes made no difference.

"We are not that way, Kyla, nor is it how we operate. Choose your side carefully. Now, use that trans hanging in the hallway, go back to Albatross, and tell your master that I will not allow him to hold my regional headquarters or its people captive. I will regain control."

As the light vanished, so did Alex's presence. Kyla was still trying to blink away the effects of the light. As she regained her senses, the table vibrated. She walked over and retrieved her phone from under a folded piece of purple fabric and held it to her ear.

"Brian? Yes, it's me. . . no, I was just in the bathroom. No, nothing is wrong."

Kyla's expression showed inward conflict as Murphy spoke into the other end. Alex's talk had made an impression, but she seemed unable to decide how she would let it affect her. She nervously bit her thumbnail, but as Murphy continued talking, she lowered her hand and clenched her jaw. Her demeanor darkened, and a flicker of defiance danced in her pupils.

"I don't care about your friends. Tell me where you are so I can come to you if you won't come to me. This has been going on long enough. I know you can stop their threats."

Kyla hung up the phone and shoved it into her pocket. She walked into the hallway toward the transit mirror. The Kaiser needed to know about this, but she was still needed at Albatross. She would have to update him from there. With a huff, she placed her hand on the mirror and vanished.

Murphy looked at the screen, surprised that she had hung up so abruptly. He chucked his phone onto this bed, stressfully ran his fingers through his hair, locking his fingers together on top of his head, and gazed outside.

Alex closed the door behind him and took a seat beside Graham.

"What did you think of the tea?"

Graham looked at the empty cup with the mushy teabag resting at the bottom.

"I think I'd rather have a Coke, but the sugar helped."

"I'll make a note of that for next time," Alex said with a smile, picking up the book beside Graham's cup. "Have you finished with this?"

"Yes. I could see a lot of people's motivations in this."

"I had a feeling you would catch on. And who did you take notice of?"

"Kel, for sure. I could see her nature in the way they described their discipline. She has a way of carrying herself. Maybe in the way she always sees things as black and white."

"Kel does have an elevated sense of justice and integrity. It guides her way of thinking. What else did you see?"

I also saw Cavaness' strictness, Damien's courage, Ailey's servant heart and. . ."

"And?"

"And I also saw that you were the one to establish it all."

Alex leaned in, resting his elbows on his knees.

"Go on."

"Well, you have lived for centuries. You could be anywhere and with anyone. You have every gifting there is. You have established all of this. I guess I just feel like I need to bow or something. . . or talk to you from the other side of the door. What did I do to deserve this attention from you?"

Alex smiled and gripped Graham's shoulder. "You didn't deserve any of it. I desire to spend time with you, Graham, to develop and establish you. You do not need to retreat from me. I hope you know by now that I am on your side. Always."

Graham couldn't help his timidity, and it showed.

"But I'm talking with one of two people who has lived since the beginning of time. That changes things. Shouldn't I kneel or something? I still don't feel I deserve to sit with you."

"Your reverence is well noted and appreciated. It says a lot about your character. There will be no need for kneeling or bowing at the moment. You have my permission to come to me as you are, as a team member and son. You are, after all, legally my son."

Graham relaxed. "So you really are immortal?"

"Yes, I am."

"So, does it hurt if you get cut or attacked?"

"In a manner of speaking, though not as you do. Since my body does not degrade, it is more of an awareness than pain."

"And your younger brother. . . he's the same way?"

"He's only my brother in the sense that we are eternal, but yes, he, too, experiences pain as I do."

"So, when the council talked about there not being a resolution between the immovable object and the unstoppable force, they did have a reason for saying it."

"There is an element of logic that supports their reasoning, but it's made without all the facts, and, therefore, illogical."

"And we are fighting against his army called Victus."

"Yes, that is the double-barreled name he has given his followers."

Graham paused, taking in the name. It did not seem overly evil or regal. He half expected it to feel evil, but it seemed pretty average.

"So, what's your plan to beat him if he can't die?"

"It's a work in progress," Alex admitted. "But that can wait. For now, we must deal with the issues at hand, which is getting you and the others developed and re-establishing connections with the other outposts.

"Tomorrow, I want you to remain in the training room once your final lesson ends instead of coming here. I believe I can help you progress."

Alex stood up and gestured toward the door.

"That is all for tonight."

Graham agreed and stood up.

Murphy was walking around the corner when the door to Alex's office opened. When he saw Graham walking out, he paused and remained partially hidden behind the wall. Alex emerged after Graham, continuing their conversation.

Alex looked directly at Murphy, who diverted his gaze and acted as if he were simply continuing his stroll down the hallway.

"Good night, Alex. Graham."

"Goodnight, Murphy," replied Graham. "Thanks for the training today."

"You bet," he said flatly as he continued down the hall.

"Good evening, Brian, and rest well. You look as though you have a lot on your mind."

Murphy stopped for a moment. He tilted his head toward Alex but never completely turned around.

"Nothing I can't handle, sir. We all have a lot on our shoulders."

"Indeed we do. Some more than others."

Murphy looked at the floor, slightly nodded, and continued around the next corner.

"Is he alright? He hasn't seemed to be himself lately," asked Graham.

Alex continued to stare down the hallway.

"No, I don't believe he is, and I fear it will get worse before it gets better."

"What do you mean?"

"Brian is carrying a burden right now that is much bigger than he realizes but will have to unravel on its own, much like your nightmare. Right now, the best thing for him is to focus on training and let it all play out."

"Okay, if that's what you say. Goodnight, Alex."

"Goodnight, Graham."

Alex walked back into his office, removed the walkie-talkie from his desk drawer, and strolled in front of the fireplace as he turned the dial back to channel six. He arched his back to stretch, adjusting his vest before asking his question.

"Agent Red, this is Falcon. Please provide a status update. Over."

Alex stared into the flames in the fireplace, tapping the

antenna on his chin until he received a response.

"Falcon, this is Red," responded the woman. "My source was good, and I believe I'm in the same town as Skyle. He's supposed to meet with a new client in four hours. I'll confirm once I have a visual."

"Wonderful news. Keep up the excellent work, and stay safe."

"Yes, sir. Red out."

Alex turned the unit off and placed it on the small table as he settled into his wingback chair, feeling quite satisfied.

"At last, we can get Graham some answers."

33

ALBATROSS

ALBATROSS OUTPOST
Remote Jungle- Argentina

It was a tight squeeze going through the opening of the spring head. Adrian had made it easy once he commanded the water to lift the stones, pulling them away from the entrance like a multi-branched candlestick. The water, which had initially streamed from the opening in the ground, had now split down the middle, holding to the sides and ceiling of the tunnel, leaving the ground dry to walk on.

They walked single-file through the narrow underground tunnel with Adrian in the lead. He held out his hand to command the water away from them and illuminate the path ahead with his catalyst band. He even acted as a tour guide as they ventured deeper underground.

"Cavaness may already know this, but long ago, before The Ancient removed the first edition of the bands from our ancestors, they built these outposts to reflect the core Aegis tenets of beliefs. Albatross was the last to be erected. The springhead we just went through– it was not always there. Just as the Israelites ventured into their promised land in ancient biblical times, they had constructed a small pillar of twelve stones to commemorate their entrance into their new homeland and acknowledge divine provision. The leaders of Albatross, though not Hebrew, decided it was a meaningful sentiment and did the same here. Fortunately for us, the stone pillar also serves a dual purpose."

"What do you mean when you say tenants?" asked Jael.

"In every organization, there are core values on which they operate. Aegis is no different. There are seven tenets, or core values, to the moral fabric of who we are, and they are represented in each outpost. Once the final outpost had been constructed, it seemed we'd reached our promised land. We had centralized access to every part of the world. At this time, we could recruit worldwide from within a solid and fully connected network. The entire world was literally at our fingertips."

"And now it is the cause of our unraveling," added Cavaness. "How much longer before we get inside? We've got to stop them before they learn of the other locations and kill Marcio."

"Another sixty meters or so. The upper wall of the canal opens up inside the training hall. I am sure you could imagine the benefits."

"No doubt," said Chase. "That would be like Branson being allowed to train in an electrical power plant."

"Indeed. You know, during construction, part of the channel was compromised. It was later fortified with dense plexiglass so we could enjoy the view of the rushing water to remind us of our vitality. One small access point was intentionally left open just before the canal wraps behind the adjacent wall so we could use the water in our training. We can climb up to that point and sneak in from there."

"And where do we go from the training facility?" asked Cavaness.

"The main hall. It's a hub for the outpost. They're side by side. Just let me lead the way once we're inside."

Cavaness nodded. "Looks like it's right up there."

Just ahead, a faint glow emanated from around the bend.

"Indeed," said Adrian. The group continued until they were a few feet from where the rock bed opened to the training room. Adrian waved his hands through the air as if playing a harp. The water channels shifted their flow pattern, allowing the team access to the left side, where hewn stairs lead to the top of the channel.

"It's best if I have a look first. Victus has been keeping every room guarded up until now," said Adrian, who then stepped forward into the wall of water as if it were the most natural thing in the world.

He peeked around the lip of where the rock and plexiglass joined. As suspected, two men were walking the perimeter of the room. Adrian turned and poked his head through the wall of water.

"We have two Vics. Intermediates by the look of them. I doubt they'll be difficult to subdue. I'll remain in the stream to distract them. The rest I leave to you."

Cavaness climbed the chiseled rungs in the rock and peeked his head over the lip. He motioned for Chase to come up with him.

"We've got two bogies, both walking counter-clockwise. From our position, there's one at five o'clock and one at eleven o'clock. Blinding them with light will be too risky. Others may see the flash, so it's just you and me. I'll take out five. You take eleven. Got it?"

"Got it," replied Chase.

"Remember, they have Marcio in the room. You've got to take him out in silence."

"Understood. I'll handle it."

"I'll pulse into this rock wall. That's your signal."

Chase nodded, as did Adrian, who acknowledged from the water.

Cavaness watched as Adrian swam further into the stream, now fully exposed. His bands illuminated at half the average brightness and cast a dull light along the massive glass wall, rippling through the current, which was more than enough to get the men's attention. They both snapped their heads around to see Adrian suspended in the water with blazing wrists and glowing eyes, his white hair wavering in the water like silk.

While the two Vics stood stunned at the odd sight of Adrian's floating form, Cavaness placed his hand on the lip of the rock and fired a pulse downward. As Chase leaped up the wall and over Cavaness' head, the pulse ejected from the wall, slamming into the man's head.

Chase propelled through the air, landed in front of the second man, scooped his leg, and flung him into the air. Chase carried his momentum up the wall a few steps and then twisted back toward the falling Victus soldier. He assisted the man's descent by landing on him like a cat. When they landed, Chase's feet pinned the man's chest to the stone floor while muffling his grunts by cupping his hand over the man's mouth and slamming his head into the stone.

Chase then bolted over to Cavaness' victim, snatching the chunk of rock from the air before it could hit the ground. He gently placed it on the ground and returned to his fallen Vic, who struggled against Chase, half coherent, but quickly passed out after Chase had grabbed his wrist to drain his energy. Chase removed his hand, keeping it a few inches above his mouth to ensure he was still breathing.

Cavaness jumped over the wall, landing behind the fallen

soldier with impressive stealth for a man his size. The dazed soldier cradled his head in one hand and tried to shuffle away from Cavaness. He took a deep breath to alert his team in the next room, but Cavaness got the man in a chokehold before he could yell. As if picking up a small rock, Cavaness held the man off the ground by his neck and placed the fingertips of his free hand to the man's temple.

"Sleep."

Cavaness fired a pulse into his head, and he went limp.

Looking very satisfied, Adrian withdrew from the stream and appeared at the top of the channel with Jael. They jumped down and joined Cavaness. Chase dragged the unconscious soldier to the other at Cavaness's feet.

Jael put a hand on each of the men's shoulders while Adrian crept toward the great hall's entrance.

"It's just like you thought. They have Marcio in the center of the next room. The last memories of these guys showed at least six men, along with Silas and Kyla. We are way outnumbered," whispered Jael.

"Adrian, is there any way to get a visual in that room?" asked Cavaness.

"The only way in and out of here is through that door," replied Adrian.

"We can't just bust down the door, guns blazing. That would be a death sentence for Marcio," said Chase.

"What about the spring? Does that lead anywhere else in this place?" asked Cavaness.

"No, it only goes further into the mountain, however. . . wait, yes, I think that may work."

"What?" whispered Cavaness.

"It's not much, but it could be enough."

Adrian walked to the wall separating the two rooms, placing a hand on the stone.

"On the other side of this wall runs a wide stream of water, which branches throughout the great hall in various streams, as I am sure you have seen before, Cavaness."

"Yes, I remember the water features."

"I believe I can use them. Marcio was the one to come up with the idea. He stumbled upon it during a training exercise. The best way to describe it is sonar, like many fishing boats have. All of the water streams connect above the ceiling. I will attempt to send my energy into that stream and down through the falls around the room. I can then bounce that energy back and forth across the room and get an indication of where people are located. The water acts as receptors."

"Interesting," said Cavaness. "Let's see what comes of it."

"I cannot promise this will go undetected. There's a very real possibility the Vics will notice the energy transmitting throughout the room."

"Then I suggest we be ready. Jael, can you pull memories as they are being recorded?"

"I have never tried, but I think so. They should be the first thing I come across."

"Good. Try to see what Adrian sees, then give us real-time intel on where everyone is positioned. This could help Adrian concentrate on suppressing energy detection."

"It's worth a shot," said Jael.

Adrian closed his eyes in concentration. Jael gripped his shoulder and did the same. Transparent ripples of energy stretched out across the giant stone wall and up into the ceiling.

In the great hall, Marcio sat on his knees, his hands bound behind his back with black, smoky chains. His thick black hair hung over his olive-green eyes, matted to his tanned skin. He looked as though he'd been in the same position for hours. His breathing was steady but shallow. His vacant stare changed when a slight glimmer of energy in the water caught his eye. His grimace curled into a grin.

From Adrian's perspective, there was complete darkness, except for the glowing yellow network of water coursing through Albatross. As he commanded faint pulses of energy through the great hall, he could see outlines of people positioned on both levels of the room.

"Unbelievable," said Jael. "There's a man on his knees in the center of the room with two men behind him. This is amazing. You have four Vics on the second level. They are at two, four, seven, and eleven o'clock from our position. Besides the two Vics behind Marcio, there are also six on the lower level. Three on each side of the room, spaced fairly evenly throughout."

"They're guarding the entrances to the other sections of Albatross," said Adrian. "And you have one other person at the far end of the hall, nearest the exit to the upper room where we would have entered through the main waterfall entrance. Suffice to say, we are indeed outmatched."

"Have we been made?" asked Cavaness.

"The two with Marcio are shifty, so possibly," said Jael.

"Alright. This is going to happen fast. Chase, we need a surge. Take out the three lining the left wall. Jael, use that and intensify the light with the waterfalls. Can you do that?"

"Of course."

"Good. Adrian, take out the second level, and I'll deal with the rest."

"Understood," said everyone.

"Marcio is counting on us," said Cavaness.

"Oh, no. Cavaness, they've pulled Marcio to his feet, and the two men are poised. We must move," said Adrian.

"Positions!" yelled a man from the other room. "We've got visitors!"

Chase positioned himself in front of the massive door, one foot back to brace for the attack. Cavaness stood beside him. Chase pulled both hands back and snapped them forward, firing a thick pulse into the door, which immediately exploded into a cloud of splinters. Shards of wood and metal burst into the hall, taking huge chunks of the stone wall with them.

With the door gone, Chase let loose a strong surge of

energy toward the three Vics lining the wall. The first was hit square in the chest, propelling him backward into the second. The third Vic dove to the ground in time to dodge her friends flying over her head. She tried to get up but was nearly paralyzed by the blinding light that emanated from the energy wave.

Jael used the waterfalls to reflect that light, directing it to blind whomever she wished. Most everyone in the hall blocked the light with an outstretched hand, all except the Aegis team, who were aided by it.

As Chase attacked, Cavaness ran through the door, analyzing the positions of the Vics on the main floor. He then turned his back to the room and slammed both palms into the wall next to the door he had just destroyed. Pulses rippled through the stone into the adjacent wall and floor, which soon exploded. Chunks of stone ripped from the wall, hitting all three men positioned on the wall opposite Chase. They all fell to the ground, pinned under the cascading rocks. The ground erupted underneath Marcio and his two captors. The two Vics were sprayed with pebbles and dirt, knocking them sideways off their feet, but Marcio was simply thrust forward onto his chest.

Meanwhile, Adrian was busy commanding tendrils of water to pin the four men on the second floor to the walls.

"Chase, take out the ones holding Marcio!" yelled Adrian.

"I've got them," said Cavaness. "Get the ones on the upper level! Jael, take the one at the back of the room."

Jael was already in pursuit. She twisted the light to blind her target, but two wide discs formed from the Vic's hands to block the rays. She squinted to see Jael approaching and threw the formed discs at her. Jael strafed and ducked to avoid the attack, keeping her pace. As she grew close, she could see Kyla's wicked scowl.

Jael gritted her teeth and snarled. She threw a blast and deflected another attack from Kyla with the shield from her band. She tucked her body behind it and used it as a battering ram, slamming it into Kyla. She stumbled backward but quickly regained her balance. She grabbed the glowing shield and braced against it while her feet slid back across the floor.

Purple rods stretched vertically from Kyla's hands like prison bars. They penetrated the stone floor, bringing Jael to a dead stop. She then circled Jael, grabbed her by the shoulders, and threw her onto her back. Using the momentum, Jael tucked her feet and sunk both feet into Kyla's chest, kicking her like a mule.

Kyla hit the ground with a thud, though she kept her chin tucked to her chest, preventing her head from hitting the floor. As Jael got up, Kyla threw up a purple wall of energy as wide as the hall and as high as the ceiling. Slowly standing, she could see the shadowy form of Jael trying to find a way around it.

"Get around that, you stubborn coward! I'm surprised you–"

Kyla suddenly yelped and fell forward to the floor. Streaks of blurred motion circled around her, causing her hair and clothing to whip and whirl like she was in the center of a vortex. The force and increased pressure made Kyla dizzy. Her nose began to bleed. Her eyes rolled in her head, and her wall of energy faded. Just as she appeared to give in, her eyes snapped back into focus. Her teeth bared, and with a shaky hand, she threw shafts of light forward, tripping Chase. He tumbled to her right, rolling over one of the unconscious Vics from Cavaness' attack.

Marcio threw an elbow into a Vic's collarbone. The man cried out and fell to the side. The second man reached for Marcio, but Cavaness clamped both shoulders and picked him up off his feet. His feet flailed in the air as he twisted his torso to escape the big man's grasp. Cavaness' wrists regained their luminosity as he sent a pulse of energy from both hands through the man's body, which incapacitated him immediately.

By this time, Adrian had climbed one of the two staircases leading to the upper level. He had already taken out one Vic on his way to the second.

"Marcio! To your right!" Adrian screamed.

The two Vics on the other side of the balcony had escaped the water and were poised on top of the railing, ready to attack Marcio. As they left from the handrail, Marcio held his hands outstretched, then brought them quickly together, twisting his palms toward his chest. The towering waterfalls on either side of the men vomited their liquid streams toward each other under Marcio's direction. The two sheets of water slammed into one another just below the Vics, catching them in a suspended water net hovering between the two levels.

The men fell into the liquid trap. At first, they swam to the surface. Once they had realized what had happened, they decided to swim toward the bottom and escape, but Marcio had caused a current to push them back to the top, trapping the men in the suspended whirlpool.

Kyla darted past, forming a purple, diamond-shaped shield. As she sunk it into Cavaness's torso, she also fired a wave from its surface, knocking the big man off his feet, retrieved three silver throwing knives from a small holster in her belt, and hurled them toward Marcio. The force of hitting Cavaness carried Kyla in a backward somersault, letting her continue toward the nearest doorway. She opened the door and looked back in time to see Marcio fall to the ground with two of the three knives protruding from his chest and abdomen.

"No!" Adrian screamed, the intensity of his yell muffled by the echo of the massive wooden door slamming behind Kyla.

34

HAWKSNEST

HAWKSNEST OUTPOST
Nobbys Headland: Newcastle, Australia

Lucas looked up in time to see a blast fly through the air. He sheltered the young boy from the attack, taking the blow to his back. Sonia cast the women aside and braced for impact. The two Vics landed just in front of them, one quiet like a cat, the other with a heavy boom.

The whole room shook. Lucas held onto the railing, still hunched over the boy. Sonia quickly fell to all fours to keep balance. With Aegis on the defense, the attackers fired more bursts without regard to the boy or the other women.

Bale ran awkwardly to the fight, trying to keep his balance amidst the quaking. He ran behind the Pusher and kicked the back of his knee, making his leg buckle. Bale pulled his fist back for a punch, forming a circle of light the size of a basketball around his hand. Bale swung hard with a right hook. The orb connected and cracked like a shotgun blast. The attacker was thrown sideways into the wall. His head bounced off the stone, and with a second burst, he slammed into the wall again and crumpled to the ground.

Lucas fired a dart at the second man, hitting him in the shin. He yelped and retaliated with a surge. Lucas shielded the attack and threw more darts at the man's feet. He danced around them, hoping from one foot to the other, cringing every time he landed on his injured leg. Sonia threw a wall of fire between her and the man. He scurried away from the heat, shuffling in front of the stairs. He braced for another surge, but Lucas fired first, throwing darts at the floor in front of him, making a semicircle of small holes around his feet.

The stair tread cracked and broke off as the last dart pinned a hole into the stone. The Vic disconnected his hands, flailing and falling backward down the stairs. He somersaulted in all sorts of painful angles, gaining speed as he fell.

Lucas and Sonia were so distracted by the immediate threat that they did not see the third man still concealed among the wooden beams above.

By this time, Corbin had laid the unconscious survivor down and was climbing up the stairs to help his team. He saw the tumbling Vic roll toward him, so he instinctually threw up a golden wall on the stair tread in front of him. The Vic slammed into it hard with his shoulder and upper back, stopping his descent.

While the man was dazed, Corbin grabbed the trans, placed The Vic's hand to the glass, and sent him through to the Wastelands.

Bale heard a gasp and turned to see Sonia held from behind in a chokehold. The third Vic from above had grabbed her while everyone else was distracted. He held a jagged sliver of stone to her neck.

"Back down or she dies!" yelled the man.

Lucas held his hands in the air, as did Bale.

"And place your hands over your chest!"

Lucas obeyed, crossing his arms like a mummy.

"Okay, see? We are not fighting back. There's no reason to hurt her now. Just tell me what you want."

"Want? What do I want? You call yourselves protectors, but it's all a guise, a license to murder. All you're doing now is hindering the inevitable. So, what I want is for you to work with us like nature intended or die."

Bale took one step toward the man, keeping his hands up.

"If you hurt her, you know you're not leaving here alive, right?" said Bale.

"I've been in worse situations than this. You'd be surprised how I can– Hey, stop! Stop right there!"

Corbin froze on the staircase upon seeing the shiv tight against Sonia's neck.

"Whoa, now. Let's ease up, baby. Why don' we talk dis through."

"Ease up? It's four on one. Three if you take another step!"

"Alright, no one's movin', so why don' you tell us how dis is gonna play out."

"You, Cajun. How did you get here?" As he asked the question, he pulled the shiv tighter to Sonia's neck. "And don't lie to me."

"Through a trans, just like you, I imagine."

"And I assume you have another one to get back home?"

Lucas glanced at Corbin and Sonia. Corbin did not look back but kept his attention on the threat.

"Yes, we got one with us."

Lucas grunted under his breath.

"Then go and get it, and remember. . . her life depends on your ability to follow instructions. You are the leader of this group, are you not?"

"Yes, I am."

"Then order them to stand down. I see the determination in their eyes."

"Look, Mr. Vic, no one's doing anything, so be cool while I get what you asked for."

"Do it!" the man spat as he yelled. A ripple of purple mist transferred from his hand into the slate shard. The sliver of stone radiated from within, then absorbed the light, regaining its normal appearance.

"Do what I ask, or I'll make sure this can never be pulled out of her."

Corbin held his hands up a little further. "I'm going. Just ease up." He slowly turned around and marched down the stairs to retrieve the satchel.

A thin red line was beginning to appear on Sonia's neck like she was allergic to the shiv. She pulled her head back to get relief, but the man held her tight.

"Just how long have you been activated?" asked Bale.

"Long enough to take out four Aegis at once."

"You did tear this place apart, I'll give you that," said Bale. "Tell me, what did your master tell you when you came here?"

"He said to shut them up if they keep asking questions."

Bale stared at the young man like he was reading a book.

"You have never met him, have you?"

"Hey! This isn't twenty questions, alright? I want that mirror up here, and I want it without being questioned by any of you! Is that clear?"

"Crystal," replied Lucas as Corbin trotted up the stairs.

Corbin pulled the strap over his head and set the satchel on the ground. He unzipped the top pouch and retrieved a small mirror.

"What's your name?" asked Corbin.

"Doesn't matter," the man replied.

"Well, if you don' want us to keep callin' you Mr. Vic, then at least give us a name," replied Corbin.

"Seth, and don't think I believe that is the trans you use to get back home. Now, put that away and get the real one."

"Alright, Seth. . . just Seth? I had to move this out of the way to get to the other. Just give me a second."

"Ashman. Seth Ashman. Let that name burn in your memory, just like my slaughtered brother's name is burned in mine."

"Slaughtered?"

"Yes, because of you, he was found near one of our camps with a knife in his chest. Believe me when I say that I won't hesitate to do the same to any one of you."

"We don't operate like that," said Lucas. "Surely you don't think a member of Aegis would blatantly murder, even a member of Victus."

"I think. . . if you do not give me that mirror, you are all dead."

Corbin reached the bottom of the pack and retrieved two larger trans, which Alex had made. He set them down amidst the rubble.

"Alright, where would you like to go? You got my place here," he said, pointing to the first mirror. "And you got Alex here," he said, pointing to the second. "Both destinations will not end well for you. You'll be outnumbered, and in the heat of the confusion, I can't promise you won't be killed."

Seth looked at both mirrors, plotting his next move.

"There is a third option here," said Lucas. "Surrender now, and we can help you figure out what happened to your brother."

Seth looked at Lucas with rage and disgust.

"I already know what happened to him, and so do his wife and daughters. Did you think killing him would be one less *Vic* to worry about? All you did was galvanize our entire community against you."

"We didn't kill your brother. It goes entirely against who we are. Such a vile thing–"

"Enough! The conversation is over! I'm going to your main headquarters to kill Alex and find Graham, and I'll be doing it alone."

Seth raised the shiv to stab Sonia. As he reared back, Sonia shifted just enough to expose his lower half.

Lucas threw darts at his exposed leg, but Seth was quick to strafe. Corbin threw a tiny orb between Sonia and the shiv. As it hovered between the two, it expanded into a flat disc. The shiv penetrated it, turning it a dark purple from the middle out, like ink permeating a glass of water.

The moment of resistance gave Bale enough time to run in and form coiled bands around Seth's body. Sonia was able to slip from his grasp as his hands were pinned to his side. Bale then grabbed each side of his head and fired two waves of energy through his temples. Seth went cross-eyed and crumpled to the floor. He landed on his side, his eyes wide and unfocused. Bale dissolved the bonds, letting Seth's arm slide onto the ground.

Sonia got to her feet, rubbing the red line on her neck. Corbin's disk had vanished, leaving the shiv at Sonia's feet. She bent to retrieve it, but Lucas held her back.

"No, don't touch that. This man is a Weaver, and that is still dangerous."

35

ALBATROSS

ALBATROSS OUTPOST
  Remote Jungle- Argentina

Adrian ran down the stairwell to Marcio, followed by Chase and Jael. Cavaness went to where Kyla had fled.

"Where does this lead?" asked Cavaness.

Adrian answered but did not take his eyes off Marcio as he surveyed the damage.

"It goes into the west wing, but only one passageway leads up to the main entrance. The rest go deeper underground."

"You must. . . must stop her," mumbled Marcio. "She is next in command under Silas. She knows wha. . . what he knows."

"Save your energy," said Adrian.

"I'll rest when I am dead," Marcio replied.

He looked down to see the curvature of the hilts protruding from his shoulder and lower abdomen just to the left of his belly button, with blood rings growing around them.

"I'll live. You have to go after her. Now."

Marcio winced and pulled the blade from his shoulder.

"Go," commanded Cavaness. "You two, go now. Make sure Kyla does not escape."

Chase and Jael wasted no time. Chase took Jael by the hand and sped off through the doorway.

Cavaness and Adrian helped Marcio to his feet. Cavaness then walked over, ripped the sleeves from one of the unconscious Victus soldiers, and started tearing them into strips. By the time he returned to Marcio, he had already taken the second knife from his torso, painfully removing his garment to inspect the damage. He extended a hand and commanded a small stream of water into it, forming a small liquid ball. He grabbed the sleeve of his shirt and bit down on it.

He then forced the water into the wound in his oblique. He groaned and tensed as the water flowed in and out of the gash. The crystal blue water began to turn a milky red as Marcio cleaned the wound. Once satisfied, he let the water spill to the floor. He removed his gag and panted.

"Cavaness, you need to go help those two." Marcio winced again. He was pale, and his knees nearly buckled under him. Adrian bent down to help catch him. "I'm okay, I'm okay," he said, throwing a hand up, begging for a moment to catch his breath. "You do not want them to suffer like this. Please, go. Adrian is more than capable of helping me from here."

Cavaness agreed and left the room.

"Please, help hold me up for this one," Marcio said as he bit his garment again and held his breath. He retrieved another stream of water and forced it into the gash in his shoulder. His muffled scream echoed throughout the great hall.

"Do you know your way around this place?" asked Chase.

"No, I've never visited Albatross before," replied Jael. "Just keep going up."

Chase was pulling Jael so fast she could hardly keep her feet underneath her, much less talk.

Calculating the route in his mind as fast as he was running, Chase zipped through the tunnels, but every so often, he would make a wrong turn, and they would have to backtrack. Chase would grunt in frustration and change course.

"Chase, stop. Just for a moment."

"Why?"

"Because you need to clear your head. You are a rapid thinker, right?"

"Yes, but we don't have time for that."

"We don't have time to backtrack. You need to think clearly and try to concentrate."

"You don't understand. When I analyze as a Surge, it takes all my bandwidth. I can't do anything else. I can't even move. Besides, it's not the twisted pathways I'm thinking about. It's you and her."

Chase grabbed Jael by the hand and sprinted up a ramp to the left. Once they got to the top, they stopped again.

"If you aren't careful, Kyla will have a vendetta. You don't want someone like that to make it her life's purpose to kill you."

Chase made his decision and sprinted up another hallway.

"I can handle her," said Jael, out of breath. "She destroyed Raven and killed my friends. Maybe it isn't her who has a vendetta."

"I get it. I really do, but when you get blinded by your anger, you make mistakes, and you cannot afford mistakes with her."

Jael ripped her hand from Chase's. "I'm fine. This is my business. You couldn't possibly understand."

Chase looked around the room and then took Jael's hand back.

"I'm just concerned. I haven't known you long, but I like having you around." Chase pointed to the right. "This way."

Another long ramp led them up to a vaulted area with a single stairway leading to a pointed arched entryway. Chase could hear the faint roar of a waterfall through the walls. Kyla was sprinting up the stairs, already near the top.

Jael released a blast, blowing out the treads beneath Kyla's feet. Kyla grabbed the railing to steady herself and pulled her feet to the next available step. Chase darted toward the left wall. He jumped, stuck a brief landing with one foot, and then pushed off the wall toward the staircase. As Kyla regained her balance, Chase sprinted up the stairs, lunged forward, and tackled her. The force of the collision cracked the stone railing, propelling them both over the side. In mid-descent, Chase tucked his feet against Kyla and pushed off her, which flung her even harder to the ground. Chase fell on his side, absorbing most of the impact by rolling over his shoulder. Kyla tried to carry her force into a backward roll, but she was too close to the staircase wall and slammed into it hard with her shoulder.

She cradled her head and held up a glowing shield with the other as Chase hurled blasts at her. Jael released a surge, connecting with the staircase wall a few feet from Kyla. Like a welder, she carved an arc around Kyla. The stone rumbled and cracked, and a large portion of the wall crumbled on top of her. Kyla stole one final glance at Jael before being buried, and her scowl would be an image forever burned into Jael's mind.

Chase shuffled to his feet as the chunks of rock and dust settled. Cavaness sprinted into the room behind Jael and looked at the heap of rubble.

"Kyla?"

"Yes, sir."

"Was this necessary?"

Jael stared directly into his eyes. "Absolutely."

Chase looked a bit bewildered, not quite sure what had just happened. He glanced back over to the rubble while Cavaness walked to him.

"You alright?"

"Unclear," said Chase, staring at the heap.

"Can you pull memories from the dead?" asked Cavaness to Jael.

"If it's within the first fifteen minutes or so, yes, I believe so."

"Then start digging."

"I buried her for a reason. I don't think I could stand to look at her again."

"Then keep your eyes shut. We need to know what they're planning. You say this was necessary. So be it, but don't waste this chance to get ahead of the firefight."

Jael stood stiff, eyes unfocused, lost in an evident elaborate web of emotion as Cavaness turned to leave.

A small cascade of pebbles tumbled down the heap of stone and dirt, followed by a slight rumble. Dust particles danced in small shafts of light now emanating from underneath the rock. The rumbling grew more intense as muffled screams echoed from the pile.

"Get down!" yelled Cavaness.

Jael froze in disbelief. Chase sprinted over and tackled her to the ground with his shield, protecting them just in time to shelter them from the explosion. Kyla burst from her tomb with an intense blast of light. She had formed a cocoon around herself as she was buried, and the intensity of the shell grew with her anger. The explosion was as intense as exploding dynamite. Rock sprayed all around, littering the room with the debris.

Kyla darted around the staircase. Jael felt her footsteps just beyond her head, tensing in expectation of retaliation, but none came. The railing blew into pieces as Kyla looped around and approached the stoop. Cavaness threw another burst, but Kyla had already constructed a wall of her own, which rested on top of the fractured banister, reaching up to the tall ceilings.

Chase jumped to his feet to pursue, but Cavaness intervened.

"No, wait until she's through the door."

"But she's getting away!" said Chase.

"She'll bring that formed wall on top of you. It's a trap she wants you to follow. Wait until it dissipates."

As Kyla continued her ascent, Jael pushed the rubble to the side to get up. She watched as the destructor of her home reached the top of the stairs and disappeared through the arched doorway. Jael took a chunk of rock in her hand and slammed it into the floor with a burst of energy behind it, crushing it into smaller pieces.

After Kyla was gone, her formed wall faded away, imploding into darkness like a dying star.

Cavaness turned up the staircase with the others close behind until they reached the top. Once through the doorway, they entered a narrow corridor with another arched doorway on the other side.

"The entrance behind the main falls is through there," said Cavaness in mid-stride.

He grabbed the handle. The knob twisted, but the door would not budge.

"Stand back."

Canvases also took a few steps back until he was satisfied with his positioning. Pulses fired from his hands into the castle-style wooden door. The door splintered and erupted, blowing apart nearly parallel to the wall, giving them a clear path to run through.

The roar of the waterfall was deafening as they ran into the cavern. The main entrance of Albatross was a giant, hewn cave hidden behind the watery curtain. The cave was completely bare and open, having only two doorways at the rear, one of which had just been obliterated. The door on the other side was halfway open.

Cavaness looked to the back wall, where Marcio stood pale and limp, being propped up by Adrian. He had put his garments back on, but the bloodstains had expanded.

"Always finding a way when there seems to be none. That has always been your strength, old friend."

Cavaness looked toward the falls to see Silas holding a walking cane with a satchel hanging by his side. Kyla was standing next to him. Two men from downstairs were also present, standing to each side of their leaders. One held a hand with a formed dart protruding from his palm, aimed at Marcio.

"Silas, stop this," commanded Cavaness.

"You know, I genuinely thought you were dead when I destroyed your facilities, your *catalyst grove* in Portfield. You are one tough cookie, I'll give you that."

"Haven't you seen by now that you're disposable, no matter how far up the food chain you may go? You and I know that better than most."

"My motives are my own business, though maybe I just enjoy killing you off, one by one."

"What then? You kill us and take over Albatross. That's your plan? You know by now that the mirrors connecting to the other facilities are deactivated and useless. You won't find the other outposts. So, what's the point in all this?"

"Who says there needs to be a point? Maybe I'm just that kid on the beach who wants to feel good by stomping on your sandcastle."

"You're not here because of your narcissism. Neither Alex nor Graham is with us, as you can see. I know that's what you really want, so what now? Engage in a useless death match to control an outpost which both sides know the location of?"

"That sounds rather nice. As I understand, your lady friend has a bit of a grudge against Kyla. Why don't we let them settle their issues?"

"No."

Silas glanced at the man beside him, who threw sparks, scathing the floor at their feet. The Snype fired his dart, which pelted the stone inches from Marcio's head, leaving a small, gunshot-like hole. Marcio did not flinch.

"Leverage is such a great bargaining tool," Silas mocked. "Now then. Your team pinned Kyla to a wall, helpless and outnumbered, then buried her under a pile of rocks. That seems very dark to me."

Silas looked at Jael. "What is your name, dear?"

"Jael," she said flatly.

"Jael. What a unique name. And what power do you have? Show me your wrist."

Jael glanced at her team and held her arm up. She made her bands show, along with the symbol of her gifting.

"Another Lumos. How fascinating. Please, step away from your friends and go over there."

Jael met Silas' eyes as she walked to where he had pointed.

"Jael, you buried someone under a heap of stone. How unsavory."

"And destroying Portfield Manor and Raven was a favor to us? Save me your hypocritical monologs."

"Ohh, spicy," said Silas. "Alright then, I can cut to the chase." Silas dumbed down his speech as if addressing a child. "Jael, what you did to Kyla was quite nasty, and there is something she would like to say to you."

Kyla fired two purple blasts into Jael's stomach, causing her to double over onto her knees. She then sprinted over and kicked her with a glowing foot, using a burst to enhance the attack. Jael was lifted from her hands and knees, toppling onto her side. It was evident that she wanted to cry out in pain, but she clenched her jaw and steadied her gaze.

"It's best if you just get it all out. The worst thing you could do in a situation like this is to bottle it up inside," said Silas, snickering at his own wit.

Chase's eyes begged Cavaness to think of something. In a very Cavaness-esque way, he kept eye contact for a moment, then calmly looked away. Chase looked relieved.

Adrian continued to hold Marcio up by the arm, but he was slouching even more now. His skin was clammy, and his eyes were becoming increasingly unfocused. His breathing was shallow and rapid.

"We've got to get you help. Stay with me," said Adrian, firmly patting Marcio's cheek.

"No, we need to stop this. . . to stop them," replied Marcio in slurs. "He will toy with her like a cat with a trapped mouse until he gets bored. Then they will kill her."

"That was quite the load you dumped on me," said Kyla.

A vaporous horseshoe flung from her palm, hooking around Jael's neck and pinning it to the stone slab like a choke collar. Two more pinned her hands to the floor beside her head.

"I didn't know if I would get out of there. I bet that's what your friends felt as they suffocated under the remains of your precious outpost."

Jael fought against her bonds, but she had no room for leverage.

"I would like to return the favor. I should let the ground beneath you crumble, but I want to see your face. I want to see the life drain from your eyes."

Kyla licked her lips in a twisted expression of anticipation.

"How about a few minutes of a constant surge? That should satisfy."

Silas commanded the others to ready their powers to

attack Chase and Cavaness should they try to intervene. He, too, held up the tip of his cane, almost as a taunt.

"Please, just give me a reason," Silas said to Cavaness.

Kyla reared back and launched a wave of dark energy. Jael writhed and squirmed. Her eyes clenched, and her fists shook violently under the bonds. She tried not to scream, but eventually, she cried out.

The glow of Kyla's attack caused shadows to dance at odd angles over her expression, making her seem outright monstrous. While Kyla was exacting her revenge, Marcio leaned into Adrian.

"Get them to safety at all costs. It has been an honor serving with you, brother."

Marcio shoved Adrian to the floor. He took a deep breath and stretched out his hands to command the waterfall to spew inward, flooding the cavern and almost taking Kyla's legs from under her. She stumbled and stopped the surge. Jael took a deep breath as she disappeared under the sheets of rushing water.

Marcio sprinted toward Kyla and Silas. Kyla was too distracted by the water, but Silas had enough awareness to understand what was happening. Marcio opened his arms to tackle Kyla, but just before he reached her, Silas grabbed her by the arm and flung her to the side, replacing her with the man to his right.

Marcio wrapped him up and continued his sprint until they both disappeared behind the waterfall.

"Marcio!" screamed Adrian.

Chase searched and found Jael's shadow under the water's surface and dove toward her. He felt for her under the water until he grabbed a fist, which was fighting against Kyla's formed cuffs. Chase gripped the cuff around her neck and fired a burst into it. The cuff crumbled and disintegrated. Cavaness fired a pulse, which made the floor underneath Jael quake and splinter, freeing her hands.

In a similar style to Marcio, Adrian held his hands out to

command the water. This time, Kyla was able to anticipate. She saw the liquid tendrils reach out from the water around them, so she grabbed the Snype to her left and threw him in the path of Adrian's attack.

Silas reached into his satchel and retrieved a laptop-sized trans. He held it to Kyla's hand, allowing her to travel through.

"Until next time," said Silas to Cavaness.

Cavaness tried to fire a burst at him, but Silas had already placed his fingers into the wooden divots beside the glass and pushed his thumb to its center, taking the mirror with him. The yellow blast of light cut through the vapor, still in the shape of Silas's body.

After seeing that Jael was freed, Adrian ran to the edge of the waterfall and commanded it to part in the center like curtains, allowing him to search for Marcio. He could see the white water crashing against the crags below but saw no sign of Marcio or the man he took with him.

Jael continued to cough up water. Chase had her in his arms, pounding her back to get the water out of her lungs. As she regained her composure, she wrapped her trembling arms around Chase and held tight.

36

"Graham, you and I have not had much time to spend together since the final adoption," said Kel, reclining in one of the wingback chairs. "What do you think of all this. . . the missions and the training, I mean?"

Graham sat in the other chair, sipping on more sugar tea.

"I think we're lucky. Life at Greenwood has seemed so meaningless compared to all this. And look at what I have now. What we have."

Kel leaned in. "And what do we have?"

"We have a family and a reason to protect it. That means a lot more to me than having superpowers."

"Yeah, we are family, aren't we? It still seems a little strange to say. I mean, before I had Ailey, but now. . ." Kel paused and cleared her throat. "Now, I have more than just her. Do you know what I mean?"

"Sure, it means you have all of us now."

Kel deflected her gaze and sunk back into her chair, seemingly disappointed by his answer, and Graham noticed. He wondered why that would have been a bad answer. *It's true. We have an entire family now. Me, Damien, Alex. . . oh, wait a second.* Graham's cheeks grew red very fast.

"I, um. . . we have each other," Graham stammered in a terrible attempt to rebound.

Kel smiled. "We will always have each other, right? No matter what?"

Graham's heart raced. "Sure. No matter what."

"Graham, I don't know what's going to happen in the next few days, weeks, or however long this battle is going to last. I want to be ready to fight, and I want you to be ready too, but I am scared of what could happen when we are ready."

"I feel the same way, but after learning all I have from Alex, I don't think he'll let us get in over our heads. Plus, you know that if I can help it, I won't let anything happen to you or the others."

"I know you won't, but it may not always be up to you," said Kel, placing a hand on Graham's. "But, something tells me that Alex will prepare you the best he can. And remember that no matter what, I will always have your back."

Graham stared at her hand on his long enough to make it awkward, but Kel didn't seem to mind. He looked at her and smiled. She smiled back. As Graham began to speak, however, Alex appeared behind him.

"Graham, I need to see you in the training room."

Kel quickly pulled her hand away, bit her lip, and smirked. Graham sat in disbelief at Alex's poor timing, wanting nothing more than to keep Kel's hand on his.

"Yes, sir."

Alex looked at Kel and smiled.

Graham followed Alex into the center of the training room. Alex turned to face him.

"Graham, everyone up until now has been able to hone and develop their specific gifting except you. This has allowed them to level up nearly to the point of deployment, and now it is time to focus on getting you to the same place. I have a hunch that I need to confirm but to do so; I need to ask you to do something that will make you very uncomfortable."

"Um, okay. What is it?"

I need you to go against your natural inclinations and trust me, though you may fear the worst. I need you to expend yourself as you did in the cavern," said Alex. "To release the fullness of your energy, here and now."

Graham was stunned. "But I don't know how I broke loose, and besides, didn't you say it nearly killed me?"

"Yes, it came quite close to destroying you and everyone else, but I was not there to help. Your gifting is the magnitude of your power. Fortunately, this is a power that can both destroy and sustain. Eventually, you will go out into the real world and fight, but you must be able to harness your strength and confidently hold the reins. I can help you do that. There is more to your power than just its strength, but you must unleash it as you did in the cavern before I can know for sure.

"Alex, you know I would do anything if it meant helping you and the team, but I don't know if I can do what you're asking me to do right now."

"All you need to do is trust me. Follow my instructions and have faith. I know you can do that, and remember that these walls will absorb your power, even at your level."

Graham felt as though a rock had sunk into his stomach. The last thing he wanted to do was go back into a coma for another three days or more. He gritted his teeth. His heart wanted to say no, but his obedience to Alex overruled his internal desire. Meanwhile, Branson entered the room.

"I'll try."

"Alright. Branson, please bring in Kel."

Graham's eyes darted toward the door.

"What? No."

"Yes, Graham. She needs to be a part of this. I promise you that no harm will come to her."

"But what if you're wrong? What if you can't control me? It'll be like my parents all over again."

Kel entered and quickly noticed Graham's panicked expression.

"It's okay, Graham. Alex told me what he's trying to do, and I told him I'm willing to help."

"But you could get hurt! I could accidentally kill you!"

"You won't, and besides, this is my decision. We are together, no matter what, right?"

Graham began to feel like a dog being backed into a corner, and he hated it. Branson closed the door and approached Graham with a serious look of intent.

"Stop. Why are you looking at me like that, Branson? What's going on?"

Alex stood with his hands clasped behind his back, staring at Graham, expressionless.

Graham was shaking. He could not process what Alex was trying to do but felt that Alex was somehow creating his growing panic. Graham's breathing became shallow, feeling his heightened blood pressure pulse behind his eyes.

"I said stop!" Graham said to Branson.

Alex spoke softly. "Don't hold it back, Graham. Your power is reactionary. React."

Alex nodded at Kel, who quickly crumpled to her knees and began to scream at the top of her lungs.

Branson kept his pace, walking in between Graham and Kel. He held up both hands and fired a surge at Graham.

Graham dove out of the way. "STOP! Alex, tell them to

stop!" screamed Graham.

Graham could hear Alex's voice in his mind. "*React. Trust me.*"

Just then, Damien and Ailey burst through the door in a panic. They looked as though they were being chased. They started screaming just as loud as Kel.

"Just react," Alex whispered again in Graham's mind. Graham held his hands to his ears. He wanted to shut down, but he couldn't. He couldn't do anything in the confusion of what was happening.

"React!"

Branson pulled his glowing hands to his chest and fired another surge. The onslaught of panic overtook him. Graham screamed even louder than Kel, his fists clenched at his side. His arms were so tense that he felt his biceps would rip out of his skin. Without thinking, Graham exploded in an inferno of energy. Branson's surge was quickly absorbed by it. The emission would have encapsulated them all, but the instant Graham released his energy, Alex caught and contained the raw power in a five-foot perimeter around Graham.

Alex held both hands out from a distance, seemingly molding the blast around Graham, holding it in place to protect the others.

Kel stopped her wailing, eyes wide in awe of the spectacle before her. Graham was completely engulfed in raw energy. His eyes were glowing embers. Even Branson seemed like this was something no one had ever witnessed.

Alex moved his hands to command and send pulses of Graham's energy back through his body, infusing him with the strength to endure the stresses it was putting on him. Graham felt a sturdy balance of the inward force feeding him and the outward force pressing against him.

"Do you feel it, Graham? Can you feel the balance of power? That is how you control it and harness it."

He could hear Alex speak but could not see his mouth

moving.

Alex slowly relaxed his hands and allowed Graham to assume more control of what was happening until only Graham was holding his own power at bay. He stood in a mixture of intense yellow and orange fire as it swirled around him like a hurricane.

Once Alex could fully retract his protection, he took hold of a pipe and hurled it at Graham.

In reaction, Graham held his hand up and fired a blast, which hit the pipe and did two things. First, the pipe blew into shreds. The second thing confirmed Alex's suspicions. As the glow wore off, the small pieces of pipe remained suspended in the air, rotating slowly as if gravity no longer affected them.

Alex quickly retrieved a chair and threw it at Graham.

Graham held his hand up again to attack.

"Surge this time, Graham, and don't stop."

Graham changed his position and connected his hands, firing a steady stream of energy at the chair, which blew apart instantly. As the surge continued, a small, vertical line appeared in mid-air, about the length of a pencil, opening up like a tear in a garment. The tear slowly grew wider and longer as the power continued to flow until Alex was satisfied with the result.

"Perfect, Graham. That is enough. You can stop."

Graham disconnected his palms and ceased fire, but he still felt like a fully charged battery.

"Now, breathe. Let the inward power overtake the external and allow it to dissipate," said Alex's disembodied voice inside Graham's head.

He struggled to adjust the power levels, not wanting the exhilaration to end. He wanted to feel this way all the time.

"I know it feels good, Graham, but it is time to stop. You must relinquish, or it will master you. You must master *it*."

Graham stood still, allowing the power to continue to flow. He couldn't let go.

"Graham, it's over. You can stop now."

It took him a moment to realize that it was no longer Alex who was speaking. Graham looked to his left and saw Kel standing there, asking him to stop. As his focus shifted, the power began to fade.

Damien stood stone-faced. "Wha. . ."

"Well done, Graham, well done! How do you feel?" Alex asked.

"I feel. . . everything. Confused, angry, happy, excited."

"And did you get a feel for how to consume your own power to counterbalance the strain?"

"Yes, I think so."

"So, what now? We get Graham in front of Silas and that Kaiser guy and let him blow his top?" asked Damien.

"Not exactly, Damien. Further development is needed before we get to that *Kaiser guy*."

Kel elbowed Damien in the ribs. "Really? You are seriously an idiot."

"What? That was a legit question."

"To answer your question, Damien, now we wait for your power level assessments and the return of our teammates. Graham, do you need any other questions answered?"

"Yes, what just happened?"

"Your team agreed to help their leader lead. They acted at my request to force you into another energy release and to great success, I might add."

Graham looked at the others, who were happily guilty, especially Damien.

Alex waved the kids back out of the room. Kel squeezed Graham's hand before departing. "I knew you could."

Graham blushed.

Graham stayed for a while longer to talk to Alex about his

experiment. A nagging question remained in his head after a full explanation of Alex's suspicions. He turned back around to find Alex, who was about to walk out the door.

"Alex, your brother, or whoever he is. . . you have mentioned before that Kaiser is not his real name."

"No, that's the name his followers have given him, and unfortunately, it's one that the Council has also adopted."

"So, he has a given name, just as yours is Alexander."

"Yes, he does, though no one has spoken it for a long time. He has his own way of adapting it to remain hidden in plain sight over the centuries. Long ago, others thought he would become more powerful if you spoke his name, so they simply did not say it. I suppose the tradition has continued."

"Will it?"

"Speaking one's name neither empowers nor disables. Their real fear is acknowledging his true nature as history has shown him to be. In the beginning, his name had the connotation of being a bold and regal steward, but as he grew more evil and vile, his nature changed the meaning."

"Then, can I ask what his name is?"

Alex nodded.

"I am glad you are not timid to ask or mention it aloud."

Alex held eye contact with Graham.

"Many of his followers today likely know him only as Kaiser, but in the beginning, his name was Bale."

37

ALBATROSS

ALBATROSS OUTPOST
Remote Jungle- Argentina

Adrian could not pull himself from the edge of the falls. He stood searching for any sign that his friend and co-worker was still alive, but he could see no such evidence. The rapids below looked as they always had.

Jael kept a tight grip on Chase, coughing in between breaths. Chase rubbed her back, unable to offer any words of comfort, but Jael did not seem to mind.

Cavaness went to console Adrian. He stood beside him, placing his hands on his hips and looking out from the gap in the falls.

"That was a courageous thing he did. It probably saved

Jael's life."

"Yes, he was like that, always making split-second decisions in the heat of the moment, without regard for his own wellbeing."

"Not seeing him might be a good thing. Maybe he made it to the bank and retreated into the forest," said Cavaness.

"Or maybe the current pinned him under its mighty hand. But it's pointless to speculate, though I thank you for the sentiment. Our people downstream will know eventually, one way or the other."

"You have a network downstream? How many?"

"A few hundred scattered over about twenty miles. They're probably wondering why we sent them some Vics earlier today. I should make contact and provide updates while you gather your team. I can get you all some dry clothes as well."

Adrian allowed the water to fall back to its natural flow and turned to go inside. As he passed Cavaness, he laid a gentle hand on his cannonball-sized shoulder.

"Thank you. . . Thank you and your team for coming to our aid and salvaging Albatross. I doubt I would have seen the end of this day had you not come."

"I don't think we salvaged much," said Chase, looking around the cavern.

"Castles and kingdoms can always be rebuilt," said Adrian.

"Or sometimes, they need to be demolished and started over," said Chase to Jael.

Jael remained emotionless.

"Come on, let's get you up. You'll probably feel better if you walk around," said Chase.

Jael used Chase as a crutch as they all re-entered the great hall of Albatross. As the others continued, Jael stopped and stared at the floor.

"Chase, I owe you an apology."

"What for?"

"If you knew me. . . the me before the attack on Raven, you would have met a very different person than you did today. I'm not a person who usually holds such anger and revenge."

"You can't let one day define who you are, whether it was the day Raven fell or today."

"I know, but I'm a Lumos. I should have known better. I do know better. I have advised people against situations just like this."

"It's a little different when your emotions take over. Give yourself a little grace. That is what the matron of my old orphanage used to tell me."

"She seems pretty wise." Jael looked up at Chase as they descended the stairs of the great hall. "I'll work on forgiving myself as long as you do."

"Deal. Just don't give Kyla that kind of power over you."

"I'll try, but I cannot promise to remain steadfast when I see her. It takes over me. For now, I'll try to make it down the stairs."

Chase let go of her waist. Jael slipped her arm from around his shoulders and grabbed the stone railing. Taking one slow step after another, she regained her sense of balance.

"Okay, I think I'm good."

Cavaness walked among the remaining Victus attackers. One began to stir. Without bothering to look, he fired a burst, hitting the man square in the chest. The man did not stir anymore.

Jael looked around for her satchel, forgetting where she had dropped it. Cavaness must have caught her shuffle out of the corner of his eye. He had already grabbed one of the unconscious men by the collar and was dragging him to the middle of the hall.

"It's in the training room," he said, casting the man aside like a ragdoll.

"Adrian, can you show me where your library is?" asked

Chase.

"Certainly. Is there something in particular you're looking for?"

"Yes, it's something Alex wanted."

"Come, I will take you. It appears that Cavaness has everything else under control."

Jael emerged from the other room with the army-tan satchel draped over her shoulder. Cavaness had gone upstairs to retrieve the two men, one over each shoulder, carrying them easily as if carrying a couple of pillows and setting them down next to the others.

Jael took to a knee and retrieved a mirror from the bag. She held it up and placed it against the palm of the first man, who vanished in a purplish mist. She repeated the process until all the remaining attackers were gone.

"Where do they go, anyway?" asked Jael.

"It is a type of prison. Alex designed it to hold enemy combatants until he could speak with them one-on-one. As I'm sure you can imagine, he's good at persuasion. Those that refuse are relieved of their abilities and deactivated."

"Deactivated? Is that even possible?"

"Anything is possible."

Jael exhaled heavily and put a hand to her head.

"You okay?"

"Yeah, I think so. I'll be fine. I just need to rest."

"Let's set the outpost trans and get you back to Falcon."

Chase and Adrian met Jael and Cavaness in the hallway and maneuvered through several hallways until they reached a vaulted room with dozens of transit mirrors. There were fewer than Falcon, but it was still a nice collection. What would have previously been a majestic scene had now turned into a depressing display of sacrifice. The mirrors were in sets, one row just over their heads and then a cascading series of mirrors like tree roots reaching down toward the ground. Every mirror was broken, having been struck in the center of the glass, leaving them in fragments. Adrian noticed their curiosity.

"Fascinating and heart-breaking, isn't it? That is. . . it was our entire network. The single trans at the top was our country hub. The rest are the outlying facilities throughout the country and beyond."

Adrian traced the edge of a mirror with his fingertips, his tone grim and despondent.

"Did Victus do this?" asked Chase.

"Victus? Heavens, no. They would have used our network to destroy everything and everyone. No. Marcio and I destroyed these as soon as we knew of their arrival. We could not let Victus leverage our communications to steal, kill, and destroy. To our dismay, we even had to break our tie with the other regional offices."

Adrian took them back to the entrance of the room. Hanging near the doorway was a large golden sun, the Aegis Sun, as wide as Cavaness was tall, with a shattered mirror in the center.

"When I broke this, I thought all was lost. We were completely cut off from the outside world, yet you came. Have you ever felt completely void of hope? I pray you never feel that way."

Adrian turned, facing Cavaness.

"How did you know? How did you know we were still alive?"

"We didn't. Alex's best guess was that they wanted to lure us here by holding you captive. Turns out, he was right."

Jael pulled a large trans from the bag and gave it to Cavaness, who removed the broken trans from the wall and replaced it with the newly fashioned one that Alex had created.

"Does this lead to Falcon?"

"Yes. We are replacing all of the old Trans with these. Alex wants to brief you as soon as possible, but first, you must activate it."

Adrian nodded and hovered his palm inches from its

glossy surface. His bands grew bright, with their light swirling toward the center of the glass. Yellow energy filled it like droplets of ink merging on paper until the entire mirror was filled with bright, yellow light. The intensity was subtle at first, but once the trans was filled, the light intensified tenfold, causing everyone to retreat behind the crook of their arms. The blinding light flashed quickly before absorbing into the glass like a black hole. A soft ripple stretched out to the wooden frame, and Falcon's mirror room appeared in the glass.

Adrian peered inquisitively into the mirror, as did the rest.

"I remember these walls being full of mirrors. Are you sure this is Falcon?"

Chase looked to see well over half the trans missing from the walls. Only dingy outlines remained.

"What? Where are all the mirrors? Did Falcon get attacked while we were out?"

"No, we would have heard," said Cavaness, pointing to Chase's COM unit. "I'm sure Alex will brief us once we're back."

Cavaness clapped an encouraging hand on Adrian's shoulder as the two men shook hands.

"This is not over. Be on guard. Silas will not take this one lying down, nor will Kyla. We bruised their egos, and they *will* retaliate."

"Yes, I imagine they will, but we will be ready when they do. Thank you again, Cavaness, to all of you."

"I hope you find Marcio," said Jael. "He could have survived the fall, especially being an Aquatic."

"Time will tell, and I will keep you updated. Something tells me we will meet again soon."

"I hope so, Adrian. You know, we found another Aquatic just before all this went down," said Chase. "You would be impressed. He's pretty remarkable, especially for being only fifteen."

"Then I should hope to meet the boy very soon and introduce him to his true culture."

Cavaness nodded, then ushered his team through the trans back to Falcon.

"Stay here, Adrian. I'll get Alex as soon as we're through. He's eager to make contact and know you are safe."

"I'll be right here."

Adrian bowed his hand and pounded his chest with his fist and glowing band. Cavaness returned the salute and vanished through the mirror.

Once he was alone, Adrian allowed himself to grieve for his friend. His breathing was rapid but rhythmic, controlling the apparent storm of anger and sadness inside. He turned to face the network of broken mirrors. Standing tall, he clasped his hands behind his back and closed his eyes in meditative thought. Tears pricked behind his clenched eyes, but he forced them back.

Thin trickles of water that naturally fell down the room's walls intensified and poured harder until the floor started to flood. Water licked the sides of Adrian's feet, but he didn't move. As he caused the increase in the water's flow, the broken mirrors began to detach from the walls. Soon, all the mirrors rained down with the streams of water, crashing to the floor. The walls were stripped bare in seconds, and a shallow sea of water and glass surrounded Adrian.

Adrian detected light emanating from the mirror behind him, the only mirror still in its place. The water flow quickly died down to its natural trickle as Alex spoke.

"Adrian, you could not begin to know how happy I am to see you alive and well."

Adrian turned toward Alex. The water and glass at his feet parted, giving him a dry and clean path to the mirror as Alex continued.

"We have a lot to talk about."

38

HAWKSNEST

HAWKSNEST OUTPOST
Nobbys Headland: Newcastle, Australia

"We need to defuse his power from the shiv," said Corbin.

The purple hue still shimmered from within the stone sliver in the right light. Seth was still unconscious, yet his eyes were half-open. Lucas bent down and held two fingers to Seth's neck.

"He's alive, but I've never seen anyone like this before," said Lucas. "He seems catatonic."

"He'll be like that for a day or two," said Bale. "Don't worry, though. He'll come out of it. Hopefully, in a more secure facility than this."

Lucas stood and dusted the dirt from his black cargo

pants. "Do you believe he was speaking the truth of his brother?"

"Yes," said Bale. "Yes, I believe so. He seemed very convinced."

"That sounds like a Victus tactic to me. Killing one of their own and framing us to rally their community to war."

"Never underestimate Victus and their tenacity," said Bale.

"There truly are no limits to what they will do, are there?" replied Lucas.

"They've played their hand. It's time for us to step up and play ours," said Corbin, forming an orb in his hand.

The orb descended on Seth's shiv and encapsulated it. With a flick of his wrist, the orb flew through the room and crashed into the stone wall, shattering into tiny pebbles. As it disintegrated, purple vapors rolled into the air.

"No object, no infused power," said Corbin. "Dis fella is dangerous. We need to get him outta here. Sonia, hand me the small trans."

Sonia grabbed it from the floor next to the satchel and handed it to him. Corbin placed it in Seth's hand. His band illuminated slightly, like a dull nightlight, and he was gone.

"Alright now. Let's set the new outpost trans and get the heck outta Dodge. Lucas, get topside and give us an assessment. Bale will need to know how to keep this place safe until the rest of the mirrors are set at the other outposts."

Bale looked confused. "Wait, you want me to stay here? No, I can better serve if I'm with you and your team."

"Sorry, my man. We've got to get the rest of the trans set before we leave an outpost unsecured. They must all be connected with the new mirrors before they become fully activated. Until that happens, we must protect them."

"If you need anyone here to guard this place, it's Braxton. I wouldn't know where to begin. You don't want me here as the sentinel," replied Bale. "The only rightful person to guide this ship is its captain."

"And if Braxton agrees, you want to relocate to EagleEye and be with us?" asked Corbin.

"I think we've done pretty well together so far," said Bale.

Corbin glanced at Lucas.

"I'm sorry, Bale, but I don't think we should consider anything until headquarters have fully vetted you," said Lucas.

"About dat. I asked about Bale during my last status update. Alex is aware of who Bale is." Corbin turned to Bale. "Between that and your work here in fighting off the Vics, I'd say you are clear to join us if Braxton agrees to stay."

Corbin then addressed his team. "What do ya think? Should we add a fourth?"

"Why not? He did save me from that shiv," replied Sonia. "And your fighting style ain't half bad."

"Lucas? I'm not gonna do anything without everyone's approval," said Corbin.

Lucas turned to Bale, analyzing him.

"We are a close-knit team. We look out for each other. Are you willing to sacrifice yourself for us?"

"Lucas, I am willing to make any sacrifice necessary for the cause."

"And you understand that we all must be of one mind?" asked Corbin.

"How else are we supposed to operate?" replied Bale. "Every good team member follows a vision just as closely as their leader."

Lucas nodded at Bale's final remark. "In that, you have my approval."

"Let's ease into this. You're fortunate we even have an opening on our team. Let's take dis one step at a time. You're probationary. You've shown your worth just now, but you still have a ways to go. We will review some ground rules when we return home and take a test run. We let one decision lead to the next. You agree?"

"Agreed. I want nothing more than to assist in connecting the outposts."

"Den, let's get this thing placed. Lucas, grab the big one. Bale, show us where the old one is."

Lucas took the new transit mirror, and they all followed Bale down beyond the leadership commons and to the outpost's communication room. The room was deep underground, dark and musty. Since HawksNest was an underground silo, each room had long solar tubes in the ceiling, which provided the necessary light during the daytime. They were well placed to illuminate the expanse of the room, and three additional tubes were strategically placed to highlight the wall holding the outpost trans.

Corbin took the tattered mirror from the wall, careful not to let any broken shards fall from the frame. He laid it down to the side as Lucas mounted Alex's new mirror. Once set, Lucas placed his hand over the carving of the outpost's crest in the frame's crown. His band flashed, and a ripple of light ran over the mirror's surface.

Bale watched Lucas activate the mirror and then walked over to the broken one. He knelt to one knee and surveyed the damage.

Corbin took a COM unit in hand and held it to his mouth. The unit crackled to life.

"Home base, this is Eagle One, over."

Only a few seconds ticked by until Alex replied.

"Eagle One, this is home base. What is your status?"

"Status complete. The facility is secure, and we've set the trans. We've relocated the remaining survivors to EagleEye for medical care and assessments."

Bale stood to his feet at the sound of Alex's voice, staring intently at the COM unit.

"And your team?"

"We're all in good shape, boss. Lucas needs some first aid from a Snype shot to the shoulder, but nothing serious. We'll seal off the room and return to EagleEye to await further instructions."

"How many survivors were found?"

"I got a head count of thirty-seven. I'm unsure of how many were here at the initial attack. I want to say they've all been able to escape, but we do have confirmed casualties. I have personally seen four bodies while searching. What shall we do with the remains?"

Alex appeared in the glass of the Trans. Corbin shifted so he was directly in front of the mirror and tossed the COM unit to Sonia. Bale moved into the shadows, acting busy.

"My heart breaks at this news," said Alex. "We will tend to our dead, but at the right time. Falcon One has also completed its mission. Six of the seven outposts are now secured with the new mirrors in place. The only one remaining is Raven. We must secure it at once. Take your team and go back to EagleEye. Get Lucas back in shape and replenish your supplies. Eric Branson is finishing a tactical map of our approach to Raven. Once it and you are ready, we'll have a briefing and move in."

"Yes, sir. Understood."

"Corbin. I also want a full report on who was sent to attack HawksNest and your assessment of Victus's endgame. Knowing who they sent to destroy the outpost will tell much about their intentions."

Bale continued to rifle through drawers and bookcases, pretending to be helpful, but kept his ear toward the conversation.

"You will have my full report as soon as we return."

"Very good, Corbin, and well done. Please extend my gratitude to Sonia and Lucas as well."

"Thank you, sir," said Lucas, bowing to Alex. "It is my honor and privilege."

"Thank you, Alex," said Sonia.

"Rest up. The biggest challenge is yet to come," said Alex.

"Yes, sir," replied Corbin. "Eagle One, out."

Bale returned to the others once Alex was gone.

"What, no intros for the new guy?"

"Hey, if you want to be recognized, you gotta jump in. What were you doing back there, anyway?" said Corbin.

"Just looking for anything Victus may have left behind. I don't like being idle."

"Whatever you say, baby. Let's get home and get ready for the big one," said Corbin.

Sonia retrieved the trans for EagleEye and propped it against the wall. She went through first, followed by Lucas. Corbin looked back to Bale.

"Take it with you when you go through. You know how?"

"Yes, I know how to take a trans with me to the other side."

"Alright, den. Let's finish dis fight."

Corbin held a hand to the trans and transported to the other side.

Bale looked around the room, fully content. A sinister grin stretched across his face as he exhaled with a twisted sense of pleasure.

"Yes, Corbin. Let's finish it, once and for all."

Bale placed his fingers in the divots of the wood frame, pressed his thumb to the center of the glass, and vanished.

39

FALCON

FALCON HQ
Portfield, Pennsylvania

Alex stood with Cavaness in the training room. It was dimly lit so that they would not be disturbed.

"I've found our leak, and it's not what you or I imagined it would be."

"What happened?" Cavaness said, the anger in his voice apparent.

"It's best if it came straight from the source. Not even he realizes the impact of his secrecy."

"Just tell me, Alex."

"You'll think I've misinterpreted if I tell you. You must see it for yourself. It explains why I could never detect it. Call an immediate group meeting downstairs, and be sure Murphy is the last to know."

"I knew it! That backstabbing–"

"Control yourself, Cavaness," Alex commanded. "Things are not as they appear. Please assemble everyone as I have asked."

"Yes, sir," Canvass said, seething.

Murphy jogged down the stairs to greet the rest of the group circled in the main foyer. Most looked confused, but Cavaness appeared nearly out of control.

"What's going on?" asked Murphy.

Alex stood at the base of the stairs.

"I thought it would be best for you to clear the air," said Alex.

"Clear what air?" Murphy said in an unconvincing tone.

"Stop hiding your actions, Brian. Why would you even make it a secret in the first place?"

Murphy cleared his throat, nervously shifting from side to side.

"Look, I didn't want to burden anyone else with my problems. I can handle it, alright. There's no need for an intervention."

Graham was genuinely confused, along with everyone else in the room.

Cavaness was about to draw blood from his fingernails digging into his palms.

Murphy looked agitated, nervous, and upset about how he was being treated.

"Fine, I used scouts outside of the compound. It's not a big deal. I'm helping a friend with a problem."

Everyone remained still.

"Look, she was reporting threats made against her. I told

her I would help her out. She thinks I work for the police, so I told her I would send out scouts to do some surveillance. I wasn't lying. I did send scouts. . . they just weren't the human kind."

Murphy appeared relaxed, as if this admission was lifting a heavy weight from his shoulders.

"Careless!" screamed Cavaness. "She could track you! Do you think she's innocent? She's working for Victus!"

"Hey, back off! You don't know what you're talking about! She's not activated, which means she's not capable, and besides, even if she was working for them, I never bring my scouts back. We already talked about this. I'm not being careless."

Alex calmly stepped in between the two men.

"She is not just a friend, is she?"

"How do you know that? No, Kyla is my cousin. She doesn't have any other family, so–"

"Kyla?" shouted Jael. "She nearly killed us all!"

Murphy shook his head in disbelief.

"Whoa, now. Stop. Just stop right there! You must be talking about someone else. The Kyla I know is hard-headed and a pain to deal with sometimes, but she's no killer."

Alex again intervened. "Did you check on her while the children were going through the catalyst process?"

"What?"

"Did you send scouts to her house while Graham and the others were going through the catalyst process?"

"I. . . wha. . . yes, I did. I had some time on the rooftop just after they'd fled the warehouse. What does that matter?"

Alex slumped his shoulders. "Unfortunately, it means everything, Brian. Her cry for help was a ruse to find our location."

"But I didn't allow the scout to return. I don't see the problem."

"That's because you didn't think your own blood would betray you. It is rare, but when blood relatives connect orbs, they can see through each other's eyes. Kyla is a very skilled Former who could latch onto your scout undetected and use the blood connection to see exactly where we were." Alex sighed. "Your position on the rooftop gave her enough information to find us."

The color in Murphy's face drained.

Cavaness charged him in a rage. He grabbed Murphy by the collar, slammed him into the closest wall, and punched a hole in the sheetrock beside his head, sinking his arm halfway up his forearm. He pulled it out and punched a half-dozen more holes while grunting in a rage.

"People died, Brian! Good people! What were you thinking? Or do you even think anymore?"

Murphy barely flinched under Cavaness' anger. He stood with weak knees as the color continued draining from his skin. Cavaness' grip on his throat was the only thing holding him up now. The rest of the team, even Jael, were speechless.

"Cavaness, enough. Brian was betrayed," said Alex. He then turned to address Murphy. "How long have you been looking out for her?"

Murphy tried to answer, but as he opened his mouth to speak, he began to dry heave. He pushed Cavaness' hand away, fell to his knees, and threw up on the floor. His arms were rubber, and he nearly fell into the vomit pooling around his hands.

Cavaness pulled his fist out of the drywall, making bits of sheetrock fall to the floor. Panting heavily, he turned and waited for an answer.

After a few more dry heaves, Murphy was able to mumble his answer as tears pooled around the veins bulging under his eyes.

"For about six or seven months."

"Then it's safe to say she's been using the Former's blood connection for that long, feeding intel back to the others."

"Wha. . . what have I done?" Murphy said. He could not

keep his composure. He remained on all fours, shaking and weeping bitterly.

"I. . . I did this. I did this," he mumbled in anguish.

"You should not have hidden your actions, Brian. We don't have secrets here, but in the end, you're not to blame," said Alex. "I know you and understand that you are not one to turn your back on us. This betrayal is something that was masterminded by Bale and tested by Kyla. You were simply their lab rat."

Cavaness dusted off his arm. His demeanor completely changed as he watched Murphy grieve.

He knelt beside Murphy and put a hand on his back. "Come," said Cavaness. He helped him to his feet, wrapped Murphy's arm around his shoulders, and took him into the next room.

Kel and Ailey were both teary-eyed, clearly sympathetic to Murphy's position. Jael held a good poker face.

"Are you okay?" asked Alex.

Jael slid her thumb along her cheek to remove a tear.

"No, I don't think I am. How can I look at him? He's related to the woman who destroyed everything I cared about."

"Your feelings are understandable, but we cannot control who we're related to, nor what they decide to do with their lives. I'm not saying it will be easy to forgive Brian, but I hope you can empathize with his brokenness. His detest for Kyla now matches your own."

Jael's expression closed off. Her eyes narrowed.

"Even still," said Jael, ice-like.

"The decision is yours to make," said Alex in a tone of finality.

Jael nodded and left the room. Graham joined Damien and the others. They stood together in silence. How do you say anything after that? Murphy unknowingly helped Victus kill thousands of Aegis members. Graham felt terrible for him and didn't know how Murphy would make it through. How could a man live with something like that?

"Do you think he will be okay?" signed Ailey.

"I don't think he'll ever be the same," replied Kel. "I don't think anyone could."

"At least he wasn't one of them," said Damien. "I know he has it rough, but I'm glad he's still one of us."

"He's hardly anything now," said Graham, hearing Murphy's uncontrolled wailing from the other room. "I don't think he'll be able to do anything for a while. I don't see any way he could go to Raven, for sure."

"I think it best to call it an evening," said Alex. "When Brian comes back out, he will need time alone."

"Of course," said Kel. They all started to walk down the hall toward their rooms.

"Graham, I need you to stay for a moment."

"Yes, sir."

Alex waited for the others to turn the corner before continuing.

"Tell me what you're thinking right now."

"About Murphy?"

"Yes. How does this make you feel?"

"I feel really bad for him. I think he's pretty messed up after that. I don't think he meant for any of this to happen."

"And what if he did mean to?"

"I'm not sure I follow."

"What if Brian did betray us all? What would you do if he stood here as a guilty man?"

This question caught Graham off guard. Why bother speculating? The question made him a bit uncomfortable, but since Alex asked, he allowed himself to think it through.

"Let me ask it a different way. If Kyla was standing here, what would you do?"

That's something he could answer without much thought.

"I would want her to suffer the same fate as the people she killed. I definitely wouldn't let her escape."

Alex searched Graham's eyes, which made Graham feel

very exposed.

"Would you really be willing to bring judgment on someone without all the facts? What if you thought Murphy was guilty? Would you condemn him to death as well?"

Graham was speechless. This was the first time he'd felt reprimanded.

"Bale sees this world as his chessboard and has mastered using the pieces. You have not been given the authority to judge the pieces. Graham, this is extremely important. You must use discernment and look beneath the surface to see things as they truly are. This is Bale. It always is. He is moving the pieces. Though we fight physically against his people, our ultimate battle is against him— The game's mastermind. Do you understand what I am saying?"

"But Kyla is responsible for people dying. She's the one who wants destruction. How can you tell me not to want her punished?"

"I'm not telling you how to feel, Graham, but I am trying to teach you how to react. Remember what I told you when your power was finally revealed. You have to keep yourself pure. Wanting someone dead, though their actions may deserve it, will corrupt you. You will never have all the details. It's a lure Bale will pull you in with. This very well could be the biggest struggle you will ever face, more than facing physical harm, but you must take this to heart. You must see Victus combatants as blinded pawns instead of the main enemy. You never know how they might change with the right motivation. You must see Bale's strategy and use it to your benefit."

"I don't know if that's possible. It feels like proper justice that someone like that should be punished for their evil actions."

"Make no mistake. Kyla will be punished for her actions, but remember that ultimate justice is not yours to deliver. Bale will test your resolve, and you have the power to sway the course of humanity by the way you react. That level of responsibility comes with the gift you have been given."

40

FALCON HQ
Portfield, Pennsylvania

Chase stuck his head through the door to Graham's room.

"You've got ten minutes, little bro."

"Okay, I'll be there. Hey, how's Murphy doing?"

Chase cracked open the door a little more and stepped into the room.

"He hasn't come out all night. I don't think he's doing well at all."

"Can I do anything to help?"

"Right now, the best thing is to give him some space when he wants it and encouragement when he decides he needs it."

Chase began to close the door, but Graham stopped him.

"Chase? You came face to face with Kyla, right?"

"Yes."

"If you had the chance to make sure she didn't hurt any more people, wouldn't you take it?"

"Do you mean, would I kill her if I had the opportunity?"

"If it meant protecting our own."

"That's a very situational question. Would I want her dead? Absolutely. She's a monster, but I've been doing this long enough to know that Bale is very persuasive. I would make sure she was captured and neutralized, but to kill her would be a mistake in the long run."

Graham stared at Chase.

"I don't get it. Why shouldn't she die? She killed thousands."

"You mean Bale killed thousands through her. That's an important distinction."

"What?"

"Graham, I get it, and I felt the exact same way you do now about other Victus members. Really, I understand. I know what Alex said to you, and he is right. It takes time for that to sink in, but trust me and trust him. It's the right mindset and one you must have."

"But why do I have to? It seems so unjust."

"We are protectors, not judges. Many bad people can turn it around once they are out from under Bale's influence. You even know one of them."

"What? Who?"

"If you had been around twenty years ago and acted on the way you feel right now, you would have killed Cavaness."

"What! Cavaness was one of them?"

"You think those scars on his wrist were from fights? No, those came from removing his Victus bands."

Graham thought Murphy's situation was a curveball, but Cavaness? A former bad guy?

"We can talk later. We have to get downstairs. You don't need to worry about Cavaness now. He is Aegis to his core. Finish up, and I'll meet you in the den."

"It's what I would do," said Branson. "Tactically, it's the best option."

"Then we must act quick," replied Cavaness.

Graham came downstairs and slipped in beside Damien. Everyone was gathered in the large den, listening to Branson's proposal.

"What are we doing quickly?"

"Taking back the last outpost," whispered Damien. "All of us."

"You mean we are going too?" said Graham excitedly.

"He didn't come right out and say it, but it looks that way."

"Tell me how you would proceed," said Alex.

If we're using everyone, we should split into three groups and stage our approach so we remain undetected as we surround from all sides. We have enough COM equipment to space out around Raven and stay in contact with one another. We must take each section in succession to throw them off guard."

"I agree," said Alex. "I want you all to understand that this is the last chance Victus will have to thwart our efforts and gain access to our network. This will not just be a fight. It will be a full-scale attack to take control. I fully expect them to funnel us into the outpost to surround us. We must allow them to believe they are succeeding and use the element of surprise from within Raven. Not only to catch them off guard but also to protect the lives of the civilians on the outside. Remember, Raven is in the heart of Brussels, and the casualty rate will be very high if our war occurs on the streets."

"I've set out the necessary COM units for everyone in the training room. We are on channel three," said Branson.

"We must loop Corbin in on this assault. He still has an important role to play in this," said Alex. "He has taken the survivors of HawksNest back to EagleEye. He has reconnected his new trans. We can communicate and provide the necessary equipment from there. Also, there will no longer be a need for code names. All communication will flow through each team leader. Corbin will lead his team. Chase will remain with Graham, but Graham is to remain as the team leader. Are you willing to take that responsibility, Graham?"

Graham looked around nervously at all the seasoned veterans. *You want me to lead a team into a full-scale attack and operate on the same level as these people?*

"If that is what you want me to do, then I will do it." *Crap! We're dead. Why did I say that? Take it back.* Graham shot a panicked look at Chase, who simply winked at him confidently. Graham adjusted himself and refocused back on Alex.

"Are you sure I'm ready? Did we all reach level ten in our training?"

"Indeed you have. That is the assessment from your teachers as well as myself. Normally, we would celebrate, but given the circumstances, we must applaud your achievements by immediately testing them. I'm confident you and your team are ready for what lies ahead. Should anything go wrong, Chase will be there as support. I will take Cavaness with me. Eric— you and Jael will go with Brian in the lead."

"Murphy? Forgive me, Alex, but he is in no position to run point!" said Jael, much more bluntly than she anticipated.

"Brian is a victim just as you were, Jael. He is broken and shamed, and this is the quickest way to restore him. He will happily give his life before he makes the same mistake again."

"But I. . . I don't think I can work with him."

"I am not just pairing you two together for his sake. I trust you both can do the right thing."

Branson stepped in. "Are you certain he will even agree to go?"

"Let me take care of Brian."

"Of course."

"I will go to him now. I need you to go upstairs and get Corbin and his team equipped and brought up to speed." Alex looked down at the black tactical watch on Branson's wrist. "We leave in one hour."

"Yes, sir."

"Everyone, we will meet back in this room at sixteen hundred hours to review our plans. Make your final preparations."

41

FALCON

Alex knocked a few times. After no reply, he did so again –
nothing. He decided not to knock a third time but enter as if
he had permission. The door cracked open to reveal Murphy
sitting in a wingback chair at the far corner of the room,
looking very much like Abraham on the Lincoln Memorial
with his arms resting on the high arms of the chair. He did
not acknowledge Alex's entrance. His eyes remained fixed
on the glass of the French doors.

Alex, in turn, made no effort to talk to Murphy. He
walked past the scattered furniture and personal effects,
knowing that Murphy had torn his room apart in despair,

and stood in front of the same glass door. He stuck his hands in his pockets and decided to simply be in the room with Murphy.

"I heard a lot of the chatter over the radio. Sounds like you had your hands full over there," said Branson.

The vaporous after-effects of traveling through the mirror still lingered around Corbin's legs.

"Yeah, well, dose fools almost had us. Dat outpost was in a good' n strategic location. Dey musta cased dat place in a hurry cause they knew deir way around the inside pretty well."

"Even so, we took it back in the end. Well done on the op."

"Much obliged."

Branson retrieved the duffle bag resting at his feet and handed it to Corbin.

"Here's all the gear for Raven. You have COM units, sketched tactical entry points, and protective training gear. With you and Murphy providing aerial views, we can launch a multi-staged attack successfully. We'll take the least guarded entrance first, followed by the second and third, making our way to the facility's center. Can your scouts cut through the brick and plaster enough to lead us in?"

"No problem on the visual. What you've got ta worry 'bout are the Snypes and other Formers taking care of long-range surveillance. After takin' back Albatross and HawksNest, you know dey gonna be ready for us now."

"They may have the place covered, but we have Jael. She's already provided sketches of the most concealed routes leading up to Raven. Your suggested route is already in your bag. The plan is to leave our outpost at sixteen hundred hours. From there, we will all be on channel three, giving a radio check every fifteen minutes on our current

ETA until we're all in position."

Branson reached over, took a small mirror from the desk, and handed it to Corbin.

"We will be in three teams, each going to a different location. You, Sonia, and Lucas will use this trans and the routing provided by Jael. We will do the same with ours. I heard you were able to bring survivors back to EagleEye. Is there anyone strong and experienced enough to go with you?"

Corbin glanced back at the trans to EagleEye. "We rescued a handful, yeah." Corbin thought for a moment. "Maybe one or two could help, but I'm still weighing my options."

"It's your call. I put two extra units in the bag. We need to know who we are dealing with on this op. Once you make up your mind, tell us your final count. All communication will flow through the team lead. That's you, Cavaness, Murphy, and Graham."

"Whoa, now. Graham? You tellin' me you plan to let a kid lead an op like dis?"

"Alex's orders. Graham is the game changer and needs to develop as quickly as possible. He will have Chase by his side, but yes, he's the team lead."

Corbin appeared skeptical but spoke from his relaxed, laid-back nature.

"Alright, den. If Alex said it, we'll go with it."

"We're set then. I'll have my COM in place in ten minutes. Should you have any more questions, just ask."

"I got it, my man. See you on the other side."

Murphy broke the silence first.

"You're wasting your time, Alex." A long pause followed. "I know you mean well, but I'm done."

Alex remained still and silent.

"There has been so much destruction and death, all because of me. I helped usher in the apocalypse, Alex. Bale has the upper hand because of me. You might as well let me go into Raven as bait. That's all I'm good for now."

Murphy looked at Alex for any sign of accepting his words, but he remained emotionless. Murphy got up out of his chair and stood in front of Alex.

"You see that, right? No one will trust me now. I'm forever written in the pages of Aegis history as the one who opened the door for Bale's rule. Alex. . . I couldn't even see that Kyla was activated! You might as well remove these bands and throw me back into the normal world!"

Alex allowed Murphy to vent, expressing the frustration, pain, and despair of his ignorant actions. Once Murphy had finished his woeful rant, Alex turned to him and spoke with authority.

"You are who I say you are, and history will see you as such. Bale should never be underestimated, but do you not think I carry as much power as he does?"

Alex paused for an answer.

"Answer me, Brian. Your identity is not in your actions, your successes or failures. I am tasked with humanity's safety, and my authority declares your worth. Do you understand what I am telling you?"

"I–"

Alex held his hand out to cause Murphy's band to shine.

"You know the connection those bands give me, correct?"

"Yes."

"So, you understand how I know when is turning against me?"

"Yes."

"Then surely you can understand my vexation over knowing that one of you had given Silas our whereabouts while at the same time knowing that no one from this outpost had betrayed us. I can read your heart, Brian. I can feel your loyalty, and it has not shifted since the day you were activated. To the contrary, it has only strengthened."

Murphy had trouble lifting his eyes to Alex. His shame continued to pull his head downward.

"You may see it that way, and I believe what you're saying, but I don't think the others will see it that way downstairs."

"The level of sorrow you expressed is difficult to fake. I put you on the spot yesterday for a purpose. It was not just to make you understand the truth. It was just as much for them as for you."

"Do you really think everyone, even Jael, will just accept me after this?" Murphy asked in a doubtful tone.

"Some will take more time than others, but I've already set you up as a team lead to take back Raven. They know how I feel about you, and for most of them, that is enough."

The thought of leading a team was enough to bring Murphy's head up.

"You want me. . . to lead the next op? Why?"

Alex lowered his hand and put it back in his pocket.

"Did you hear about the story of the pilot who nearly died in an aerial show?"

"What?"

"Yes, many years ago, a pilot flew with a crew that entertained thousands. One day, the team was scheduled to perform their aerial acrobatics for the people of a town they had visited many times before, only this time, the pilot crashed and nearly died. After investigating the crash, they concluded that the crew member who had fueled the plane before the show had accidentally put the wrong fuel in the tank. As I'm sure you can imagine, the young crewman was devastated by the knowledge that he had almost caused the pilot's death. Do you know what the pilot did?"

"Fired the guy and ensured he never touched another plane?"

"I'm sure he may have felt that way, but actually, he did the exact opposite. He threw his helmet to the young man and told him not to worry about it because he was certain he would not make the same mistake the next day."

"That's a pretty bold move."

"I thought so, but think about it for a moment. How many times do you think that man checked the fuel type each time he filled the tank?"

"Enough to be sure."

"And how many opportunities will you allow Kyla, or anyone else, to pull the wool over your eyes again?"

Murphy's jaw tightened in silence.

"That's why you are the team lead."

Corbin set the bag on the stone slab of EagleEye's strategy room in between Sonia and Lucas. They each pulled out the necessary gear, strapping throat mikes around their necks and stuffing earwigs into their ears.

As Corbin relayed the plan to his team, Bale stepped through the door.

"The rest of the people from HawksNest are still in pretty bad shape. They're having a hard time understanding where or who they are."

Bale took notice of the preparations.

"Where are you all going?"

Corbin continued sifting through the bag. He nodded at Lucas.

"We've only got one outpost left to take back," replied Lucas. "Alex has just instructed us on how to go in."

"Then let me come," said Bale in a controlled tone.

"I don't know 'bout that," replied Corbin. "Ya see, we three work real good as a team. You saw dat back in Aussie land. I said we would take it one step at a time, but this is a colossal step."

"Maybe, but do you really want to be left wondering if I

could have made a difference if the worst happens? I can stay with one of you and learn your tactics, but I think it would be a mistake to not take an able-bodied man with you. If this is the last one, don't you think Victus will do anything in their power to hold onto it?"

"No offense, Bale, but if we were to take anyone else with us, it would be Jack. He's worked with us before. You are better suited to stay here and care for the wounded."

"I disagree," said Sonia. "Bale's power is better suited for this op. Jack is good, but Bale is stronger and more motivated."

Corbin listened to both sides of the conversation. His eyes darted between the three of them.

"The people here still need a leader and caretaker. Jack can be both," said Sonia.

"And I'm sure Bale could be equally as effective," replied Lucas. "Yes, he is motivated by what happened in Australia, but the fact remains that Jack has fought with us before."

"So has Bale, and more recently," replied Sonia. "Having two Formers on one team could give us untold advantages."

Corbin continued listening, but something else caught his eye. He saw Jack at the other end of the room, carrying a tray of food to one of the younger children rescued from HawksNest. The little boy was crying. Jack knelt down, laid the tray next to the boy and put a hand on his shoulder. He was able to get the boy's attention and calmed him enough to be able to whisper into his ear. The boy wiped his tears away with his sleeve, listened intently, and nodded occasionally. Then, to Corbin's surprise, Jack made his band glow and saluted the boy. In turn, the boy got to his feet and did the same, then fell into Jack's arms.

Corbin lingered in the moment, and then shifted back to his team.

"Bale is with us. Sonia is right. Jack's place is here to be with the people. We need tenacity and gall, both of which Bale has. You with me, Lucas?"

"Respectfully, sir, I think this is a mistake," replied Lucas.

"Lucas, use that vision of yours to see into the situation. I don't look at just the next step, my man. I look at the coming months and years and make my judgment. I want you to do the same. Bale is stronger and offers more than Jack can, and speakin' of– look over there. Jack can serve better here. He's already built relationships with these people."

Lucas looked across the room to see the young boy still wrapped up in Jack's arms, one hand on the back of his head and one rubbing his back in comforting circles. The boy's anguish melted away in the tenderness of Jack's care.

"Alright. You want my trust, sir, and you will have it."

"Music to my ears, my man. Let's get ready for the grand finale."

42

Into The Heart of Europe

FALCON HQ
Portfield, Pennsylvania

The clock on the wall counted down the final minutes to the siege. Graham's heart was pounding out of his chest. The tactical gear was cumbersome, especially with the training clothing underneath. He awkwardly tugged at the band around his throat, which held the small microphones, and twisted the small rubber earpiece in his left ear. Though he wanted to puke, he swallowed hard and looked at his team in forced confidence.

"You guys ready for this?"

"Not really," replied Kel. "Before, it seemed fun, but now, it's all too real."

"I know. I feel the same way, but knowing Alex is coming with us makes it easier. Having a guy on our team that can't die is a big plus."

Graham felt a bit awkward at the silence that followed. He was grateful that his friends believed in him, so in a paltry effort to show his gratitude, he pounded his chest with his fist and bowed slightly to his team. He was even able to cause his band to glow slightly.

Ailey was the first to return the salute, followed by Kel, Damien, and even Chase.

"We are going to be a part of Aegis history tonight," said Graham, his words weightier than he wanted.

"And you are going to help lead us there," added Chase. "I'm proud of you, little bro."

Alex gathered the three sets of teams, encouraging them and checking for any last-minute needs. He was also dressed in Aegis tactical gear and loose-fitting cargo pants. A wide, thin belt provided a place for the COM units, among other supplies.

"Corbin, radio check. Come in."

"Confirming radio check," crackled Corbin's voice in everyone's earwig. "Hear you loud and clear, Alex."

"Corbin, use your trans and move into Position *A*. Go now and await further instruction."

"Roger dat. Moving in."

Murphy joined the others, looking rather ragged with ruffled hair, pale skin, and dark rings under his eyes.

Graham did not think his heart could beat any harder, or it would literally pound out of his chest. Hearing Corbin's team made things more real than he ever imagined– even more than when they were in the cabin at Catalyst Grove.

"We haven't a moment to lose. Everyone must move swiftly into position around the Grand Place and the large courtyard in front of it. Corbin's trans will position them in the northern quarter. The rest of us will be coming from the east. Since we are all using the same trans from here, we will travel in teams, spaced out by twenty minutes, to avoid suspicion. Murphy, you are to travel to Position B. Cavaness, me to Position C, and Graham's team to Position D."

Alex reached into Graham's bag and removed a folded map.

"Branson has provided each team with a map showing the specified routing. I'll give you a few minutes to review the routing one last time, and then we move in."

Each team huddled together to review their map. A blue, green, and yellow line mapped the route for each team, beginning from St. Michael's Cathedral to surround the nearby square titled 'Grand Place.' Once Alex saw that Graham was finished moving his finger over the highlighted blue path, he asked him to come over.

"Graham, you are the youngest member of Aegis to ever lead a team in a mission of any significant magnitude. Your mind will want to tell you you're too young, inexperienced, and weak to complete such a task. It's human nature to feel this way, so do not let this upset you. When you begin to panic, I want you to remember what I'm about to tell you. Do you understand?"

Graham was shocked at how accurately Alex had just described his feelings.

"Yes, sir. I'm listening."

Alex smiled. "Good. I have led generations of men and women over many centuries. Would you agree that this experience qualifies the accuracy of my judgment?"

"I would say that you would probably know people better than they know themselves."

"Well said. So, in times of doubt, know this. I have called you to a time such as this and have done so in full confidence of who you are. You are equipped for the task because I have said you are. Do you believe this?"

Until this very moment, Graham would have said no, but once Alex spoke, it felt like his words infused him, just like his power did in the training room.

"Oddly, I do, I think."

Alex looked pleased with Graham's reply. He gave Graham a few encouraging pats on the back and walked to the other team. Murphy was scheming while Jael stared a hole through him with crossed arms and a clenched jaw. Despite the scowl, Murphy spoke.

"We have the longest route to the west side of the square. I can keep an eye in the sky. Jael, if I point out any Vics, you can blind them with lights of the surrounding buildings and street lamps. Branson, you will be fairly limited with the electricity, but I'm sure you can get creative."

Jael bit her lip. Murphy glanced up and took notice, as did Alex as he approached.

"Go ahead and say it," said Brian.

"Say what?" replied Jael.

"Whatever you're holding back. You despise me, and I don't blame you. I don't like me right now either, but this can't affect the mission. Not now, and especially not Raven. I am trying to make this right."

Jael turned a hard shoulder to Brian as she teared up.

"I want to forgive you, but I can't. I live in torment every day because of what happened, and you let your cousin start it all."

Alex stood close by, listening.

"Jael, I despise Kyla for what she did, but I didn't know she was even activated. I was trying to protect her, and she used me. She used our blood connection to see through my eyes. You have no idea how violated I feel. . . how used. We are both victims here."

Jael did not reply or make any attempt to reconcile, so Alex moved in.

"It sounds to me that it's not Brian who you need to forgive."

Jael turned to Alex, perplexed.

"What?"

"Before we can forgive other people, we usually have to forgive ourselves first."

Jael's cheeks flushed, and her eyes softened at his remark.

"Jael, you won't forgive yourself for escaping and surviving. Would you rather be among the dead?"

"Why do I deserve to be alive when they died while fighting off Victus? A coward should perish before a warrior does."

"You are alive because you still have a purpose to serve, but you will never be able to fulfill that purpose carrying this burden of guilt. You must drop that yoke and be free to serve. Chasing Kyla nearly got you killed. Don't let your despair do the same."

Jael looked as though her inner parts were trying to escape her body. She took a deep, controlled breath. A tear streaked down her cheek, but a slight smile caught it and diverted it around the corner of her mouth.

"There, now we have some progress," said Alex.

Murphy clapped Jael's shoulders and looked into her eyes.

"I will show you that I'm on your side. Just give me the chance to."

Jael peeked up and nodded, wiping the tear from her jawline.

"Okay. I think I can do that."

Alex looked at the clock on the wall.

"In that spirit, Brian, take your team through. We will follow as described earlier. Tell us when you are in position."

"Yes, sir."

Murphy and his team traveled through the mirror, leaving wafts of vapor behind.

After waiting the allotted time, Graham took his team through, followed twenty minutes later by Alex and Cavaness.

The light pouring in from the narrow windows cast eery,

iridescent rays through the remaining vapor, which filled the empty room until Adrian stepped through the door and disrupted the colorful array. He was accompanied by three other men, who began removing all the transit mirrors from the walls. Adrian retrieved the small trans, which the teams had traveled through, and looked into its shiny surface.

"And so the beginning of the end has come."

43

CONVERGENCE

RAVEN OUTPOST
Grand Place, Brussels

Corbin's team wove through the back streets coming from the north quarter of Brussels with impressive speed. After arriving at Rue du Danier, they quickly passed by Hotel Metropole, cutting the corner of Rue de I'Ecuyer and plowing through the surrounding buildings of Les Galeries Royales, arriving at the northern side of the ornate building of Grand Place.

"Corbin in position A." Corbin's voice was rushed and hurried. "No Vics in sight."

"Copy that, Corbin," said Alex. "We are closing in. Stand by and await further instruction."

"Roger that," replied Corbin.

Graham was the first to exit the back room of Saint Michael's Cathedral. As he stepped into the main sanctuary, he was mesmerized by the splendor of the vaulted stone archways scissoring across the ceiling. He followed the arches down to the large bricked columns, each holding a statue of a man on a pedestal. He had never seen such elaborate detail in all his life.

"Stay out of the main aisle and stick to the sides, but act normal," said Chase. "We need to blend in until we can get to the side streets. Now, lead us on."

Graham nodded, trying his best not to get distracted by the Cathedral's beauty. As they exited the side entrance, Graham pulled out the map.

"Alright, we need to go left down Cantersteen and cut through Rue Duquesnoy to get into position D."

The sun was fading behind the skyline, turning the sky into a palette of purples and pinks. Graham looked up to see what appeared to be a mirage in the sky. They did not have to worry about being noticed by the crowd because most people in the streets were also looking at it.

The veil that covered Raven was getting so thin that it was slightly visible to the outside world. Graham could see the faint outline of the top half of the building hovering above the Grand Place Courtyard with nothing visible underneath for support. It was like staring at the upper half of a ghost that faded into empty space.

Graham held the small tablet up, seeing his position marked on the map with a yellow circle and the small blue arrow creeping slowly toward it. He glanced back to ensure his team was keeping pace. Chase was just a stride or two behind with the others on his heels. It was easy to keep up with their movement because the cars in the street were at a standstill, with the drivers staring at the top third of Raven suspended in the sky like a vaporous, stone cloud.

"We need to take a right in a few blocks," said Graham. "And we're sticking out like lions among sheep in this crowd. We're the only ones moving. Do you detect any Vics?"

"Corbin said he saw nothing, so I'll trust that for now, at least until we can get closer," replied Chase, now side by side with Graham. "And let's stick to the east side of the buildings so we can stay in the shadows. I don't think anyone around us cares about what we're doing, but if Victus has scouts, then we are the sheep among lions."

Graham pushed into Chase as he took a sharp right. The others trailed behind, gathering in an alleyway, sheltered by a ceiling of drying clothes on wires and power lines. They all gathered around the faint light of Graham's tablet, staring at the tiny blue arrow pointing due west.

"We're not far. . . maybe another ten minutes. Y'all alright?" asked Graham.

"We're good," said Kel. Ailey nodded.

Damien also nodded as he peeked around the corner, surveying the next street. "I think we're clear."

Kel stepped out to confirm Damien's assessment. The canopy of hanging clothes opened up to the painted sky and the ghostly apparition of Raven.

"Yeah, we can move forward. The closer we get, the more mesmerized people are."

Graham stared at the thinning veil and the remnants of the building behind it. He leaned to Chase, nudging to get his attention.

"What does this mean? You know, now that people know something paranormal is going on?"

"I don't know, little bro. It could go a lot of different ways, but in my opinion– get ready for a downhill ride."

Murphy and his team were already on Rue de Midi, heading north. Branson took the lead on foot, allowing Murphy to keep a hand on his shoulder while he viewed the route through his scout in the sky. They moved swiftly and stealthily in the shadows, darting from street to alley and back to the street. Thanks to Jael, they remained in the dark. As they ran, she would manipulate the light of the street lamps to pour their light in the opposite direction.

"This would be a little more impressive if it made any difference," she said in a heavy European accent. Being back home must have pulled the heaviness of her speech back out.

"I can't blame them," said Branson. "I'd be captivated too if I saw a transparent, floating castle."

"The next two blocks are clean. I'm not seeing any Vics."

"You sure about that?" asked Jael.

Branson jogged a few more meters before realizing that Murphy had stopped. His irises had turned back to their usual color, and he was staring deep into Jael's eyes.

"You're still not over it, are you? Just get it out," said Murphy. "If we go in there divided, we lose."

Jael rolled her eyes, and her ponytail whipped to the side as she trotted toward Raven. Before she could get far, Murphy grabbed her wrist and pulled her back. When she turned around, her eyes were on fire.

"Let go of me, Brian."

"Hit me."

"What? No, I'm not going to–"

"I said hit me. You didn't get it all out at Falcon, so let's get it out now. I'm ultimately responsible for your pain, right? I got played like a fiddle by my cousin through an incredibly rare connection, and because of that, hundreds, maybe thousands died."

Murphy's Adam's apple was bobbing up and down, choking back the emotional impact of his words. He tilted his jaw forward for an easier target.

Jael looked as though she were seriously contemplating the offer. Her gaze was like a dagger. She pulled her right arm back. Her wrist rippled with light, activating her band. She gritted her teeth. Her cheeks were flushed red, and her eyes pooled with hot tears. She tried to throw the punch but was unable to throw it. She grunted, clenching her jaw tighter until her arm fell like a heavy sack.

Murphy never flinched or blinked. He stood ready to absorb Jael's anger. Instead, she fell into his arms, weeping.

Murphy hugged her tight but remained silent.

"I'm sorry, Brian. I'm sorry."

Murphy pulled back to look at her directly.

"We got played. All of us, but most of all me." He pointed to Raven.

"Our true enemy is in there– your home. We can already see that it's a shambles. You better believe I will dump my emotional payload on them when I get in there. If you can do the same at the right time, we will take Raven back, but I need to know you can be calculated in your retaliation."

Jael rubbed her thumbs under her eyes to dry them, nodding.

"I've made enough mistakes these past few days. I can do this the right way."

Branson consulted his tablet and pulled them toward their final position. Once set, they squatted in the tight alleyway, peering into the massive courtyard.

Murphy turned his COM unit on, checking the proper channel.

"Murphy in position B and ready to tear it up."

Cavaness and Alex darted through the streets and alleys as if they had one mind. One would take the lead, confirming a clear way forward, while the other ensured they were not being followed, and then they would switch. They leapfrogged in tactical precision beyond Place d'Espagne until they had a visual of their predetermined position.

Cavaness spoke into the COM. "Cavaness on approach. Three minutes out. Advancement instructions to follow."

All three teams on the other end acknowledged.

With no one in proximity paying even a hint of attention, Cavaness and Alex walked casually as if they were part of the crowd. Though Raven stood nearly over them, they did not marvel at its visibility. They continued forward, analyzing the old and elaborate buildings around them. As Alex surveyed the architecture, he noticed dancing shadows among the ornate carvings.

"We are not alone, Cavaness."

"And right you are, Alexander," said a man, stepping out from the darkness in a fedora and a tweed overcoat.

Cavaness immediately poised for attack, but Silas simply wagged a finger at him, shaking his head.

"Ah ah ah," said Silas, pointing skyward.

Alex surveyed the rooftops again and held his hand against Cavaness' chest. A legion of Victus emerged, each having a broken rooftop statue carving at perilous angles, ready to crash down on the unsuspecting crowd below.

Silas looked at his soldiers and flashed a half grin at Alex.

"Wise decision. Now that I have your attention, why don't you contact your other teammates and tell them to hold their positions. We have a few things we need to discuss."

44

FROM THE SHADOWS

"I've done as you requested," said Alex. "Now, tell your men to stand down."

"My orders do not come from you, Alexander," replied Silas. "As long as you do what you are told, there will be no bloodshed. But cross me one time, and you will see the true meaning of rage."

Cavaness took a step closer to Silas.

"And what if I kill you before you have time to signal to your friends?"

"We both know the likelihood of that scenario."

Silas lifted his cane, rested the tip on Cavaness' chest, and pushed him back a step.

"You know I value my personal space, Cavaness, and I don't particularly enjoy your brand of stench."

"What are your demands, Silas?" asked Alex. "What bidding of your master have you come to collect? I can see your determination. I've seen that same look many times before. Did Bale give the ultimatum of taking our lives or yours should you fail?"

Silas shifted his feet. He snarled at Alex's remark, trying to conceal it with a half smile.

"It's more about the pleasure of finally meeting you in person, Alexander. It's not every day one is in the presence of an immortal being. . . well, it is true enough for me, but now, I get to see two in one day." Silas mockingly shivered as if a cold wind had blown over him. "How thrilling."

"You're in a strong position here, Silas. I won't deny it. You had us cornered before our arrival, but let's say, just for argument's sake, that we overtake you tonight. We thwart your well-laid plans and gain the upper hand. If you survive, how many more mistakes will Bale allow you to make before he makes good on his threat? Mercy was never his strong suit, believe me. So, before we go any further, I want you to make peace with your next words. They may very well pull you into your own grave."

"Now that is psychology at its finest. Well said, Alex. I could not manipulate any better if I tried."

Alex did not acknowledge that Silas had even spoken. "On the other hand, you can always walk away from Victus and join us. Turn from these evil ways and accept my power, and what you have done will be forgiven. I do not hold my people under the threat of perfect performance."

"No, that's not the way of the Protectors of the unseen world. You give them perceived freedom, but never allow them to look up and see their marionette strings in your hand." Silas looked to Cavaness with a cold stare. "Honestly, I still have a hard time with your inability to see that. You had everything at your fingertips. We had *everything*, and you threw it all away for what? A prison cell that you cannot see? You are a slave, Cavaness. You are all slaves to this buffoon. You only use your power to further his agenda. We forge our own destiny. My power is under my direction and mine alone."

"You speak of perceived freedom," replied Cavaness, "but you don't see the chains around your own wrists. Bale gives you what you think you want, but it's only because he can control you through it." Cavaness extended his arm, baring a mangled, scarred wrist. "Those bands come at a terrible price but are ultimately removable. They are poison, Silas. Why can't you understand that? You are on the wrong side of the dividing line and will only serve Bale for as long as it profits him. You are expendable to him, just like his bands."

"Enough of this!" spat Silas. "I did not meet you here to have a lesson in morality and ethics. You and your teams are breathing right now simply because I'm allowing it, and that is a power you will never possess, Cavaness. Never. Now, command the others to move forward with their siege."

"You just said to wait," replied Cavaness.

"Because I like telling you what to do. Now, I'm telling you to allow them to continue."

"And send them to their slaughter? I don't think so."

Silas calmly raised his cane high in the air. The end ignited in purple flame. The soldiers on the rooftops began to move, holding the various heavy objects, ready to bombard the crowds below.

"Are you willing to sacrifice innocent lives because you are a stubborn mule?"

Alex's gaze never left Silas, as if he were reading the man like a book. He pushed a button on his COM unit. "Move in."

Cavaness shot Alex a questionable glance. Alex simply met his gaze.

"I knew all those centuries of life produced some measure

of wisdom," Silas scoffed. "Now, I trust you will come along without a fuss."

"Only after I have certainty that your men on the rooftops will stand down," replied Alex. "I have given you a show of compliance. Now, you do the same."

Silas snickered and held his cane in the air again, this time with a crimson flame. The soldiers on the rooftops set the objects down and melted back into the shadows.

"And how will we know they will not return once we are inside?" asked Cavaness

"You won't. I suppose you will have to trust me," replied Silas.

"Trust the man who tried to bury me? Not likely."

"Then I shall trust you," Alex cut in. "If Bale has something to prove to me, he will do it with a focus on those closest to me. There is no strategic advantage in holding these people hostage any longer. The pawns have played their part. He wants us inside, together. Let's move, shall we?"

Murphy led his team swiftly through the ornate corridor of the west side of Raven, having entered via a secret passage in the central courtyard of the Hotel de Ville de Bruxelles. Much like HawksNest, Raven was in shambles, barely recognizable as a castle in many places. Flagstone floors looked like a mined rock quarry. The walls were half torn down. Long hallways would end abruptly in a heap of stone and rubble.

The team bobbed and weaved through the debris, following the pre-described route. Murphy kept a scout ahead of them, though keeping his vision connected proved difficult as he navigated the remains of the outpost.

What must have been a library opened into a smaller room containing six large mirrors. As they entered, they met up with Corbin and his team, who were already scattered throughout. They had reached the rendezvous point without a hint of opposition.

"Corbin, did you run into any Vics?" asked Murphy.

"Na, we could have marched in here playin' jazz and not have attracted anyone. Dis place is a ghost town."

"This makes no sense. If they were smart, they would have brought their whole army. Surely after the other outposts, they would have suspected we were coming."

"I hear ya. Maybe dey have other plans. I wouldn't put your guard down just yet."

As Corbin and Murphy continued discussing the oddness of the mission, Graham and his team entered the room from the eastern wing, keeping in the shadows until they saw the others.

"What are you guys doing out in the open like that?" asked Graham.

"Because there's no one here to hide from," replied Sonia. "It doesn't seem like anyone wants to fight today."

"This is impossible," said Jael. "This place was overrun by Victus months ago. They would not have packed up and left. No ruler in history would have overtaken a territory and left it vacant to be reclaimed by the people it was taken from."

"So, what next?" asked Kel. "I agree, this doesn't make sense, but what do we do? Do we need to search the rest of the outpost?"

"Makes sense to me," said Lucas. "Why not split up and search before setting the final trans?"

"Because it wasn't our directive," said Corbin. "We meet up here with everyone, den we move on to the next part. Let's just sit tight until Alex and Cavaness get here. Should be any minute now."

Damien and Ailey turned their attention to the condition of the outpost.

"Looks like a king's robe was trampled by a herd of pigs,"

said Damien as he rubbed his hand down a tattered curtain.

Ailey nodded, flinching as she rubbed the scar on her neck. Damien was too involved in his surroundings to notice her discomfort. It wasn't until he saw her head jerk to the side like she had been stung by a hornet that he realized something was wrong.

"Hey, Ailey. You okay? What's wrong with your neck?"

I don't know, she signed, rubbing the scar furiously.

"It's this place," said a stranger from beyond the curtain.

"Who are you?" asked Damien.

"Corbin and his team at HawksNest rescued me. I have a lot of nicknames, but you can call me Bale."

Ailey's cheeks were beginning to turn red and her eyes straining under the peculiar pain.

"I assume you didn't hurt like this before you got here."

Ailey nodded.

"What is it? Why is she hurting?" asked Damien.

"I would wager by the look on your face that whatever created that scar was not purely natural, but supernatural. I've seen and studied this type of phenomenon before. The force infused in whatever struck you is present here, amplifying its effect. Think of it like a lightbulb on a dimmer switch. You have been stricken with a malevolent force, my dear, and that evil is present tonight."

While Graham was in mid-conversation with Kel, he glanced over his shoulder, taking notice of the new person with his friends. For some unknown reason, his insides rolled over like he was on a rollercoaster. Nothing he felt seemed natural or good. It felt just the opposite.

Kel's voice trailed off as Graham fell into a sort of nightmarish trance. The room twisted and darkened as he stared at Bale. Graham blinked hard to focus, but he was becoming increasingly disoriented. Whoever this man was, he was not on their side. He could not explain why he knew this. He just knew, in the pit of his stomach.

"Graham, what's happening right now?" asked Kel.

Graham held up a hand, begging for a moment, then approached Ailey and the threat beside her.

"Ailey, come over here now. Damien. . . now."

His tone left no room for objection. They immediately obeyed, and Bale made no effort to restrain them. He simply clasped his hands behind his back in a regal posture and smiled at Graham. In a split second, a picture from his nightmare flashed in front of his eyes. A black panther, enveloped in a black mist, leapt toward him and disappeared as quickly as it had appeared. Of course, this was all in Graham's head, but Bale looked at him as if he had seen it too. . . as if he had made it appear. The look on his face was devilish.

Graham reacted to the illusion by stumbling backward, covering himself with a defensive hand, and started panting. The thuds of his heart were punching the inside of his ribcage.

Chase jogged to Graham's side as the others turned to see what would have made Graham do such a thing.

"What? You alright?" asked Chase.

"No, I would say he is thoroughly terrified," said Silas, entering from the south wing.

All of Aegis, in unison, held outstretched arms with illuminated bands. All that is, except for Corbin and Sonia. Alex held an authoritative hand in the air as an unspoken request to stand down. Cavaness silently joined the others.

"Someone please tell me what's happening right now," said Murphy, still poised to strike.

"What is happening is checkmate," replied Silas. "A clash of Titans, if you will. An inevitable collision of the immovable object and the unstoppable force."

"Tell me you have a plan, Alex," said Branson. "Why did you guys walk in with him?"

"Because they have the upper hand right now, and we do not want any unnecessary bloodshed."

"Who said any of this is unnecessary?" asked Bale, joining

the group from the shadows. "War always produces bloodshed, isn't that right, brother?"

45

FACE TO FACE

RAVEN OUTPOST
Grand Place, Brussels

"What does he mean by brother?" Lucas asked Corbin. "You said Alex vetted this guy."

"I said Alex knew about Bale, and so he does," replied Corbin.

"Lucas, if Corbin has implied that I permitted this man to be a part of your team, then you have been misled," said Alex.

"What are you doing, Corbin? What is the meaning of this?" asked Lucas.

"It means these two finally get to settle their centuries-old rivalry," Corbin replied. "And it's about freakin' time."

Lucas took a step back from Corbin in disgust. He then turned to Bale. "But you had the catalyst band. I don't understand."

"You mean this?" Bale pulled up his sleeve.

A gold band appeared around his wrist. As he held his arm up for all to see, the band morphed into an odd-looking cylinder and then moved from his wrist into the palm of his hand. He smiled as it formed into a ball of energy, hovering a few inches from his hand. He threw the orb down at Lucas' feet, cracking the stone.

"You faked your bands?" Lucas asked in disbelief.

Bale straightened and clasped his hands behind his back, looking quite satisfied with himself. Fearing no retaliation from Lucas, he turned toward Alex. "You haven't returned any of my calls, dear brother."

"You have not given me anything worth talking about," replied Alex, not breaking outside of his usual demeanor. "And please stop calling me that. You know there are better ways of getting my attention, Bale."

"Yes, but why ruin all the fun? How long has it been, Alexander? Seventy-plus years since our last conversation? Are you still so eager to protect those who are not even aware of your existence? Will you still hold your hand out to them when they turn on you like the dogs they are?"

Alex stepped closer to Bale, almost nose to nose. He stuffed one hand in his pocket and leisurely directed his train of thought with the other.

"You see, it is exactly that attitude that has caused your fall. It's not about the people's reactions to me. It's about how I view them. We were tasked to shepherd the human race. To help them build a world to live and thrive in, both physically and mentally. You took the mantle that was given you and used it to enslave them, trying to be like the Ancient himself."

"They are slaves to their ignorance of our world, Alex and every slave needs a slave master."

"And they should be following a person worthy enough to be followed."

Bale's air of superiority cracked beneath that statement. His grin morphed into a snarl, baring teeth like a wolf. His empirical demeanor snapped into a defensive banter.

"Enough of this. I know you well enough to know you will never see what I see. So be it. All that means is that you will watch all those close to you die at my hand. You claim to be close to your people, yet you somehow failed to see that two of them have turned against you."

Bale motioned for Corbin and Sonia to take their place at his side. As they did, Branson stepped forward from behind Murphy.

"What is the meaning of this? Explain yourself, Corbin!"

Lucas stood silently as he watched his teammates publicly disown him and Alex.

"Oh, come on now, y'all. Surely you don' think dis is ever gonna end. The council has made their case with Bale, and he has agreed to come to an agreement. Alex just needed a little push to get here, so we helped."

"Look at reality," said Sonia. "Aegis is crippled beyond any conceivable repair. Our outposts have either been compromised or destroyed. It was only a matter of time before they got to them all. Why not be on the winning side?"

Sonia reached out to Lucas. "Come on. You know it's true. We're fighting a war that can't be won. This has been going on way too long, Lucas. The table had to turn so that all this could finally stop."

Lucas looked at Sonia with a blank stare. He shifted to look at the others, appearing lost. His face displayed a gambit of emotion, from shock to outrage to confusion.

Eventually, after a heavy sigh, he walked over to Sonia and held her head in his hands. She smiled as he stepped forward.

Corbin gave him a hearty slap on the back. "My man!"

Lucas kissed Sonia on the cheek, wiping away a falling tear as he looked at his partner and friend.

"I will truly miss your company."

Sonia's happiness faded.

"You are wrong in this," said Lucas, looking at the two of them. "You both are. What you have done is nearly unforgivable. You allowed Bale to infiltrate our ranks and exposed me to his toxic presence, and for what? In hopes that I would see things the way you have twisted them to be?"

Lucas had to breathe between sentences to keep his composure.

"No, I love you both, but no. I forgive your trespass against me. I long to remain with you but will not join you."

Lucas turned to rejoin the others. Bale rolled his eyes and threw a black dart at him as he did.

Lucas arched his back and shrieked in pain as the misty dart passed through his chest. He crumpled to the ground as blood seeped from the entrance and exit wounds.

"No!" screamed Kel.

"Lucas!" yelled Branson, running to his aid.

"One step closer, and I command my people outside to crush the innocents below them. Understand?" said Bale. "Do what I say, and I will let you help him, though he hardly seems worth saving."

Bale held a hand out to Graham. "Come here, young man."

"Don't do it!" yelled Damien.

"Are you going to let poor Lucas bleed to death? That doesn't sound very heroic."

Graham shifted nervously, weighing his fate against that of Lucas, who was now in the fetal position, clutching his chest as blood ran down his pale knuckles. A small stream of blood had already begun to drip from the corner of his lips. Graham clenched his jaw. He wanted to stay back, to shrink back into the shadows, but his conscience would not allow him to. He remembered what Alex had told him after waking from his coma-- the degree to which they would protect him, and that thought seemed to take the first step for him.

Graham walked past Lucas toward Bale.

"Hang in there, Lucas. We'll get you out of here."

"Graham, no. My life is not worth yours," he murmured.

"Now, that is what I like to see. A boy with a little gusto," said Bale.

Graham stood just a few feet from Bale. He wanted to melt away but forced his legs to stand firm without trembling.

"The infamous Graham Dawson. We meet at last."

Bale clasped his hands around Graham's shoulders. Graham gritted his teeth and forced himself to show no emotion.

"You are a slippery one. I thought we had you, but you had to go on and nearly blow up my people, and your own, for that matter. Rather die than be captured; is that it?"

Graham remained speechless. Bale grinned and took Graham by the wrist and twisted it so his hand was palm up.

"Make it appear."

Graham swallowed his repulsion and closed his eyes. He balled his fingers into a fist. As he did, his band appeared under his skin. Bale stared at the dagger-shaped rods that held the Aegis Sun. Graham opened his eyes and watched him, trying to analyze his expression, but all he could see was a sadistic delight.

"So, it is true. You are the one to offset the balance. How remarkable. You may put your arm down now."

Graham unclenched his fist and allowed his band to fade.

"See, quite painless. You see, Alex would like you to believe that I will keep you under my harsh rule, but to the contrary, with you at my side, we shall rule together as kings."

Graham did not break eye contact nor give a reply.

"Of course, you will need time to understand the state of events. That's reasonable, so for now, I only want that satchel you are carrying."

Graham had forgotten that he was even wearing it. The mirrors were so lightweight that it felt like just another layer of clothing. He looked back to Alex, knowing what Bale wanted. His eyes begged Alex to intervene, but all he did in reply was give the nod of approval.

Graham lowered his head and slipped the strap off his shoulder. He held it out for Bale to take.

"I'll let you do the honors."

Silas raised his cane and proceeded to blast all six Trans mirrors off the wall. Each shattered in a spray of glass and wood shards, giving Graham space to hang the new ones.

Jael shifted nervously and whispered, "Alex, do something. We can't just let him take all the outposts."

Alex held a hand up for silence.

"My dear, he can and he will. You see, I know Alexander quite well, and he will not sacrifice his precious humans, the so-called innocent people outside these walls. It's his weakness, you see. Compassion will get you nowhere. He will never do what is necessary to prevail."

Lucas coughed and moaned.

"Are you done?" asked Alex. "Graham is doing as you requested, and I am restraining my team as I see necessary. Now, let us tend to Lucas as you promised."

"Live today to die tomorrow. I see no point in it, but if you insist, you may have one person tend to him."

Branson leaped forward, kneeling at his side. He removed supplies from his duffel bag and patched Lucas while Graham set the new trans. Lucas was pale. His eyes began to lose focus and roll back into his head. Branson lightly slapped his cheek to help him refocus.

"Stay with me, Lucas. Look at me. . . there you go. That was pretty bold, something for us all to aspire to. Talk to me.

I don't care what you say, just talk."

As Lucas whispered incoherently, Graham walked back over to Alex's side.

"It's done."

"Activate them," Bale commanded Alex. "Or so help me, I will make sure the entire Grand Place courtyard is filled to the brim with the blood of the people of Brussels."

All eyes followed Alex as he walked over to the mirrors. Everyone stood frozen in anticipation of Alex's next move. He rolled up one sleeve and held his hand to the first mirror.

"I want you to be sure of this, Bale. You've already openly declared war by your heinous acts on my training facilities, but if you do this, you will solidify our division. So, consider what you are about to do. There is still time for you to turn this around."

"I hardly think you're in a position to negotiate. Do you honestly think I did all this to turn back now? Should I move my king when I have a checkmate? Stop stalling and activate your mirrors."

"Very well, but in the end, I want you to look back at this moment and know you had the choice."

Alex's hand erupted in pure white flame. He pressed it to the center of the mirror. As he did, each mirror lit up with white beams of light stretching out from the pits and cracks in the wood, lighting up the room. The rays grew increasingly bright, culminating in one thick beam, which leaped from the center of each trans, one after the other. Everyone shielded their eyes until the light dissipated, and the room fell dark again, except for a faint glow around each mirror.

Bale was exuberant, yet even with a joyous expression, his sinister nature remained. His joy was a twisted version of the genuine thing. He did not have delight for delight's sake but for the sake of destruction.

"Now, stand down."

Alex calmly took a few steps backward to allow room for

Bale to stand in front of the mirrors. Bale held a hand up, much like Alex did, but instead of a white flame, a purplish-black flame appeared around his hand. He grinned at Alex in sick delight, beaming with a twisted pride.

"You really are a fool," said Bale, slamming his palm into the mirror. "Really? You are not going to resist at all? I knew I could control you, but I'll be honest, I didn't expect you just to roll over and go belly up." Bale was now laughing as he spoke. "I mean, nothing! You just sacrificed your entire network without so much as an objection. Why the Ancient called you out is beyond me, honestly. You're weak and gullible, and this is undeniable proof."

Bale allowed a surge of energy to rush into the mirrors. Each one transitioned from a soft white to a deep radiant purple, smoldering as black smoke billowed out between the wood frame and the glass. He closed his eyes and raised his chin to the sky, breathing in the success of his plan. His eyes fluttered as he gained some type of power and knowledge from the trans. He clenched his teeth while maintaining his nefarious grin until he had gathered what he needed.

Once he had finished the infusion of his power, he signaled Silas, who walked over to a lever on the wall.

"There is nowhere to run," spat Bale. "You thought the destruction of your precious training facilities was bad? You just dealt your own death blow. Beginning immediately, I will command my forces to hunt your people down and destroy them now that I have the location of all your headquarters and your entire network!"

With those words, Silas pulled the lever. The lever loosed a series of chains in the room's corners, which released a giant mirror the size of a swimming pool from the ceiling. Silas ran over to the others, as did Bale. In its descent, Bale fired a blast into the mirrored surface, causing it to activate and glow. Everyone in the room was absorbed and transported through the mirror before it crashed to the floor, shattering into a sea of splintered wood and fractured glass.

46

VICTUS HQ

A vast, dank room waited to embrace its new tenants. It was strikingly similar to the room from Raven, yet the decor gave it a much more depraved feel. The floor was made of wide flagstone, the walls textured plaster filled with old paintings spaced out between giant marble statues. There was also an elaborate timber truss system for the roof, but instead of warm and welcoming arches, it was constructed of sharp and jagged lines as if the whole room was in the jaws of a giant lion.

In the center of this room, a large mirror hung, prominently displayed and framed with purple curtains.

The surface rippled, causing the curtains to breathe and flutter. Growing from the center outwards, the glass filled with smoke and rippled until it vomited its inhabitants onto the icy stone floor.

Bale and Silas landed on their feet, but the others fell to the ground with heavy thuds, rolling like logs along the stone floor. Alex was the first to rise, and then he helped the rest of his team to their feet. He dusted off his vest and shirtsleeves as he surveyed the room with its many eclectic art pieces.

Silas sauntered over at once to the room's entrance. He raised the tip of his cane, pressed a button on an intercom box, and casually strode back over to Bale.

Graham checked on his team for any scrapes and bumps. He wished he could be big enough to shelter them all, but he knew that was impossible. He'd been so eager to get out into the front lines to fight, to make a difference. Now, he was terrified of making a single move and getting someone on his team hurt or worse. It was paralyzing. One that kept his chest in a vice, restricting his every breath.

They had been through one real simulation, which hardly gave him comfort or confidence. He looked at Alex, walking toward Bale, and knew he had to trust Alex's instincts. If Alex brought them here, then they were ready. Faith was never Graham's strong suit. Graham shifted in front of the others as best he could and waited for Alex to make the next move.

"Welcome to my humble abode," said Bale, holding his hands high.

"Not very humble, in my opinion," replied Alex.

"Come now, Alexander. There is no harm in reflecting on one's achievements."

"If it points to a worthy success, I would agree. This, however, is self-attesting narcissism."

"You don't like it?" asked Bale, pointing to the paintings adorning the room's four walls.

Each painting was a different portrait of an ancient god. Zeus sitting on this throne wielding a lightning bolt, A tall, swarthy Anubis statue, Krishna's blue bust, Allah's hand outstretched toward Muhammad, the feathered serpent of the Mayans, and many others. Each painting had a gold nameplate near the bottom with the name of the god portrayed.

"Those who have been in my presence have reported their encounter in many different forms over the last few millennia. Far be it from me to be so crass as to reject their worship."

"You never could look past yourself. That is why you will never win this battle. It goes against the very reason we were given the power we possess. Why can you not see that?" said Alex almost pleadingly.

"Why I will never win? Are you delusional, Alexander? I have just discovered the location of all your regional headquarters, which I will put under my boot, and you say I am the disadvantaged one?"

As Bale continued his quarrel with Alex, a group of ten men and women poured into the room, led by Kyla and Seth with immense determination in their stride.

"Perfect timing, Seth," said Bale. "And now you are also outnumbered in unfamiliar territory. Am I still the underdog?"

Lucas stared at Seth in disbelief.

"What? How? You were sent to the Wastelands."

"Whoops. Must have used the wrong mirror," replied Corbin with a grin.

Alex remained silent as Bale continued.

"Precisely what I thought. Now that we have that settled, here's my offer. Hand over the boy to me now, and I will ensure that the rest of your team will be given a quick and painless death. No pain and no drama. As for you, dear brother, you can either live to be made a spectacle of and see your followers die at my hand, or you can voluntarily forfeit your power and die alongside them, which is infinitely more preferable."

Bale grinned, enjoying the proposition, although he began to show signs of irritation when Alex seemed unaffected by his ultimatum.

"As I said, Bale, your greed has always been your Achilles' heel and serves as blinders that restrict your vision. After all this time, did you believe I came here unaware of your plans? Do you think me so naive that I would not recognize one of my own who had turned against me?"

The corners of Bale's mouth pulled down into a malicious sign of discontent.

"I have a connection with my people you will never have or understand. It's how I knew of Corbin and Sonia's betrayal and Brian's innocence. I let you play your hand so I could play mine, and in all sincerity, I must thank you."

Graham looked at Damien, vexed beyond belief. "Alex is thanking Bale? What the heck for?"

Damien shrugged, not taking his eyes off Alex.

Bale tapped his head with his index finger. "I will not let you mess with me, Alexander. I know better."

"It's not a mind game, Bale. You destroy. It's your nature. To ensure the safety of my people, I knew all I needed to utilize is what you have mastered. . . destruction."

Bale wore the same perplexed expression as Graham.

"Still not connecting the dots? Very well. You took down several of my outposts to eventually claim them all. You did so to cripple my network and capture Graham. This would give you the upper hand, and I knew you would stop at nothing to get it, so I let you have what you wanted, with one small caveat. I indeed set all the new Transit mirrors to connect to one another, which you know. The only thing I required of you was the influx of destructive energy. That is where you were kind enough to assist."

Bale's perplexed stare began to morph into rage.

"My intention was never to save the outpost facilities. I

wanted to rescue the leadership over them. When you put your palm on that mirror, you only secured their safety. When you arrive at their locations, I'm afraid you will find vacant lots of rubble, nothing more. I imagine the men and women in Brussels had quite a spectacular sight as they watched Raven dissolve behind the protective veil."

Bale's body radiated a purple mist. His teeth were mashing together so hard that Graham thought they would shatter. His view of Bale began to ripple and blur like heat waves on hot asphalt. The same nausea he felt in Raven when he first saw Bale intensified ten-fold. His eyes rolled into the back of his head as he fell to his knees, cradling his head in his hands.

"Graham!" yelled Kel as Damien knelt beside him.

Graham felt vomit in his throat, but he choked it back down, giving into dry heaves.

"What's happening with you? Please, talk to me," said Kel, clearly stressed.

Graham wanted to but couldn't. He could hardly move.

"None of that matters!" spat Bale. "All you did was delay the inevitable. You still led your team into my trap, where I have the home-field advantage and the bigger army. I will kill them, take Graham, and hold you captive until I have eradicated every last one of the Aegis members! Nothing has changed!"

The last remark lingered as Bale sprinted toward Alex, throwing purple blasts. Alex sidestepped the attacks, turned full circle, and fired a surge into Bale's ribcage. At the last second, Bale formed a purplish-black shield and skidded backward across the floor as he blocked the wave of yellow energy.

Bale deflected the power skyward and fired bolts of electricity in return. Alex strafed, tucking into a side roll, and returned to his feet, flinging a pulse of energy into the flagstone floor. The ground rumbled and quaked, causing everyone to ground themselves in the tremor. Bale jumped into a back handspring, narrowly missing the explosion of dirt and rock that was unearthed.

Bale then sprinted through the dust cloud quicker than Chase could ever move. Alex matched his speed, and the room lit up like fireworks for the next few minutes as Alex and Bale fired the gambit of attacks at one another at the speed of sound. Tumultuous cracks of thunder accompanied the showers of light as the dueling immortals repeatedly hit Mach-One and beyond.

Graham gave up trying to follow the fight with his eyes. He just cupped his ears and tried to view the whole room using his peripheral vision, catching glimpses of pluming lights and bubbling air ripples as the sound barrier was repeatedly broken. The ground would erupt with a Pusher attack in retaliation to a Snype maneuver, followed by bolts of electricity, met with Former scout orbs dancing through the air like fireflies. Purple orbs arched upward and then hurled toward the Aegis members but were quickly dismantled by pursuing yellow orbs.

The fight continued for what felt like hours. Graham was sure that the apocalypse was being birthed before his very eyes. He braced for Silas or any one of the others to attack while Alex and Bale fought, but they seemed just as surprised to see the fight as he was. Graham turned to his three teammates.

"This can't last much longer, or the building will collapse."

"I hope it lasts long enough for Alex to tear Bale a new one," replied Damien, ducking to miss small pieces of debris.

Kel continued to follow the motion of the fight but finally stopped to look at the others. "What do we do? They can fight all they want, but neither can die, so it seems a bit pointless. We aren't here to watch this. We're here to stop *them*," she said, pointing to Silas and the others.

"When this settles, I'm sure we will. I think I know what Alex has in mind. When I tell you to, I want the three of you to stay directly behind me."

"We didn't come all this way to hide, amigo."

"Just trust me, okay? Last time, it didn't get quite as intense from behind. Once I have it under control, then attack. Got it?"

"Are you saying what I think you're saying?" asked Kel.

"You said it pretty well," replied Graham. "They can't beat one another because they have nearly the same power level. There's only one person who can change that."

Ailey continued to rub her neck in growing discomfort, kneading it like a lump of dough.

"Just hold on, okay?" asked Graham.

Ailey nodded unconvincingly.

"We'll figure it out once this is over, I promise."

She nodded again.

Alex and Bale were now returning to normal speeds. Bale landed a glowing punch to Alex's midsection, yet Alex did not seem to feel it. Without a flinch, he returned with a burst attack to the side of Bale's head. Bale toppled back, holding his ear, shaking it off with a laugh.

"You're fighting in vain, Bale. You always have," said Alex without a single strained breath.

"Oh, I hardly call this a fight. I just needed to stretch my legs for a bit," replied Bale, shaking off the pain in his ear. "It's been a few decades since we got to play."

"It has never been about play for me."

"I know, I know. . . always hopeful I will see the error of my ways. The usual."

"No. Actually, I know the leopard's spots do not usually change, no matter how much I wish them to. I allowed you to indulge for two reasons."

"You allowed me, did you? Haha. How kind. Did you ever think that I may also have played a few steps ahead?"

"I've seen how you're setting up the chess board, letting us take the outposts back and ensuring the battle in Australia was captured on the news. You're playing on many levels by cutting our numbers and turning the public against us."

"I know, and with a gentle nudge, they have now named the global threat. They say the group is cunning enough to label themselves as protectors, though their true motives are now being shown as just the opposite. Care to guess what that name could be?"

Alex smiled. "As I was saying, two reasons. First, your team needed to witness the simple truth that we are every bit as strong as you claim Victus to be. They must see that despite all your efforts over the past months. We are by no means crippled, but we are, in fact, many steps ahead. And by the time this is over, they will see the rising of the Sun and definitively decide to stand beside the one they will serve."

Graham perked up. Did he just? His heart jumped to his throat. Alex said the words, and he was now about to walk into a battle that had been waging for centuries. Graham forced his legs to move as Alex finished his talk, walking to his side.

"That brings me to the second reason," said Alex as Graham came alongside.

Graham focused on the ground in front of him, balling his fingers into fists. His eyes changed quicker than they had ever before. His body began to radiate with raw energy as the dust and debris around him launched skyward in its wake.

"The second reason — the reason why I allowed my team to walk into your trap — is so you could see, first-hand, the means of your destruction."

Alex rested a hand on Graham's shoulder, infusing him with enough power to fully release his own. Graham's back arched, and he screamed as he unleashed his energy in its entirety.

47

THE RIFT

VICTUS HQ
Location unknown

Silas, Seth, and the others were blown backward by the blast. Bale had shielded himself behind another formed barrier, his feet planted yet sliding across the stone floor.

Graham was right. Most of the eruption happened in front and to his sides. Though he knew Alex was again helping him contain it, he felt as though he was partially in control of his power. He could feel himself directing some of his energy back into his body to sustain the pressures it created. He called out to his team when he thought he had enough control.

"Guys! Now!"

As Graham commanded his team, Alex did the same with a simple nod to Cavaness, and when Silas and the others returned to their feet, Aegis attacked. Murphy and Jael took off toward Kyla, while Chase and Branson took Seth and his henchmen.

Damien and Kel positioned themselves as close to Graham as his power would allow, but Ailey took off, running to their left.

"Get me something to work with," said Damien.

Kel fired a few pulses into the ground until she seemed satisfied with a particular result. "There we are. Just give me a second." Cupping her hands together, she fired a stronger pulse into the same place as the previous one. A few seconds later, the ground rumbled and quaked—a small crack formed in the floor, growing wider as the Pusher energy rebounded. Damien could feel the surge flying upward, his hair whipping in reaction to its invisible force. Moments later, water bubbled to the surface.

Damien looked at Kel, shocked.

"What? There was a spring?"

"There's no time to explain. . . just use it!"

Damien raised his hands and commanded the water forward, taking out a Vic at the end of the pack. "Boo-ya! Take that, henchman!"

Kel was already busy with her own attack now. She saw the woman beside Seth plant her feet and rear back with glowing wrists. She quickly analyzed the distance and fired another pulse into the ground, which caused a mound of earth to explode upward in front of the woman just before she released her attack. Her two bursts bounced off the mound and flew back into her chest, knocking her backward into the puddle of water her friend was lying in.

Murphy sprinted at Kyla to attack from behind, but she sidestepped in anticipation. Jael hurled burst after burst, but Kyla strafed and blocked each one.

Murphy met Jael's eyes and looked skyward. He then flung a large disc fifteen feet or so in the air. Jael threw another few bursts at Kyla and then shot a blast at the disc. Kyla easily blocked the paltry attacks but failed to see what was happening above her. As the blast approached, Murphy adjusted and angled the disc. The yellow comet of energy bounced off the disc's shiny yellow surface and redirected. Kyla looked up just in time to feel the pain in her chest. As she fell backward, Jael caught her by the front of her shirt, pulled her close, cocked her arm, and landed a punch directly to Kyla's cheekbone. Her head hit hard against the floor, and her eyes crossed in a daze.

Seth ran to her aid but fell at her side in convulsions as Branson's electric tentacles took hold of him. The rest of the Vics with Seth attacked with bursts and surges, but each was dismantled or deflected by rapid attacks from Chase.

Corbin formed a small army of orbs between Seth and Chase, giving him time to shake off the effects of Branson's attack and rebound to his feet. The orbs then connected and arched toward Chase, Murphy, and Jael. Lucas continued sprinting and stretched out his hand as yellow streaks of light flowed from his fingertips into his palm. His blazing amber eyes met Corbin's as a Snype dart tore through his thigh muscle and another through his tricep.

Corbin fell with a shriek of pain, not knowing which injury to grab first. The wall of interconnected orbs quickly dissolved.

Lucas looked for Sonia and eventually found her unconscious in a pool of water. He then allowed himself to collapse to his back. The bleeding had mostly stopped, but he had lost a lot already. He held his injured arm close to his chest and pulled himself behind the others with his good arm. He propped himself against the cold stone wall and popped shots off as long as he could keep his eyes open.

Pound for pound, Aegis and Victus traded shots, but Victus was not faring well with their veterans down. Silas looked to his master, seeing him still crouched behind his formed barricade, unable to move away from Graham's surge. So long as Alex had his hand on the boy's shoulder, the combined power was too strong.

Silas laid his cane down and aimed for the small gap between Alex and Graham. He connected the heels of his hands and pulled back for the attack. A shimmer caught the edge of his peripheral vision, and he quickly ducked to avoid a burst from Cavaness, which flew over his head. He looked up to see Cavaness fire a few more rounds at him until Ailey ran up and grabbed his arm.

Jael sprinted toward Kyla, seemingly eager to finish what she had started. Seth rose and lunged at her, but Murphy quickly tackled him back to the ground. As Kyla stood, Jael surged, throwing Kyla into the wall. She surged again, but Kyla dodged it by ducking and rolling under the wave of light. Like a wrestler, she wrapped her arms around Jael's leg and pushed against it with her shoulder, flinging her backward.

The two wrestled on the ground, firing bursts and throwing punches.

Jael grabbed Kyla's arms and barrel-rolled, gaining the upper hand. She kept Kyla's arms pinned to the ground.

"You killed him!" she said, struggling to keep Kyla incapacitated.

Kyla grinned. "And I enjoyed it."

Kyla worked a leg free and kneed Jael in the ribs. Jael grunted but kept her grip. Kyla threw her knee into Jael's side a few more times until her grip conceded. The two women scrambled to their feet.

"I'll kill you. I swear I will," said Jael.

"No, you won't because if you do, you'll be like me. What would poor Leon think?"

"Do not speak his name!" Jael screamed, lunging for Kyla.

Kyla sidestepped and kicked her feet out from under her. Jael caught herself on her hands but could not stand. Vertical purple shafts penetrated the ground around her, caging her inside of formed bars.

Jael shuffled to the center of her cell while Kyla dusted off her jacket.

"Let's see you work your way out of that. I love a good fight, but even you are a little too wild for my taste."

"I won't stop. You're going to have to kill me first."

"Oh, I see that plain as day, honey. I know revenge when I see it, trust me."

"Why? Why did you have to kill him?"

Kyla thought for a moment. "I wish I had a reason for you that made his death meaningful, but I honestly did it just because I could. I was there for information, and he wouldn't give it to me. That's all."

Jael's gaze fell to the ground. "He was my fiancé, you know." She straightened up on her knees and looked at her hands. One began to glow with increasing intensity. She then looked up and stared Kyla right in the eye. "You took away my whole life."

The light around Jael's hand forged what appeared to be a glove around it. She grabbed one of the formed bars with it.

The bar flickered and vibrated. Jael squeezed with all her strength, and the bar snapped. She then held her other hand in the gap over her head like an umbrella and formed a shield from her band, which severed the surrounding bars. She ducked through the hole and out from under the cage while throwing bursts at Kyla's feet.

Jael quickly stood, braced herself, and fired a surge.

Cavaness looked irritated at the distraction. He shot another burst at Silas before attending to Ailey.

"What?"

Ailey wrapped both arms around Cavaness' forearm as if carrying a big log of firewood. She pulled back with impressive strength for a girl her size, making Cavaness follow. As they gained momentum, she slid her arm down and held his hand so she could turn and run a little easier. Cavaness fired bursts as he was able to while weaving through the others.

Ailey wasted no time in getting to where she wanted to be. When she stopped beside Graham, she let go of Cavaness' hand and pointed to the ground. She stared at Cavaness with arched eyebrows until he acknowledged.

Cavaness took his usual pre-pulse stance, and as he did, Ailey placed one hand on the small of Graham's back. The color of her eyes intensified like an arc welder. She took a deep breath as she made contact, adjusting to the influx of Graham's power. Before Cavaness could throw his pulse, Ailey grabbed his wrist.

Cavaness jerked upright with the influx, much as Ailey had just done. He watched Ailey begin to radiate with the same yellow aura as Graham as it approached his arm. The semi-transparent glow grew from Ailey's hand to his arm, quickly covering him like a foggy blanket. The glow of his eyes intensified, and his bands were nearly too bright for Ailey to look at.

With a forceful push, Cavaness' pulse leaped into the ground. For a moment, there was nothing but an eerie calmness as if the pulse had brought balance to the chaos. But soon, there was a rumble like the earth was experiencing hunger pains. As the pulse worked its way further down into the tectonic plates beyond the earth's crust, it caused them to shift, creating the beginnings of a massive earthquake.

Everyone scrambled to steady themselves, which forced a cease-fire. Jael lost her footing and stumbled backward from Kyla as a crevasse formed between them. It was as if the ground was a sheet of paper tearing into two jagged pieces. As the ground split, the earth bellowed with heated breath. Not a single person remained on their feet, not even Graham and Alex. The fortress they were in moaned and sighed under the quake. A wooden pillar split in half vertically and lost its foundation. It came crashing down on the edge of the crevasse, knocking a chunk down into the dark oblivion, following its trail shortly after.

The split in the ground grew until it was roughly the width of a two-lane road. Once the worst tremors had passed, Aegis and Victus braced for battle.

"It's useless, Alex!" screamed Bale. "Go ahead and turn my house to rubble. I have many others. Bring it down, and you will only destroy yourselves. There is no escape from here. You don't even have the slightest idea of where you are."

As he steadied himself, Bale could not hold back a wicked grimace. The rumblings slowly ceased, and the racket died down enough for one to yell to the other from across the divide.

"Look deep into the abyss, Bale," replied Alex. "Such a fate is waiting for you with open arms." Alex looked from Bale to the others. "This fate lies for all who follow this man! Is the veil so thick over your eyes that you cannot see the light of truth? Bale does not care for you. He crafts his own version of the truth, calling it *The Way*, but it's all a means to his own gain and glory. What promises has he deceived you with? Has he pledged status in his ranks? Wealth? Power? Trust me when I say you will lose all of what he has promised as soon as your purpose in his twisted plan is fulfilled."

"Blah, blah, blah. Every time you feel the need to preach. It's far from endearing. Enough talk. Give the boy to me, and I will make your deaths quick."

"My nature is not yours. None of my people will be sacrificed or traded."

"Is that so? Well, let's put that to the test, shall we?" Bale turned to Corbin and leaned in close to whisper. "It's time to prove your worth."

Bale grabbed Corbin by the collar and the back of his shirt. He pivoted, and in one fluid motion, he flung Corbin into the crevasse.

Corbin screamed as he flailed his arms and legs like a maimed duck. Kel gasped, covering her mouth with one hand and reaching for Corbin with the other if only to acknowledge a slight hint of compassion toward him.

Graham stood still. He struggled with conflicting emotions. The terror in Corbin's eyes sent a chill down his spine. It wasn't just terror but also confusion. Graham could empathize with that mixture but couldn't deny the feeling of relief in his heart, maybe even a hint of justice. The punishment for his betrayal was being carried out. Graham's conversation with Chase flashed in his mind. He did not want to hear it. He wanted justice– for a wrong to be made right, but Chase's words wouldn't leave his mind.

Graham watched as Corbin's body fell past the lip of the rock; the whites of his eyes streaked with red veins. When he thought it was over, he saw four fingers clamping down on a protruding rock. Graham stepped closer and saw Corbin swaying like a pendulum as he held onto the ledge with one hand.

"Kill them!" screamed Bale, seizing the window of opportunity. Streaks of yellow and purple filled the air, though all sound faded into the background like white noise. Graham was acutely aware of the battle peaking to its climax, yet time seemed to stand still. He knew his team would keep the evil at bay. All he could do – wanted to do, was stare at Corbin. This man's life was now in his hands, and it troubled him to think that he was not inclined to save it. This man had led them to slaughter. Why should he be saved? But Chase's words cut through the darkness of his thoughts, as did Alex's on the day he woke from his coma.

> You may not believe it now, but this gifting would not have been given to you unless you had the physical and moral capacity to wield it. You mustn't allow an open door for corruption. A power of this magnitude will sway entire armies at the proper time. Part of your responsibility will be to keep yourself and your motives pure.

Graham clenched his eyes shut, unable to shake the storm of opposing emotion inside. How could anyone deny justice? On the other hand, how could anyone wield the power to bring the judgment of death? It was an impossible decision to make. Maybe he did not have to make one at all. If Corbin could climb out, fate allowed him to live. If he fell, then it was meant to be. Was making no decision the right one?

The muscles in his jaw tightened. His forehead wrinkled with thoughts flowing through his mind, and Graham knew what he had to do just when he thought indecision would win. His eyes opened and met Corbin's. This was the last thing that Graham wanted, but at his core, in the far reaches of his subconscious, he knew it was the right thing to do.

Corbin's expression begged for rescue. Graham clenched his teeth. The aura around him returned, as did the amber irises. His bands gleamed as he held both hands toward

Corbin, not in an attempt to pull him up but as an attack. All the debris around him levitated and surrounded him. Graham bared his teeth, and a yellow ball of light sprang from his hands. It broke off the rock Corbin was clinging to, and he fell into the darkness. He could only hear his scream of terror as he fell, having lost his only hope of survival.

48

TO LIVE OR LET DIE

A tear left a trail of clean skin through the smeared dirt on Graham's face. Though the deed was done, he still held his hands out, staring into the darkness below. Alex made no attempt to sway Graham's decision. Though he was engaged in the battle, Alex kept a sovereign eye on Graham, shielding him from being hit and giving him the mental space to make his choice. And once the decision was made, Alex smiled.

Graham's eyes were red and puffy. He was still under intense concentration and focus. His hands were outstretched and rotating as if he were steering a car. His fingers were curled and facing upward, summoning some unknown object from the deep. The first object to rise beyond the lip of the crevasse was a shard of stone, followed by dozens of pieces of rock and dirt. Then, Corbin's head crested, his eyes wild in bewilderment. The anti-gravitational effects of Graham's heightened power levels had transferred to his energy attack.

He allowed Corbin to rise nearly ten feet above the ground. He rotated his hand clockwise, commanding Corbin to do the same. Graham again met his eyes. He did not speak but willed Corbin to understand the impact of his decision. In his mind, Graham warned Corbin that he had no strength to make this choice again. He wanted him to know. . . to feel the full impact of his treason. Graham told Corbin all these things through a simple stare, and for a moment, he thought Corbin got the message. Then, with a flick of the wrist, Graham sent Corbin hurling back to Victus. He landed beside Silas with a heavy thud, then held himself up on his elbows, staring blankly at Graham.

Even Bale seemed to have trouble understanding Graham's decision. He scowled and bellowed a battle cry. "You will never leave here alive!" Electricity leaped from one hand, and Snype shots fired from the other.

Alex formed a curved barrier between them, parrying his Bale's attack. "Our purpose here is done. It's time we retreat."

"How? We can't leave this place. We don't even know where we are," replied Graham.

"The second part is true enough, though I have an educated guess. As for our exit plan, you will be the one to open the door for us."

"What?"

"Power up, Graham. Call upon your full strength and trust me to do the rest."

Graham exhausted most of his energy on the one decision to save Corbin and not let him plummet to his death. He felt like he had just finished running a marathon, but Alex had always been right, so Graham would do what he could, praying it would be enough to succeed in whatever Alex had in mind.

"Don't throw any attacks," whispered Alex. "Just release everything you have."

Graham nodded, and Alex dissolved the barrier between them and Bale. Graham balled his fists, arched his back, and screamed. Power erupted from him with the intensity of an exploding star, and the brightness nearly matched. Alex again stood behind Graham, catching and containing the raw power. He pushed some through Graham's body and focused the rest on a singular point just beyond the crevasse between them and Bale.

Graham held his arms out, watching in amazement how the energy streams funneled into a single point like a laser beam. They were aimed at Bale, but they did not reach him. The power penetrated the air just in front of him, and a small rift tore the very fabric of space. Graham watched as Bale's head and body split in two. Not his physical body, but rather the space between them, as if reality itself was being torn in two, revealing another world hidden on the other side. Then, it made sense. They were in a stronghold. . . an outpost belonging to Bale, which was probably covered by a veil like Falcon, concealing it from the outside world, and he was tearing through it.

The rift continued to open, growing until it was long enough for a person to pass through. Graham could see a darkened blue sky and green grass through the slit in space that starkly contrasted the dungeon-like hall they were currently fighting in. He was having a hard time understanding what was real. He could see the broken flagstone floor at his feet and the chasm created by Cavaness, yet as he peered through the rift, there was no gap in the ground, no tattered buildings, and no Vics. It was as if he was staring into a living painting on the wall of another place in time, seeing the blades of grass bend with a gentle breeze.

"Now!" commanded Alex to the others.

Chase corralled Kel and Ailey and jumped through the rift. Damien was not far behind. Branson and Murphy pulled Lucas to his feet, dipped under his arms, and assisted him through. Jael raised a hand to fire a burst at Kyla, but Alex's voice intervened.

"Not now, Jael."

"But she–"

"There's a time and a place. This is neither. You need to go through, and you need to go now."

Jael kept her stance, clenched her jaw, and screamed. She eventually let her arm drop and dove through the tear.

"Just a bit longer, alright?" said Alex.

Graham nodded. He was tired, but not nearly as much as he had anticipated after learning to consume more energy for himself instead of Alex pushing it through him. He could see the Victus attacks of the others hurling at him, but they thinned and dissolved under the immense power pulsating around him as they approached.

"Keep it steady, Graham. I'm going to pick you up."

Alex was still helping Graham control his strength. He took small, precise steps, entering the shell-like energy surrounding Graham. He bowed his head slightly and shielded his eyes from the intensity of it. Even Alex seemed to have to focus on stabilizing himself within it. As he reached Graham, he tucked his head under Graham's arm and wrapped his arms around his waist.

Graham looked down into the darkness of the crevasse and then to the rift which hovered just above it.

"If ever there was ever a time to keep your focus, it is now," said Alex, grunting.

Graham swallowed hard. He felt his feet lift from the floor. He could feel Alex's muscles tighten as he lunged forward. Graham wanted to reach a hand out to touch the fringes of the rift, to see if it had a texture, but he would not dare move his hands. Just before he passed through, he caught a glimpse of the left side of Bale's face, consumed with anger, and his eyes flickered as if to contain the world's rage within them. Maybe it was just the effects of the rift, but he thought he even saw Bale's face twist, blacken, and morph into a form that was not human.

Then, a cold breeze blew over him, and he knew they were on the other side.

49

RETREAT TO THE FIRE

Graham turned and flopped onto his back, panting. Rain clouds formed overhead, and soon, tiny droplets peppered his forehead. The coolness was beyond refreshing. He did not want to move. Wherever they were, it was, at that very moment, the most comfortable place on earth. He welcomed the break, but before he could take another sigh of relief, he heard the shuffling of feet behind him.

"They're on the lawn!" yelled a man's voice off in the distance.

What lawn? Graham asked himself. *Were they at someone's house? I bet it would be a shock to see a group of people fall from nowhere onto your front lawn. But I'm sure Alex will be able to explain it somehow.* Graham looked to his left and quickly felt a streak of panic bolt through his stomach. They were not on *a* lawn. They were on *the lawn*, and he understood why the man's voice had an air of urgency. The White House looked enormous from ground level, with its gleaming white columns adorning the front entrance.

Graham quickly got to his feet, turning around to see hundreds of people staring at him through the black iron fence along the street.

"They're attacking the White House!" screamed a woman.

"It's them! The terrorists! It's Aegis!" yelled another.

Armed guards pushed the civilians aside, aiming black machine guns at them. Graham looked up to see if the rift was still there, but it had already closed. It was not a permanent tear, a relief, but a small one compared to the soldiers outside and the Secret Service agents on fast approach.

Branson yelled for everyone to follow him. He entered a cluster of shrubbery near the south end, around the corner of the building. As Graham took his first steps, he felt a terrible pain in his left shoulder, nearly throwing him forward. He looked over his shoulder to see the Secret Service open fire. Graham grabbed his arm and ran.

Chase doubled back for Graham, and in a blur, he yanked him up and bolted to the shrubs. Damien was already there holding a hand up to fire back, but Cavaness slapped it down.

"No, don't retaliate. It won't help."

"I wasn't. I was going to throw up my shield."

"It's a good thought, but no. It will only make matters worse."

Cavaness took Damien by the scruff of the neck and threw him down into the shrubs and through the trans which Branson had set up. More bullets tore through the air as they all shuffled toward the bushes. As the Secret Service agents rounded the corner, Kel and Ailey had already traveled through, and Chase was dragging Lucas and Graham. The rest quickly followed with Alex at the rear, and as he traveled through, he placed his thumb in the small divot, taking the mirror with him.

Graham poured out from the hanging mirror onto a white wooden floor. He landed on his injured shoulder, yelling out in pain. He curled into a ball and held his leg, unsure if it hurt worse than his shoulder. Chase laid Lucas beside him, who was pale and with eyes half open. Seeing him struggle to remain conscious, Graham did not hurt as badly. Once Kel was through, she sunk to her knees beside Graham.

"What hit you? Was it Silas? Bale? How bad is it?" Kel pulled his hand out of the way. "You're bleeding!"

Graham looked at his arm. Blood had already trailed down his arm and between his fingers. Thankfully, the bullet had only grazed him.

"I'll live. It wasn't Victus. It was the soldiers. I think I'd rather have been hit by Silas."

"Oh, thank heavens. You scared me," said Kel, nudging him in the shoulder, which happened to be very close to the gash in his arm.

Graham grunted and doubled over in pain.

"Oh, no! Sorry Graham. I get a little crazy when I'm scared. Are you okay?"

"How about a hug or something next time?"

Kel blushed a little as Graham cracked a grin. "Sure, that seems better."

Ailey sat close by, massaging the scar on her neck. Her eyes pooled with tears. Jael ran over and knelt beside her.

"What is it? Did you get hit?"

Ailey signed to her, telling her what Bale had said.

"I've heard of this kind of thing before. If what he said is true, then this is not an ordinary scar, and now that we're away from that place, the pain should dissipate."

Ailey's lip trembled as she fought back the tears.

"Don't worry. We'll figure it out together. First, let's get cleaned up and get you something to eat. If the pain fades within the hour, we'll have enough information to take the next step."

Damien ran over to Graham and slapped him on the injured shoulder.

"Dude, what the heck was that? You just tore a wormhole in space! Are you kidding me? That was the coolest party trick ever."

Graham collapsed on his side, clutching his shoulder.

"Oh, are you hurt, amigo?"

"Slightly," said Graham, holding back hot tears. Damien did not seem to notice the injury.

"Oh, my bad. So, really, you've got to tell me what that was all about."

Graham steadied his breathing. "I'll tell you the secrets of the Kennedy Assassination if you'll just stop hitting my shoulder." Graham took another couple of deep breaths. "Go and help Lucas."

Damien looked over his shoulder and was startled by a man in a blue tunic and long white hair entering the room. Damien froze, not knowing who the stranger was. The last time he met a stranger, it ended up being the eternal epitome of evil.

"Adrian, over here," said Branson. "His name is Lucas, from EagleEye. Corbin and Sonia betrayed us. Lucas stayed true to Aegis and was attacked for it. He needs your expertise and quickly."

"Understood, Eric. How thankful I am to see you all back and alive. That was a perilous mission. What was the result?"

"Just get him some medical attention, please. We'll give everyone the full debrief as soon as we can."

"Of course." Branson took Lucas' feet, Adrian took his hands, and together, they took him to another room for treatment. As Adrian passed by Damien, he glanced over and smiled warmly. Damien, a bit confused, smiled back.

"Who was that guy?" Damien asked no one in particular.

"That was the leader of Albatross," replied Jael, wiping away grime from her cheek. "He's an Aquatic, like you. I think he already knew that by the look on his face."

Damien perked. "Another Aquatic? Really? Do you think I can meet him?"

"I'm sure Adrian wouldn't be thrilled."

Without looking, Damien reached around and accidentally slapped Graham on the shoulder again.

"Did you hear that, man? Another Aquatic!"

Graham yelped and slapped Damien twice as hard. "Ow! Seriously, man, I'm injured! I hurt. Lighten up, for the love of all that is sacred! I need my arm for things."

"Oh, lo siento."

Alex had been watching Graham with pity. He walked over to him, rubbing his hands together in yellow flame. He approached Graham from behind and gently grasped him by both shoulders. Graham flinched as the energy from Alex's hands soaked into his muscles, soothing and relieving the pain. Graham nearly melted into the floor.

"Better?" asked Alex.

"You have no idea. Thanks for that," replied Graham.

"Good. You more than earned it. I want you to be in good spirits when I introduce you to the others."

Graham looked around him. He knew everyone here and had just been introduced to Adrian.

"Who else is here?"

50

SKYVIEW

SKYVIEW
Location unknown

Once everyone had eaten and cleaned up, Alex led them through a series of hallways until they were in a large, open room with a massive oval table in the center. The interior was completely white, and it looked like a forest of trees had twisted together to make a mansion. Stark-white tree trunks and branches stretched throughout the inside, but they had not been cut and placed. Each looked as though they were still a living tree. Entryways were made of adjacent branches, arching to touch one another at the peak. Instead of molding around doorways and ceilings, the smaller branches twisted and weaved into elegant Celtic-like patterns.

Twelve men and women sat around the table, all faces Graham had never seen before, except Adrian.

"Everyone, please take a seat. I promise to be brief so you can rest," said Alex.

Jael looked inquisitively across the table to Ailey. She pointed to her neck and gave a thumbs-up, asking if Ailey was okay. Ailey smiled weakly and nodded, giving her a thumbs-up in return.

Graham grabbed the seat in front of him. Damien walked over and took a seat beside Adrian. Everyone else fell in place around the table while Alex remained standing.

"Good evening, and welcome to the Skyview situation room. Most of you know one another, but allow me to make introductions to those who do not," said Alex. Adrian and a rehabilitated Marcio stood with Jael and the new people, as did Cavaness.

"Marcio, how are you?" asked Alex.

"Never better," he replied, looking more radiant than before being wounded.

"I'm glad to hear that, and thank you for your bravery in Albatross."

"It is my honor to serve, Alex."

Alex smiled and then looked at Graham and his team. "After all this running about, I'm sure you're wondering, in the end, what it was all for." Alex swept his hand around the room, pointing to everyone standing.

"Allow me to introduce you to the seven Pillars, well, six at the moment with Corbin's absence." Alex walked the room, introducing the outpost Directors in pairs, beginning with Adrian and Marcio and ending with Cavaness as the Director from Falcon, with Branson as Assistant Director.

Graham nodded as they were introduced but needed clarification on one point. "I thought the outposts were the pillars?" he asked.

"The outposts were our seven headquarters, but Aegis is

built on people, not places."

"But we did take back the outposts," said Kel.

"Yes. We most certainly did, but only as a means to an end. The mission all along was to secure our people and communication network. I would never risk human lives for wood and stone. We recaptured the outposts to set the transit mirrors and re-connect them. But those mirrors were designed to create a chain reaction to destroy the physical buildings."

"So, these people knew about your plan?" asked Graham.

"Yes, they did and made the necessary preparations leading up to the connection. Adrian and others safely removed all the necessities and additional trans from Falcon before it was destroyed."

Alex then addressed the other leaders who were not a part of the fight. "Bale had already found a number of the outposts, so it would only be a matter of time before he found the rest. That is why we are all assembled in one place, for now, until I can arrange something more sustainable. As you may have noticed, Corbin and Sonia are not with us. Because of their betrayal, we have lost many of our own and find ourselves in our current predicament. They have turned to Victus, believing them to be the stronger side. When Lucas recovers, he will assume the position of EagleEye's Director alongside an Assistant Director of his choosing."

Alex then made his way around the table to Graham.

"Now, I would like you all to meet our final recruits. This is Kel and her close companion, Ailey. They came from the same orphanage and are practically sisters. Their giftings are a Pusher and Bridge, respectively. Damien is a near neighbor to Adrian. He is originally from Peru but has lived most of his life in the States alongside Graham Dawson. Damien is a rapidly developing Aquatic, and as you are already keenly aware, Graham is the one who wields the Sun."

At the mention of the Aegis Sun, each Director and Assistant Director pounded their chest and bowed their head—even Cavaness. Graham didn't know how to receive the salute. He stood awkwardly with a half-smile and flushed cheeks until he thought it a good idea to return the salute. He forced his bands to shine, pounded his chest with his fist, and bowed.

"Marvelous," said Alex. "Now, I would like to elaborate further on how the destruction of the outposts was a success. Bale took our bait, acting on his greed, and used the mirrors to learn their location. In doing so, his destructive nature fused with the power I placed within them and destroyed them all, along with any trail leading to our networks. Conversely, he had also set a trap for us, which sent us back to his headquarters, which was a splendid turn of events."

Graham looked at Alex in shock of his gratitude at being tricked.

"We gained two advantages there. The first and most obvious is knowing the location of his base of operations, having built his home over the most powerful house in the most powerful country on earth. No doubt it is a symbol of his perceived authority." Alex looked at Graham. "Perceived," he repeated, with a note of distinction. "The second advantage was the partial fulfillment of the prophecy. Graham successfully produced the phenomenon known as The Rift. For those unfamiliar with the specifics, the prophecy predicts that near the end of the age, the veil separating our world from the normal world will be torn, and the nations will take their sides in the great war."

The adults shook their heads in acknowledgment and excitement while Kel, Ailey, and Damien remained expressionless. Alex took note and continued.

"In the story of the Unseen War, you will remember that in the end, a dagger was used to cut through the veil. The story never revealed which leader wielded the dagger, but many believe it was the Younger. The thing about prophecy is that things tend to be symbolic. In the story, a physical dagger splits the veil. In reality, it is a person with a very sharp mind."

Kel looked over at Graham with wide eyes. Graham blushed again and looked down at the underside of his wrists, tracing the outline of the dagger-like shape around the Aegis Sun. *So, that is why it changed.*

"Bale witnessed this event first-hand. Graham successfully performed The Rift so we could escape. For the first time in centuries, we have been able to strike a measure of fear into Bale's evil heart, and it gives us some much-needed momentum as we take our next steps. This is a great encouragement but also shows a great need for caution. The enemy is now on the defense, poised in the grass like a lion ready for attack, and we must all be aware of his ferocity."

"So, what is our next step, Alex?" asked Adrian.

"Our next step is to spread this news among your networks. They need to know that our location is secure and that Bale has been given a black eye. They need to know that we are no longer the underdog and that every action will culminate in victory over Victus. With the balance of power tipping in our favor, we can finally end this war. This news must spread like wildfire throughout your networks, reaching the highest members of the Council as well. They must understand that all prospects of a peace treaty are futile."

Alex picked up a remote control from the table, turning on the four flat TV screens positioned back to back above the center of the table. They crackled to life, each displaying the current news story. The news anchor recapped the story of an attempted attack on the White House, showing footage taken by people outside of the White House gate on their cell phones. It showed the Aegis team scurrying away from the agents and into the shrubs. Graham melted into his seat as he watched himself collapse after being shot.

The footage then switched to previous footage recorded in Australia, which showed Corbin and his team advancing on HawksNest. Finally, the screen displayed a shot of the silhouette of Raven as it disappeared from view. Graham's heart sank into his feet as he saw a granular photo of himself, along with Alex, Cavaness, and the others. "Terrorist members identified," said the newscaster. "Armed and dangerous," he continued. "Organization identified as a group who calls themselves Aegis."

"This has been Bale's plan, along with the capture of our outposts," said Alex, cutting through the heaviness of the report. "He's turning the very people we are trying to liberate and protect against us. And I must say, he has done an excellent job of it. I've been watching it build, and no doubt the main reason for his forces on the rooftops around Raven was to not only capture us inside but also to capture our identities. He wanted to hit us from all sides, and he has succeeded. We must continue our fight underground now, outside the public eye, even in everyday life."

Graham had no words. They had not been a part of Aegis for more than half a year, and now, Bale had forced them into exile from the rest of humanity. He watched their faces circulate on the news channel's big screen, and all he could do was shake his head in disbelief. What now? How could they fight Victus and the rest of humanity at the same time? This did not sound like having the upper hand at all.

Alex could see their distress, so he ended with one final word.

"Make no mistake. The end of days is quickly approaching, and we must be ready to greet it with a drawn sword."

51

A Midnight Visitor

Nearly everyone had gone to bed. Only Alex, Chase, Graham, and Cavaness remained in the situation room, huddled together near the end of the oval table.

"So, where are we?" asked Graham.

Alex was leaning forward with his elbows on his knees and fingers laced together.

"We are still in North America, but it is best to leave it at that for now until I can decide our level of discretion in the public eye.

"So, we can't leave Skyview at all?"

"The general area around this place is also cloaked, so

you'll have a bit of freedom," Cavaness interjected, "but, yes. For the time being, it's best to remain here. You only got a small glimpse of what Bale is capable of. Don't underestimate him."

Graham glanced at Cavaness' wrists and remembered what Chase had told him. He decided to take him at his word.

"And you know his power first-hand," Graham said, more than asked.

"Yes. Unfortunately, I do," Cavaness replied. "Silas and I moved up through the ranks of Victus together, but as his lust for destruction grew, it ate away at me. I've seen Bale's charm with his followers, promising them the world and all its pleasures, but in the end, it leaves you empty and broken. Every word that escapes his tongue is a lie."

"Sometimes you need to walk through the darkness to understand the true value of the light, right Graham?" said Chase. "Remember that?"

"Yes, I remember. That's what Ms. Winstone kept telling you."

"And it is a good bit of advice," said Alex. "In some ways, those who have been to one extreme can operate more effectively on the other because they know precisely what they are fighting against. It's another level of wisdom. Our next obstacle, however, is a bit more complicated than that."

"What next obstacle?" asked Graham.

"What I told the group earlier was true, but another piece of the story pertains especially to your next steps. Over the past few months, I have been diligently searching for a man who is neither Aegis nor Victus. He has visited both extremes and has settled in an obscure gray area in the middle that serves neither. He is a powerful mercenary who contracts his powers for money without concern for outcomes. The cause for which he fights only matters in currency."

Alex stopped there as they all turned their attention

toward the entrance after hearing the heavy thuds of the metal door knocker.

"I could not have timed it any better," said Alex, getting to his feet. "Come. We will finish this talk with our new guest."

"Who is it? Do I know him?" asked Graham.

"*Her*. While on mission, her covert name is Agent Red, but now that she is here, I will let her do the intros," said Alex.

They went through a long, narrow hallway, vaulted nearly three stories high, to the arched front entryway. Alex opened the door, revealing the new arrival covered in a long trench coat and a hood draped over her head, sheltering her from the pouring rain. The sound of the rain was shocking as Alex opened the door. It was as if there were a monsoon outside.

"Come in, come in." Alex stepped to the side to allow the woman to enter.

She turned her back to Graham, removed her coat, and hung it on a wall hook. She shuddered a bit with the cold chill, wiping away the remains of the rain splattered on her forearm.

"Oh, hello, dear! Heavens, it is much too late for you to be up, Graham."

Graham gasped. "Ms. Winstone?" he said in utter disbelief.

"Indeed, my dear," she said with a radiant smile that could cut through the gloom outside.

"You're Aegis?"

"Well, it would be a little awkward right now if I wasn't. Skyview is not exactly a Motel Six on the side of the interstate, dearie."

"But you. . . You're. . ."

"I have been placed in a job where I can be most useful, my dear. Playing a part in Aegis does not always mean embarking on perilous journeys with a threat of constant mortal danger. Sometimes, the most effective mission is influencing others in the ordinary, day-to-day things."

"But, you never. . . why didn't you say anything after I took the bands?"

"Because I had orders and a mission. It just wasn't the right time."

"Speaking of which, I thought you were gone with family issues."

"Well, this is my family, Graham, so yes, I suppose I have been."

Graham could not believe his eyes. He could not even form a coherent sentence in his head. He just stared at her with an open mouth. Ms. Winstone patted Graham on the cheek and smiled again.

"There will be plenty of time to chat. First things first." She turned to Alex and continued. "I have found Skyle, and it wasn't easy. He's terribly good at masking his energy signature."

"And you're certain it was him?"

"No one can forget that mask. I am positive."

"Was he aware of your presence?"

"No, he was too engaged in his current business proposition."

"Wait," Graham cut in, "you said mask. What mask? Who is Skyle?"

Alex nodded for Chase to explain.

"Skyle is the mercenary Alex was telling you about. He was once one of us but was captured by Victus and experimented on because, for a long time, he was thought to be who you are. . . the Aegis dagger. We sent him on a mission, but he was captured and tortured. Somehow, he escaped, but not until after he was horribly disfigured. Many called him a faceless specter, but we know him as Skyle. He wears a mask to conceal his disfigurement, but now it's his identity."

"And what does this have to do with me?" asked Graham.

"Because many years ago, Skyle retrieved a two-year-old boy from the woods after an attack on his family," said Alex.

A bolt of lightning streaked through Graham's chest. His heart was nearly in his throat.

"Wait. You're saying that a faceless mercenary rescued me from the woods?"

"He was not a mercenary at the time, but yes. He is the one your subconscious has been recalling in your most current nightmares," Alex replied. "He holds information key to understanding what Bale has planned next. If Bale tried to use him as the dagger to cause the Rift, then he has the insight we need but will not give it willingly. We need you to persuade him."

"Alex, surely not!" Ms. Winstone snapped. "That is much too dangerous for Graham."

"Olivia, I understand your concern, but Graham will not be alone in this, and you know why it must be him."

"Yes, I understand, but isn't there another way?"

"I would not suggest it if there was."

"Why am I the only one who can talk to him?" asked Graham.

Chase picked back up. "Because he blames you for being what he is."

"Me? Why?"

"When he rescued you in those woods, your power was already so strong that he absorbed a lot of it somehow. We think it's because of his Weaver gifting. Regardless, he was so powerful after that day that Victus thought he was the Aegis dagger from the prophecy."

"Not only that. . ." said Cavaness, ". . .but he also has answers you need. He placed a heavy hand on Graham's shoulder. "Your parents' bodies were never found, so we suspect they are still alive, but you must know that it's only speculation. Only Skyle can attest to your parents' condition."

Graham felt like he was going to throw up. So many days he'd spent wondering about them, and now, there's someone who can explain what happened that day. There were answers to his muddied past, all from a person who likely wanted to kill him. Graham held a hand to his head and sat down on a nearby bench.

"What if he killed them?" Graham said, finally able to say something.

"That's unlikely," said Alex. "As I said before, Skyle was one of us then. Victus had not yet tainted him, but more than that, he would not have harmed them because they were not just your parents. They called Skyle to rescue you, Graham, because he is your older brother."

LUMOS

Any typical Lumos wields the power to bend physical light, increase or decrease the intensity, and use it as they please. They can also retrieve knowledge and personal experiences through physical touch in the advanced stages. Aging Lumos' are highly reflective and eventually become the elders of the rest of the AEGIS groups, freely giving and teaching others in their advanced knowledge. They are also influential strategists and can think many steps ahead of the other groups.

SNYPE

Snypes use their ability to create and fire small darts of energy from the palm of their hands with unparalleled precision and with the force of a 50-caliber bullet while focusing their sight at remarkable distances. Initially, this gifting was used for carving and sculpting large stones for building projects such as the pyramids, but in times of war, they are most often used for long-range attacks. They are known for their patience and meticulous detail.

SCORCHER

Scorchers are the adrenaline junkies of the supernatural world. The Scorcher can create and control the element of fire and remain unscathed from the elbows to their fingertips. Fire can be ignited, intensified at will, and propelled in small bursts as far as 100 yards. Longer streams of flame can be expelled at shorter distances. They have a habit of running into the heat of battle and making decisions as they go.

WEAVER

Weavers are patient and introverted. Their power

requires long periods in isolation as they infuse their *dynamis* power into objects. This power will remain until the Weaver has passed away. Weavers who construct Transit Mirrors are highly skilled and are usually heavily guarded, as they are the literal gatekeepers of the passages for their team.

***

NEMESIS REVEALED

V I C T U S

Declared enemy of AEGIS, led by the immortal- Bale.

ABOUT THE AUTHOR

Hey there, fellow adventure reader. My name is Nathan
Roten - author of the AEGIS Series. If you are new to my
writing, then let me help you out. My niche that I know and
love is action/adventure contemporary fantasy fiction for
middle school and Young Adults (though many adults have
told me they love it just as much as their kids). The fantasy
is set in the real world with fantastical powers. No dragons,
elves, vampires, etc... Think the audiences of Chronicles Of
Narnia, Percy Jackson, Harry Potter & Michael Vey.

All my books are guaranteed to be adventurous, thrilling,
engaging, and free from course language and sexual content.
Ain't nobody got time for that! I write clean fiction with
Christian influences that you will likely trade in late-night
hours to finish.

Nathan would like to invite you to connect with him

wherever you are in cyberspace:

Website: www.NathanRoten.com
Facebook: facebook.com/TheNathanRoten
Instagram: https://www.instagram.com/thenathanroten/

And don't forget to join the vibrant community of fellow adventurers who love a little awesome sauce in their daily lives by signing up for the *Adventure Seekers* Newsletter. Get the latest news on the development of the Aegis Series, free books, sneak peeks, connect with Nathan and other fans of the series, and much more. You can sign up here: NathanRoten.com/adventure